I0577224

William S. Baker

Washington After the Revolution

MDCCLXXXIV - MDCCXCIX

William S. Baker

Washington After the Revolution
MDCCLXXXIV - MDCCXCIX

ISBN/EAN: 9783337230487

Printed in Europe, USA, Canada, Australia, Japan

Cover: Foto ©Andreas Hilbeck / pixelio.de

More available books at **www.hansebooks.com**

WASHINGTON AFTER THE REVOLUTION

MDCCLXXXIV—MDCCXCIX

BY WILLIAM SPOHN BAKER

AUTHOR OF "ITINERARY OF GENERAL WASHINGTON, 1775–
1783," "EARLY SKETCHES OF GEORGE WASHINGTON," "EN-
GRAVED PORTRAITS OF WASHINGTON," "MEDALLIC PORTRAITS
OF WASHINGTON," "CHARACTER PORTRAITS OF WASHINGTON,"
"BIBLIOTHECA WASHINGTONIANA," ETC.

J. B. LIPPINCOTT COMPANY

PHILADELPHIA MDCCCXCVIII

INTRODUCTORY NOTE.

On the 23d day of December, 1783, Washington resigned his commission as Commander-in-Chief of the armies of the Revolution to the Congress of the United States, then in session at Annapolis, Maryland. After a simple but most impressive ceremony, made memorable by the singular beauty and dignity of his address, he left for Mount Vernon, where he arrived toward the close of the following day. It was the evening before Christmas when Washington returned to that home which through the long and weary struggle was ever in his mind, and where he hoped, to use his own words, "to spend the remainder of his days in cultivating the affections of good men, and in the practice of the domestic virtues." But the end was not yet! There was to be but a brief period of repose; other and more trying years were before him; other and more trying duties were to be imposed. But when they came, when the new duties and responsibilities were to be met, the old firmness and courage, judgment and decision, were displayed, and, strong alike in peace as in war, the great soul, responsive to the call, was found equal to the task.

We propose, as a sequel to the Itinerary of the Revolution (1775–1783), to follow Washington through the remaining years of his life, keeping our notes as closely as possible to his personal movements, although at times it may be difficult to separate his public acts from those of a more private and personal nature.

W. S. Baker.

Philadelphia.

WASHINGTON
AFTER THE REVOLUTION.

1784.

THURSDAY, JANUARY 1.

At Mount Vernon : "The public and other papers, which were committed to your charge, and the books in which they have been recorded under your inspection, having come safe to hand, I take this first opportunity of signifying my entire approbation of the manner in which you have executed the important duties of recording secretary, and the satisfaction I feel in having my papers so properly arranged, and so correctly recorded."— *Washington to Richard Varick.*

In the month of May, 1781, General Washington made arrangements, by authority of Congress, to have all his official papers recorded in volumes. He appointed Colonel Richard Varick to superintend this work,—to classify the papers according to a plan furnished by himself, and to engage such a number of copyists as he should deem expedient. These volumes, thirty-seven in number, containing transcripts of Washington's entire correspondence, official and private, from the beginning to the end of the Revolution, are now the property of the national government, and form one of the most valuable features of its archives. They were purchased with a large amount of other papers in August, 1834, from George Corbin Washington, to whom they were bequeathed by his uncle, Judge Bushrod Washington, the original devisee under the will of General Washington.

SATURDAY, JANUARY 10.

At Mount Vernon : "When you have finished my portrait which is intended for the Count de Solms, I will thank you for handing it to Mr. Robert Morris, who will forward it to the Count de Bruhl (Minister from His Electoral High-

3

ness of Saxe at the Court of London), as the channel pointed out for the conveyance of it."— *Washington to Joseph Wright, at Philadelphia.*

Under date of August 4, 1785, the Comte de Solms, "De la Fortress de Königstein en Saxe," acknowledged the receipt of this portrait in the following terms: "My General and my Hero.—I have just received your picture, and I am entirely taken up to give it a sufficient embellishment by placing it between the King of Prussia and his illustrious brother Henry. You see that this is a trio very harmonical. . . . It must be that the picture resembles, for I regard it as the greatest ornament of my fortress."

The sittings for this portrait must have been given in December, 1783, Washington having been in Philadelphia from the 5th to the 15th of that month. Another portrait by Wright—a three-quarter length, presented by Washington to Mrs. Samuel Powel, of Philadelphia, and still in possession of the family at Newport, Rhode Island—may have been executed at the same time. It is signed and dated "J. Wright, 1784." The *Powel Portrait* is known through an etching executed by Albert Rosenthal, the frontispiece to Baker's "Bibliotheca Washingtoniana," Philadelphia, 1889.

WEDNESDAY, JANUARY 14.

At Mount Vernon: "I am truly sensible, Sir, that the extract from the instructions of the executive of Pennsylvania to their delegates, contains another most flattering proof of the favorable opinion they are pleased to entertain of my past services. Every repeated mark of the approbation of my fellow citizens, especially of those invested with so dignified an appointment, demands my particular acknowledgment. Under this impression, I cannot but feel the greatest obligations to the Supreme Executive Council of the commonwealth of Pennsylvania. But, as my sentiments on the subject of their instructions have been long and well known to the public, I need not repeat them to your Excellency on the present occasion."— *Washington to Thomas Mifflin.*

Under date of December 16, 1783, the Supreme Executive Council of Pennsylvania forwarded a paper to the delegates in Congress from that State, instructing them to bring to the early attention of Congress the fact that, as the admiration of the world might make the life of Washington in a very

considerable degree public, and his very services to his country subject him
to expenses, some testimonial of public gratitude would be proper under the
circumstances.   The instructions, drawn in a most delicate manner, were
transmitted to Washington by President Mifflin before submitting them to
Congress.   The reply as given above, in accordance with his determination,
made known when he received his commission as Commander-in-Chief, to
accept no compensation from his country for his services other than his
expenses, prevented any further action on the subject.

SUNDAY, JANUARY 18.

At Mount Vernon : " The disinclination of the individual
States to yield competent powers to Congress for the federal
government, their unreasonable jealousy of that body and
of one another, and the disposition, which seems to pervade
each, of being all-wise and all-powerful within itself, will,
if there is not a change in the system, be our downfall as a
nation."— *Washington to Benjamin Harrison.*

THURSDAY, JANUARY 22.

At Mount Vernon : " If my commission [as Commander-
in-Chief] is not necessary for the files of Congress, I should
be glad to have it deposited among my own papers.   It may
serve *my grandchildren*, some fifty or a hundred years hence,
for a theme to ruminate upon, if *they* should be contempla-
tively disposed."— *Washington to Charles Thomson.*

" *Annapolis*, February 7th.—With respect to your *commission*, I have to
inform you, that, previous to the receipt of your letter, it had been in agitation among the members to have an order passed for returning it to you
in a gold box.   A motion has accordingly been made to that effect, which
was received with general approbation, and referred to a committee to be
drawn up in proper terms.   The committee have not yet reported.   But I
have not the least doubt of its being returned to you in a way, that will be
satisfactory; and I heartily wish, that this sacred deposit may be preserved
by your *children* and children's children to the latest posterity, and may
prove an incentive to them to emulate the virtues of their worthy and great
progenitor."—*Charles Thomson to Washington.*
    This intention, it seems, was never fulfilled.   The original commission was
retained, and is deposited in the Department of State of the United States.

SUNDAY, FEBRUARY 1.

At Mount Vernon: "At length, my dear Marquis, I am become a private citizen on the banks of the Potomac; and under the shadow of my own vine and my own fig-tree, free from the bustle of a camp, and the busy scenes of public life, I am solacing myself with those tranquil enjoyments, of which the soldier, who is ever in pursuit of fame, the statesman, whose watchful days and sleepless nights are spent in devising schemes to promote the welfare of his own, perhaps the ruin of other countries, as if this globe was insufficient for us all, and the courtier, who is always watching the countenance of his prince, in hopes of catching a gracious smile, can have very little conception."— *Washington to the Marquis de Lafayette.*

WEDNESDAY, FEBRUARY 11.

Leaves Mount Vernon: On this day Washington set out for Fredericksburg, to pay a visit to his mother, which had been delayed on account of the severity of the weather. He did not return until the 19th.

"We have been so fast locked up in snow and ice since Christmas, that all kinds of intercourse have been suspended; and a duty which I owed my mother, and intended ere this to have performed, has been forced to yield to the intemperance of the weather."— *Washington to Charles Thomson,* January 22.

FRIDAY, FEBRUARY 20.

At Mount Vernon: "I am just beginning to experience that ease and freedom from public cares, which, however desirable, takes some time to realize; for, strange as it may seem, it is nevertheless true, that it was not till lately I could get the better of my usual custom of ruminating, as soon as I waked in the morning, on the business of the ensuing day; and of my surprise at finding, after revolving many things in my mind, that I was no longer a public man, nor had anything to do with public transactions."— *Washington to General Knox.*

THURSDAY, MARCH 25.

At Mount Vernon : "I will frankly declare to you, my dear Doctor, that any memoirs of my life, distinct and unconnected with the general history of the war, would rather hurt my feelings than tickle my pride whilst I live. I had rather glide gently down the stream of life, leaving it to posterity to think and say what they please of me, than by any act of mine to have vanity or ostentation imputed to me."— *Washington to Dr. James Craik.*

The letter from which the above extract is made was in reply to an application made by a Mr. Bowie, through Dr. Craik, for permission to examine such papers as would be necessary to enable him to prepare a memoir of the General, which he had in contemplation. Washington, deeming it improper to have the papers connected with his career during the Revolution made public until Congress thought proper to open its archives to the historian, and as, in his opinion, no accurate history of his life could be written without consulting them, denied the request, not unwillingly, as it appears.

MONDAY, APRIL 12.

At Mount Vernon : " The estate of General Washington not being more than fifteen leagues from Annapolis I accepted an invitation that he gave me to go and pass several days there, and it is from his house that I have the honor to write to you. After having seen him on my arrival in this continent, in the midst of his camp and in the tumult of arms, I have the pleasure to see him a simple citizen, enjoying in the repose of his retreat the glory which he has so justly acquired. . . . He dresses in a gray coat like a Virginia farmer, and nothing about him recalls the recollection of the important part which he has played except the great number of foreigners who come to see him."—*Chevalier de la Luzerne to Rayneval*, April 12, 1784.

SATURDAY, MAY 1.

At Philadelphia : " On Saturday last [May 1] his Excellency General Washington our late worthy and much respected Commander in Chief arrived in the city, from his seat in Virginia."—*Pennsylvania Gazette*, May 5, 1784.

"On Saturday, *the first of May*, the sons of St. Tammany* met at Mr. Pole's seat on Schuylkill in order to celebrate the day. The company having learned that general Washington dined with the financier general [Robert Morris], they marched with the music before them to his door, where they halted and gave his excellency thirteen cheers, and at the same time thirteen cannon were fired on the banks of the Schuylkill."—*Pennsylvania Packet*, May 6, 1784.

SATURDAY, MAY 15.

At Philadelphia : " We have been amazingly embarrassed in the business that brought us here. It is now drawing to a conclusion, and will soon be given to the public."— *Washington to Philip Schuyler*.

Washington visited Philadelphia at this time for the purpose of attending the first general meeting of the Cincinnati. The society met at the City Tavern, Second Street above Walnut, every morning at nine o'clock (Sundays excepted) from Tuesday, May 4, to Tuesday, the 18th, when it adjourned. The session of the 18th was short, and Washington in all probability left for Mount Vernon the same day.

The embarrassment in the business referred to by Washington arose from his desire to overcome the popular dissatisfaction excited by the institution of the society, produced mainly by the provision of hereditary distinction. He, therefore, submitted a paper to the meeting, suggesting alterations to the institution, and most of his suggestions were embodied in a proposed amended institution, which was recommended to the State societies for adoption. The State societies, however, regarding the prevailing excitement as a passing storm, withheld their approval and ratification of the proposed amendments, and the society stands now on the same footing that it did on its organization in 1783.

---

* This society, organized for social purposes, took its name from TAMA-NEND, an ancient Indian chief of the Lenni Lenape confederacy, remarkable for his good and noble qualities. The fame of this great man extended among the whites, and in the Revolutionary war his admirers among the Pennsylvania troops established him as the Patron Saint of America, under the name of *St. Tamany*. His festival was celebrated on the first day of May in every year. The noted political organization of New York, the " Tammany Society," derives its name from this chief.

FRIDAY, MAY 21.

At Annapolis, Maryland : " His excellency general Washington arrived at Annapolis from Philadelphia the 21st. ult. and the next day set off for his seat in Virginia."—*Pennsylvania Packet,* June 8, 1784.

WEDNESDAY, JUNE 2.

At Mount Vernon : " I did not hear of your late appointment until I arrived at Annapolis, where I remained but one day, and that occasioned by the detention of my carriage and horses on the Eastern Shore."—*Washington to David Humphreys.*

David Humphreys, of Connecticut, an aide to Washington from 1780 until he resigned his commission, accompanied him on his return to Mount Vernon, where he remained until the middle of January.   He was the last officer of the army to take leave of the General.

On the 12th of May, Colonel Humphreys was appointed secretary to the commission for negotiating treaties of commerce with foreign powers.   He sailed from New York for France in July.   The commission was composed of Benjamin Franklin, John Adams, and Thomas Jefferson.

THURSDAY, JUNE 24.

At Alexandria, Virginia : Attends the Masonic festival of St. John the Baptist, and dines with the Master and brethren of Lodge No. 39.   The following record was made : " The Worshipful Master, with the unanimous consent of the brethren, was pleased to admit his EXCELLENCY GENERAL WASHINGTON, as an honorary member of Lodge No. 39."

MONDAY, JULY 5.

At Mount Vernon : " The General being in want of a House Joiner & Bricklayer who understand their respective trades perfectly, would thank Mr. Rumney for enquiring into the terms upon which such workmen might be engaged for two or three years."—*Washington to William Rumney.*

At this time Washington was engaged in the prosecution of improvements at Mount Vernon, the principal being additions to the house originally built by Lawrence Washington (1744), which was of the old gable-roofed style, with only four rooms upon each floor. It was about one-third the size of the present building, and in the alteration it was made to occupy the central portion, the two ends having been built at the same time. The mansion, when completed by General Washington, at the close of 1785 (and as it now appears), was of the most substantial framework, two stories in height, ninety-six feet in length, thirty feet in depth, with a piazza fifteen feet in width, extending along the eastern or river front.

Mr. William Rumney, a shipping merchant of Alexandria, to whom the above-quoted letter was addressed, was about to leave for England, and hence the request.

THURSDAY, JULY 15.

At Mount Vernon : Answers an address of the General Assembly of Virginia, voted on the 22d of June, and presented to him at Mount Vernon, a few days afterward, by a joint committee of the two Houses, headed by James Madison.

FRIDAY, AUGUST 20.

At Mount Vernon : " I thank you for your favor of the 16th of June by the Marquis de Lafayette, who arrived here three days ago."— *Washington to Count de Rochambeau.*

Lafayette arrived at New York on the 4th of August, after a passage of thirty-four days from France. He remained a short time in New York to receive the congratulations of the citizens, and also in Philadelphia, and then hastened forward to Mount Vernon, which place he reached, as stated, on the 17th. He stayed at Mount Vernon twelve days.

WEDNESDAY, SEPTEMBER 1.

Leaves Mount Vernon : "*September* 1.—Having found it indispensably necessary to visit my Landed property West of the Apalacheon Mountains, and more especially that part of it which I held [in Fayette County, Pennsylvania] in Co-partnership with Mr Gilbert Simpson.—Having determined upon a tour into that Country,—and having made the necessary preparations for it,—I did, on the first day of this Month (September) set out on my journey.

" Having dispatched my equipage about 9 o'clock A.M. ; consisting of 3 Servants & 6 horses, three of which carried my Baggage, I set out myself in company with Doctor James Craik ; and after dining at Mr Sampson Trammells (ab^t 2 Miles above the Falls Church) we proceeded to Difficulty Bridge, and lodged at one Shepherds Tavern 25 Miles."— *Washington's Diary.*

" *September* 2.—About 5 o'clock we set out from Shepherds ; and leaving the Baggage to follow slowly on, we arrived about 11 O'clock ourselves at Leesburgh where we Dined—The Baggage having joined we proceeded to Mr Israel Thompsons & lodged mak^s ab^t 36 M. *September* 3.—Having business to transact with my Tenants in Berkeley ; & others were directed to meet me at my Brothers (Col^o Charles Washington's*) I left Doct^r Craik and the Baggage to follow slowly, and set out myself about Sun Rise for that place—where after Breakfasting at Keys' ferry [on the Shenandoah] I arrived about 11 O'clock—distant ab^t 17 Miles. Col^o Warner Washington,† Mr Wormeley, Genl [Daniel] Morgan, Mr Trickett and many other Gentlemen came here to see me. *September* 4.—Having finished my business with my Tenants . . . and provided a Waggon for the transportation of my Baggage to the Warm Springs (or Town of Bath) to give relief to my Horses, which from the extreme heat of the Weather began to Rub & gaul, I set out after dinner and reached Captn Stroads a substantial farmers betw^n Opecken [Opequan] Creek & Martinsburgh—distant by estimation 14 Miles from my Brothers. *September* 5.—Dispatched my Waggon (with the Baggage) at daylight ; and at 7 o'clock followed it.—bated at one Snodgrasses, on Back Creek—and dined there, about 5 o'clock P.M. we arrived at the Springs—or Town of Bath [now Berkeley Springs, Morgan County, West Virginia] after travelling the whole day through a drizling Rain, 30 Miles."— *Washington's Diary.*

MONDAY, SEPTEMBER 6.

At Bath, Virginia : " *September* 6.—Remained at Bath all day, and was showed the Model of a Boat constructed by the ingenious M^r [James] Rumsey for ascending rapid cur-

---

* Charles Washington resided at what is now Charlestown, Jefferson County, West Virginia, laid out in 1786, and named from his Christian name.

† A son of John Washington, the elder brother of Augustine, the father of General Washington. He resided at Fairfield, Frederick (now Clarke) County, Virginia.

rents by mechanism; the principles of this were not only
shown & fully explained to me, but to my very great satisfaction, exhibited in practice in private under the injunction
of Secrecy, until he saw the effect of an application he was
about to Make to the Assembly of this State, for a reward.
. . . Having obtained a Plan of this Town (Bath) and ascer-
tained the situation of my lots therein . . . & Mr Rumsey
being willing to undertake those Buildings [a dwelling-
house, kitchen, and stable], I have agreed with him to have
them finished by the 10th of next July."— *Washington's
Diary.*

"*September* 7.—Having hired three Pack horses—to give my own greater
relief—I sent my Baggage of this day about one O'clock, and ordered those
who had charge of it, to proceed to one Headricks at 15 Miles Creek, distant
ab^t ten Miles, to night, and to the old Town next day. *September* 8.—Set
out about 7 o'clock with the Doct^r (Craik) his son William and my Nephew
Bushrod Washington, who were to make the tour with us,—about ten
I parted with them at 15 Miles Creek, & recrossed the Potomack (having
passed it ab^t 3 Miles from the Springs before) to a tract of mine on the Virginia Side, which I find exceedingly Rich, & must be very valuable. . . .
After having reviewed this Land I again crossed the River [to Maryland] &
getting into the waggon Road pursued my journey to the old Town where I
overtook my Company & baggage—lodged at Col^o [Thomas] Cresaps—ab^t
35 Miles this day. *September* 9.—The day proving rainy we remained here
[Old Town]. *September* 10.—Set off a little after 5 oclock altho' the morning was very unpromising,—finding from the Rains that had fallen, and
description of the Roads, part of which between the old Town & this place
(old Fort Cumberland) we had passed, that the progress of my Baggage
would be tedeous, I resolved (it being necessary) to leave it to follow; and
proceed on myself to Gilbert Simpson's. . . . Accordingly, leaving Doct^r
Craik, his Son, and My Nephew with it, I set out with one Servant only—
dined at Mr Gwins at the Fort [? Fork] of the Roads leaving [? leading] to
Winchester and the old Town, distant from the latter ab^t 20 Miles & lodged
at Tumbersons [Tumbelson] at the little Meadows [Somerset County, Penn-
sylvania] 15 Miles further. *September* 11.—Set out at half after 5 oclock
from Tumbersons, & in about 1½ Miles came to what is called the little
crossing of the Yohiogany. . . . Breakfasted at one Mounts or Mountains,
11 Miles from Tumbersons; the Road being exceedingly bad, especially
through what is called the Shades of death.—Bated at the great crossing
[of the Youghiogheny River or Braddock's road, now Somerfield] which is
a large Water, distant from Mounts* 9 Miles, and a better Road than be-

tween that and Tumbersons—Lodged at one Daughertys a Mile & half short of the Great Meadows . . . distant from the crossing 12 Miles."—*Washington's Diary.*

SUNDAY, SEPTEMBER 12.

At Fayette County, Pennsylvania: "*September* 12.—Left Daughertys about 6 oclock—stopped awhile at the Great Meadows and viewed a tenement I have there . . . is a very good stand for a Tavern. Dined at Mr Thomas Gists [Mount Braddock] at the Foot of Laurel, distant from the Meadows 12 Miles, and arrived at Gilbert Simpsons about 5 oclock 12 Miles further."—*Washington's Diary.*

The tenement at Great Meadows, in what is now Wharton Township, Fayette County, Pennsylvania, and which Washington considered "a very good stand for a Tavern," was on a tract of land containing two hundred and thirty-four acres, acquired by him in 1767. It included the site of *Fort Necessity,* a stockade hastily constructed by Washington, when a colonel in the Virginia service, to resist the attack of a superior body of French and Indians under the command of M. Coulan de Villiers, and made memorable by its surrender to that officer on July 3, 1754. The entire tract was sold by the executors of the last will and testament of Washington to Andrew Parks, of Baltimore. In the notes to the schedule attached to the will this property is referred to as follows: "This land is valuable on account of its local situation and other properties.—It affords an exceeding good stand on Braddock's Road from Fort Cumberland to *Pittsburgh* and besides a fertile soil possesses a large quantity of natural meadow fit for the scythe. —It is distinguished by the appellation of the Great Meadows, where the first action with the French in the year 1754 was fought."

MONDAY, SEPTEMBER 13.

At Fayette County, Pennsylvania: "*September* 13.—I visited my Mill, and the several tenements on this Tract (on which Simpson lives)—I do not find the land in *general* equal to my expectations of it."—*Washington's Diary.*

The tract referred to, "on which Simpson lives," comprised about sixteen hundred acres, and was situate at and near the present town of Perryopolis, Perry Township, Fayette County, Pennsylvania. It was located for Washington by Captain William Crawford in 1769, and was visited by him in 1770. Gilbert Simpson, who had superintended the erection of a mill on the premises, which, however, was not finished until the spring of 1776, seems also to have been a copartner in the management of the estate. The property was sold in 1795 to Colonel Israel Shreve, of New Jersey, under articles of agreement, and in 1802 the executors of the last will and testament of Washington conveyed it to the heirs of Colonel Shreve, who had died in 1799.

TUESDAY, SEPTEMBER 14.

At Fayette County, Pennsylvania: "*September* 14.—Remained at Mr Gilbert Simpsons all day,—before Noon Col° Wm Butler and the officer Commanding the Garrison at Fort Pitt a Capt° Lucket came here—as they confirmed the reports of the discontented temper of the Indians and the Mischiefs done by some parties of them—and the former advised me not to prosecute my intended trip to the Great Kanahawa, I resolved to decline it."— *Washington's Diary.*

"*September* 15.—This being the day appointed for the Sale of my moiety of the Co-partnership Stock—many People were gathered (more out of curiosity I believe than from other motives) but no great Sale made.—My Mill I could obtain no bid for. *September* 16.—Continued at Simpsons all day in order to finish the business which was begun yesterday--Gave leases to some of my Ten^{ts} on the Land whereon I now am. *September* 17.—Detained here by a settled Rain the whole day—which gave me time to close my Acc^{ts} with Gilbert Simpson, & put a final end to my Partnership with him."— *Washington's Diary.*

SATURDAY, SEPTEMBER 18.

At Washington County, Pennsylvania: "*September* 18.—Set out with Doct^r Craik for my Land on Millers Run (a branch of Shurtees [Chartiers] Creek—crossed the Monongahela at Deboirs [Devore's] Ferry—16 miles from Simpsons—bated at one Hamiltons about 4 Miles from it, in Washington County and lodged at a Col° Cassons [Canon] on the Waters of Shurtees Creek—a kind, hospitable Man; & sensible."— *Washington's Diary.*

"*September* 19.—Being Sunday, and the People living on my land apparently very religious, it was thought best to postpone going among them till to-morrow." - *Washington's Diary.*

MONDAY, SEPTEMBER 20.

At Washington County, Pennsylvania : " *September* 20.—
Went early this Morning to view my Land & to receive the
final determination of those who live upon it."—*Washington's Diary.*

The land on Miller's Run, in what is now Mount Pleasant Township,
Washington County, Pennsylvania, was held by Washington under a military patent from Lord Dunmore, Governor of Virginia. It comprised two
thousand eight hundred and thirteen acres, and was described as "being in
Augusta County, Vir. on the waters of Miller's Run, one of the branches
of Chartiers Creek, a branch of the Ohio." A number of families (Scotch-Irish) had settled on this land, and Washington passed most of Monday,
September 20, in endeavoring to arrange with them for the purchase of the
whole tract. No agreement, however, could be made, and subsequently
ejectment suits were brought, which were successful. The tract was sold in
June, 1796, for twelve thousand dollars.

Washington passed the night of the 20th at the house of Colonel John
Canon, the site of the present Canonsburg, laid out in 1787.

TUESDAY, SEPTEMBER 21.

Leaves Washington County : " *September* 21.—Accompanied by Colᵒ Casson & Captⁿ Swearingin [sheriff of the
county] who attended me to Debores ferry on the Monongahela which seperates the Counties of Fayette & Washington, I returned to Gilbert Simpson's in the afternoon; after
dining at one Wickermans [Wickerham's] Mill near the
Monongahela."—*Washington's Diary.*

" *September* 22.—After giving instructions to Major Thomas Freeman respecting his conduct in my business, and disposing of my Baggage which
was left under the care of Mʳ Gilbert Simpson . . . I set out for Beason
[Beeson] Town [now Uniontown, the county-seat of Fayette County] in
order to meet with & engage Mʳ Thoˢ Smith to bring Ejectments & to prosecute my Suit for the Land in Washington County. . . . Reached Beason
Town about dusk (about the way I came) 18 Miles . . . my Baggage under
the care of Doctʳ Craik and Son, having, from Simpsons, taken the Rout by
the New (or Turkey foot) Road as it is called (which is said to be 20 Miles
near than Braddocks). . . . My Nephew and I set out about Noon [on the
23d], with one Colᵒ Philips for Cheat River."—*Washington's Diary.*

THURSDAY, SEPTEMBER 23.

At Fayette County, Pennsylvania: "*September* 23.—Arrived at Col° Philips ab' five oclock in the afternoon 16 Miles from Beason Town & near the Mouth of Cheat River. . . .

"*September* 24.—Set of in the Morning of the 24th (accompanied by Col° Philips) and crossed it [Cheat River] at the Mouth, as it was thought the River was too much swelled to attempt the ford a little higher up."— *Washington's Diary.*

Washington passed the night of the 24th at the house of Captain Samuel Hanway, about three miles south of Cheat River, in Monongalia County, Virginia, now West Virginia. Captain Hanway was the surveyor of Monongalia County. On the 25th he resumed his journey, setting out before sunrise and lodging that night in the rain, with no shelter or cover other than his cloak. On the 26th he reached a Mr. Logston's, and left a little after daybreak on the following day, crossing the Stony River after a ride of four miles, gaining at ten miles "the summit of the Alligany Mountain," and arriving at "Col° Abrah^m Hites at Fort pleasant on the South Branch [of the Potomac] about 35 miles from Logstons a little before the Suns setting," where he remained all of the next day, the 28th.

WEDNESDAY, SEPTEMBER 29.

Leaves Fort Pleasant, Virginia: "*September* 29.—Having appointed to join Doct^r Craik and my Baggage at Col° Warner Washingtons, but finding it required only one day more to take the Rout of Mr Tho' Lewis's (near Stanton) . . . I sent my Nephew Bushrod Washington to that place to request the Doct^r to proceed & accompanied by Capt^a Hite son to the Colonel I set out for Rockingham, in which county Mr Lewis now lives since the division of Augusta." — *Washington's Diary.*

The night of the 29th was passed on the North Fork of the Shenandoah, at the house of one "Fishwaters in Brocks gap, about Eight Miles from the foot of the Mountain—12 from Rudibort's [where he had dined] & 36 from Colon' Hites," arriving at Mr. Lewis's on the 30th "about Sundown, after riding about 40 Miles—leaving Rockingham C^t House to the right about 2 Miles." Washington remained at Mr. Lewis's until October 2, setting off very early on that day, accompanied by Mr. Lewis, "to the foot of the bleu

Ridge at Swift run gap, 10 Miles," where he baited and proceeded over the mountain, lodging at night at a Widow Yearly's, twelve miles farther. On the following day, October 3, he took breakfast at Culpeper Court-House, and lodged at Captain John Ashby's.

MONDAY, OCTOBER 4.

At Mount Vernon : " *October* 4.—Notwithstanding a good deal of Rain fell in the Night and the continuance of it this morning (which lasted till about 10 oclock) I breakfasted by Candlelight, and Mounted my horse soon after day break ; & having Capt^a Ashby for a guide thro' the intricate part of the Road (which ought tho' I missed it, to have been by Prince William old Court H°) I arrived at Colchester,* 30 Miles to Dinner; and reached home before Sun down ; having travelled on the same horses since the first day of September by the computed distances 680 Miles."— *Washington's Diary.*

An interesting description of Washington and the life at Mount Vernon at this period has been written by Charles Varlo, an Englishman, who visited this country in 1784. Landing at Philadelphia on July 23 of that year, Mr. Varlo made an excursion to the eastward as far as Boston, and afterward journeyed to the southward, arriving at Mount Vernon in the month of October. The following is transcribed from vol. ii., p. 90, of his work, entitled " Floating Ideas of Nature, suited to the Philosopher, Farmer, and Mechanic," published at London in 1796 :

" I crossed the river from Maryland into Virginia, near to the renowned General Washington's, where I had the honour to spend some time, and was kindly entertained with that worthy family. As to the General, if we may judge by the countenance, he is what the world says of him, a shrewd, good-natured, plain, humane man, about fifty-five years of age, and seems to wear well, being healthful and active, straight, well made, and about six feet high. He keeps a good table, which is always open to those of a genteel appearance. He does not use many Frenchified *congees*, or flattering useless words without meaning, which savours more of deceit than an honest heart ; but on the contrary, his words seem to point at truth and reason, and to spring from the fountain of a heart, which being good of itself, cannot be suspicious of others, till facts unriddle designs, which evidently appeared to me by a long tale that he told me about Arnold's manœuvres, far-fetched schemes, and deep-laid designs, to give him and his army up, above a month

---

* Ten miles southwest of Mount Vernon.

2

before the affair happened ; and though he said he wondered at many things that he observed in Arnold's conduct, yet he had not the least suspicion of any treachery going on, till the thing happened, and then he could trace back and see through his intentions from the beginning; which, from the General's behaviour to him, I am well apprized, seems to be the highest sin of ingratitude that a man could be guilty of.

"The General's house is rather warm, snug, convenient, and useful, than ornamental. The size is what ought to suit a man of about two or three thousand a year in England. The out-offices are good, and seem to be not long built; and he was making more offices at each wing to the front of the house, which added more to ornament than real use. The situation is high, and commands a beautiful prospect of the river which parts Virginia and Maryland, but in other respects the situation seems to be out of the world, being chiefly surrounded by woods, and far from any great road or thoroughfare, and nine miles from Alexandria in Virginia. The General's lady is a hearty, comely, discreet, affable woman, some few years older than himself; she was a widow when he married her. He has no children by her. The General's house is open to poor travellers as well as rich; he gives diet and lodging to all that come that way, which indeed cannot be many, without they go out of their way on purpose. . . .

"I have travelled and seen a great deal of the world, have conversed with all degrees of people, and have remarked that there are only two persons in the world which have every one's good word, and those are—the Queen of England and General Washington, which I never heard friend or foe speak slightly of."

SUNDAY, NOVEMBER 14.

At Richmond, Virginia : "Last Sunday [November 14], in the afternoon, came to this city, his Excellency General George Washington, Esq. The next day was ushered in with the discharge of thirteen cannon, when every countenance showed the most heartfelt gladness on seeing our illustrious and beloved General in the Capital of the State, and in the bosom of peace. In the evening the city was illuminated and every demonstration of joy was shown on the pleasing occasion. The corporation of the city waited on his Excellency with an address, which he answered."—*Richmond paper*, November 20, 1784.

"On Thursday [November 18], the merchants of the city gave an elegant dinner to his Excellency General Washington; the same day came from Boston, the Marquis de la Fayette, accompanied with Captain Grandchain, of the navy of his most Christian Majesty, and the Chevalier Caraman. The two Houses of Assembly appointed committees to wait upon his Excellency and the Marquis de la Fayette, who severally addressed them."—*Idem.*

FRIDAY, NOVEMBER 19.

At Richmond : "Last night [November 19] the corporation of the city gave an elegant ball in honor to our illustrious and much beloved visitor General Washington."— *Richmond paper*, November 20, 1784.

Washington visited Richmond for the purpose of meeting the Marquis de Lafayette, who, after leaving Mount Vernon in August, had made a tour of the Eastern States. At Boston he embarked on board the French frigate "Nymphe," for the Chesapeake Bay, and landed at Yorktown. He met Washington at Richmond on the 18th of November (as stated) and accompanied him to Mount Vernon, where he made a second visit of about a week.

THURSDAY, NOVEMBER 25.

At Mount Vernon : "I have had the honor to receive your favor of the 11th of June, accompanied with your *Remarks and Inquiries concerning America.* The honorable mention, which you make of me in both, is far above my deserts. . . . It is a matter of regret to me, that my want of knowledge in the French language will not allow me to become acquainted with all the beauties of your *Spectator.*" — *Washington to Joseph Mandrillon.*

Joseph Mandrillon was born at Bourg-en-Bresse, France, in 1742. Having embraced the mercantile profession, he established himself at Amsterdam, from whence he made a voyage to the United States, and afterward published the results of his observations in a 12mo volume, entitled "Le Spectateur Américain," Amsterdam, 1784, a copy of which he seems to have sent to Washington. From his "Portrait of General Washington" in this book we make the following extract :

"If ever mortal enjoyed his whole reputation during his lifetime, if ever a citizen has found in his own country a reward for his services and abilities, it is my hero; every where fêted, admired, caressed, he every where sees hearts eager to render him homage ; if he enters a town, or if he passes through a village, old and young men, women and children, all follow him with acclamations; all load him with blessings; in every heart he has a temple consecrated to respect and friendship. How I love to imagine to myself the French general (M. de Rochambeau) equally the idol and the hero of his army, saying at table as he sat near Washington, that he had never known what true glory was, nor a truly great man, until he became acquainted with him. When America, overthrown by the dreadful revolutions of nature, shall no longer exist, it will be remembered of Washington, that he was the defender of liberty, the friend of man, and the avenger of an oppressed people."

MONDAY, NOVEMBER 29.

At Annapolis, Maryland : " On Monday, the 29th of November, 1784, general Washington arrived at Annapolis, accompanied by the Marquis de la Fayette. On the day following, the general assembly of this State, being then in session, to manifest their gratitude and attachment to those distinguished men, directed an elegant ball to be provided for their entertainment. The evening was crowned with the utmost joy and festivity, the whole company being made happy by the presence of two most amiable and all-accomplished men, to whom America is so deeply indebted for her preservation from tyranny and oppression."—*Annals of Annapolis.*

At Annapolis, Washington bade a final adieu to Lafayette. From thence the marquis proceeded to Trenton, where Congress was then sitting, reaching that place on December 8. On the 25th of the month he embarked at New York for France, on board the frigate " Nymphe."

SUNDAY, DECEMBER 5.

At Mount Vernon : " I met the Marquis de La Fayette at Richmond—brought him to this place, conducted him to Annapolis, saw him on the road to Baltimore, and returned." — *Washington to General Knox.*

" *December* 8.—The peregrination of the day in which I parted from you ended at Marlborough [Maryland]. The next day, bad as it was, I got home before dinner. In the moment of our separation, upon the road as I travelled, and every hour since, I have felt all that love, respect, and attachment for you, with which length of years, close connexion, and your merits have inspired me. I often asked myself, as our carriages separated, whether that was the last sight I ever should have of you ?"—*Washington to the Marquis de Lafayette.*

TUESDAY, DECEMBER 14.

At Mount Vernon: "The Assemblies of Virginia and Maryland have now under consideration the extension of the inland navigation of the rivers Potomac and James, and opening a communication between them and the western waters. They seem fully impressed with the political as well as the commercial advantages, which would result from the accomplishment of these great objects, and I hope will embrace the present moment to put them in a train for execution."— *Washington to Richard Henry Lee.*

The importance of connecting the western with the eastern territory by a system of inland navigation had from an early period attracted the attention of Washington, and prior to the Revolution he had made some efforts to bring the subject to public notice. During his western trip in September the matter was constantly in his mind, and after his return he wrote a long letter to Benjamin Harrison, Governor of Virginia, in which he detailed the advantages, both in a commercial and political point of view, which might be derived from opening the Potomac and James Rivers as high as should be practicable. This letter was communicated to the Assembly of Virginia, and led to the organization of the James River and Potomac Canal Companies. Thus it will be seen that during the first year after the close of the Revolution, Washington set in motion that vast scheme of internal improvements which has had a powerful and salutary influence upon the destinies of the country.

THURSDAY, DECEMBER 23.

At Annapolis: "I am here [since December 20] with General Gates, at the request of the Assembly of Virginia to fix matters with the Assembly of this State respecting the extension of the inland navigation of the Potomac, and the communication between it and the western waters." — *Washington to the Marquis de Lafayette.*

An exact conformity between the acts of Virginia and of Maryland being indispensable to the improvement of the Potomac, Washington was requested to wait upon the Assembly of Maryland, in order to agree on a bill which might receive the sanction of both States.

TUESDAY, DECEMBER 28.

At Annapolis: " The proceedings of the conference, and the Act & Resolutions of this Legislature consequent thereupon (herewith transmitted to the Assembly) are so full & explanatory of the motives which governed in this business, that it is scarcely necessary for me to say any thing in addition to them; except that this State seem highly impressed with the importance of the objects w'ch we have had under consideration,—and are very desirous of seeing them accomplished. . . .

" It is now near 12 at Night, and I am writing with an Aching head, having been constantly employed in this business since the 22d, without assistance from my Colleagues —Gen'l Gates having been sick the whole time & Col° Blackburn not attending."— *Washington to James Madison.*

" I am just returned from Annapolis to which place I was requested to go by our Assembly (with my bosom friend Genl. G—tes, who being at Richmond contrived to edge himself into the commission) for the purpose of arranging matters and framing a Law which should be similar in both States, so far as it respected the river Potomack which separates them. I met the most perfect accordance in that legislature; and the matter is now reported to ours, for its consideration."— *Washington to General Knox,* January 5, 1785.

1785.

At Mount Vernon : "*January* 1.—Col° Bassett, who brought his daughter Fanny to this place to remain on the 24th of last Month set off on his return to the Assembly now sitting at Richmond."— *Washington's Diary.*

Colonel Burwell Bassett, of " Eltham," New Kent County, Virginia, marrie for a second wife Anna Maria Dandridge, a sister of Mrs. Washington. His daughter Fanny married George Augustine Washington, a nephew of General Washington (son of his brother Charles), at Mount Vernon, October 15, 1785.

MONDAY, JANUARY 3.

At Mount Vernon : " *January* 3.—Doct' Stuart—his wife —Betcy & Patcy Custis who had been here since the 27th Ulto returned home."— *Washington's Diary.*

" Betcy & Patcy Custis" (Eliza Parke and Martha Parke Custis) were the eldest children of Mrs. Dr. Stuart, by her first husband, John Parke Custis, the son of Mrs. Washington, who died November 5, 1781. The younger children, Eleanor (" Nelly") Parke and George Washington Parke, had been adopted by Washington and were living at Mount Vernon. With the exception of the latter, all the others were born at " Abingdon," a plantation on the Potomac River immediately above Alexandria, and where the family were living at this time. Dr. David Stuart married Mrs. Custis, who was the daughter of Benedict Calvert, of Mount Airy, Prince George's County, Maryland, in the fall of 1783. He was a frequent visitor at Mount Vernon, and was held in much respect by Washington.

WEDNESDAY, JANUARY 19.

At Mount Vernon : " *January* 19.—Employed until dinner in laying out my Serpentine Road & Shrubberies adjoining.—Just as we had done dinner a M' Watson—late of the House of Watson & Cossoul of Nantes—came in, and

23

stayed all Night. *January* 20.—Mr Watson went away after breakfast."— *Washington's Diary.*

"I had feasted my imagination for several days in the near prospect of a visit to Mount Vernon, the seat of Washington. No pilgrim ever approached Mecca with deeper enthusiasm. I arrived there, in the afternoon of January 23d [?] '85. . . . I found him at table with Mrs. Washington and his private family, and was received in the native dignity and with that urbanity so peculiarly combined in the character of a soldier and eminent private gentleman. He soon put me at ease, by unbending in a free and affable conversation. . . .

"The first evening I spent under the wing of his hospitality, we sat a full hour at table by ourselves, without the least interruption, after the family had retired. I was extremely oppressed by a severe cold and excessive coughing, contracted by the exposure of a harsh winter journey. He pressed me to use some remedies, but I declined doing so. As usual after retiring, my coughing increased. When some time had elapsed, the door of my room was gently opened, and on drawing my bed-curtains, to my utter astonishment, I beheld Washington himself, standing at my bed-side, with a bowl of hot tea in his hand."—*Memoirs of Elkanah Watson.*

THURSDAY, JANUARY 27.

At Mount Vernon: "*January* 27.—Made M^r & Mrs Lund Washington a morning visit—from thence I went to Belvoir and viewed the ruined buildings of that place."— *Washington's Diary.*

Lund Washington, manager of the Mount Vernon estate during the Revolution, was a third cousin of General Washington. He resided at "Hayfield," a plantation about four miles northwest of Mount Vernon. "Belvoir," the estate and residence of Sir William Fairfax, a cousin and agent of Lord Thomas Fairfax, the owner of an immense landed estate in the Northern Neck of Virginia, was situated on the Potomac, four miles below Mount Vernon. On the death of Sir William in 1757, it descended to his son George William Fairfax, the friend and neighbor of George Washington. Mr. Fairfax went to England in 1773, and died at Bath, April 3, 1787. As he had no children, "Belvoir" was devised to Ferdinando, the son of his brother, the Rev. Bryan Fairfax. The mansion-house was destroyed by fire shortly after his leaving America.

WEDNESDAY, FEBRUARY 2.

At Mount Vernon: "*February* 2.—Employed myself (as there could be no stirring without) in writing Letters by the

Post and in Signing 83 Diplomas for the members of the
Society of the Cincinnati—and sent them to the care of
Col° Fitzgerald in Alexandria—to be forwarded to General
[Otho H.] Williams of Baltimore—the Assistant Secretary
of the Society."— *Washington's Diary.*

SATURDAY, FEBRUARY 5.

At Mount Vernon : " Captain Haskell, in the ship Mary,
arrived at Alexandria a few days ago ; but a frost, which at
present interrupts the navigation of the river, has prevented
my sending for the chimney-piece. By the number of cases,
however, I greatly fear it is too elegant and costly for my
room and republican style of living."— *Washington to Benjamin Vaughan,* at London.

This chimney-piece, one of the special ornaments of the mansion at
Mount Vernon, was originally made for Samuel Vaughan, a resident of
London, and a great admirer of Washington. It was wrought in Italy
from the finest white and sienite marbles for Mr. Vaughan's own use. At
the time of its arrival in England, that gentleman was informed of the improvements then in progress at Mount Vernon, and, without unpacking it,
he directed his son (Benjamin Vaughan) to send it at once to Washington.
An interesting description of this work of art will be found in Lossing's
" Mount Vernon and its Associations."

SATURDAY, FEBRUARY 12.

At Alexandria, Virginia : " *February* 12.—Received an
Invitation to the Funeral of Wm Ramsay Esqr of Alexandria
—the oldest Inhabitant of the Town ; & went up—walked in
procession as a free mason—Mr Ramsay in his life time being
one & now buried with the ceremony & honors due to one."
— *Washington's Diary.*

TUESDAY, FEBRUARY 22.

At Mount Vernon : " *February* 22.—Removed two pretty
large & full-grown lilacs to the N° Garden gate—one on
each side taking up as much dirt with the roots as c^d be well
obtained. . . . I also removed from the woods and old fields,
several young trees of the sassafras, Dogwood & Redbud, to

the Shrubbery on the N° side the grass plot. *February* 28. —Planted all the Mulberry trees, Maple trees, & Black gums in my Serpentine walks—and the Poplars on the right walk." — *Washington's Diary.*

Washington took great pleasure in planting trees and shrubbery, and the diaries of 1785-86 show that in these years he was much engaged in that business. On the west front of the mansion he laid out a fine lawn upon a level surface of about twenty acres, and around it made a serpentine carriage-way, on each side of which he planted a great variety of shade-trees, some of which are still standing. The lawn, the oval grass-plot, and the gardens were laid out according to a plan drawn by himself, and still remain unchanged as to form.

TUESDAY, MARCH 8.

At Mount Vernon : "Some imperfect miniature cuts I send you under cover with this letter. They were designed for me by Miss D' Hart of Elizabethtown, and given to Mrs. Washington, who, in sparing them, only wishes they may answer your purpose. For her I can get none cut yet." — *Washington to William Gordon.*

A silhouette published in volume four of the illustrated edition of Irving's "Life of Washington," inscribed "From the original (cut with scissors) by Miss De Hart, Elizabethtown, N. J. 1783," is, we presume, a reproduction of one of the "imperfect miniature cuts" referred to in the above letter. It is extremely unlike any known profile of Washington. Miss De Hart visited Mount Vernon in October, 1786. She remained from the 26th to the 28th.

SUNDAY, MARCH 20.

At Mount Vernon : "*March* 20.—Major Jenefir came here to dinner—and my carriage went to Gunston Hall to take Col° Mason to a meeting of Com^rs at Alexandria for settling the Jurisdiction of Chesapeak Bay & the River Potomack & Pocomoke between the States of Virginia & Maryland.—The Commissioners on the Part of Virginia being Col° [George] Mason—The Attorney General [Edmund Randolph]—M^r [James] Madison & M^r [Alexander] Henderson—on that of Maryland, Major [Daniel of St.

Thomas] Jenifer, Thom⁸ Johnson, Tho⁸ Stone & Sam¹ Chase
Esqⁿ. *March* 21.—Major Jenifer left this for Alexandria
after Dinner."—*Washington's Diary.*

TUESDAY, MARCH 22.

At Alexandria: " *March* 22.—Went to Alexandria—
dined & returned in the Evening."—*Washington's Diary.*

THURSDAY, MARCH 24.

At Mount Vernon: " *March* 24.—Sent my Carriage to
Alexandria for Col⁰ Mason according to appointment—who
came in, about dusk. *March* 25.—About One o'clock
Major Jenifer, Mʳ Stone, Mʳ Chase, & Mʳ Alexʳ Henderson
arrived here. *March* 27.—Mʳ Henderson went to Colchester after dinner to return in the morning."—*Washington's Diary.*

MONDAY, MARCH 28.

At Mount Vernon : " *March* 28.—Mʳ Henderson returned
to the Meeting of the Commissioners abᵗ 10 Oclock—and
Mʳ Chase went away after dinner."—*Washington's Diary.*

The commissioners,* after preparing the terms of a compact between Virginia and Maryland for the jurisdiction over the waters of the Chesapeake
Bay and the rivers that were common to both States, took up matters of
general policy, and decided to recommend to the two States a uniformity of
duties on imports, a uniformity of commercial regulations, and a uniformity
of currency. From this resulted (January, 1786) a proposition from Virginia
that a convention from all the States should be held to regulate the restric-
tions on commerce for the whole, the commissioners to meet at Annapolis
on the first Monday in September, 1786. The invitations to the States were
made through the executive of Virginia, although Maryland had made
(December, 1785) the first move in the matter.

TUESDAY, MARCH 29.

At Mount Vernon : " *March* 29.—Major Jenifer, Mʳ
Stone and Mʳ Henderson went away before breakfast &

---

* Three of the commissioners, Edmund Randolph and James Madison on
the part of Virginia, and Thomas Johnson on the part of Maryland, were
not present at any of the meetings either at Alexandria or Mount Vernon.

Col° Mason (in my Carriage) after it; by the return of
which he sent me some young Shoots of the Persian Jessa-
mine & Guilder Rose."—*Washington's Diary.*

MONDAY, APRIL 18.

At Alexandria: "*April* 18.—Rid to Alexandria to the
Election of Delagates for this County and dined at Col°
Fitzgeralds—Col° Lynne & Doct' Stewart were chosen,—&
for whom I gave my support."—*Washington's Diary.*

THURSDAY, APRIL 21.

At Abingdon, Virginia: "*April* 21.—After an early dinner, I went up in my Barge to Abingdon, in order to bring
M' John Lewis (who had lain there sick for more than two
months) down—Took my Instruments, with intent to Survey the Land I hold by purchase on 4 Mile Run [three
miles above Alexandria] of Geo: & Ja' Mercer Esqr' Called
at Alexandria & staid an hour or two."—*Washington's
Diary.*

"*April* 22.—Took an early breakfast at Abingdon; & accompanied by
Doct' Stewart & Lund Washington, and having sent for M' Moses Ball
(who attended); I went to a Corner of the above Land, within about 3 poles
of the Run (4 Miles Run) a white Oak, 18 inches in diameter, on the side
of a hill ab' 150 yards below the Ruins of an old Mill & 100 below a small
Branch which comes in on the N° E' side.—and after having Run one course
& part of another, My Servant William * (one of the Chain Carriers) fell,
and broke the pan of his knee w'b put a stop to my surveying; & with much
difficulty I was able to get him to Abingdon, being obliged to get a sled to
carry him on, as he could neither Walk, stand, or Ride:—At M' Adams
Mill I took Lund Washingtons horse & came home."—*Washington's Diary.*

SUNDAY, APRIL 24.

At Mount Vernon: "*April* 24.—An Express arrived with
the acc' of the Deaths of M" Dandridge & M' B.[artholo-

* William ("Billy") Lee was Washington's body-servant during the Revolutionary war. He survived his master, who, by his will, gave him his
freedom and an annuity of thirty dollars.

mew] Dandridge, the Mother and Brother of Mrs Washington."— *Washington's Diary.*

THURSDAY, APRIL 28.

At Mount Vernon: "*April 28.*—To Dinner Mr Pine a pretty eminent Portrait & Historical Painter arrived in order to take my picture from the life & to plan it in the Historical pieces he was about to draw.—This Gentleman stands in good estimation as a Painter in England;—comes recommended to me from Col° Fairfax—Mr Morris—Govr Dickenson—Mr Hopkinson & others."— *Washington's Diary.*

Robert Edge Pine, a painter of considerable merit, was born in London in the year 1742. He came to America in 1784, for the purpose of obtaining portraits of the heroes and patriots of the Revolution, in order to introduce them in historical pictures commemorating the events of that period. Pine remained three weeks at Mount Vernon, leaving May 19, and besides that of Washington, painted also the portraits of the two grandchildren of Mrs. Washington. He died at Philadelphia, November 19, 1788, before carrying out his design of painting the historical pictures.

FRIDAY, APRIL 29.

Leaves Mount Vernon : "*April 29.*—I set off for the appointed meeting of the Dismal Swamp Company * at Richmond.—Dined at Dumfries & lodged at My Sister Lewis's † (after visiting at my Mother) in Fredericksburgh."— *Washington's Diary.*

"*April 30.*—Dined at General [Alexander] Spotswoods, and lodged at M^r Jn° Baylor's (New Market). *May 1*—Took a late breakfast at Hanover C^t House—Went from thence to Mr Peter Lyon's where I intended to dine, but neither he nor Mrs Lyon being at home, I proceeded to, & arrived at

* In January, 1764, a company was formed and chartered by the Legislature of Virginia for the purpose of draining and rendering fit for cultivation the Great Dismal Swamp, between Norfolk and Albemarle Sound. Washington was one of the company. In October, 1763, he penetrated the swamp and examined it in various parts.

† Washington's sister Betty married Colonel Fielding Lewis, of Fredericksburg, in 1760. Colonel Lewis died December, 1781.

Richmond about 6 oclock in the aftern⁰—Supped, & lodged, at the Governors [Patrick Henry]."—*Washington's Diary.*

MONDAY, MAY 2.

At Richmond: " *May 2.*—Received, and accepted an invitation to dine with the Sons of Saint Tammy, at M⁺ Andersons Tavern, and accordingly did so, at 3 oclock. About Noon, having assembled a sufficient number of the Proprietors of the Swamp, we proceeded to business in the Senate Chamber; & continued thereon 'till dinner, when we adjourned 'till nine oclock next day."—*Washington's Diary.*

" *May 3.*—Met according to adjournment. & finished the business by 3 oclock—Dinner at the Governors. *May 4.*—After doing a little business, & calling upon Judge Mercer and the Attorney General, I left Richmond about 11 oclock—Dined at one Winslow's ab⁺ 8 Miles from the City, & lodged at Clarks Tavern 10 Miles above Hanover Court House. *May 5.*—Breakfasted at Bowling Green—Dined with my Sister Lewis in Fredericksburgh—spent half an hour with my Mother—and lodged at Stafford C⁺ House (at one Taylors Tavern). *May 6.*—Breakfasted at Dumfries, & dined at home."—*Washington's Diary.*

SUNDAY, MAY 15.

At Mount Vernon: " *May 15.*—General [John] Cadwallader came here yesterday. *May 17.*—General Cadwallader went away after Breakfast."—*Washington's Diary.*

TUESDAY, MAY 17.

At Alexandria: " *May 17.*—I went to Alexandria to the appointed meeting of the Subscribers to the Potomack Navigation. Upon comparing & examining the Books of the different Managers, it was found, including the Subscriptions in behalf of the two States, & the 50 Shares which the Assembly of Virginia had directed to be Subscribed for me (& which I then declared I would only hold in trust for the State) that their were 403 Shares Subscribed: which being more than sufficient to constitute the Company under the Act—the Subscribers proceeded to the choice of a

President & 4 Directors;—the first of which fell upon me the votes for the other four fell upon [Ex] Governors [Thomas] Johnson & [Thomas Sim] Lee of Maryland—and Colonels [John] Fitzgerald & [George] Gilpin of this State. —Dined at Lomaxs and returned in the afternoon."— *Washington's Diary.*

THURSDAY, MAY 26.

At Mount Vernon : "*May 26.*—Upon my return [from riding to the plantations] found Mr Magowan, and a Doct^r Coke & a Mr Asbury here—the two last Methodist Preachers recommended by Genl Roberdeau—the same who were expected yesterday. . . . After Dinner Mr Coke & Mr Asbury went away."— *Washington's Diary.*

"*May 26.*—Mr. Asbury [Francis Asbury, Bishop of the M. E. Church] and I set off for General Washington's. We were engaged to dine there the day before. The General's seat is very elegant; built upon the great river Potomawk; for the improvement of the navigation of which, he is carrying on jointly with the State some amazing Plans. He received us very politely, and was very open to access. He is quite the plain, Country-Gentleman. After dinner we desired a private interview, and opened to him the grand business on which we came, presenting to him our petition for the emancipation of the Negroes, and entreating his signature, if the eminence of his station did not render it inexpedient for him to sign any petition. He informed us that he was of our sentiments, and had signified his thoughts on the subject to most of the great men of the State; that he did not see it proper to sign the petition, but if the Assembly took it into consideration, would signify his sentiments to the Assembly by a letter. He asked us to spend the evening and lodge at his house, but our engagement at Annapolis the following day would not admit of it. We returned that evening to Alexandria."—*Journal of the Rev. Thomas Coke.*

MONDAY, MAY 30.

At Alexandria : "*May 30.*—I went to Alexandria to meet the Directors of the Potomack C^o—Dined at Col^o Fitzgerald and Returned in the Evening."— *Washington's Diary.*

SATURDAY, JUNE 4.

At Mount Vernon : "*June 4.*—In the Afternoon the celebrated Mrs Macauly Graham & Mr Graham her Husband arrived here. *June* 8.—Placed my Military Records into the Hands of M⁫ Macauly Graham for her perusal & amusement. *June* 14.—About 7 oclock Mr Graham & M⁫ Macauly left this on their Return to New York—I accompanied them to Mr Digges's * to which place I had her Carriage & horses put over—Mr Digges escorted her to Bladensburgh." — *Washington's Diary.*

Mrs. Catharine Macaulay Graham, historian and controversialist, was the youngest daughter of John Sawbridge, Esq., of Olantigh, Kent, England. Her first husband (1760) was Dr. George Macaulay, her second (1778) William Graham. Her most famous production was the " History of England from the Accession of James I. to that of the Brunswick Line," eight volumes, 1763–1783, which attracted great attention at the time, but has now dropped into oblivion. Her visit to America was solely for the purpose of seeing Washington, with whom she had previously maintained a correspondence. She died in 1791, at the age of sixty.

THURSDAY, JUNE 30.

At Mount Vernon: " *June* 30.—Dined with only M⁫ Washington which I believe is the first instance of it since my retirement from public life."— *Washington's Diary.*

FRIDAY, JULY 1.

At Alexandria: " *July* 1.—Went to Alexandria to a meeting of the Board of Directors, who by Advertisement were to attend this day for the purpose of agreeing with a Manager and two assistants to conduct the Undertaking of the Potomack Navigation—but no person applying with proper Credentials the Board gave the applicants until thursday the 14th to provide these & for others to offer.

" Returned in the Evening accompanied by Col° Bassett & Col° Spait [Richard D. Spaight], a Member of Congress for the State of N° Carolina."— *Washington's Diary.*

* Mr. George Digges was a wealthy planter on the Potomac, in Prince George's County, Maryland. His estate, known as " Warburton," was in full view of the mansion at Mount Vernon, and the intercourse between the two families was frequent and very friendly.

TUESDAY, JULY 5.

At Mount Vernon: *"July* 5.—After dinner Mr Govourn^r^ Morris and Mr Wm Craik came in."—*Washington's Diary.*

" *July* 6.—General [Benjamin] Lincoln & his Son came to Dinner & returned afterwards. *July* 7.—Mr Govourn^r^ Morris went away before Breakfast as did Mr Craik—Col^o^ Bassett & Mr Geo: Washington accompanied the former as far as Alexandria—Mr Arthur Lee came to Dinner, to which Col^o^ Bassett & G. W. returned."— *Washington's Diary.*

THURSDAY, JULY 14.

At Alexandria: *"July* 14.—Went through my Harvest field at Muddy hole to Alexandria, to a meeting of the Directors of the Potomack Company—Agreed with Mr James Rumsey to undertake the Management of our Works—and a M^r^ [Richardson] Stuart from Baltimore as an Assistant—Gave them directions—passed some acc^ts^—paid my quota of the demand for these purposes to M^r^ [William] Hartshorne the Treasurer—Made Mrs Dalby a visit—and came home in the evening.

" Found Mr Bryan Fairfax* & his son Ferdinando here at my return who had come down before dinner."— *Washington's Diary.*

TUESDAY, JULY 26.

At Mount Vernon : " *July* 26.—On my return [from dining with Lund Washington], found Mr Will Shaw whom I had engaged to live with me as a Book Keeper, Secretary &c. here."—*Washington's Diary.*

Mr. Shaw remained at Mount Vernon in the capacity of book-keeper, etc., until August 25, 1786, when he left for Philadelphia, to embark for the West Indies.

---

* Brother of George William Fairfax, of " Belvoir," and rector of Christ Church, Alexandria, 1790–1792.

WEDNESDAY, JULY 27.

At Mount Vernon : "*July* 27.—Mⁿ Fendal, Miss Lee (eldest daughter of the Presid^t of Congress) Miss Nancy Lee, Grand daughter of Richd Lee Esqr of Maryland—Mr Chas Lee—& Mr Law^e Washington, Lund Washington & their Wives—and Mr Law^e Washington, Son of Lawrence & Mr Thos Washington Son to Robert all dined here and went away in the Afternoon."— *Washington's Diary.*

MONDAY, AUGUST 1.

At George Town, Maryland : "*August* 1.—Left home at 6 Oclock P. [? A.] M. and after escorting Fanny Bassett to Alexandria I proceeded to Doct^r Stuarts [at Abingdon] where I breakfasted; and from thence went to George Town to the Annual Meeting of the Potomack Company appointed to be held at that place. . . . Dined at Shuters [Suter's] Tavern, and lodged at Mr Oneals."— *Washington's Diary.*

"*August* 2.—Left George Town about 10 Oclock, in Company with all the Directors except Govr Lee. . . . We dined at Mr Bealls Mill 14 Miles from George Town and proceeded to a Mr Goldsboroughs, a decent Farmers House at the head of the Seneca Falls,—about 6 Miles and 20 from George Town. *August* 3.—Having provided Canoes and being joined by Mr Rumsay the principal Manager, & Mr Stewart an assistant to him, in carrying on the Works. we proceeded to examine the falls; and beginning at the head of them went through the whole by Water, and continued from the foot of them to the Great Falls. . . . Returned back by the way of Mr Bealls Mill to our old Quarters at Mr Goldsboroughs,—the distance as estimated 8 Miles. *August* 4.—Engaged nine labourers with whom to commence the Work."— *Washington's Diary.*

FRIDAY, AUGUST 5.

At Frederick Town, Maryland : "*August* 5.—After Breakfast, and after directing Mr Rumsey when he had marked the way and set the labourers to work to meet us at Harpers ferry on the Evening of the Morrow (at the conflux of the Shannondoah with the Potomack) myself and the Directors set out for the same place by way of Frederick Town

(Maryland)—Dined at a Dutchmans 2 Miles above the M°
of Monocasy & reached the former about 5 oclock—Drank
Tea—supped—and lodged at Gov' Johnsons."—*Washington's Diary.*

" In the Evening the Bells Rang, & Guns were fired; & a Committee
waited upon me by order of the Gentlemen of the Town to request that I
w'd stay next day and partake of a publick dinner which the Town were desirous of giving me—But as arrangements had been made, and the time for
examining the Shannondoah Falls, previous to the day fixed for receiving
labourers into pay, was short I found it most expedient to decline the
honor."—*Washington's Diary.*

SATURDAY, AUGUST 6.

At Harper's Ferry: " *August 6.*—Breakfasted in Frederick
Town, at Gov' Johnsons, and dined at Harpers Ferry—
took a view of the River, from the Banks as we road up the
bottom from Pains falls to the Ferry, as well as it could be
done on Horse back.—Sent a Canoe in a Waggon from the
Ferry to Keeptriest Furnace in ord' to descend the Falls
therin to-morrow."—*Washington's Diary.*

" *August 7.*—About Sunrising, the Directors & myself Rid up to Keep-
trieste, where Canoes were provided, in which we crossed to the Maryland
side of the River and examined a Gut, or swash, through which it is supposed the Navigation must be conducted. . . . Having examined this passage, I returned to the head of the fall and in one of the Canoes with two
skilful hands descended them with the common curr' in its natural bed.
. . . Here (at the Ferry) we breakfasted; after which we set out to explore
the Falls below; . . . At the foot of these Falls The Directors & myself
(Gov' Lee having joined us in the Evening before) held a meeting. . . .
Gov' Lee left us at this place—the rest of us returned to the Tavern at Harpers Ferry."—*Washington's Diary.*

MONDAY, AUGUST 8.

At Harper's Ferry: " *August 8.*—This being the day appointed for labourers to engage in the work we waited to
see the issue until Evening. . . . Many Gentlemen of the
Neighbourhood visited us here to day. . . . A few hands
offered and were employed."—*Washington's Diary.*

"Having provided a light & convenient Boat—hired two hands to work her—and laid in some Stores, Colonels Fitzgerald & Gilpin, and myself embarked in it about 6 Oclock P. M.   In this Boat we passed through the Spout, and all the other Falls and Rapids, and breakfasted at a Capt⁰ Smiths on the Maryland side; to which place our horses had been sent the Evening before—after which and dining on our prog at Knowlands Ferry (about 15 Miles from Harpers) we lodged at the House of a Mʳ Taylor, about three Miles above the Mouth of Goose Creek, and about 10 M. below Knowlands. *August* 10.—Before Sun rise we embarked, and about Nine Oclock arrived at the head of the Seneca Falls and breakfasted with our old Landlord Mʳ Goldsborough to which place our horses had proceeded the over Night from Capt⁰ Smiths. . . . After Breakfasting, and spending some time with the labourers at their different Works, of blowing, removing Stone, and getting Coal wood &c—we left the Seneca Falls about 2 oclock A. [? P.] M., & crossing the River about half a mile below them and a little above Capt⁰ Trammels we got into the great Road from Leesburgh to Alexandria and about half after Nine O'clock in the Evening I reached home after an absence from it of 10 days."—*Washington's Diary.*

SATURDAY, AUGUST 13.

At Mount Vernon : " The great object for the accomplishment of which I wish to see the inland navigation of the rivers Potomack and James improved and extended is to connect the western territory with the Atlantic states. All others with me are secondary; though I am clearly of opinion that it will greatly increase our commerce and be an immense saving in the article of transportation and draft cattle to the planters and farmers who are in a situation to have the produce of their labor water-borne. . . . I have already subscribed five shares to the Potomack navigation ; and enclosed I give you a power to put my name down for five shares to that of James river."— *Washington to Edmund Randolph.*

WEDNESDAY, AUGUST 31.

At Mount Vernon : " *August* 31.—This day I told Doctʳ Craik that I would contribute One hundred Dollars pʳ Annum, as long as it was necessary, towards the Education of His Son Geo Washington either in this Country or in Scotland."— *Washington's Diary.*

Dr. James Craik, a graduate of the University of Edinburgh, was born in Scotland, and settled in Virginia in the year 1753. He joined the expedition to the Ohio in 1754, and was with Colonel Washington at the battle of the Great Meadows and the surrender of "Fort Necessity," in July of that year. Dr. Craik was in the Braddock campaign of 1755, and remained attached to the Virginia troops until about 1763. He also served as a surgeon in the Revolutionary war. The friendship formed between Washington and the doctor in 1754 lasted through their lives, and he was a frequent and most welcome guest at Mount Vernon. He attended the General in his last illness, and was remembered in his will as his "compatriot in arms and old and intimate friend." Dr. Craik died February 6, 1814, at the age of eighty-two.

THURSDAY, SEPTEMBER 1.

At Mount Vernon : "The hounds which you were so obliging as to send, arrived safe, and are of promising appearance."— *Washington to the Marquis de Lafayette.*

"*September* 19.—Rid to the Plantations at the Ferry, Dogue run, and Muddy hole—took my French Hounds with me for the purpose of Airing them & giving them a knowledge of the grounds about the place. *November* 29.—Went out after Breakfast with my hounds from France. *December* 1.—Took the Hounds out before Sun Rise. . . . 3 or 4 of the French Hds discovered no greater disposition for Hunting to day than they did on tuesday last. *December* 5.—It being a good scenting Morning I went out with the Hounds. . . . My French Hounds performed better to day."— *Washington's Diary.*

SATURDAY, SEPTEMBER 3.

At Mount Vernon : "*September* 3.—In the Evening James Madison Esq. came in. *September* 5.—Mr Madison left this after Breakfast."— *Washington's Diary.*

TUESDAY, SEPTEMBER 6.

At Mount Vernon : "*September* 6.—A Mr Taylor Clerk to the Secretary for Foreign Affairs came here whilst we were at Dinner, sent by Mr Jay, by order of Congress, to take Copies of the Report of the Commissioners who had been sent in by me to New York, to take an Acct. of the Slaves which had been sent from that place (previous to the evacuation) by the British."— *Washington's Diary.*

FRIDAY, SEPTEMBER 9.

At Alexandria: "*September* 9.—Rid up to Alexandria with M⁸ Washington, who wanted to get some Cloathing for little Washington Custis; and for the purpose of seeing Col° Fitzgerald & Col° Gilpin on the business of the Potomack Company—Returned home to Dinner."—*Washington's Diary.*

SATURDAY, SEPTEMBER 10.

At Mount Vernon : "*September* 10.—Rid with Fanny Bassett, M⁸ Taylor and M⁸ Shaw to meet a Party from Alexandria at Johnsons Spring (on my Land where Clifton formerly lived) where we dined on a cold dinner brought from Town by water and spent the Afternoon agreeably—Returning home by Sun down or a little after it."—*Washington's Diary.*

TUESDAY, SEPTEMBER 20.

Leaves Mount Vernon : "*September* 20.—About Noon, agreeably to an appointment I set off for the Seneca Falls—dined at Col° Gilpins and proceeded afterwards with him to M⁸ Bryan Fairfaxs * where we lodged."—*Washington's Diary.*

"*September* 21.—The Rain continuing without intermission until 10 or 11 oclock, and no appearances of fair weather until Noon, we did not leave M⁸ Fairfaxs 'till a little after it and then meeting much difficulty in procuring a vessel, did not get to the Works at the Seneca falls until the labourers had quit them.—we then went to our old quarters at M⁸ Goldsboroughs were lodged—M⁸ Fairfax accompanied us. *September* 22.—About 10 oclock we left M⁸ Goldsboroughs & in a boat passed down the Seneca falls to the place where the workmen were blowing Rocks. . . . After viewing the works we crossed to the Virginia side and proceeded to the Great Falls where by appointment we were to have met Col° Fitzgerald—and Vessels to take us by Water to the little Falls in order to review the River between the two.—The

---

* The Rev. Bryan Fairfax resided at " Towlston," about three miles from the Great Falls of the Potomac. In the latter years of his life he lived at " Mount Eagle," between Alexandria and Mount Vernon, where he died in 1802.

latter we found, but not the first, & parting with Mʳ Fairfax here, and
sending our Horses by Land to Mʳ Hipkins's at the Falls Warehouse we
embarked about 3 oclock; Colᵒ Gilpin myself & one hand in one Canoe, and
two other people in another Canoe, and proceeded down the River to the
place where it is proposed to let the Water again into a Canal to avoid the
little Falls. . . . Lodged this Night at Mʳ Hipkins's at the Falls warehouse
where we arrived at Dark. *September* 23.—After taking an Early breakfast
at Mʳ Hipkins's I set out and reached home about 11 oclock."—*Washington's Diary.*

MONDAY, SEPTEMBER 26.

At Alexandria: "*September* 26.—Went up to Alexandria
to meet Colonels Gilpin & Fitzgerald on business of the
Potomack Compʸ. Dined at the New Tavern, kept by Mʳ
Lyle."— *Washington's Diary.*

SUNDAY, OCTOBER 2.

At Mount Vernon : " *October* 2.—Went with Fanny Bassett, Burwell Bassett, Doctʳ Stuart, G. A. Washington, Mʳ
Shaw & Nelly Custis to Pohick Church; to hear a Mʳ
Thompso ⸱ preach, who returned home with us to Dinner,
where I found the Rev. Mʳ Jones,* formerly a Chaplin in
one of the Pennsylvania Regiments.—After we were in
Bed (about Eleven oclock in the Evening) Mʳ Houdon, sent
from Paris by Doctʳ Franklin and Mʳ Jefferson to take My
Bust, in behalf of the State of Virginia, with three young
men assistants, introduced by a Mʳ Perin a French Gentleman of Alexandria arrived here by Water from the latter
place. *October* 7.—Sat this day, as I had done yesterday
for Mʳ Houdon to form my Bust."— *Washington's Diary.*

The General Assembly of Virginia having passed a resolution (June 22,
1784) that " The Executive be requested to take measures for procuring a
statue of General Washington, to be of the finest marble and best workman-
ship," Governor Harrison directed Thomas Jefferson, then in Paris, to
engage the services of a suitable person for the purpose. Mr. Jefferson
thereupon contracted with the celebrated statuary, Jean Antoine Houdon,

---

* David Jones, of Chester County, Pennsylvania, chaplain of General
Anthony Wayne in the Revolutionary war and the Indian war of 1794-95.

to undertake the work. Mr. Houdon was unwilling to do so without seeing Washington, and accordingly arrangements were made for his visiting the United States. He remained at Mount Vernon until October 19, during which time he made a cast of the face, from which a bust was modelled, and took minute measurements of the figure of Washington. The statue was completed in 1788, but was not put in position in the Capitol at Richmond until May 14, 1796. The figure has been pronounced by Lafayette "a fac-simile of Washington's person," while the bust is held as the acknowledged likeness of the great American.

MONDAY, OCTOBER 10.

At Mount Vernon: "*October* 10.—A Mr Jno Lone, on his way to Bishop Seabury for ordination, called & dined here —could not give him more than a general certificate founded on information, respecting his character—having no ac-quaintance with him, nor any desire to open a Correspond-ence with the *new* ordained Bishop."— *Washington's Diary.*

Dr. Samuel Seabury was elected Bishop of Connecticut, by the Church of England clergy of that State, at Woodbury, March 25, 1783, and finally consecrated November 14, 1784, at Aberdeen, Scotland, by Bishops Kilgour, Petrie, and Skinner, representing the episcopate of the Scottish Church. He was the first Bishop of the American Church.

WEDNESDAY, OCTOBER 12.

At Mount Vernon: "*October* 12.—Mr Livingston son of Peter Vanbrugh Livingston of New York came to Dinner & stayed all Night—and in the Evening Mr Madison ar-rived."— *Washington's Diary.*

"*October* 13.—Mr Livingston, notwithstanding the Rain, returned to Alexandria after dinner. *October* 14.—Mr Madison went away after Break-fast."— *Washington's Diary.*

SATURDAY, OCTOBER 15.

At Mount Vernon: "*October* 15.—The Reverend M^r [Spence] Grayson, and Doct^r [David] Griffith; Lund Wash-ington, his wife, & Miss Stuart came to Dinner—all of whom remained the Evening except L. W.—After the Candles were lighted George Augt Washington and Frances Bassett were married by Mr Grayson."— *Washington's Diary.*

MONDAY, OCTOBER 17.

Leaves Mount Vernon : " *October* 17.—Set out to meet the Directors of the Potomack Navigation at George Town, —where having all assembled, we proceeded towards the Great Falls, and dispersing for the convenience of obtaining Quarters, Govr Johnson & I went to Mr Bryan Fairfax."— *Washington's Diary.*

" *October* 18.—After an early breakfast at Mr Fairfax's Govr Johnson & I set out for the Falls (accompanied by Mr Fairfax) where we met the other Directors—and Col^o Gilpin in the operation of levelling the ground for the proposed cut or Canal from the place where it is proposed to take the Water out to the other where it will be let into the River again. . . . After dark I returned to Mr Fairfax's. *October* 19.—Immediately after breakfast I set out for my return home—at which I arrived a little after Noon.—And found my Brother Jno [Augustine] his Wife, Daughter Milly, & Sons Bushrod & Corbin, & the Wife of the first.—Mr Willm Washington & his Wife & 4 Children."— *Washington's Diary.*

FRIDAY, OCTOBER 21.

At Alexandria : " *October* 21.—My Brother [and] Mr Willm Washington and his Wife went up with me to this days Races at Alexandria—We dined at Col^o [Dennis] Ramsays & returned in the Evening. *October* 22.—Went up again to day, with my Brother and the rest of the Gentlemen to the Race & dined at M^r [William] Herberts."— *Washington's Diary.*

SATURDAY, OCTOBER 29.

At Mount Vernon : Declines, in a letter to Patrick Henry, Governor of Virginia, to accept fifty shares in the Potomac Company and one hundred shares in the James River Company, voted to him January 5 by the General Assembly of the State ; " it being their wish in particular, that those great works of improvement, which, both as springing from the liberty which he has been so instrumental in establishing, and as encouraged by his patronage, will be durable monuments of his glory, may be made monuments also of the gratitude of his country."

In this letter, after referring to his fixed determination of refusing every pecuniary recompense for his services to his country, Washington wrote, " But if it should please the General Assembly to permit me to turn the destination of the fund vested in me, from my private emolument, to objects of a public nature, it will be my study in selecting these to prove the sincerity of my gratitude for the honor conferred on me, by preferring such as may appear most subservient to the enlightened and patriotic views of the legislature." This proposition the Assembly acceded to, such disposition to be made either during his lifetime or by testamentary writing.

By his last will and testament Washington bequeathed the one hundred shares in the James River Company to the " Liberty Hall Academy in the County of Rockbridge, in the Commonwealth of Virga," now the Washington and Lee University of Lexington ; and the fifty shares of the Potomac Company " towards the endowment of a University to be established within the limits of the District of Columbia, under the auspices of the General Government."

MONDAY, OCTOBER 31.

At Mount Vernon : " *October* 31.—A Captain [Richard] Fullerton came here to Dinner on business of the State Society of the Cincinnati of Pensylvania; for whom I signed 250 Diplomas as President.—went away after."— *Washington's Diary.*

FRIDAY, NOVEMBER 4.

At Mount Vernon : " *November* 4.—In the Evening a Mʳ Jnº Fitch came in, to propose a draft & Model of a Machine for promoting Navigation, by means of a Steam."— *Washington's Diary.*

John Fitch, who in April, 1785, first conceived the idea of steam as a motive-power for vessels, and had a few months later (September) submitted a model for his steamboat before the American Philosophical Society, visited Virginia at this time, in order to petition the Legislature for assistance to complete his invention.

Washington does not seem to have taken any interest in the object of his visit, and even when at Philadelphia in 1787, in attendance on the Constitutional Convention, was not present at the successful attempt made by Fitch (August 22) to propel a boat of some size on the Delaware, although a number of the members of the Convention seem to have witnessed it.

SATURDAY, NOVEMBER 5.

At Mount Vernon : " *November* 5.—Mr Robert Washington of Chotanck—Mr Lund Washington & Mr Lawrence Washington dined here as did Col° Gilpin & Mr Noah Webster—the 4 first went away afterwards—the last stayed all Night."—*Washington's Diary.*

Noah Webster, LL.D., the author of the "American Dictionary of the English Language," first published in 1828, had previously visited Mount Vernon (May 20). His journey to the Southern States was for the purpose of petitioning their Legislatures to enact a copyright law. It is stated that when at Mount Vernon, Dr. Webster presented Washington with a copy of his pamphlet entitled "Sketches of American Policy," published in 1784, in which he argued that a new system of government was necessary for the country, in which the people and Congress should act without the constant intervention of the States. This is believed to have been the first movement toward a national constitution.

TUESDAY, NOVEMBER 8.

At Mount Vernon : " *November* 8.—A Captn Lewis Littlepage came here to Dinner. . . . This Captn Littlepage has been Aid de Camp to the Duke de Crillen—was at the Sieges of Fort St. Phillip (on the Island of Minorca) and Gibralter; and is an extraordinary character."—*Washington's Diary.*

Lewis Littlepage, son of Colonel James Littlepage, was born in Hanover County, Virginia, December 19, 1762. He was graduated at William and Mary College in 1778, and being a relative of John Jay, then minister to Madrid, he joined him in the winter of 1779–80. He volunteered in the expedition of the Duc de Crillon against Minorca in 1782, and at the attack on Gibraltar was blown up from one of the floating batteries, but saved. He subsequently made the tour of Europe, established himself at Warsaw, and went to St. Petersburg as ambassador from Poland. He died at Fredericksburg, Virginia, July 19, 1802.

THURSDAY, NOVEMBER 10.

At Alexandria : " *November* 10.—Went up to Alexandria to meet the Directors of the Potomack Company.—Dined at M^r [Philip Richard] Fendalls (who was from home) and returned in the Evening with M** Washington."—*Washington's Diary.*

WEDNESDAY, NOVEMBER 16.

At Mount Vernon : " *November* 16.—Richard Henry Lee, lately President of Congress ; * his son Ludwell, Col° Fitzgerald, and a M* Hunter (Merch*) of London came to Dinner & stayed all Night."—*Washington's Diary.*

" *November* 16.—We arrived at Mount Vernon by one o'clock—so-called by the General's eldest brother, who lived there before him, after the Admiral of that name. When Colonel Fitzgerald introduced me to the General I was struck with his noble and venerable appearance. It immediately brought to my mind the great part he had acted in the late war. The General is about six feet high, perfectly straight and well made ; rather inclined to be lusty. His eyes are full and blue and seem to express an air of gravity. His nose inclines to the aquiline ; his mouth is small ; his teeth are yet good and his cheeks indicate perfect health. His forehead is a noble one and he wears his hair turned back, without curls and quite in the officer's style, and tyed in a long queue behind. Altogether he makes a most noble, respectable appearance, and I really think him the first man in the world. . . . When I was first introduced to him he was neatly dressed in a plain blue coat, white cassimir waistcoat, and black breeches and Boots, as he came from his farm. After having sat with us some time he retired and sent in his lady, a most agreeable woman about 50, and Major Washington his nephew, married about three weeks ago to a Miss Bassett : She is Mrs. Washington's niece and a most charming young woman. She is about 19. After chatting with them for half an hour, the General came in again, with his hair neatly powdered, a clean shirt on, a new plain drab coat, white waistcoat and white silk stockings. At three, dinner was on the table, and we were shewn by the General into another room, where everything was set off with a peculiar taste, and at the same time very neat and plain. The General sent the bottle about pretty freely after dinner, and gave success to the navigation of the Potomac for his toasts, which he has very much at heart, and when finished will I suppose be the first river in the world. . . .

" After tea General Washington retired to his study and left us with the President, his lady and the rest of the Company. If he had not been anxious to hear the news of Congress from Mr. Lee, most probably he would not have returned to supper, but gone to bed at his usual hour, nine o'clock,

---

* Richard Henry Lee was President of Congress from November 30, 1784, to November 4, 1785.

for he seldom makes any ceremony. We had a very elegant supper about
that time. The General with a few glasses of champagne got quite merry,
and being with his intimate friends laughed and talked a good deal. Before
strangers he is generally very reserved, and seldom says a word."—*Diary of
John Hunter, Pennsylvania Magazine,* vol. xvii. p. 76.

THURSDAY, NOVEMBER 17.

At Mount Vernon : " *November* 17.—Col° Lee & all the
Company [including Mr. Hunter] went away after Breakfast."—*Washington's Diary.*

" *November* 17.—I rose early and took a walk about the General's grounds
—which are really beautifully laid out. He has about 4000 acres well cultivated and superintends the whole himself. Indeed his greatest pride now is,
to be thought the first farmer in America. He is quite a Cincinnatus, and
often works with his men himself—strips off his coat and labors like a common
man. The General has a great turn for mechanics. It's astonishing with
what niceness he directs everything in the building way, condescending even
to measure the things himself, that all may be perfectly uniform. The style
of his house is very elegant, something like the Prince de Condé's at Chan-
tille, near Paris, only not quite so large ; but it's a pity he did not build a
new one at once, as it has cost him nearly as much repairing his old one. His
improvements I'm told are very great within the last year. . . . It's astonishing what a number of small houses the General has upon his Estate for
his different Workmen and Negroes to live in. He has everything within
himself—Carpenters, Bricklayers, Brewers, Blacksmiths, Bakers, etc , etc.,
and even has a well assorted Store for the use of his family and servants. . . .
The General has some hundreds of Negroes on his plantations. He chiefly
grows Indian corn, wheat and tobacco. . . . The situation of Mount Vernon
is by nature one of the sweetest in the world, and what makes it still more
pleasing is the amazing number of sloops that are constantly sailing up and
down the River."—*Diary of John Hunter.*

MONDAY, NOVEMBER 21.

At Alexandria : " *November* 21.—I went up to Alexandria
with G. Washington to meet the Directors of the Potomack
Com* and to a Turtle feast (the Turtle given by myself to
the Gentlemen of Alex*). Returned in the Evening and
found the Count Doradour, recommended by & related to
the Marq* de la Fayette here."—*Washington's Diary.*

FRIDAY, NOVEMBER 25.

At Gunston Hall: "*November 25.*—Set out after breakfast, accompanied by M* G. Washington, to make M* Mason
at Colchester a visit, but hearing on the Road that he had
removed from thence I turned into Gunston Hall where we
dined and returned in the Evening & found Col° Henry Lee
& his Lady here."—*Washington's Diary.*

Gunston Hall, on the Potomac, near the mouth of the Occoquan River,
below Mount Vernon, was the residence of George Mason, author of "The
Virginia Bill of Rights." The house, erected by Mr. Mason about the year
1758, is still standing, although no longer in possession of the Mason family.

FRIDAY, DECEMBER 2.

At Mount Vernon: "*December 2.*—Col° & Mⁿ [Daniel]
Macarty came here to Dinner—as did Colonels Fitzgerald
and Gilpin—and M* Cha* Lee & Doct* Baker."—*Washington's Diary.*

SUNDAY, DECEMBER 4.

At Mount Vernon: "*December 4.*—Last Night Jn° Alton,
an Overseer of mine in the Neck—an old & faithful Servant
who had lived with me 30 odd years died—and this evening
the wife of Tho* Bishop, another old Servant who had lived
with me an equal number of years also died."—*Washington's
Diary.*

John Alton, a Welshman by birth, attended Washington in the Braddock
campaign of 1755. Thomas Bishop (the death of whose wife is noted in the
Diary) came to America in 1755, as a military servant to General Braddock,
and at the battle of the Monongahela (July 9) was detailed by that commander to wait upon Washington, who had barely recovered from a severe
attack of illness. After the death of Braddock he took service with the
young Virginia colonel, and was in attendance upon him the day of his first
interview with the widow Custis. Bishop was deemed too old for active
service in the Revolution, and remained at Mount Vernon. He died in
January, 1795, aged eighty years.

THURSDAY, DECEMBER 8.

At Mount Vernon : " *December* 8.—Captᵃ Fairley [James Fairlie] of New York came here in the Afternoon."— *Washington's Diary.*

" *December* 12.—Majʳ Farlie went away before breakfast, with 251 Diplomas which I had signed for the Members of the Cincinnati of the State of New York, at the request of General MᶜDougall Presedent of that Society.—
" After an early breakfast George Washington Mʳ Shaw & Myself went into the Woods back of Muddy hole Plantation a hunting and were joined by Mʳ Lund Washington and Mʳ William Peake.—About half after ten Oclock (being first plagued with the Dogs running Hogs) we found a fox near Colᵒ Masons Plantation on little Hunting Creek (West fork) having followed on his Drag more than half a Mile ; and run him with Eight Dogs (the other 4 getting, as was supposed after a Second Fox) close and well for an hour—When the Dogs came to a fault and to cold Hunting until 20 Minutes after 12 When being joined by the missing Dogs they put him up a fresh and in about 50 Minutes killed up in an open field of Colᵒ Mason's—every Rider & every Dog being present at the Death."—*Washington's Diary.*

SATURDAY, DECEMBER 17.

At Alexandria : " *December* 17.—Went to Alexandria to meet the Trustees of the Academy in that place—and offered to vest in the hands of the said Trustees, when they are permanently established by Charter, the Sum of One thousand pounds, the Interest of which only, to be applied towards the establishment of a charity School for the education of Orphan and other poor Children—which offer was accepted—returned again in the Evening."— *Washington's Diary.*

MONDAY, DECEMBER 19.

At Mount Vernon : " My homage is due to his Catholic Majesty for the honor of his present. The value of it is intrinsically great; but it is rendered inestimable by the manner, and the hand it is derived from. Let me entreat you, therefore, Sir, to lay before the King my thanks for the jackasses, with which he has been graciously pleased to compliment me."— *Washington to Count de Florida Blanca*, Spanish Minister of State.

The King of Spain, hearing that General Washington was endeavoring to procure in Europe asses of the best breed, for the purpose of rearing mules on his estates, made him a present of three, a jack and two jennies, and sent over with them a person who was acquainted with the habits of these animals and the mode of treating them. He arrived at Mount Vernon early in December, and after his instructions were taken down in writing by Washington, left on the 20th. The jack, called the *Royal Gift*, was about fifteen hands high.

THURSDAY, DECEMBER 22.

At Mount Vernon : " *December 22.*—Went a Fox hunting with the Gentlemen who came here yesterday [Daniel Dulany, Jr., Benjamin Dulany, Samuel Hanson, Thomas Hanson, Philip Alexander, and a Mr. Mounsher], together with Ferdinando Washington* and Mr Shaw, after a very early breakfast—found a Fox just back of Muddy hole Plantation and after a Chase of an hour and a quarter with my Dogs, & eight couple of Doctor Smiths (brought by Mr Phil Alexander) we put him into a hollow tree, in which we fastned him, and in the Pincushion put up another Fox which, in an hour & 13 Minutes was killed—We then after allowing the Fox in the hole half an hour put the Dogs upon his Trail & in half a Mile he took to another hollow tree and was again put out of it but he did not go 600 yards before he had recourse to the same shift—finding therefore that he was a conquered Fox we took the Dogs off, and came home to Dinner."— *Washington's Diary.*

" Breakfast was served, on hunting mornings, at candle-light, the general always breaking his fast with an Indian-corn cake and a bowl of milk ; and, ere the cock had 'done salutation to the morn,' the whole cavalcade would often have left the house, and the fox be frequently unkennelled before sun-rise. Those who have seen *Washington on horseback* will admit that he was one of the most accomplished of cavaliers in the true sense and perfection of the character. He rode, as he did everything else, with ease, elegance, and with power. The vicious propensities of horses were of no moment to this skilful and daring rider ! He always said that he required but one good quality in a horse, *to go along*, and ridiculed the idea of its being even pos-

---

* A nephew of General Washington, son of his brother Samuel.

sible that he should be unhorsed, provided the animal kept on his legs. Indeed the perfect and sinewy frame of the admirable man gave him such a surpassing grip with his knees, that a horse might as soon disencumber itself of the saddle as of such a rider.

"The general usually rode in the chase a horse called *Blueskin*, of a dark iron-gray color, approaching to blue. This was a fine but fiery animal, and of great endurance in a long run. . . . There were roads cut through the woods in various directions, by which aged and timid hunters and ladies could enjoy the exhilarating cry, without risk of life or limb; but Washington rode gaily up to his dogs, through all the difficulties and dangers of the ground on which he hunted, nor spared his generous steed, as the distended nostrils of *Blueskin* often would show. He was always in at the death, and yielded to no man the honor of the brush."—GEORGE WASHINGTON PARKE CUSTIS, *Recollections of Washington.*

SUNDAY, DECEMBER 25.

At Mount Vernon: " *December* 25.—Count Castiglioni came here to dinner. *December* 29.—Count Castiglioni went away after breakfast, on his tour to the Southward." — *Washington's Diary.*

THURSDAY, DECEMBER 29.

At Mount Vernon: " *December* 29.—I went [after breakfast] to my Dogue run Plantation to measure, with a view to New Model, the Fields at that place—did not return until dark nor finish my Surveys. *December* 30.—Went to Dogue Run again to compleat my Surveys of the Fields which I did about 2 o'clock."— *Washington's Diary.*

1786.

MONDAY, JANUARY 2.

At Mount Vernon: "*January* 2.—Immediately after an early breakfast I went out with the Hounds but returned as soon as it began to Rain, without touching upon the drag of a fox."— *Washington's Diary.*

"*January* 4.—After breakfast I rid by the places where my Muddy hole & Ferry people were clearing—thence to the Mill and Dogue Run Plantations—and having the Hounds with me in passing from the latter towards Muddy hole Plantation I found a Fox which after dragging him some distance and running him hard for near an hour was killed by the cross road in front of the House. *January* 10.—Rid to my Plantation in the Neck and took the hounds with me—about 11 Oclock found a fox in the Pocoson * at Sheridan's point and after running it very indifferently and treeing it once caught it about one Oclock. *January* 14 —Went out with the Hounds & run a fox from 11 oclock untill near 3 oclock when I came home and left the Dogs at fault after which they recovered the Fox & its supposed killed it."— *Washington's Diary.*

SATURDAY, JANUARY 21.

At Mount Vernon: "*January* 21.—Rid to my Plantations at Muddy hole and Dogue run—from thence to the Mill."— *Washington's Diary.*

The Mount Vernon estate proper comprised nearly forty-five hundred acres of land. For the purpose of systematic arrangement it was divided into the Mansion-House Farm and four plantations, known as the Union Farm, the Dogue Run Farm, the Muddy Hole Farm, and the River Farm, the latter of which, separated from the others by Little Hunting Creek, included several plantations in what was known as the Neck. The four plantations contained thirty-two hundred and sixty acres of arable land, and the Mansion-House Farm about four hundred and fifty acres with

---

* A word used in Virginia and other Southern States, signifying a reclaimed marsh. Both Webster and Worcester cite Washington as authority.

large bounds of woodland. Each one of the plantations had its own overseer and its independent outfit and plant. A map of the Washington
farms at Mount Vernon, reduced from a drawing made by himself, will be
found in volume xii. p. 316 of Sparks's "Writings of George Washington."

Washington, when at home, visited these farms almost every day, mounting his horse after breakfast and returning shortly before three o'clock,
when he dressed for dinner. The tour of the farms might average ten to
fifteen miles per day. The afternoon was usually devoted to the library
and the evening to his family and friends; at nine o'clock he retired for the
night, as he was an early riser.

SATURDAY, JANUARY 28.

At Mount Vernon: "*January* 28.—Went out after breakfast with my hounds—found a Fox on the Branch within
Mr Thomson Masons Field and run him some times hard
and sometimes at cold hunting from 11 oclock till near two
when I came home and left the huntsman with them who
followed in the same manner two hours or more longer,
and then took the Dogs off without killing."— *Washington's
Diary.*

WEDNESDAY, FEBRUARY 1.

At Potomac Falls: "*February* 1.—Not being able to
leave here yesterday (as I intended) for the appointed meeting of the Directors of the Potomack Navigation at the
Great Falls this day, I set out this Morning at the first
dawning of day for this purpose, and after as disagreeable
a ride as I ever had for the distance, arrived, at the Falls at
half after 11 oclock where I found Col^o Gilpin (who had
been there since Sunday Night) levelling &c—and Col^o
Fitzgerald who got there just before me.

"Spent the remainder of this day in viewing the different
grounds along which it was supposed the Canal might be
carried and after dining at the Huts went in the evening
accompanied by Col^o Fitzgerald & Mr Potts [clerk to the
board of managers] to a Mr Wheelers in the Neighbourhood (ab^t 1½ Miles off) to lodge."— *Washington's Diary.*

" *February* 2.—Spent this day in examining the ground more attentively, and levelling the different ways we had discovered yesterday. . . . Dined again at the Hutts. . . . After 7 Oclock at Night Col⁰ Fitzgerald Mʳ Potts & myself left the Hutts, & came to Mʳ William Scotts about 6 Miles on this side of the Falls where we lodged. *February* 3.—After an early breakfast we left Mʳ Scotts ; and about noon I reached home."—*Washington's Diary.*

TUESDAY, FEBRUARY 28.

Leaves Mount Vernon : " *February* 28.—Set out, by appointment, to attend a meeting of the Board of Directors of the Potomack Company at the Great Falls—Dined and lodged at Abingdon, to which place Mʳˢ Washington and all the Children accompanied me."—*Washington's Diary.*

" *March* 1.—After a very early breakfast at Abingdon I set off for the meeting at the Great Falls & passing near the little falls arrived at the former about 10 Oclock ; where in a little time, assembled Govʳ Johnston Col⁰ Fitzgerald, and Col⁰ Gilpin. Little or no business done to day. . . . I went to Mʳ Fairfax's (about 3 Miles off) where I lodged. *March* 2.—Accompanied by Mʳ Fairfax I repaired again to the Falls where we arrived about 8 oclock . . . the day was so stormy, that we could neither level, nor Survey the different tracks talked of for the Canal. . . . Col⁰ Fitzgerald & Mʳ Potts accompanied Mʳ Fairfax & myself to Towlston. *March* 3.—The Snow which fell yesterday & last Night covered the ground at least a foot deep ; and continuing snowing a little all day, & blowing hard from the N⁰ West, we were obliged tho' we assembled at yᵉ huts again to relinquish all hopes of levelling & Surveying the ground this trip. . . . I again returned (first dining at the Hutts) with Col⁰ Fitzgerald to Towlston, in a very severe evening. *March* 4.—After breakfast Col⁰ Fitzgerald and myself set off on our return home & parted at 4 Mile run.—about half after four I got to Mount Vernon, where Mʳˢ Washington, Nelly and little Washington had just arrived."—*Washington's Diary.*

SUNDAY, MARCH 5.

At Mount Vernon : " *March* 5.—Mʳ Richᵈ Bland Lee came here to dinner and stayed all Night. *March* 6.—Mʳ Lee went away about 10 Oclock and Mʳ Thornton Washington [son of Samuel Washington] came in after we had dined and stayed all night."—*Washington's Diary.*

SUNDAY, MARCH 12.

At Mount Vernon: "*March* 12.—About dusk Mr William Harrison (a delegate to Congress from the State of Maryland) and his Son came in on their way to New York. *March* 13.—Mr Harrison and son went away after breakfast."— *Washington's Diary.*

SUNDAY, MARCH 19.

At Mount Vernon: "*March* 19.—A Gentleman calling himself the Count de Cheiza D'arteignan officer of the French Guards came here to dinner; but bringing no letters of introduction, nor any authentic testimonials of his being either: I was at a loss how to receive or treat him—he stayed dinner and the evening."— *Washington's Diary.*

"*March* 21.—The Count de Cheiza D'artingnon (so calling himself) was sent, with my horses, to day, at his own request, to Alexand^a."— *Washington's Diary.*

SATURDAY, MARCH 25.

At Mount Vernon: "I feel very sensibly the honor conferred on me by the 'South Carolina Society for promoting and improving Agriculture and other Rural Concerns,' by unanimously electing me the first honorary member of that body."— *Washington to William Drayton.*

In communicating to General Washington, under date of Charleston, November 23, 1785, the above intelligence, Mr. Drayton added, "This mark of their respect, the Society thought, was with peculiar propriety due to the man, who, by his gallantry and conduct as a soldier, contributed so eminently to stamp a value on the labors of every American farmer; and who, by his skill and industry in the cultivation of his fields, has likewise distinguished himself as a farmer."

FRIDAY, APRIL 7.

At Mount Vernon: "*April* 7.—Mr George Washington went to Alexandria and engaged 100,000 Herrings to Smith & Douglas (if caught) at 5/ p^r thousand."— *Washington's Diary.*

It will be seen from the above that the fisheries at Mount Vernon formed no unimportant part of the domestic economy of the proprietor. They were quite valuable and extensive, and Washington, in describing his estate to Arthur Young, in 1793, wrote, " The river which encompasses the land, is well supplied with various kinds of fish at all seasons of the year; and, in the spring, with the greatest profusion of shad, herring, bass, carp, perch, sturgeon, &c. Several valuable fisheries appertain to the estate; the whole shore, in short, is one entire fishery."

TUESDAY, APRIL 11.

At Mount Vernon: "*April* 11.—Rid to the Fishing Landing, where 30 odd Shad had just been caught at a haul,—not more than 2 or 3 had been taken at one time before this Spring."— *Washington's Diary.*

SATURDAY, APRIL 15.

At Alexandria: "*April* 15.—Rid to Alexandria to a Meeting of the Directors of the Potomack Company, who had advertised their intention of Contracting on this day with whomsoever should bid lowest for the Supplying the Company's Servants with Rations for one year. . . . Dined at Mr Lyle's tavern and returned in the Evening."— *Washington's Diary.*

" *April* 17.—Went up to Alexandria to an election of Delegates to represent this County; when the suffrages of the people fell upon Col° Mason and Doct^r Stuart. . . . Returned home in the evening."— *Washington's Diary.*

THURSDAY, APRIL 20.

At Mount Vernon: " *April* 20.—The Shad began to Run to day, having caught 100, 200 & 300 at a draught."— *Washington's Diary.*

SUNDAY, APRIL 23.

Leaves Mount Vernon: " *April* 23.—Set off after breakfast, on a journey to Richmond—to acknowledge in the General Court some Deeds for Land sold by me as Attorney for Col° George Mercer which it seems, could not be executed without. Dined at Dumfries and lodged at Stafford Court House."— *Washington's Diary.*

"*April* 24.—A good deal of Rain having fallen in the Night and it continuing to do so till after 6 ocl^k I was detained till near seven—when I set
out, dined at my Mothers in Fredericksburg & proceeded afterwards to, and
lodged at General Spotswoods. *April* 25.—Set out from General Spotswoods about Sun Rising and breakfasted at the Bowling green. . . . Dined
at Rawlins and lodged at Hanover Court House. *April* 26.—Left Hanover
Court H° about Sun Rise—breakfasted at Norvals tavern—and reached
Richmond about Noon,—put up at Formicalo's Tavern, where by invitation, I dined with the Judges of the General Court."—*Washington's Diary.*

THURSDAY, APRIL 27.

At Richmond, Virginia: "*April* 27.—Acknowledged in
the General Court a Deed to James Mercer Esqr for the
Lotts he and I bought at the Sale of his deceased Brother
Col° George Mercer—and received a reconveyance from
him of my part thereof.

"Road with the Lieu^t Govr [Beverley] Randolph, the
Attorney General and Mr George Webb to view the cut
which had commenced between Westham and Richmond
for the improvement of the Navigation of James River. . . .
Dined and spent the evening at the Attorneys—lodged
again at Formicalo's."—*Washington's Diary.*

"*April* 28.—Left Richmond about 6 oclock—breakfasted at Norvals—
Dined at Rawlins—and lodged at the Bowling. *April* 29.—Set out from
Bowling green a little after Sun rising—breakfasted at General Spotswoods
—Dined at my Sister's in Fredericksburgh—and spent the evening at M^r
[William] Fitzhughs of Chatham. *April* 30.—Set off about Sun rising
from Mr Fitzhughs—breakfasted at Dumfries—and reached home to a late
Dinner."—*Washington's Diary.*

THURSDAY, MAY 4.*

At Abingdon: "*May* 4.—After Dinner I set out for
Abingdon in order (to morrow) to Survey my 4 Miles Run
Tract; on which I had cause to apprehend trespasses had
been committed."—*Washington's Diary.*

* "*May* 4.—Sent Maj^r Washington to town [Alexandria] on Business
where he and Mr Lund Washington engaged to Mr Watson 100 Barr^{ls} of
my Flour to be delivered next week at 32/9 p^r Barr^l."—*Washington's Diary.*

The tract on Four Mile Run, which empties into the Potomac River three miles above Alexandria, contained about twelve hundred acres. Washington made several surveys of this land, the final one on April 29 and 30, 1799, and by his last will and testament devised it to George Washington Parke Custis, his adopted son.

FRIDAY, MAY 5.

At Four Mile Run : " *May* 5.—Set out early from Abingdon, and beginning at the upper corner of my Land (on 4 Miles Run) a little below an old Mill; I ran the Tract agreeably to the courses & distances of a Plat made thereof by John Hough, in the year 1766 (Nov") in presence of Col° Carlyle & M' James Mercer.—Not hav^g Hough's field Notes & no Corner trees being noted in His *Plat,* I did not attempt to look for lines; but allowing one degree for the variation of Compass since the Survey, above mentioned, was made, I run the courses and distances only. . . . Returned at Night to Abingdon, being attended in the labours of the day by Doct' Stuart."— *Washington's Diary.*

" *May* 6.—After an early breakfast I set out on my Return home & taking Muddy hole [plantation] in my way, returned about 10 Oclock."— *Washington's Diary.*

WEDNESDAY, MAY 10.

At Mount Vernon : " A measure in which this State [Virginia] has taken the lead at its last session, will, it is to be hoped, give efficient powers to that body [Congress] for all commercial purposes. This is a nomination of some of its first characters to meet other commissioners from the several States, in order to consider and decide upon such powers as shall be necessary for the sovereign authority of them to act under."— *Washington to the Marquis de Lafayette.*

This convention met at Annapolis, Maryland, September 11, 1786, to take into consideration the trade and commerce of the United States, and to provide for a uniform system in their commercial intercourse and regulations. Five States only—New York, New Jersey, Pennsylvania, Delaware, and Virginia—were represented, and when the commissioners came together they found themselves invested with such limited powers as not to enable them to act for the general purposes of the meeting. They did little else than draw up a report, to be presented to the several States, urging the necessity of a revision of the confederated system of government, and recommending a convention of delegates with larger powers to be held at Philadelphia on the second Monday of May following.

THURSDAY, MAY 18.

At Mount Vernon : " That it is necessary to revise and amend the articles of confederation, I entertain no doubt; but what may be the consequences of such an attempt is doubtful. Yet something must be done, or the fabric must fall, for it is certainly tottering."— *Washington to John Jay.*

The letter from which the above extract is made was in answer to one from Mr. Jay, dated March 16, in which he said, " Experience has pointed out errors in our national government which call for correction, and which threaten to blast the fruit we expected from our tree of liberty. The convention proposed by Virginia [for commercial purposes] may do some good, and would perhaps do more if it comprehended more objects. An opinion begins to prevail that a general Convention for revising the articles of confederation would be expedient. Whether the people are yet ripe for such a measure, or whether the system proposed to be attained by it is only to be expected from calamity and commotion, is difficult to ascertain. I think we are in a delicate situation, and a variety of considerations and circumstances give me uneasiness.''

MONDAY, MAY 22.

At Mount Vernon : " *May* 22.—Began to take up the pavement of the Piaza. *May* 23.—This day began to lay the Flags in my Piaza. *May* 27.—Finished laying 28 courses of the pavement in the Piaza."— *Washington's Diary.*

MONDAY, MAY 29.

At Mount Vernon : " *May* 29.—About 9 Oclock Mr Tobias Lear, who had been previously engaged on a Salary of 200 dollars, to live with me as a private Secretary & preceptor for Washington Custis a year came here from New Hampshire, at which place his friends reside."— *Washington's Diary.*

Tobias Lear, who remained with Washington, first as a secretary and afterward as superintendent of his private affairs, until the close of his first term as President, was born in Portsmouth, New Hampshire, September 19, 1762, and died in Washington, D. C., October 11, 1816. At the desire of Washington he resumed his duties as secretary in the summer of 1798, and was present at his death, of which he drew up a circumstantial account. (Sparks, vol. i. p. 555.)

Mr. Lear, whose relations with Washington were of the most confidential nature, has left us the following testimonial to his private character, which, brief as it is, reveals more of the truth and consistency of his manhood than could be conveyed by the most labored eulogy : " General Washington is, I believe, almost the only man of an exalted character who does not lose some part of his respectability by an intimate acquaintance. I have never found a single thing that could lessen my respect for him. A complete knowledge of his honesty, uprightness, and candour in all his private transactions, has sometimes led me to think him more than a man."

SUNDAY, JUNE 4.

At Mount Vernon : " *June* 4.—Received from on board the Brig Ann, from Ireland, two Servant Men for whom I had agreed yesterday—viz.—Thomas Ryan a shoemaker, and Caven Bou—a Taylor Redemptioners for 3 years Service by Indenture if they could not pay, each, the sum of £12 Ster^s which sums I agreed to pay."— *Washington's Diary.*

The demand for labor of a better character than that obtained from negro slaves gave rise, at an early period in the history of the colonies, to the custom of importing white men for a specified time of service. These *covenant servants* were regularly indentured under a voluntary agreement, and upon their arrival in this country were disposed of on terms seldom exceeding seven years, except in the case of very young persons. In later years the price paid to the shipper was but little in excess of the passage-money and expenses attending the importation. At the end of the term agreed upon the " redemptioners," as they came to be called, merged into the mass of the white population without any special taint of servitude. Many of them were skilled mechanics, who in the end became valuable citizens.

WEDNESDAY, JUNE 14.

At Potomac Falls : " *June* 14.—After an early breakfast in Company with Col° Serf, I set out for our Works at the great falls ; where we arrived about 11 Oclock and after viewing them set out on our Return & reached Col° Gilpins where we lodged."— *Washington's Diary.*

" June 15.—Took Alexandria—My Mill dam Meadow at Dogue Run and the Plantation there—as also the Ferry Plantation in my way home."— *Washington's Diary.*

SATURDAY, JUNE 17.

At Mount Vernon : *" June* 17.—Mʳ Hough, Butcher in Alexandria, came here this afternoon & purchased from me three fatted Beeves (2 in the Neck & 1 at Dogue run) for which he is to pay next week £42—also the picking of 12 Weathers from my flock at 34/ pʳ head—if upon consulting my Farmer & they could be spared, he was to have 20."— *Washington's Diary.*

MONDAY, JUNE 19.

At Mount Vernon : *" June* 19.—A Monsʳ Andri Michaux a Botanest sent by the Court of France to America (after having been only 6 Weeks returned from India) came in a little before dinner with letters of Introduction & recommendation from the Duke de Lauzen, & Marqˢ de la Fayette to me—he dined and returned afterwards to Alexandˢ on his way to New York, from whence he had come; and where he was about to establish a Botanical garden."— *Washington's Diary.*

In pursuance of his commission from the French government, André Michaux established nurseries for the cultivation of trees and shrubs, to be naturalized in France, at Bergen County, New Jersey, and near Charleston, South Carolina. From the former he made one shipment, but the Revolution prevented remittances, and the work was discontinued. He, however, in prosecution of his studies, travelled extensively in America, and did not return to his native land until 1796.

His son, François André, also a distinguished botanist, was sent by the French government in 1802 to study the forests of America, which had been explored by his father. This resulted in the production of his work entitled " Histoire des Arbres Forestiers de l'Amérique," four vols., 1810-13, which laid the foundation of his reputation as a botanist. He was elected a member of the American Philosophical Society, April 21, 1809, and by his will bequeathed to it the sum of ninety-two thousand francs, invested in French three-per-cent. rentes, the interest of which is used by the Society for the advancement of botany.

SUNDAY, JUNE 25.

At Mount Vernon: "No person, who shall come with your passport, will be an unwelcome guest. . . . My manner of living is plain. I do not mean to be put out of it. A glass of wine and a bit of mutton are always ready; and such as will be content to partake of them are always welcome. Those who expect more will be disappointed."— *Washington to George William Fairfax.*

SUNDAY, JULY 2.

Leaves Mount Vernon: "*July* 2.—About Noon I set out for the intended meeting (to be held to morrow) at the Seneca falls—Dined at Col° Gilpins; where meeting with Col° Fitzgerald we proceeded all three of us to M[r] Bryan Fairfax's and lodged."— *Washington's Diary.*

"*July* 3.—After a very early breakfast (about Sun rise) we left M[r] Fairfax's and arriving at the head of the Seneca falls (where a Vessel was to have met us) was detained till near ten oclock before one arrived to put us over to our place of rendezvous at M[r] Goldsboroughs. *July* 4.—The Directors determined to prosecute their first plan for openting the Navigation of the River in the bed of it. . . . These matters being settled Col° Gilpin and myself resolved to send our horses to the Great falls and go by water to that place ourselves. . . . After dining with M[r] Rumsey at the Great falls Col° Gilpin and myself set out in order to reach our respective homes, but a gust of wind & rain, with much lightning, compelled me to take shelter, about dark at his house, where I was detained all night. *July* 5.—I set out about sun rising, & taking my harvest fields at Muddy hole & the ferry in my way, got home to breakfast."— *Washington's Diary.*

MONDAY, JULY 24.

At Mount Vernon: "*July* 24.—After breakfast I accompanied Col° [Theodoric] Bland to M[r] Lund Washingtons; where he entered the stage on his return home.—Rid from hence to the Plantations at Dogue Run & Muddy hole. . . .

On my return home, found Col° Humphreys here."—*Wash-ington's Diary.*

Colonel Humphreys remained at Mount Vernon until August 23. He had just returned from France, and, according to Lossing, brought with him, at the request of Louis XVI., an impression of the king's full-length portrait, engraved by Bervic after the painting by Callet. This engraving, which was elegantly framed, was one of the well-known ornaments of the mansion at Mount Vernon; but as it was not executed until 1790, the statement by Lossing is incorrect. It must have been presented to Washington *after* that date.

MONDAY, JULY 31.

At Mount Vernon: "General Greene lately died at Savannah in Georgia. The public as well as his family and friends, has met with a severe loss. He was a great and good man indeed."—*Washington to Count de Rochambeau.*

Nathanael Greene, of whom Alexander Hamilton said, that "his qualifications for statesmanship were not less remarkable than his military ability, which was of the highest order," died on the 19th of July, 1786, at the age of forty-four. His death, caused by a sunstroke, occurred at "Mulberry Grove," on the Savannah River, an estate presented to him by the State of Georgia. He was *indeed* "a great and good man."

TUESDAY, AUGUST 1.

At Mount Vernon: "I do not conceive we can exist long as a nation without having lodged somewhere a power, which will pervade the whole Union in as energetic a manner as the authority of the State governments extends over the several States."—*Washington to John Jay.*

SATURDAY, AUGUST 5.

At Alexandria: "*August 5.*—Went to Alexandria to a meeting of the Directors of the Potomac Comp^y in order to prepare the Acct^s and a report for the Genl Meeting of the C° on Monday next.—Neither of the Maryland Gent^a attended—Dined at Wises Tav^a."—*Washington's Diary.*

"*August 7.*—Went to Alexandria to the Genl Meeting of the Potomack C°—Col° Humphreys accompanied me—A sufficient number of shares being present to constitute the Meeting the Acct* of the Directors were exhibited and a Gen¹ Report made—but for want of the Secretarys Books which were locked up, and he absent the Orders and other proceedings referred to in that Report could not be exhibited."— *Washington's Diary.*

SATURDAY, AUGUST 19.

At Alexandria: "*August* 19.—After breakfast I accompanied Col° Humphreys by water to Alexandria and dined with him at Cap¹ [Richard] Conways to whom he had been previously engaged."— *Washington's Diary.*

TUESDAY, AUGUST 29.

At Mount Vernon: "*August* 29.—Taken with an Ague about 7 oclock this morning which being succeeded by a smart fever confined me to the House till evening—Had a slight fit of both on Sunday last but was not confined by them."— *Washington's Diary.*

"*August* 31.—Siezed with an ague before 6 oclock this morning after having laboured under a fever all night—Sent for Doct' Craik who arrived just as we were setting down to dinner; who, when he thought my fever sufficiently abated gave me a cathartick and directed the Bark to be applied in the Morning. *September* 2.—Kept close to the House to day, being my fit day in course least any exposure might bring it on,—happily missed it. *September* 14.—At home all day repeating dozes of Bark of which I took 4 with an interval of 2 hours between."— *Washington's Diary.*

SATURDAY, SEPTEMBER 9.

At Mount Vernon: "I never mean, unless some particular circumstances should compel me to it, to possess another slave by purchase, it being among my first wishes to see some plan adopted, by which slavery in this country may be abolished by law."— *Washington to John F. Mercer.*

SUNDAY, OCTOBER 1.

Leaves Mount Vernon: "*October* 1.—The day clear and warm.—Took an early Dinner and set out for Abingdon on my way to the Great Falls to meet the Directors of the Potomack C°."— *Washington's Diary.*

" *October* 2.—Set out [from Abingdon] before Six oclock, & arrived at the Great Falls ab^t half after nine.—found Col^o Gilpin there & soon after Gov^rs Johnson & Lee, and Col^o Fitzgerald & Mr Potts arrived when the board proceeded to enquire into the charges exhibited by Mr James Rumsey the late against Mr Richardson Stuart the present Manager of the Companys business—the examination of the Witnesses employed the board until dark when the Members dispersed for Lodgings—I went to Mr Fairfaxs. *October* 3.—Returned to the Falls by appointment at 7 oclock to Breakfast: we proceeded immediately afterwards to a consideration of the evidence . . . the whole appeared (the charges) malignant, envious & trifling.—After this the board settled many acc^ts and adjourned till 8 oclock next Morning. *October* 4.—The Board having agreed to a Petition to be offered to the Assemblies of Virg^a and Maryland for prolonging the time allowed by Law for improving the Navigation of the River above the Great Falls, broke up about three oclock—When in company of Col^os Fitzgerald & Gilpin & Mr Potts I set off home.—With much difficulty on acc^t of the Rising of the Water by the Rain of last Night we crossed Difficult run and through a constant Rain till I had reached Cameron * I got home a little before 8 o'clock where I found my Brother J^no Aug^e Washington."—*Washington's Diary.*

MONDAY, OCTOBER 9.

At Mount Vernon : " *October* 9.—Allowed all my People to go to the Races in Alexandria on one of three days as best comported with their respective businesses—leaving careful persons on the Plantations."— *Washington's Diary.*

TUESDAY, OCTOBER 10.

At Alexandria : " *October* 10.—In company with Major Washington and Mr Lear went up to Alexandria to see the Jockey Club purse run for (which was won by Mr Snickers) dined by invitation with the Members of it and returned home in the evening."— *Washington's Diary.*

SUNDAY, OCTOBER 15.

At Pohick Church : " *October* 15.—Accompanied by Maj^r Washington his wife—Mr Lear & the two child^n Nelly &

---

* An estate situate two miles south of the old road from Alexandria to Mount Vernon, and about eight miles from the latter place.

Washington Custis—went to Pohick Church & returned to Dinner."— *Washington's Diary.*

Pohick Church is situated on Pohick Creek, about five miles southwest of Mount Vernon. The first building (of frame) was erected on the south side of the creek in 1732. The present structure (of brick) was put up in 1772, on the north side, two miles farther up the stream, for which Washington drew the plans, and also served on the building committee. He was chosen a vestryman in 1765, and was kept in that office for several years. His pew was No. 28, north side, next to the communion table; it was marked with his initials.

SUNDAY, OCTOBER 22.

At Mount Vernon : " *October* 22.—The Honble Wm Drayton and Mr Walter Izard came here to dinner and stayed all Night."— *Washington's Diary.*

MONDAY, OCTOBER 23.

At Mount Vernon : " *October* 23.—I remained at home all day in the evening Col° Monroe & his Lady and Mr Maddison came in."— *Washington's Diary.*

" *October* 23.—Mr. Drayton, Mr. Izard here all day. After dinner General Washington was, in the course of conversation, led to speak of Arnold's treachery, when he gave an account of it." *—Diary of Tobias Lear.*

TUESDAY, OCTOBER 24.

At Mount Vernon : " *October* 24.—Mr Drayton and Mr Izard set out after breakfast on their Rout to South Carolina. *October* 25.—Mr Maddison and Col° Monroe and his Lady set out after breakfast for Fredericksburg."— *Washington's Diary.*

SUNDAY, OCTOBER 29.

At Charles County, Maryland : " *October* 29.—I crossed the River with intention to view & survey my land [600 acres] in Charles County Maryland—Went to and lodged

---

* For this interesting statement see " Washington in Domestic Life," by Richard Rush, Philadelphia, 1857.

at Gov' [William] Smallwoods about 14 Miles from the Ferry."— *Washington's Diary*.

" *October* 30.—About One oclock,—accompanied by the Governor, I set out to take a view of my land which lay 12 Miles from his House.—After doing which and finding it rather better than I expected we returned to the Govern" having from the badness of the Weather & wetness of the ground given over the idea of surveying. *October* 31.—After breakfast I left Gov' Smallwoods & got home to dinner."— *Washington's Diary*.

TUESDAY, OCTOBER 31.

At Mount Vernon : " You talk, my good Sir, of employ-ing influence to appease the present tumults in Massachu-setts. I know not where that influence is to be found, or, if attainable, that it would be a proper remedy for the dis-orders. *Influence* is not *government*. Let us have a govern-ment by which our lives, liberties, and properties will be secured, or let us know the worst at once."— *Washington to Henry Lee*.

The popular movement in Western Massachusetts in opposition to the constituted authorities, referred to in the above letter, was of a most singular character. It began as early as 1782, and increased as popular discontent, incident on the unsettled condition of affairs at the close of the Revolution, became greater. Conventions were held and lists of grievances drawn up, the complaints being of the most irrational nature. The uprising known in history as the " Shays Rebellion," taking its name from Daniel Shays, one of the principal leaders, finally culminated in an attempt (January, 1787) to capture the arsenal at Springfield by a body of eleven hundred men under Shays, which was dispersed by a force of four thousand militia commanded by General Lincoln. Shays, after living in Vermont about a year, was par-doned and removed to Sparta, New York, where he died September 29, 1825.

MONDAY, NOVEMBER 6.

At Mount Vernon : " *November* 6.—On my return home [from riding to the plantations], found Col° Lewis Morris, and his Brother Major Jacob Morris here, who dined and returned to Alexandria afterwards where M" Lewis Morris & her Mother M" Elliot were on their way to Charleston." — *Washington's Diary*.

" November 10.—With M⁰ Washington and all the family, I went to Alexandria and dined with Doct⁰ Craik—returned in the Evening."— *Washington's Diary.*

THURSDAY, NOVEMBER 16.

At Mount Vernon : " *November* 16.—On my Return home [from riding to the plantations], found Mons Campoint sent by the Marq⁰ de La Fayette with the Jack and two she Asses which he had procured for me in the Island of Malta and which had arrived at Baltimore with the Chinese Pheasants &c had with my Overseer &c got there before me —these Asses are in good order and appear to be very fine —The Jack is two years old and the She Asses one three & the other two."— *Washington's Diary.*

MONDAY, NOVEMBER 27.

At Mount Vernon : " *November* 27.—The Rev⁴ M⁰ Keith, and the Rev⁴ M⁰ Morse dined here & returned to Alexandria in the Evening."— *Washington's Diary.*

Jedidiah Morse, D.D., whose visit to Mount Vernon is recorded in the Diary, was the author of the first American geography, published at New Haven, Connecticut, 1784. From a sketch of Washington, written by Dr. Morse for an edition of the geography issued at Elizabethtown, New Jersey, 1789, we transcribe his description of the personal habits and daily life of the *Farmer of Mount Vernon:*

" He rises, in winter as well as summer, at the dawn of day ; and generally reads or writes some time before breakfast. He breakfasts about seven o'clock, on three small indian hoe-cakes and as many dishes of tea. He rides immediately to his different farms, and remains with his labourers until a little past two o'clock, when he returns and dresses. At three he dines, commonly on a single dish, and drinks from half a pint to a pint of Madeira wine. This, with one small glass of punch, a draught of beer, and two dishes of tea (which he takes half an hour before sun-setting) constitutes his whole sustenance until the next day. Whether there be company or not, the table is always prepared by its elegance and exuberance for their reception ; and the General remains at it for an hour after dinner, in familiar conversation and convivial hilarity. It is then that every one present is called upon to give some absent friend as a toast ; the name not unfrequently awakens a pleasant remembrance of past events, and gives a new turn to the animated colloquy. General Washington is more chearful than he was in the army. Although his temper is rather of a serious cast and his countenance commonly carries the impression of thoughtfulness, yet he perfectly relishes a pleasant story, an unaffected sally of wit, or a burlesque description which surprises by its suddenness and incongruity with the ordinary appearance of the object described. After this sociable and innocent relaxation, he applies himself to business; and about nine o'clock retires to rest. This is the *rotine*, and this the hour he observes, when no one but his family is present; at other times he attends politely upon his company until they wish to withdraw."

THURSDAY, NOVEMBER 30.

At Mount Vernon: " *November* 30.—Surveying my new purchase of Manley's and French's Land, in order to lay the whole of into proper inclosures."— *Washington's Diary.*

"*December* 1.—Employed as yesterday, Running round the Lands of Manley and French. *December* 2.—Finished running round the Fields of Manleys and French's and rid afterwards to Dogue run and Muddy hole plantations."— *Washington's Diary.*

MONDAY, DECEMBER 11.

At Mount Vernon: "*December* 11.—In the Afternoon a Mr Anstey (Commissioner from England for ascertaining the claims of the Refugees) with a Mr Woodorf (supposed to be his Secretary) came in and stayed all Night."— *Washington's Diary.*

SATURDAY, DECEMBER 30.

At Mount Vernon: " *December* 30.—Staked out the fields at the Ferry Plantation to-day, according to the late modification of them—visited the Ditchers and rid to Dogue run."— *Washington's Diary.*

1787.

WEDNESDAY, JANUARY 3.

At Alexandria: "*January* 3.—Rid to Alexandria to a meeting of the board of Directors of the Potomack C°—Did the business which occasioned the Meeting dined at Lomax's & returned home in the evening."—*Washington's Diary.*

WEDNESDAY, JANUARY 10.

At Mount Vernon: "*January* 10.—I rec^d by express the acc^t of the sudden death (by a fit of the Gout in the head) of my beloved Brother Col° Jn° Aug° Washington." *—*Washington's Diary.*

Augustine Washington, of Pope's Creek, Westmoreland County, Virginia, the father of General Washington, had ten children: Butler, Lawrence, Augustine, and Jane by his first wife, Jane Butler; GEORGE. Betty, Samuel, *John Augustine*, Charles, and Mildred by his second wife, Mary Ball, to whom he was married on the 6th of March, 1731.† Augustine Washington died April 12, 1743, aged forty-nine years, at an estate in King George, now Stafford, County, on the Rappahannock River, nearly opposite to Fredericksburg, to which he had removed in 1739, seven years after the birth of his son GEORGE.

THURSDAY, JANUARY 25.

At Mount Vernon: "*January* 25.—On my return home [from a ride to the plantations] found Mr Madison here—and after Dinner Mr Griffith came in—both of whom stayed all night."—*Washington's Diary.*

---

* John Augustine Washington died at his estate on the Nominy River, Westmoreland County, Virginia.

† Three of the children died young,—Butler and Mildred in infancy, and Jane at the age of thirteen.

"*January* 26.—Mr Madison & Mr Griffith going away after breakfast, (the former to attend Congress) I rid as yesterday to all ye Plant^{ns}."—*Washington's Diary.*

TUESDAY, FEBRUARY 6.

At Mount Vernon : " *February* 6.—About Sundown Messrs Bushrod & Corben Washington [sons of John Augustine Washington] came in on their return from Berkeley County."— *Washington's Diary.*

"*February* 7.—Continued at home. *February* 8.—At home all day. *February* 9.—Mr Bushrod Washington* and his Brother Corbin went away after breakfast."—*Washington's Diary.*

WEDNESDAY, FEBRUARY 14.

At Mount Vernon: " *February* 14.—Rid immediately, after breakfast to French's Plantation to see a sick man— and intended to have gone to others but was driven back by the Rain."— *Washington's Diary.*

SATURDAY, FEBRUARY 17.

At Mount Vernon: " *February* 17.—Went into the Neck to Mark some lines for fences. . . . Received before I had done a message acquainting me that Col^o [Jeremiah] Wadsworth and a Mr Chaloner were here which brought me home."— *Washington's Diary.*

TUESDAY, FEBRUARY 20.

At Alexandria: " *February* 20.—Went with Mrs Washington to Mr Fendalls to make a visit to Col^o and M^{rs} [Henry] Lee.—dined and returned home in the Evening."— *Washington's Diary.*

THURSDAY, FEBRUARY 22.

At Mount Vernon : " *February* 22.—Rid to Muddy hole Dogue run & Frenchs Plantation. . . . On my return home

---

* The favorite nephew of General Washington, and devisee under his will of the Mount Vernon estate.

found Mr Bryan Fairfax, his wife & daughter here."—
Washington's Diary.

"*February* 23.—At home all day. In the Evening Mr Griffith came in
and stayed all Night. *February* 24.—After breakfast Mr. Fairfax, his wife
& daughter—and Mr Griffith went away."—*Washington's Diary.*

SATURDAY, MARCH 3.

At Mount Vernon: "*March* 3.—The Revd Mr Weems,
and ye Doct^r Craik who came here yesterday in the afternoon left this about Noon for Port Tob^o [Port Tobacco,
Maryland]."—*Washington's Diary.*

The visitor at Mount Vernon, Mason Locke Weems, was the author of
that curious compound of fact and fancy, religion and morality, which was
published at George-Town in 1800, with the title, "A History of the Life
and Death, Virtues and Exploits, of General George Washington; dedicated
to Mrs. Washington; and containing a great many curious and valuable
Anecdotes, tending to throw much light on the *private* as well as *public* life
and character of that very Extraordinary Man; the whole happily calculated
to furnish a feast of true Washingtonian Entertainment and Improvement,
both to ourselves and our children." The original production, after going
through several editions, was almost entirely rewritten, and issued at Philadelphia in 1808 as the sixth edition, with the title, "The Life of George
Washington; with curious Anecdotes, equally honorable to Himself, and
exemplary to his young Countrymen." This is the book in which *the
hatchet story, the cabbage-seed story*, etc., first appeared, and which, notwithstanding its fabrications and fanciful anecdotes, has been more widely known
and read than all the other biographies and sketches of Washington. Since
that date (1808) more than fifty editions have been issued, the last bearing
date 1892. In several years two editions were printed, and in 1810 three
appeared, the fifteenth, sixteenth, and seventeenth.

THURSDAY, MARCH 15.

At Mount Vernon: "*March* 15.—Went out with my
Compass in order to Mark the ground at Muddy hole intended for experiments, into half acre lotts, and two other
pieces adjoining—all in field N° 2—into 10 acre lotts—Also
to mark the lines which divide field N° 1 from N° 2 & 3—
and the fields 6 & 7 at Dogue Run."—*Washington's Diary.*

SUNDAY, MARCH 25.

At Mount Vernon: "Most of the legislatures have appointed, and the rest it is said will appoint, delegates to meet at Philadelphia on the second Monday in May next in a general convention of the States, to revise and correct the defects of the federal system. Congress have also recognised and recommended the measure."— *Washington to the Marquis de Lafayette.*

On February 21, Congress in session passed the following resolution: "That in the opinion of Congress it is expedient, that, on the second Monday in May next, a convention of delegates, who shall have been appointed by the several States, be held at Philadelphia, for the sole and express purpose of revising the Articles of Confederation, and reporting to Congress and the several legislatures such alterations and provisions therein, as shall. when agreed to in Congress and confirmed by the States, render the federal constitution adequate to the exigencies of government and the preservation of the Union."

Early in December, 1786, the General Assembly of Virginia appointed Washington one of the delegates from that State to attend a proposed general convention of all the States, to be held at Philadelphia, which was subsequently recommended by Congress in the foregoing resolution. Washington at first declined the appointment, but at the urgent solicitation of the Governor of the State (Edmund Randolph) and others,* finally consented to serve.

MONDAY, APRIL 16.

At Alexandria: "*April 16.*—Went up to Alexandria to the Election of Delegates to Represent the Country in General Assembly—when Col° Mason and Doct^r Stuart were chosen.—Returned in the Evening, accompanied by

---

* In this connection a letter from General Knox to Washington, dated March 19, 1787, will be noticed in Sparks, vol. ix. p. 238, in which, after saying that he took it for granted that Washington would be constrained to accept the position of presiding officer of the convention. the general writes, "I am persuaded, that your name has had already great influence to induce the States to come into the measure, that your attendance will be grateful, that your presence would confer on the assembly a national complexion, and that it would more than any other circumstance induce a compliance with the propositions of the convention."

Col° Mason—his two Sons William and George & his Son-in-Law Col° Cooke."— *Washington's Diary.*

THURSDAY, APRIL 26.

At Mount Vernon : "*April* 26.—Receiving an Express between 4 & 5 oclock this afternoon informing me of the extreme illness of my Mother and Sister Lewis I resolved to set out for Fredericksburgh by daylight in the Morning—and spent the evening in writing some letters on business respecting the Meeting of the Cincinnati to the Secretary General of the Society Gen¹ Knox."— *Washington's Diary.*

"*April* 26.—Though so much afflicted with a rheumatic complaint (of which I have not been entirely free for six months) as to be under the necessity of carrying my arm in a sling for the last ten days, I had fixed on Monday next for my departure [for Philadelphia], and had made every necessary arrangement for the purpose, when (within this hour) I am called by an express, who assures me not a moment is to be lost to see a mother and only sister (who are supposed to be in the agonies of death) expire ; and I am hastening to obey this melancholy call, after having just buried a brother who was the intimate companion of my youth, and the friend of my ripened age."— *Washington to General Knox.*

FRIDAY, APRIL 27.

At Fredericksburg : "*April* 27.—About sun rise I commenced my journey as intended—Bated at Dumfries, and reached Fredericksburgh before two o'clock and found both my Mother & Sister better than I expected—the latter out of danger as is supposed, but the extreme low state in wch the former was, left little hope of her recovery as she was exceedingly reduced and much debilitated by age and the disorder—Dined and lodged at my Sisters."— *Washington's Diary.*

"*April* 28.—Dined at Mrs Lewis's and Drank Tea at Judge Mercers ;—Gen¹ [George] Weedon, Col° Ch^s Carter, Judge Mercer, and M^r Jn° Lewis and his wife dined with me at my sisters. *April* 29.—Dined at Col° Charles Carters—and drank Tea at Mr John Lewis's. *April* 30.—Set out about Sun-rise on my return home.—halted at Dumfries for about an hour where I breakfasted—reached home about 6 oclock in a sm[l] shower, which did not continue (and that not hard) for more than 15 Minutes."—*Washington's Diary.*

THURSDAY, MAY 3.

At Mount Vernon : " *May 3.*—Rid to the Fishing landing —and thence to the Ferry, Frenchs, Dogue Run, and Muddy hole Plantations with my Nephew G. W. [George Augustine Washington] to explain to him the Nature, and the ord[r] of the business at each as I would have it carried on during my absence at the Convention in Philadelphia."—*Washington's Diary.*

MONDAY, MAY 7.

At Mount Vernon : " *May 7.*—At home preparing for my journey to Philadelphia."—*Washington's Diary.*

" *May 8.*—The weather being squally with Showers I defer[d] setting off till the Morning—M[r] Cha[s] Lee came in to dinner but left afterwards."— *Washington's Diary.*

WEDNESDAY, MAY 9.

Leaves Mount Vernon : " *May 9.*—Crossed from M[t] Vernon to M[r] Digges a little after Sun rise & pursuing the Rout by the way of Baltimore—dined at M[r] Rich[d] Hendersons in Bladensb[g] and lodged at Maj[r] Snowdens where feeling very severely a violent h[d] ach & sick stomach I went to bed early."—*Washington's Diary.*

" *May 10.*—Very great appearances of Rain in the morning, & a little falling, induced me, tho' well recovered to wait till ab[t] 8 oclock before I set off—At one Oclock I arrived at Baltimore—Dined at the Fountain [Inn], & Supped & lodged at Doct[r] [James] M[c]Henrys—Slow Rain in the Evening. *May 11.*—Set off before breakfast—rid 12 Miles to Skerretts for it— baited there and proceeded without halting (weather threatning) to the Ferry at Havre de gras where I dined but could not cross the wind being turbulent & squally—lodged here. *May 12.*—With difficulty (on acc[t] of the Wind) crossed the Susquehanna—Breakfasted at the Ferry house on the East side—Dined at the head of Elk (Hollingsworths Tavern)—and lodged at Wilmington at O'Flins [Tavern]—at the head of Elk I was overtaken by M[r] Francis Corbin who took a seat in my Carriage."—*Washington's Diary.*

SUNDAY, MAY 13.

At Philadelphia : " *May* 13.—About 8 Oclock Mr Corbin and myself set out, and dined at Chester (M^n Withys) where I was met by the Gen^ls Mifflin (now Speaker of the Pennsylvania Assembly) Knox and Varnum—The Colonels Humphreys and Minges [Francis Mentges]—and Majors [William] Jackson and [Francis] Nicholas—With whom I proceeded to Philad^s—at Grays Ferry the City light horse commanded by Col^o [Samuel] Miles met me and escorted me in by the Artillery Officers who stood arranged & saluted as I passed—alighted through a crowd at Mrs Houses *—but being again warmly and kindly pressed by M^r & Mrs Robt Morris to lodge with them I did so and had my baggage removed thither †—Waited on the President [of the State] Doct^r Franklin as soon as I got to Town—On my arrival, the Bells were chimed."— *Washington's Diary.*

" *Philadelphia*, May 14.—Yesterday His Excellency General WASHINGTON, a member of the grand convention, arrived here.—He was met at some distance and escorted into the city by the troop of horse, and saluted at his entrance by the artillery. The joy of the people on the coming of this great and good man was shewn by their acclamations and the ringing of bells."—*Pennsylvania Packet.*

MONDAY, MAY 14.

At Philadelphia : " *May* 14.—This being the day appointed for the Convention to meet, such Members as were in town assembled at the State H^o ‡ but only two States being represented—viz—Virginia & Pennsylvania—agreed to attend at the same place at 11 Oclock to morrow. Dined in a family way at Mr Morris's."— *Washington's Diary.*

" *May* 15.—Repaired, at the hour appointed to the State H^o, but no more States being represented than were yesterday (tho' several more members

* Mrs. Mary House kept a boarding-house at the corner of Fifth and Market Streets.

† Robert Morris resided on the south side of Market Street, below Sixth.

‡ The sessions of the Convention were held in the eastern room on the first floor, " Independence Chamber."

had come in) we agreed to meet again to morrow. Govᴿ Randolph from Virginia came in to day. Dined with the Members, to the Gen¹ Meeting of the Society of the Cincinnati. *May* 16.—No more than two States being yet represented, agreed till a quoram of them should be formed to alter the hour of Meeting at the State house to one Oclock. Dined at the President Doctᴿ Franklins—and drank Tea, and spent the evening at Mᴿ Jn° Penns. *May* 17.—Mᴿ [John] Rutledge from Charleston and Mᴿ Ch. Pinkney from Congress having arrived gave a Representation to S° Carolina—and Col° Mason getting in this Evening placed all the Delegates from Virginia on the floor of Convention. Dined at Mᴿ Powells * and drᵏ Tea there. *May* 18.—The Representation from New York appeared on the floor to day. Dined at Greys ferry, and drank Tea at Mᴿ Morris's—after which accompanied Mᴿˢ and some other Ladies to hear a Mᴿˢ O'Connell read (a charity affair) the lady being reduced in circumstances had had recourse to this expedient to obtain a little money—her performᵉ was tolerable—at the College Hall [Fourth, below Arch Street]. *May* 19.—No more States represented— Dined at Mᴿ [Jared] Ingersolls—spent the evening at my lodgings & Retired to my Room soon."— *Washington's Diary.*

SUNDAY, MAY 20.

At Philadelphia: " *May* 20.—Dined with Mᴿ & Mᴿˢ Morris and other Company at their farm (called the Hills †)— Returned in the afternoon & drank Tea at Mᴿ Powells."— *Washington's Diary.*

" *May* 21.—Delaware State was represented. Dined and drank Tea at Mᴿ Binghams ‡ in great splendor. *May* 22.—The Representation from N°

---

* Samuel Powel, mayor of Philadelphia in 1775 and 1789, lived at No. 112 Third Street, between Walnut and Spruce. The house, which is still standing, is now known as No. 244 South Third Street. Mr. Powel married Elizabeth Willing, sister of Thomas Willing, the well-known merchant. Washington was a frequent visitor at this house during his stay in the city.

† " The Hills,' which originally comprised eighty acres, lay upon the east bank of the Schuylkill River, north of Fairmount Hill, and extended to the Ridge Road. That portion of the land upon which the mansion-house stood, known in later years as Lemon Hill, is included in Fairmount Park.

‡ William Bingham, member of Congress from Pennsylvania, 1787–88, and United States Senator, 1795–1801, married Anna, daughter of Thomas Willing, October 26, 1780. Mrs. Bingham was distinguished for her beauty, elegance of manner, and profuse hospitality. The Bingham mansion, on Third Street, above Spruce, was one of the finest private residences of the day.

Carolina was compleated which made a representation for five States. Dined and drank Tea at M*r* Morris's."—*Washington's Diary.*

WEDNESDAY, MAY 23.

At Philadelphia: "*May 23.*—No more States being represented I rid to Gen*l* Mifflins * to breakfast—after which in Company with him M*r* Madison, M*r* Rutledge, and others I crossed the Schuylkill above the Falls—visited M*r* Peters † M*r* Penns Seat,—and M*r* W*m* Hamiltons.

"Dined at M*r* [Benjamin] Chews [No. 110 South Third Street]—with the Wedding guests (Col° [John Eager] Howard of Baltimore having married his daughter Peggy) —Drank Tea there in a very large Circle of Ladies."— *Washington's Diary.*

"*May 24.*—No more States represented. Dined, and drank Tea at M*r* John Ross's.‡ One of my Postilion boys (Paris) being sick, requested Doct*r* [John] Jones to attend him."—*Washington's Diary.*

FRIDAY, MAY 25.

At Philadelphia: "*May 25.*—Another Delegate coming in from the State of New Jersey gave it a Representation and encreased the number to Seven which forming a quorum of the 13 the Members present resolved to organize the body; when by a unanimous vote I was called up to the Chair as President of the body.—Maj*r* William Jackson was appointed Secretary—and a Com*ee* was chosen consist-

---

* Thomas Mifflin's country house was on the Ridge Road, at the Falls of Schuylkill, on the east side of the river, in what is now the Twenty-eighth Ward of the city of Philadelphia. The house was taken down quite recently.

† Richard Peters, Judge of the United States District Court for Pennsylvania from 1792 until his death in 1818, was a warm personal friend of General Washington. The Peters estate, on the high land west of the Schuylkill River, about one mile and a half below the Falls, and known as "Belmont," is now in Fairmount Park. The mansion-house, erected in 1745 by William Peters, is still standing and occupied as a Park restaurant.

‡ A prominent shipping merchant and importing agent of Philadelphia. A Scotchman by birth.

ing of 3 Members * to prepare Rules & Regulations for conducting the business—and after appointing door keepers the Convention adjourned till Monday, to give time to the Com⁰⁰ to report the Matter referred to them.

" Returned many visits to day—Dined at Mʳ Tho' Willings †—and spᵗ the evening at my lodgings."— *Washington's Diary.*

" *May* 26.—Returned all my visits this forenoon dined with a club at the City Tavern and spent the evening at my quarters writing letters. *May* 27. —Went to the Romish Church [St. Mary's, Fourth Street, above Spruce]— to high Mass—Dined, drank Tea, and spent the evening at my lodging."— *Washington's Diary.*

MONDAY, MAY 28.

At Philadelphia: " *May* 28.—Met in Convention at 10 Oclock. Two States more—viz—Massachusetts and connecticut were on the floor to day. Established Rules— agreeably to the plan broᵗ in by the Com⁰⁰ for the governmᵗ of the Convention & adjourned.—No com⁰ˢ without doors.‡

" Dined at home, and drank Tea in a large circle at Mʳ [Tench] Francis's."— *Washington's Diary.*

" *May* 29.—Attended Convention—and dined at home—after wᶜʰ accompanied Mʳˢ Morris to the benefit Concert [at the City Tavern] of a Mʳ Jutan [Juhan]. *May* 30.—Dined with Mʳ [John] Vaughan—drank Tea, and spent the evening at a Wednesday evening party at Mʳ & Mʳˢ Lawrences.§ *May* 31.—The State of Georgia came on the Floor of the Convention to day which made a Representation of ten States. Dined at Mʳ Francis's and drank Tea with Mʳˢ Meridith."— *Washington's Diary.*

---

* George Wythe, Alexander Hamilton, and Charles Pinckney.

† Thomas Willing, the head of the mercantile house of Willing & Morris (Robert Morris the financier), resided at the southwest corner of Third Street and Willing's Alley, below Walnut Street. He was the first president of the Bank of North America, the first bank chartered in this country, 1781.

‡ One of the rules adopted by the Convention, to be observed in their proceedings as standing orders, reads thus: " That nothing spoken in the House be printed, or otherwise published, or communicated without leave."

§ John Lawrence, mayor of Philadelphia, 1765–66, and justice of the Supreme Court, 1767–76.

FRIDAY, JUNE 1.

At Philadelphia : "*June* 1.—Attending in Convention— and nothing being suffered to transpire no minutes of the proceedings has been, or will be inserted in this diary.

"Dined with Mʳ John Penn, and spent the evening at a superb entertainment at Bush Hill given by Mʳ [William] Hamilton—at which were more than an hundred guests."— *Washington's Diary.*

The estate called "Bush Hill," purchased in 1729 by Andrew Hamilton, the eminent lawyer, was part of the Springettsbury Manor. It lay north of Vine Street, in what is now the Fifteenth Ward of the city of Philadelphia, and the mansion, erected about 1740, stood on the north side of the present Buttonwood Street, between Seventeenth and Eighteenth Streets. It was occupied by John Adams during a portion of his term as Vice-President, and was destroyed by fire about the year 1808.

SATURDAY, JUNE 2.

At Philadelphia : "*June* 2.—Mʳ [Daniel of St. Thomas] Jenifer coming in with sufficient powers for the purpose, gave a representation to Maryland; which brought all the States in the Union into Convention except Rhode Island which had refused to send delegates thereto.

"Dined at the City Tavern with the Club & spent the evening at my own quarters. *June* 3.—Dined at Mʳ [George] Clymers and drank Tea there also."— *Washington's Diary.*

MONDAY, JUNE 4.

At Philadelphia : "*June* 4.—Attended Convention.—Rep- resentation as on Saturday. Reviewed (at the importunity of Genʳ Mifflin and the officers) the Light Infantry—Cavalry —and part of the Artillery of the City.

"Dined with Genʳ Mifflin & drᵏ Tea with Miss Cadwalla- der."— *Washington's Diary.*

"*June* 4.—In the evening my wife and I went to Market Street to see that great and good man General Washington. We had a full view of him and Major Jackson, who walked with him, but the number of people who followed him on all sides was astonishing. He had been out on the field to review Captain Samuel Miles with his Troop of Horse, the light infantry and artillery."—*Diary of Jacob Hiltzheimer.*

TUESDAY, JUNE 5.

At Philadelphia: "*June 5.*—Dined at Mr Morris's with a large Company & spent the Evening there—Attended in Convention the usual hours."—*Washington's Diary.*

" *June 6.*—In Convention as usual—Dined at the Presidents (Doct^r Franklins) & drank Tea there—after which returned to my lodgings and wrote letters for France. *June 7.*—Attended Convention as usual—Dined with a Club of Convention Members at the Indian Queen [Tavern, Fourth, above Chestnut Street]—Drank Tea & spent the evening at my lodgings. *June 8.* —Attended the Convention.—Dined, drank Tea, and spent the evening at my lodg^s. *June 9.*—At Convention—Dined with the Club at the City Tavern—Drank Tea & set till 10 oclock at Mr Powells."—*Washington's Diary.*

SUNDAY, JUNE 10.

At Philadelphia: "*June 10.*—Breakfasted at Mr Powells, and in Company with him rid to see the Botanical Garden of M^r [William] Bartram; which, tho' stored with many curious plants, Shrubs & trees, many of which are exotics was not laid off with much taste, nor was it large.

"From hence we rid to the Farm of one Jones, to see the effect of the plaister of Paris which appeared obviously great. . . . From hence we visited Mr Powells own farm after which I went (by appointment) to the Hills & dined with M^r & Mrs Morris—Returned to the City ab^t dark."— *Washington's Diary.*

The Bartram gardens, the first botanical gardens in the United States, were founded in 1728 by John Bartram, a distinguished botanist of Philadelphia. They were situated on the west bank of the Schuylkill River, a short distance below the lower ferry, afterward called Gray's Ferry. The house, built by him in 1731, is still standing. John Bartram, cited by Linnæus as the greatest natural botanist in the world, died September 2, 1777; he was succeeded by his son William, who had like tastes. Both father and son travelled extensively through the United States, collecting specimens. The gardens, comprising about seven acres in what is now the Twenty-seventh Ward of the city of Philadelphia, have been lately purchased with some additional land, by the city, for a public park.

MONDAY, JUNE 11.

At Philadelphia : "*June* 11.—Attended in Convention— Dined, drank Tea, and spent the evening in my own Room." — *Washington's Diary.*

"*June* 12.—Dined and drank Tea at Mr Morris's—went afterwards to a concert [of Mr. Reinagle] at the City Tavern. *June* 13.—In Convention— dined at Mr Clymers & drank Tea there. Spent the evening at Mr Bing-hams. *June* 14.—Dined at Major [Thomas Lloyd] Moores (after being in Convention) and spent the evening at my own lodgings. *June* 15.—In Convention as usual—dined at Mr Powells & drank Tea there. *June* 16.— In Convention—Dined with the Club at the City Tavern—and drank Tea at Doct^r Shippins with Mrs Livingstons party." *—*Washington's Diary.*

SUNDAY, JUNE 17.

At Philadelphia : "*June* 17.—Went to [Christ] Church— heard Bishop White preach, and see him ordain two Gen-tlemen Deacons—after wch rid 8 Miles into the Country and dined with M^r Jn° Ross in Chester County—Returned in the Afternoon."— *Washington's Diary.*

"*June* 18.—Attended the Convention—Dined at the Quarterly Meeting of the Sons of St Patrick at the City Tav^n—Drank Tea at Dr Shippins with Mrs Livingston. *June* 19.—Dined (after leaving Convention) in a family way at Mr Morris's and spent the Evening there in a very large Company. *June* 20.—Attended Convention—Dined at M^r [Samuel] Merediths † & drank Tea there. *June* 21.—Attended Convention—Dined at Mr Pragers, and spent the evening in my Chamber. *June* 22.—Dined at Mr Morris's & drank Tea with Mr Frans. Hopkinson. *June* 23.—In Convention—Dined at Doct^r [Thomas] Ruston & drank Tea at Mr Morris's. *June* 24.—Dined at Mr Morris's & spent the evening at Mr Merediths—at Tea. *June* 25.— Attended Convention—Dined at Mr Morris's—drank Tea there & spent the evening in my chamber. *June* 26.—Attended Convention—partook of a family dinner with Govr Randolph,—and made one of a party to drink Tea

---

* Dr. William Shippen, the younger, and his daughter Anne Hume, who married Henry Beekman Livingston, son of Robert R. Livingston, March 11, 1781.

† Member of Congress 1787–88, and **Treasurer of the United** States from 1789 to 1801.

at Grays Ferry.* *June* 27.—In Convention—Dined at M* Morris's—drank Tea there also—and spent the evening in my own chamber. *June* 28.—Attended Convention—Dined at M* Morris's in a large Company (the news of his Bills being protested arriving last Night a little Mal-apropos)—Drank Tea there & spent the evening in my chamber. *June* 29.—In Convention—Dined at M* Morris's and spent the evening there."— *Washington's Diary.*

SATURDAY, JUNE 30.

At Philadelphia: "*June* 30.—Attended Convention—Dined with a Club at Springsbury [? Springettsbury]—consisting of several associated families of the City—the Gentlemen of which met every Saturday accompanied by the females of the families every other Saturday—this was the ladies day."— *Washington's Diary.*

Of this dining club, known as the "Cold Spring Club," we have been unable to obtain any information other than the fact that Tench Francis, the first cashier of the Bank of North America, acted as treasurer for it in the summers of 1786 and 1787. It is presumed that the place of meeting must have been at some point in the Springettsbury Manor, a large tract of land adjoining the city of Philadelphia on the northwest, and in which there were a number of large springs. Besides the Saturday above mentioned, Washington dined with the club, as appears by his Diary, on July 7, 14, 21, 28, on August 11 and 25, and on September 8.

SUNDAY, JULY 1.

At Philadelphia: " Every body wishes, every body expects something from the convention ; but what will be the final result of its deliberation, the book of fate must disclose. Persuaded I am, that the primary cause of all our disorders lies in the different State governments, and in the tenacity

---

* The garden at Gray's Ferry, on the west side of the Schuylkill River, three miles southwest of the city, was one of the most popular resorts of the day. The grounds were laid out with pleasant walks and ornamental shrubbery, and every means, such as concerts, fireworks, and the like, were used to make the place attractive. Out-of-door parties attended by the best people of the city were frequently held at the garden, and on several public occasions fêtes were given by the proprietors, George and Robert Gray. Manasseh Cutler, who visited the garden at Gray's Ferry, July 14, 1787, gives in his journal an elaborate description of the beauty and arrangement of the grounds.

6

of that power, which pervades the whole of their systems."
— *Washington to David Stuart.*

"*July* 1.—Dined and spent the evening at home. *July* 2.—Attended Convention—Dined with some of the Members of Convention at the Indian Queen. Drunk Tea at Mr Binghams, and walked afterwards in the State house yard. Set this Morning for Mr Pine who wanted to correct his port^t of me." *—*Washington's Diary.*

TUESDAY, JULY 3.

At Philadelphia : "*July* 3.—Sat before the meeting of the Convention for M^r [Charles Willson] Peale who wanted my picture to make a print or Metzotinto by.† Dined at Mr Morris's and drank Tea at M^n Powells—after which in Company with him, I attended the agricultural Society at Carpenters Hall." ‡— *Washington's Diary.*

"*July* 3.—Returning from a visit to my meadow before breakfast, with my daughter Hannah, we met His Excellency General Washington taking a ride on horseback, only his coachman Giles with him."—*Diary of Jacob Hiltzheimer.*

WEDNESDAY, JULY 4.

At Philadelphia : "*July* 4.—Visited Doct^r Shovats Anatomical figures—and (the Convention having adjourned for the purpose) went to hear an Oration on the Anniversary of Independence delivered by a Mr Mitchell a student of Law.—After which I dined with the State Society of the

---

* The portrait painted by Mr. Pine at Mount Vernon in May, 1785.

† Mr. Peale made several copies of the bust portrait resulting from this and the subsequent sittings noted in the Diary, under dates of July 6 and 9. The mezzotinto executed from it is well known to collectors, although impressions of it have become extremely rare. A description of this interesting print will be found on page 18 of Baker's " Engraved Portraits of Washington."

‡ This building, in which the sessions of the Congress of 1774 (the First Continental Congress) were held, and to which Washington was a delegate, was erected by " The Carpenters Company of the City and County of Philadelphia" in 1770. It is still standing in perfect preservation, back from the south side of Chestnut Street, below Fourth.

Cincinnati at Epplees Tavern [No. 117 Race Street], and drank Tea at Mʳ Powells."— *Washington's Diary.*

The *Pennsylvania Journal* of July 4, in the following notice of this celebration of the anniversary of independence, gives a different name for the orator of the day from that in the Diary: "THIS MORNING, at the hour of eleven being the *Anniversary of Independence*, an *Oration* will be pronounced by *James Campbell*, esquire, in honor of the day, at the Reformed Calvinist Church, in Race-street [below Fourth, south side]—the business of the day to be introduced by Prayer, by the Rev. *William Rogers*, and the doors to be opened at 10 o'clock."

THURSDAY, JULY 5.

At Philadelphia: "*July* 5.—Attended Convention—Dined at Mʳ Morris's and drank Tea there—spent the evening also."— *Washington's Diary.*

"*July* 6.—Sat for Mʳ Peale in the Morning—attended Convention—Dined at the City Tavern with some members of Convention—and spent the evening at my lodgings. *July* 7.—Attended Convention—Dined with the Club at Springsburg—and drank Tea at Mʳ Merediths."— *Washington's Diary.*

SUNDAY, JULY 8.

At Philadelphia : "*July* 8.—About 12 Oclock rid to Doctʳ Logans * near Germantown where I dined—Returned in the evening and drank Tea at Mʳ Morris's."— *Washington's Diary.*

"*July* 9.—Sat in the Morning for Mʳ Peale—Attended Convention—Dined at Mʳ Morris's—& accompanied Mʳˢ Morris to Doctʳ [John] Redmans 3 Miles in the Country where we drank Tea and returned. *July* 10.—Attended Convention—Dined at Mʳ Morris's—Drank Tea at Mr. Binghams & went to the Play [at the Southwark Theatre]. *July* 11.—Attended Convention—Dined at Mʳ Morris's and spent the evening there. *July* 12.—In Convention—Dined at Mʳ Morris's & drank Tea with Mʳˢ Livingston. *July* 13.—In Convention—Dined, drank Tea & spent the Evening at Mʳ Morris's.

---

* Dr. George Logan resided at "Stenton," on the Germantown road, a short distance below Germantown. The house built in 1728 by his grandfather James Logan is still standing. Washington passed the night of August 23, 1777, at "Stenton," when on his way to meet the British army under General Howe, at the Chesapeake.

July 14.—In Convention—Dined at Springsbury with the Club—and went to the play in the Afternoon. *July* 15.—Dined at M[r] Morris's & remained at home all day. *July* 16.—In Convention - Dined at M[r] Morris's and drank Tea with M[rs] Powell."— *Washington's Diary.*

TUESDAY, JULY 17.

At Philadelphia: "*July* 17.—In Convention—Dined at M[rs] House's, and made an excursion with a party for Tea to Grays Ferry."— *Washington's Diary*

"*July* 17.—In the afternoon went with my wife, Matthew Clarkson, and Mr. & Mrs. Barge to Mr. Grays ferry, where we saw the great improvements made in the garden, summer houses, and walks in the woods. General Washington and a number of other gentlemen of the present Convention, came down to spend the afternoon."—*Diary of Jacob Hiltzheimer.*

WEDNESDAY, JULY 18.

At Philadelphia: "*July* 18.—In Convention—Dined at M[r] [Robert] Milligans—and drank Tea at M[r] Merediths."— *Washington's Diary.*

"*July* 19.—Dined (after coming out of Convention) at M[r] John Penn the Youngers—Drank Tea & spent the evening at my lodgings. *July* 20.—In Convention—Dined at home and drank Tea at M[r] Clymers. *July* 21.—In Convention—Dined at Springsbury with the Club of Gentl[m] & Ladies—Went to the Play afterwards."— *Washington's Diary.*

SUNDAY, JULY 22.

At Philadelphia: "*July* 22.—Left Town by 5 oclock A.M. —breakfasted at Gen[l] Mifflins—Rode up with him & others to the Spring Mills * and returned to Gen[l] Mifflins to Din-

---

* On the Schuylkill, a short distance below Conshohocken, the *Matson's Ford* of the Revolution. The old mill, said to be the oldest grist-mill in Pennsylvania, is still in operation. Washington visited Spring Mill for the purpose of inspecting the vineyard and bee colony established there by Peter Legaux, a Frenchman of intelligence who came to this country in 1785. The following entry in Mr. Legaux's manuscript diary refers to this visit: "*July* 22, 1787.—This day Gen. Washington, Gen. Mifflin and four others of the Convention did us the honor of paying us a visit in order to see our vineyard and bee houses. In this they found great delight, asked a number of questions, and testified their highest approbation with my manner of managing bees, which gave me a great deal of pleasure."

ner after which proceeded to the City."—*Washington's Diary.*

" *July* 23.—In Convention as usual—Dined at Mr Morris's and drank Tea at Lansdown * (the Seat of Mr Penn). *July* 24.—In Convention—Dined at Mr Morris's, and drank Tea, by appointment & part^r Invitation at Doct^r [Benjamin] Rush's. *July* 25.—In Convention—Dined at Mr. Morris's, drank Tea & spent the evening there. *July* 26.—In Convention.—Dined at Mr Morris's, drank Tea there, and stayed within all the Afternoon."—*Washington's Diary.*

FRIDAY, JULY 27.

At Philadelphia: " *July* 27.—In Convention, which adjourned this day, to meet again on Monday the 6th of August† that a Com^ee which had been appointed (consisting of 5 members‡) might have time to arrange, and draw into method & form the several matters which had been agreed to by the Convention as a Constitution for the United States. " Dined at Mr Morris's, and drank Tea at Mr Powells."— *Washington's Diary.*

" *July* 28.—Dined with the Club at Springsbury—Drank Tea there—and spent the Evening at my lodgings. *July* 29.—Dined and spent the whole day at Mr Morris's principally in writing letters."—*Washington's Diary.*

MONDAY, JULY 30.

Near Valley Forge: " *July* 30.—In company with Mr Govr [Gouverneur] Morris, and in his Phæton with my

---

* " Lansdowne," originally comprising about two hundred acres and immediately south of " Belmont," the seat of Judge Peters, was one of the finest properties on the west bank of the Schuylkill. The mansion-house, erected by John Penn the elder, was destroyed by fire July 4, 1854. In 1797 " Lansdowne" became the property of William Bingham, from whom it descended to the Barings, which family retained possession of it until about 1866, when it was purchased by citizens of Philadelphia, ceded to the city, and is now included in Fairmount Park.

† According to the Journal of the Convention in the archives of the Department of State, Washington, D.C., the adjournment to August 6 was made on July 26, and not on the 27th, as stated by Washington.

‡ John Rutledge, Edmund Randolph, Nathaniel Gorham, Oliver Ellsworth, and James Wilson.

horses; went up to one Jane Moores in the vicinity of
Valley Forge to get Trout."— *Washington's Diary.*

The Jane Moore referred to was the owner and occupant of two hundred
and seventy-five acres of land in Upper **Merion** Township, Montgomery
County, Pennsylvania. The property was situated about one mile west of
the Schuylkill River, on Trout Creek, a stream which has its source in
Chester County near the present village of Berwyn, and empties into the
Schuylkill three miles *below* Valley Forge. It has been stated that "Moore
Hall," the seat of William Moore, Esq., three miles *above* Valley Forge, was
the objective point of the excursion recorded in the Diary. This is undoubtedly an error. William Moore died May 30, 1782, and his widow William-
ina, December 6, 1784, after which the family removed to Philadelphia.
"Moore Hall" was advertised for private sale July 5, 1787, and offered at
public vendue October 17, 1787. It was probably not occupied in July of
that year. The mistake doubtless had its origin in an item printed in the
Pennsylvania Packet (and other Philadelphia papers), Wednesday, August
1, 1787: "Monday his Excellency General Washington set out for Moore
Hall in order to visit his old quarters at the Valley Forge in this State." A
statement at variance with the Diary entry.

TUESDAY, JULY 31.

At Valley Forge: "*July* 31.—Whilst Mr Morris was fishing I rid over the old Cantonment of the American [army]
of the Winter 1777 & 8—visited all the Works wch were in
Ruins; and the Incampments in woods where the ground
had not been cultivated. . . . On my Return to Mrs Moores
I found Mr Robt Morris & his Lady there."— *Washington's
Diary.*

"*August* 1.—About 11 o'clock, after it had ceased raining, we all set out
for the City—and dined at Mr Morris's. *August* 2.—Dined, Drank Tea &
spent the Evening at Mr Morris's."— *Washington's Diary.*

FRIDAY, AUGUST 3.*

At Trenton, New Jersey: "*August* 3.—In company with
Mr Robt Morris and his Lady—and Mr Gouv^r Morris I went

* "*Philadelphia*, August 4.— His Excellency General Washington attentive
to every thing interesting to his country, yesterday [August 3] visited and
examined the steel furnace belonging to Nancarrow and Matlack, lately rebuilt, in this city. It is much the largest and best constructed furnace in

up to Trenton on another Fishing party—lodged at Col°
Sam Ogdens at the Trenton [Iron] Works—In the Evening
fished, not very successfully."— *Washington's Diary.*

" *August* 4.—In the morning, and between breakfast & dinner, fished
again with more success (for ^perch) than yesterday—Dined at Gen¹ [Phile-
mon] Dickenson's on the East side of the River a little above Trenton &
returned in the evening to Col° Ogden's. *August* 5.—Dined at Col° Ogdens,
early ; after which in the company with which I came, I returned to Philadelphia at which we arrived abᵗ 9 Oclᵏ."— *Washington's Diary.*

MONDAY, AUGUST 6.

At Philadelphia : " *August* 6.—Met according to adjourn-
ment in Convention, & received the Repᵗ of the Committee
—Dined at Mʳ Morris's and drank Tea at Mʳ Meridiths."
— *Washington's Diary.*

" *August* 7.—In Convention—Dined at Mʳ Morris's and spent the evening
there also. *August* 8.—In Convention—Dined at the City Tavern and remained there till near ten o'clock. *August* 9.—In Convention—Dined at Mʳ
[John] Swanwicks and spent the Afternᵒ in my own Room—reading letters
and accᵗˢ from home. *August* 10.—Dined (after coming out of Convention)
at Mʳ Binghams and drank Tea there—spent the evening at my lodgings.
August 11.—In Convention—Dined at the Club at Springsbury and after
Tea returned home. *August* 12.—Dined at Bush-hill with Mʳ William
Hamilton—Spent the evening at home writing letters. *August* 13.—In Convention—Dined at Mʳ Morris's, and drank Tea with Mʳˢ Richard Bache, at
the President's. *August* 14.—In Convention—Dined, drank Tea, and spent
the evening at home. *August* 15.—The same as yesterday. *August* 16.—
In Convention—Dined at Mʳ Pollocks * & spent the evening in my chamber.
August 17.—In Convention—Dined and drank Tea at Mʳ Powells. *August*
18.—In Convention—Dined at Chief Justice [Thomas] McKeans—spent
the afternoon & evening at my lodgings."— *Washington's Diary.*

America, being charged with fourteen tons of iron at that time, converting
into steel ; and His Excellency was pleased to express his approbation of it."
—*Pennsylvania Packet.*
  * Oliver Pollock, an Irishman by birth and at one time a prominent merchant in New Orleans. He espoused the cause of the Colonies and rendered
substantial pecuniary aid during the war for independence. Mr. Pollock died
in Mississippi, December 17, 1823, at an advanced age.

SUNDAY, AUGUST 19.

At Whitemarsh, Pennsylvania : *"August 19.*—In company
with M*r* Powell rode up to the White Marsh—traversed my
old Incampment,* and contemplated on the dangers which
threatened the American Army at that place—Dined at
Germantown—visited M*r* Blair M*c*Clenegan †—drank Tea
at M*r* Peter's [Belmont] and returned to Philadelphia in the
evening."— *Washington's Diary.*

"August 20.—In Convention—Dined, drank Tea and spent the evening
at M*r* Morris. *August 21.*—Did the like this day also. *August 22.*—In
Convention—Dined at M*r* Morris's farm at the Hills—visited at M*r* Powells
in the Afternoon. *August 23.*—In Convention—Dined, drank Tea & spent
the evening at M*r* Morris's. *August 24.*—Did the same this day. *August 25.*
—In Convention—Dined with the Club at Springsbury & spent the afternoon at my lodgings. *August 26.*—Rode into the Country for exercise 8 or
10 miles—Dined at the Hills and spent the evening in my chamber writing
letters. *August 27.*—In Convention—Dined at M*r* Morris's and drank Tea
at M*r* Powells. *August 28.*—In Convention—Dined, drank Tea, and spent
the evening at M*r* Morris's. *August 29.*—Did the same as yesterday.
August 30.—Again the same. *August 31.*—In Convention—Dined at M*r*
Morris's and with a Party went to Lansdale [Lansdowne] & drank Tea with
M*r* & M*rs* Penn. *September 1.*—Dined at M*r* Morris after coming out of
Convention and drank Tea there. *September 2.*—Rode to M*r* Bartrams and
other places in the Country,—Dined & drank Tea at Grays ferry and returned
to the City in the evening."— *Washington's Diary.*

MONDAY, SEPTEMBER 3.

At Philadelphia : *" September 3.*—In Convention—visited
a Machine at Doct*r* Franklins (called a Mangle) for pressing,
in place of Ironing, clothes from the wash—Which Machine
from the facility with which it dispatches business is well
calculated for Table cloths & such articles as have not pleats

---

* The Continental army was encamped at Whitemarsh, twelve miles north
of Philadelphia, from November 2 to December 11, 1777.

† Blair McClenachan, a prominent merchant of Philadelphia, was at this
time a resident of the historic Chew House (Cliveden) at Germantown, still
standing, which he had purchased from Benjamin Chew in September, 1779.
He retained the ownership until April, 1797, when he reconveyed the property to Judge Chew.

& irregular foldings and would be very useful in all large families—Dined, drank Tea & spent the evening at Mr Morris's."— *Washington's Diary.*

"*September* 4.—In Convention—Dined &c at Mr Morris's.   *September* 5. —In Convention—Dined at Mrs Houses & drank Tea at Mr Binghams. *September* 6.—In Convention—Dined at Doct^r [James] Hutchinsons and spent the afternoon and evening at Mr Morris's.   *September* 7.—In Convention—Dined, and spent the afternoon at home (except while riding a few Miles).   *September* 8.—In Convention—Dined at Springsbury with the Club—and spent the evening at my lodgings.   *September* 9.—Dined at Mr Morris's after making a visit to Mr Gardoqui (Minister from Spain) who as he says came from New York on a visit to me.   *September* 10.—In Convention—Dined at Mr Morris's & drank Tea there.   *September* 11.—In Convention—Dined at home in a large Company with Mr Gardoqui—drank Tea— and spent the evening there.   *September* 12.—In Convention—Dined at the President's and drank Tea at Mr Pines."— *Washington's Diary.*

THURSDAY, SEPTEMBER 13.

At Philadelphia : " *September* 13.—Attended Convention, Dined at the Vice Presidents Chas Biddles *—Drank Tea at Mr Powells."— *Washington's Diary.*

" When he [Washington] was in the Convention I dined several times in company with him, and had the honor of his company to dine with me. When he was elected President of the United States, he lived during the whole of the time he was in Philadelphia nearly opposite to me.   At that time I saw him almost daily.   I frequently attended his levees to introduce some friend or acquaintance and called sometimes with Governor Mifflin. The General always behaved politely to the Governor, but it appeared to me that he had not forgotten the Governor's opposition to him during the Revolutionary war.   He was a most elegant figure of a man, with so much dignity of manner, that no person whatever could take any improper liberties with him.   I have heard Mr Robert Morris, who was as intimate with him as any man in America, say that he was the only man in whose presence he felt any awe.   You would seldom see a frown or a smile on his countenance, his air was serious and reflecting, yet I have seen him in the theatre laugh heartily."—*Autobiography of Charles Biddle,* p. 284.

---

* Charles Biddle was Vice-President of Pennsylvania from October 10, 1785, to October 9, 1787.

FRIDAY, SEPTEMBER 14.

At Philadelphia: "*September* 14.—Attended Convention —Dined at the City Tavern, at an entertainm* given on my acc* by the City light Horse.—Spent the evening at M*r* Meridiths."— *Washington's Diary.*

The "City light Horse," now known as the "First Troop Philadelphia City Cavalry," was organized November 17, 1774. Of this crack company it has been said, "That troop proved time and time again, as Lee's and Washington's Legion subsequently proved in the Carolinas, that there is room in society for the order of gentlemen, and that in time of stress it is well for the State to have a class to call on who will die as gayly as they dance, and will pour out their blood, as they were wont to do their fortunes, for faith and honor, for sentiment and ideals." *

SATURDAY, SEPTEMBER 15.

At Philadelphia: "*September* 15.—Concluded the business of Convention all to signing the proceedings; to effect which the House sat till 6 oclock; and adjourned till Monday that the Constitution which it was proposed to offer to the People might be engrossed—and a number of printed copies struck off—Dined at M*r* Morris's & spent the evening there.

"M*r* Gardoqui set off for his return to New York this forenoon."— *Washington's Diary.*

"*September* 16.—Wrote many letters in the forenoon—Dined with M*r* & M*rs* Morris at the Hills & returned to town in the Even*g*."—*Washington's Diary.*

MONDAY, SEPTEMBER 17.

At Philadelphia: "*September* 17.—Met in Convention when the Constitution received the unanimous assent of 11 States † and Col° Hamilton's from New York (the only

* Bradley T. Johnson, "Life of General Washington," p. 159.

† When it appeared that the consent of eleven States was recorded in favor of the Constitution, Franklin, looking toward a sun which was blazoned on the President's chair, said of it to those near him, "In the vicissitudes of hope and fear I was not able to tell whether it was rising or setting; now I know that it is the rising sun."

delegate from thence in Convention) and was subscribed to by every Member present except Govʳ Randolph and Col° Mason from Virginia—& Mʳ Gerry from Massachusetts.

"The business being thus closed, the Members adjourned to the City Tavern, dined together and took a cordial leave of each other—after which I returned to my lodgings—did some business with, and received the papers from the Secretary of the Convention, and retired to meditate on the momentous w^k which had been executed, after not less than five, for a large part of the time Six, and sometimes 7 hours sitting every day [except], sundays & the ten days adjournment to give a Com^ee opportunity & time to arrange the business for more than four Months."—*Washington's Diary.*

In transmitting to the President of Congress the full text of the proposed Constitution, Washington wrote, "In all our deliberations on this subject we kept steadily in our view, that which appears to us the greatest interest of every true American, the consolidation of our Union, in which is involved our prosperity, felicity, safety, perhaps our national existence. This important consideration, seriously and deeply impressed on our minds, led each state in the Convention to be less rigid on points of inferior magnitude than might have been otherwise expected ; and thus the Constitution, which we now present, is the result of a spirit of amity, and of that mutual deference and concession which the peculiarity of our political situation rendered indispensible."

TUESDAY, SEPTEMBER 18.

Leaves Philadelphia: "*September* 18. — Finished what private business I had to do in the City this forenoon—took my leave of those families in wch I had been most intimate dined early at Mʳ Morris's with whom & Mʳ Gouvʳ Morris I parted at Grays ferry—and reached Chester in Company with Mʳ [John] Blair who I invited to a seat in my Carriage 'till we should reach Mount Vernon."—*Washington's Diary.*

"*September* 19.—Prevented by Rain (much of which fell in the Night) from setting off till about 8 o'clock, when it ceased & promising to be fair we departed—baited at Wilmington—dined at Christiana and lodged at the head of Elk.—At the bridge near to which my horses (two of them) and

Carriage had a very narrow escape, for the Rain which had fallen the preceeding evening having swelled the water considerably there was no fording it safely I was reduced to the necessity therefore of remaining on the other side or of attempting to cross on an old, rotten & long disused bridge—Being anxious to get on I preferred the latter and in the attempt one of my horses fell 15 feet at least the other very near following which (had it happened) would have taken the Carriage with baggage along with him and destroyed the whole effectually—however by prompt assistance of some people at a Mill just by and great exertion, the first horse was disengaged from his harness, the 2ᵈ prevented from going quite through and drawn off and the Carriage rescued from hurt. *September* 20.—Sett off after an early breakfast —crossed the Susquehanna and dined in Havre de gras at the House of one Rogers—and lodged at Skirrets Tavern 12 Miles short of Baltimore. *September* 21.—Breakfasted in Baltimore—dined at the Widow Balls (formerly Spurriers)—and lodged at Major Snowdens who was not at home."— *Washington's Diary.*

SATURDAY, SEPTEMBER 22.

At Mount Vernon: "*September* 22.—Breakfasted at Bladensburgh and passing through George Town dined in Alexandria and reached home (with Mʳ Blair) about sun set after an absence of four Months and 14 days."— *Washington's Diary.*

MONDAY, SEPTEMBER 24.

At Mount Vernon : " In the first moment after my return, I take the liberty of sending to you a copy of the constitution, which the federal convention has submitted to the people of these States. . . . I wish the constitution which is offered, had been more perfect; but I sincerely believe it is the best that could be obtained at this time."— *Washington to Patrick Henry.*

WEDNESDAY, OCTOBER 3.

At Abingdon : " *October* 3.—Went up with Mⁿ Washington to Abingdon—Dined at Mʳ Herberts in Alexandria on our way."— *Washington's Diary.*

" *October* 4.—Dined at Abingdon and came home in the Afternoon—broᵗ Fanny Washington with us."— *Washington's Diary.*

FRIDAY, OCTOBER 5.

At Mount Vernon : " *October* 5.—In the Afternoon Mr Alexr Donald came in. *October* 7.—After breakfast Mr Donald went away."— *Washington's Diary.*

" I staid two days with General Washington at Mount Vernon about six weeks ago. He is in perfect good health, and looks almost as well as he did twenty years ago. I never saw him so keen for anything in my life as he is for the adoption of the new scheme of government. As the eyes of all America are turned towards this truly great and good man for the first President, I took the liberty of sounding him upon it. He appears to be earnestly against going into public life again ; pleads in excuse for himself his love of retirement and his advanced age, but notwithstanding of these, I am fully of opinion he may be induced to appear once more on the public stage of life. I form my opinion from what passed between us in a very long and serious conversation, as well as from what I could gather from Mrs. Washington on the same subject."—*Alexander Donald to Thomas Jefferson,* November 12, 1787.

SATURDAY, OCTOBER 6.

At Mount Vernon : " *October* 6.—Towards evening Mr & Mrs [Samuel] Powell of Philadelphia came in."— *Washington's Diary.*

" *October* 8.—Rid with Mr Powell to my Plantations at Muddy hole, Dogue run Frenchs & the Ferry. *October* 9.—Rid with Mr & Mrs Powell to view the ruins of Belvoir. *October* 10.—Mr & Mrs Powell going away after an early breakfast I rid to all my Plantations."—*Washington's Diary.*

THURSDAY, OCTOBER 11.

At Mount Vernon : " *October* 11.—In the evening Gen. [Charles Cotesworth] Pinkney and his Lady came in on their return to South Carolina from the Federal Convention."— *Washington's Diary.*

SUNDAY, OCTOBER 14.

At Mount Vernon : " *October* 14.—A Severe frost this Morning, which killed Pease, Buckwheat, Pumpkins, Potatoe Vines &c turning them quite black."— *Washington's Diary.*

MONDAY, OCTOBER 22.

At George Town: " *October* 22.—Went up to a meeting
of the Pot* Company at George Town—called at Muddy
hole Plantation in my way—did the business which called
the Com⁷ together—dined at Shuters Tavern and returned
as far as Abingdon at Night."— *Washington's Diary.*

" *October* 23.—After a very early breakfast at Abingdon, I arrived at
Muddy hole Plantation by 8 o'clock."— *Washington's Diary.*

SATURDAY, OCTOBER 27.

At Mount Vernon: " *October* 27.—Went to the Woods
back of Muddy hole with the hounds—unkennelled 2 foxes
and dragged others but caught none—the dogs running
wildly and being under no command."— *Washington's Diary.*

SUNDAY, OCTOBER 28.

At Pohick Church: " *October* 28.—Went to Pohick Church
—Mr Lear & Washington Custis in the Carriage with me."
— *Washington's Diary.*

THURSDAY, NOVEMBER 1.

At Alexandria: " *November* 1.—Rid by the way of Muddy
hole where the people were taking up Turnips to transplant
for Seed to Alexandria to attend a Meeting of the Directors
of the Potomack Company—also the exhibition of the Boys
of the Academy in this place.—Dined at Lehigh [? Leigh's]
Tavern & lodged at Col° Fitzgerald's after returning ab^t 11
o'clock at Night from the performance which was well executed."— *Washington's Diary.*

" *November* 2.—After breakfast I returned home by way of Muddy hole,
Dogue Run, Frenchs and the Ferry."— *Washington's Diary.*

SUNDAY, NOVEMBER 4.

At Mount Vernon: " *November* 4.—After the Candles were
lighted M^r & Mrs Powell came in."— *Washington's Diary.*

" *November* 5.—M^r & Mrs Powell remaining here I continued at home
all day. *November* 6.—M^r & Mrs Powell crossing the River to Mr Digges a

little after sun rise I accompanied them that far & having my horse carried into the Neck I rid round that and all the other plantations."—*Washington's Diary.*

THURSDAY, NOVEMBER 8.

At Alexandria: " *November 8.*—Went up to Alexandria to meet the Directors of the Potomack Comp^y—Dined at Mr Leighs Tavern and ret^d in the afternoon."—*Washington's Diary.*

" *November 15.*—Went to Alexandria to an Election of a Senator, for the district of Fairfax & Prince William. . . . Gave my suffrage for Mr Thos West who with a Mr Pope from the other County were Candidates and returned home to dinner through the midst of the Rain from an apprehension that the weather was not likely to abate in the evening."—*Washington's Diary.*

SUNDAY, NOVEMBER 18.

At Mount Vernon: " *November 18.*—To dinner came Mr Potts his wife and Brother and Mr Wilson from Alexandria —and soon after them Col° Humphreys."—*Washington's Diary.*

MONDAY, NOVEMBER 19.

At Mount Vernon: " *November 19.*—Mr Robt Morris, Mr Gou^r [Gouverneur] Morris & Doct^r Ruston came in before Dinner."—*Washington's Diary.*

" *November 21.*—Messrs Morris's & Doct^r Ruston went away after Breakfast—with the first two I rid a few Miles—and then visited my plantations at Frenchs, Dogue Run & Muddy hole on my Return."—*Washington's Diary.*

THURSDAY, NOVEMBER 29.

At Mount Vernon: " *November 29.*—In Company with Col° Humphreys Maj^r Washington & Mr Lear went a hunting, found a fox about 11 o'clock near the Pincushion—run him hard for near 3 quarters of an hour & then lost him. Mr Lund Washington who joined us, came & dined with us and returned afterwards."—*Washington's Diary.*

FRIDAY, NOVEMBER 30.

At Mount Vernon : " I have seen no publication yet, that ought in my judgment to shake the proposed constitution in the mind of an impartial and candid public. In fine, I have hardly seen one, that is not addressed to the passions of the people, and obviously calculated to alarm their fears. Every attempt to amend the constitution at this time is in my opinion idle and vain."— *Washington to David Stuart.*

SATURDAY, DECEMBER 1.

At Mount Vernon : " *December* 1.—Went with Col° Humphreys, Maj^r W. & Mr Lear a fox hunting, found a fox ab^t 9 oclock & run him hard till near 10 and lost him."— *Washington's Diary.*

" *December* 5.—Went out, in Company with Col° Humphreys, with the hounds after we had breakfasted—took the drag of a Fox on the side of Hunting Creek near the Cedar gut—carried it through Muddy hole Plantation into the Woods back of it—and lost it near the Main Road. *December* 8.—Went a hunting after breakfast; about Noon found a fox between Muddy hole & Pincushion, which the Dogs run for some time in Wood thro which there was no following them so whether they caught, or lost it is uncertain."— *Washington's Diary.*

SATURDAY, DECEMBER 15.

At Mount Vernon : " *December* 15.—A little after Sun rise, in company with the Gentlemen who came yesterday [Messrs. Rumney, Manshur, and Porter]—Col° Humphreys, Maj^r Washington & Mr Lear, went a hunting; but did not get a fox on foot nor is it certain we ever touched on the trail of one.—The Gentlemⁿ and Lund Washington (who joined us) came home to dinner & returned home afterwards."— *Washington's Diary.*

" *December* 22.—After our usual breakfasting Col° Humphreys, Maj^r Washington & myself with Mr Lear went out with the hounds—dragged up the Creek to the Gum Spring and then the Woods between Muddy hole, Dogue Run & Col° Masons Qurters without touching on the trail of a fox.— I visited the Plantations (in going out & coming home) except the Neck. *December* 26.—Col° Humphreys, the Gentlemen of the family & myself went out with the hounds but found nothing, tho much ground was gone over. *December* 28.—Went out with the hounds to day—took the drag of a fox within my Muddy hole Inclosures, and found him in Stiths field (lately Herberts) run him hard about half an hour—came to a cold drag & then lost him."—*Washington's Diary.*

SATURDAY, DECEMBER 29.

At Mount Vernon : " *December* 29.—Rid (the hollidays being end) to the Plantations at the Ferry, Frenchs, Dogue Run, and Muddy hole."—*Washington's Diary.*

1788.

TUESDAY, JANUARY 1.

At Mount Vernon: "I have the pleasure to inform you, that there is the greatest prospect of its [the Constitution] being adopted by the people. It has its opponents, as any system formed by the wisdom of man would undoubtedly have; but they bear but a small proportion to its friends, and differ among themselves in their objections. Pennsylvania, Delaware, and New Jersey have already decided in its favor, the first by a majority of two to one, and the two last unanimously."—*Washington to William Gordon.*

The National Constitution was ratified by the different States in the following order: Delaware, December 7, 1787; Pennsylvania, December 12; New Jersey, December 18; Georgia, January 2, 1788; Connecticut, January 9; Massachusetts, February 6; Maryland, April 28; South Carolina, May 23; New Hampshire, June 21; Virginia, June 25; New York, July 26; North Carolina, November 21, 1789; Rhode Island, May 29, 1790.

SATURDAY, JANUARY 5.

At Mount Vernon: "*January 5.*—About Eight oclock in the evening we were alarmed, and the house a good deal endangered by the soot of one of the Chimneys taking fire & burning furiously, discharging great flakes of fire on the Roof but happily by having aid at hand and proper exertion no damage ensued."—*Washington's Diary.*

TUESDAY, JANUARY 8.

At Mount Vernon: "There are some things in the new form, I will readily acknowledge, which never did, and I am persuaded never will, obtain my cordial approbation: but I did then conceive, and do now most firmly believe, that in the aggregate it is the best constitution that can be

98

obtained at this epoch, and that this, or a dissolution of the
Union, awaits our choice, and is the only alternative before
us. Thus believing, I had not, nor have I now, any hesita-
tion in deciding on which to lean."—*Washington to Edmund
Randolph.*

WEDNESDAY, JANUARY 9.
At Mount Vernon: "*January 9.—Col° [Edward] Carrington came here to Dinner—I continued at home all
day.*"— *Washington's Diary.*

"*January 10.—Col° Carrington left this after breakfast (on my horses) for
Colchester ; to meet the Stage.*"—*Washington's Diary.*

TUESDAY, FEBRUARY 5.
At Mount Vernon: " Perceiving that the *Federalist*, under
the signature of PUBLIUS, is about to be republished, I
would thank you to forward to me three or four copies, one
of which to be bound, and inform me of the cost."— *Washington to James Madison,* at New York.

The " Federalist," a collection of essays written in favor of the new Constitution by James Madison, John Jay, and Alexander Hamilton, under
the signature of PUBLIUS, was first published in book form at New York in
May, 1788, in two 12mo volumes. Only one copy of the book is included
in the inventory of the library at Mount Vernon, made after the death of
Washington. It was valued at one dollar and a half. These volumes,
handsomely bound, were sold at Philadelphia in November, 1876, for one
hundred dollars, and resold February, 1891, in the same city, for nineteen
hundred dollars.
   Under date of August 28, 1788, Washington wrote to Alexander Hamilton, " As the perusal of the political papers under the signature of PUBLIUS
has afforded me great satisfaction, I shall certainly consider them as claiming
a most distinguished place in my library. I have read every performance,
which has been printed on one side and the other of the great question lately
agitated, so far as I have been able to obtain them ; and, without an un-
meaning compliment, I will say, that I have seen no other so well calculated,
in my judgment, to produce conviction on an unbiassed mind, as the production of your *triumvirate.*"

WEDNESDAY, FEBRUARY 13.

At Mount Vernon : " *February* 13.—The Marq' de Chappedelaine (introduced by letters from Gen¹ Knox, M' Bingham &c⁰) Capt° Enew (a British Officer) Col° Fitzgerald, M' Hunter, M' Nelson & M' Ingraham came here to Dinner —all of whom returned [to Alexandria] after it except the last."— *Washington's Diary.*

" *February* 14.—On my return from Riding [to the plantations], I found the Marq' de Chappedelaine and Docter Lee here—both of whom stayed all Night. *February* 15.—Let out a Fox (which had been taken alive some days ago) and after chasing it an hour lost it. The Marquis de Chappedelaine & M' Ingraham returned to Alexandria after Dinner."— *Washington's Diary.*

FRIDAY, MARCH 14.

At Alexandria : " *March* 14.—Went with M" Washington to Alexandria—Visited Capt° Conway Doct' Craik, Col⁰ Sam¹ Hanson, M' Murray, & M' Porter with the last of whom we dined—returned in the Even."— *Washington's Diary.*

" *March* 17.—Went up [to Alexandria] (accompanied by Col⁰ Humphreys) to the Election of Delegates to the Convention of this State (for the purpose of considering the New form of Governm¹ which has been recommended to the United States); When Doct' Stuart and Col⁰ [Charles] Simms were chosen with out opposition—Dined at Col⁰ Fitzgeralds and returned in the Evening."— *Washington's Diary.*

TUESDAY, MARCH 18.

At Mount Vernon : " *March* 18.—M' Madison on his way from New York to Orange [County] came in before dinner and stayed all Night. *March* 20.—M' Madison (in my Carriage) went after breakfast to Colchester to fall in with the Stage."— *Washington's Diary.*

SUNDAY, APRIL 6.

At Mount Vernon : " *April* 6.—Sent my two Jackasses to the Election at Marlborough in Maryl⁴ that they might be seen."— *Washington's Diary.*

TUESDAY, APRIL 8.

At Abingdon : "*April 8.*—About 10 oclock, in company with Col° Humphreys, Mrs Washington, Harriott Washington * and Washington Custis I set of for Abingdon—where we dined and stayed all Night. *April 9.*—Dined at Abingdon and returned home in the evening—all, except Harriot Washington."— *Washington's Diary.*

SUNDAY, APRIL 13.

At Alexandria: "*April 13.*—Went to Church at Alexandria accompanied by Col° Humphreys Mr Lear, & Washington Custis—brought Hariot Washington home with us who had been left at Abingdon & came to Church with Mr Stuart."— *Washington's Diary.*

At Alexandria, Washington attended Christ Church (Protestant Episcopal), erected in 1773, and still standing, the present rector being the Rev. Berryman Green. The Rev. David Griffith, chaplain of the Third Virginia Regiment in the Revolution, and who was a frequent visitor at Mount Vernon, officiated from 1780 until his decease in 1789. Dr. Griffith was succeeded by Bryan Fairfax, brother of George William Fairfax, of '' Belvoir,'' who served from 1790 to 1792. The Rev. Thomas Davis, toward whose salary Washington made an annual subscription of ten pounds, and who officiated at his funeral, succeeded Mr. Fairfax. The church owns a Bible, presented to it by George Washington Parke Custis, which formerly belonged to General Washington.

MONDAY, APRIL 21.

At Alexandria : "*April 21.*—Went to Alexandria to the Election of a Senator for the district and delegates for the County in the General Assembly—when Mr Pope was chosen for the first and Mr Roger West, and Doct^r Stuart for the latter—Dined at Doct^r Cr^ks and came home in the evening."— *Washington's Diary.*

MONDAY, APRIL 28.

At Mount Vernon : "All the public attention has been, for many months past, engrossed by a new constitution. It

---

* The youngest child of Samuel Washington, brother of the General, who died in 1781. She married (July 4, 1796) Andrew Parks, of Baltimore.

has met with some opposition from men of abilities, but it has been much more ably advocated. Six States have accepted it. The opinion is, that Maryland and South Carolina will soon do the same. One more State only will be wanting to put the government into execution."— *Washington to Count de Rochambeau.*

According to the provisions of Article VII., the ratification of the conventions of nine States was requisite for the establishment of the Constitution between the States so ratifying the same. Maryland accepted it on the day the above-quoted letter was written, South Carolina on May 23, and New Hampshire, the ninth State, on June 21.

WEDNESDAY, APRIL 30.

At Mount Vernon: "Influenced by a heartfelt desire to promote the cause of science in general, and the prosperity of the College of William and Mary in particular, I accept the office of chancellor in the same; and request you will be pleased to give official notice thereof to the learned body, who have thought proper to honor me with the appointment."— *Washington to Samuel Griffin.*

THURSDAY, MAY 15.

At Mount Vernon: " *May* 15.—Visited all the Plantations —and the Brick yard—where a small kiln of Brick were forming to Burn."— *Washington's Diary.*

SATURDAY, MAY 17.

At Mount Vernon: " *May* 17.—M[rs] [Robert] Morris, Miss Morris and her two Sons [Robert and Thomas] (lately arrived from Europe) came here about 11 Ocl[k]."— *Washington's Diary.*

" *May* 18.—About one oclock, Col[o] Andrew Lewis of Bottetout came in —dined, & returned to Alexandria in the afternoon. *May* 20.—Rid in company with M[rs] Morris, M[rs] Washington, the two M[r] Morris's & Col[o] Humphreys to my Mill, and returned home thro' French' & the Ferry Plantations & by the Brick yard. *May* 22.—M[rs] Morris having (by the Stage of yesterday) Received a request from M[r] Morris to proceed to Richmond, set off for that place ab[t] 9 o'clock this Morning, with her two Sons & daughter.—Col[o]

Humphreys & myself accompanied her to Colchester, & returned to dinner."
— *Washington's Diary.*

SATURDAY, MAY 31.

Leaves Mount Vernon : *"May* 31.—After an early dinner, in company with Col° Humphreys, I set out for a meeting of the Directors of the Potomack Company to be held at the Falls of Shenandoah on Monday next—reached Mʳ Fairfax's about an hour by Sun, who with his Lady were at Alexandria; but a cloud which threatened rain, induced us notwithstanding to remain there all night."— *Washington's Diary.*

"*June* 1.—About Sunrise, we set out for the Great Falls, where having met Mʳ Smith (the assistant Manager who resides at the works at the Seneca falls) we examined the Canal, banks and other operations at this place . . . from hence we proceeded by a small cut, & wall About a mile higher up the River to the Seneca falls. . . . At this place we breakfasted, and in Company with Mʳ Smith continued our journey—Dined at Leesburgh—& lodged at Mʳ Jn° Houghs. *June* 2.—About 5 oclock, after an early breakfast, we set off, pilotted by Mʳ Hugh [? Hough] thro' by Roads, over the short hills —by the House & Mill of one Belt for the M° of Shenandoah where we arrived partly by a good & partly by a rugged Road at half after eight oclock—distance about 12 Miles—Soon after came Govʳ Johnson, and about 10 oclock Govʳ Lee & Col° Gilpin arrived—We then, together crossed the River, walked up to the head of the Canal on the Maryland side & viewed all the Works. . . . After dinner the board set. . . . *June* 3.—Having accomplished all the business that came before the board by 10 oclock—the members seperated—and I (Col° Humphreys having returned the day before) went to my Brothers [Charles] about eight miles off—dined there—and continued on in the Afternoon to Colonel Warner Washington's where I spent the evening. *June* 4.—About 7 o'clock I left this place, Fairfield, bated at a small Tavern (Bacon fort) 15 Miles distant—dined at the Tavern of one Lacey 14 Miles further and lodged at Newgate 16 Miles lower down."— *Washington's Diary.*

THURSDAY, JUNE 5.

At Mount Vernon: "*June* 5.—After an early breakfast I continued my journey by the upper and lower churches of this Parish [Truro] & passing through my Plantations at Dogue Run, Frenchs, and the Ferry—and the New Barn I reached home about Noon in about 28 Miles riding where I found Col⁰ Humphreys who had just got in before me from Abingdon."— *Washington's Diary.*

MONDAY, JUNE 9.

At Mount Vernon : "*June* 9.—Capt" [Joshua] Barney, in the Miniature Ship Federalist—as a present from the Merchants of Baltimore to me arrived here to Breakfast with her and stayed all day & Night."— *Washington's Diary.*

The citizens of Baltimore celebrated the adoption of the Constitution in Maryland by a procession in which a small boat fifteen feet in length, completely rigged and perfectly equipped as a ship, called "The Federalist," was a conspicuous feature. It was mounted on wheels and drawn by four horses. Captain Barney commanded the ship. After the pageant was over, it was resolved to present the ship to General Washington, in the name of the merchants and ship-owners of Baltimore. It was launched and navigated by Captain Barney down the Chesapeake Bay to the mouth of the Potomac, and thence up the river to Mount Vernon. "The Federalist" was driven from her moorings on the night of July 23 by a high northeast wind, and sunk.

TUESDAY, JUNE 10.

Leaves Mount Vernon : "*June* 10.—Between 9 and 10 Oclock set out for Fredericksburgh, accompanied by M" Washington, on a visit to my Mother—Made a visit to M' & M" Thompson in Colchester—& reached Col⁰ [Thomas] Blackburns to dinner, where we lodged—he was from home."— *Washington's Diary.*

"*June* 11.—About Sun rise we continued our journey—breakfasted at Stafford Court House and intended to have dined at M' Fitzhughs of Chatham but he and Lady being from home we proceeded to Fredericksburgh—alighted at my Mothers and sent the Carriage & horses to my Sister Lewis's—where we dined and lodged—As we also did the next day [June 12], the first in company with M' Fitzhugh, Col⁰ Carter & Col⁰ Willis and their Ladies, and Gen¹ Weedon—The day following (Friday) we dined in a large Company at Mansfield (M' Man Page's)—on Saturday we visited Gen¹ Spotswoods dined there & returned in the Evening to My Sisters."— *Washington's Diary.*

SUNDAY, JUNE 15.

At Fredericksburg: "*June* 15.—On Sunday we went to Church [St. George's]—the Congregation being alarmed (without cause) and suppos^s the Gallery at the N° End was about to fall, were thrown into the utmost confusion; and in the precipitate Retreat to the doors many got hurt—Dined in a large Company at Col° Willis's—Where, taking leave of my friends, we re-crossed the River, and spent the evening at Chatham."— *Washington's Diary.*

"*June* 16.—Before five o'clock we left it [Chatham]—travelled to Dumfries to breakfast—and reached home to a late dinner and found that Captn Barney had left it about half an hour before for Alexandria to proceed in the Stage of Tomorrow for Baltimore."— *Washington's Diary.*

WEDNESDAY, JUNE 18.

At Mount Vernon: "We have had a backward spring and summer, with more rainy and cloudy weather than almost ever has been known; still the appearance of crops in some parts of the country is favorable, as we may generally expect will be the case, from the difference of soil and variety of climate in so extensive a region; insomuch that I hope, some day or other, we shall become a storehouse and granary for the world."— *Washington to the Marquis de Lafayette.*

SATURDAY, JUNE 28.

At Alexandria: "*June* 28.—The Inhabitants of Alexandria having received the News of the Ratification of the proposed Constitution by this State, and that of New Hampshire—and having determined on public Rejoicings, part of which to be in a dinner, to which this family was envited Col° Humphreys my Nephew G. A. Washington & myself went up to it and returned in the Afternoon."— *Washington's Diary.*

"*June* 28.—Thus the citizens of Alexandria, when convened, constituted the first public company in America, which had the pleasure of pouring a libation to the prosperity of the ten States, that had actually adopted the general government. The day itself is memorable for more reasons than one. It was recollected, that this day is the anniversary of the battles of Sullivan's Island and Monmouth. I have just returned from assisting at the entertainment."—*Washington to Charles Cotesworth Pinckney.*

FRIDAY, JULY 4.

At Mount Vernon: "*July* 4.—In the Afternoon, Mr Madison and Doct^r Stuart, with a Son of Mr Willm Lee arrived from Richmond. *July* 5.—I remained at home all day with Mr Madison. *July* 7.—After dinner—Mr Madison and the Son of Mr Lee went (in my Carriage) to Alexandria in order to proceed on to New York in the Stage tomorrow."—*Washington's Diary.*

WEDNESDAY, JULY 9.

At Mount Vernon: "*July* 9.—A Captn Gregory (a french Gentlem^n who served in the American Navy last War & now in the Service of Rob Morris Esqr) came here by Water from Dumfries—Dined, Supped and returned."—*Washington's Diary.*

SATURDAY, JULY 12.

At Mount Vernon: "*July* 12.—To a late Breakfast M^r & Mrs Robt Morris, their two Sons & Daughter and Mr Gouv^r Morris came."—*Washington's Diary.*

"*July* 15.—About 11 o'clock Mrs Washington & myself accompanied Mr Mrs Morris &c. as far as Alexandria on their return to Philadelphia—We all dined (in a large Company) at Mr Willm Hunters; after which Mr Morris & his family proceeded and Mrs Washington, Col^o Humphreys & myself ret^l."—*Washington's Diary.*

SUNDAY, JULY 20.

At Mount Vernon: "You will permit me to say, that a greater drama is now acting on this theatre, than has heretofore been brought on the American stage, or any other in the world. We exhibit at present the novel and astonishing spectacle of a whole people deliberating calmly on what

form of government will be most conducive to their happiness ; and deciding with an unexpected degree of unanimity
in favor of a system, which they conceive calculated to
answer the purpose."— *Washington to Sir Edward Newenham.*

TUESDAY, JULY 29.

At Mount Vernon : " *July* 29.—A M* Vender Kemp—a
Dutch Gent* who had suffered by the troubles in Holland
and who was introduced to me by the Marquis de la Fayette
came here to Dinner. *July* 30.—M* Vender Kemp returned."— *Washington's Diary.*

Francis Adrian Vander Kemp, at one time a minister of the Mennonite
congregation at Leyden, and who subsequently had a command in the army
of Holland, arrived with his family at New York, May 4, 1788. The following reference to his visit at Mount Vernon, taken from his manuscript
journal, is furnished by the Rev. Roswell Randall Hoes : " I arrived at last
at Mount Vernon, where simplicity and order, unadorned grandeur and
dignity had taken up their abode. . . . There seemed to me, to skulk somewhat of a repulsive coldness—not congenial with my mind, under a courteous
demeanor ; and I was infinitely better pleased by the unassuming modest
gentleness of the Lady, than with the conscious superiority of her Consort.
There was a chosen Society—Col. Humphrey was there. I was charmed
with his manners—his conversation ; He knew, how to please—he knew,
how to captivate, when he deemed it worth."

Mr. Vander Kemp first settled at Esopus (now Kingston) on the Hudson
River, and finally at Trenton, New York, originally called Oldenbarneveld.
On February 22, 1800, he delivered at Oldenbarneveld a eulogy on Wash-
ington, which was published at Amsterdam, the same year, under the title,
" Lofrede op George Washington, te Oldenbarneveld, den 22 sten van
Sprokkelmaand, 1800 in Oneida District, Staat van New York, in de En-
gelsche taale uitgesprooken, door FRANC. ADR. VANDER KEMP." 8vo,
pp. 30.

MONDAY, AUGUST 4.

At Alexandria : " *August* 4.—Went up to Alexandria to
a meeting of the Potomack Company ; the business of
which was finished about Sun down—but matters which
came more properly before the Directors obliged me to stay
in Town all Night—Dined at Wises—and lodged at Col°
Fitzgeralds. *August* 5.—The business before the Board of

Directors detaining till near two oclock (I dined at Col⁰
Fitzgeralds) and returned home in the aftern".—*Washington's Diary.*

TUESDAY, AUGUST 12.

At Warburton, Maryland: "*August* 12.—The whole
family, accompanied by Col⁰ Humphreys and Mʳ [George]
Calvert crossed the River—dined with Mr. Geo: Digges—
& returned in the Evening."—*Washington's Diary.*

WEDNESDAY, AUGUST 20.

At Alexandria: "*August* 20.—Went up to Alexandria
with Mʳˢ Washington—dined at Mʳ Fendalls and returned
in the evening."—*Washington's Diary.*

THURSDAY, AUGUST 28.

At Mount Vernon: "On the delicate subject [the Presi-
dency] with which you conclude your letter, I can say
nothing, because the event alluded to may never happen,
and because, in case it should occur, it would be a point of
prudence to defer forming one's ultimate and irrevocable
decision, so long as new data might be afforded for one to
act with the greater wisdom and propriety."—*Washington
to Alexander Hamilton.*

From Colonel Hamilton's Letter.—"I take it for granted, Sir, you have
concluded to comply with what will, no doubt, be the general call of your
country in relation to the new government. You will permit me to say,
that it is indispensable you should lend yourself to its first operations. It is
to little purpose to have introduced a system if the weightiest influence is not
given to its firm establishment in the outset."—*August* 13.

THURSDAY, SEPTEMBER 11.

At Mount Vernon: "*September* 11.—Mʳˢ Plater and her
two daughters, and Mʳ George Digges and his Sister came
here to dinner and stayed all Night."—*Washington's Diary.*

"*September* 13.—Rid with Mʳˢ Plater and Mʳˢ Washington to the Mill
and New Barn. Col⁰ [George] Plater, Mʳ Hall & a Mʳ Mathews came here

(from Mͬ Digges's) just after we had dined—stayed all Night. *September*
14.—Colᵒ Plater, his lady & daughters Mͬ Digges & his Sister; and Mr.
Hall; and Mͬ Mathews went away after breakfast."— *Washington's Diary.*

MONDAY, SEPTEMBER 22.

At Mount Vernon: "I am glad Congress have at last
decided upon an ordinance for carrying the new government into execution."— *Washington to Henry Lee.*

"*September* 13, 1788.—Whereas, the convention assembled in Philadelphia, pursuant to the resolution of Congress, of the 21st of February, 1787,
did, on the 17th of September, in the same year, report to the United States,
in Congress assembled, a constitution for the people of the United States;
whereupon, Congress, on the 28th of the same September, did resolve unanimously, 'That the said report, with the resolutions and letter accompanying
the same, be transmitted to the several legislatures, in order to be submitted
to a convention of delegates, chosen in each state by the people thereof, in
conformity of the resolves of the convention, made and provided in that
case;' And whereas the constitution so reported by the convention, and by
Congress transmitted to the several legislatures, has been ratified in the
manner therein declared to be sufficient for the establishment of the same,
and such ratifications, duly authenticated, have been received by Congress,
and are filed in the office of the secretary; therefore,—

"*Resolved*, That the first Wednesday in January next be the day for
appointing electors in the several states, which, before the said day shall
have ratified the said constitution; that the first Wednesday in February
next, be the day for the electors to assemble in their respective states, and
vote for a president; and that the first Wednesday in March next, be the
time, and the present seat of Congress [New York] the place for commencing
proceedings under the said constitution."— *Journal of Congress.*

FRIDAY, OCTOBER 3.

At Abingdon: " *October* 3.—Went with Mͬˢ Washington
to Abingdon, to visit Mͬˢ Stuart who was sick.   *October* 4.
—At Abingdon still.   *October* 5.—Returned home after
breakfast—and reached it about 11 ocᵏ."— *Washington's
Diary.*

TUESDAY, OCTOBER 21.

At Alexandria: " *October* 21.—Went up to Alexandria to
move the Court to appoint Commissioners to settle the
Accᵗˢ of the Administration of Colᵒ Thoˢ Colvills Estate to

whose Will I was an Executor. . . . I dined at Mr Fendalls
& came home in the Afternoon."— *Washington's Diary.*

SUNDAY, OCTOBER 26.

At Pohick Church: " *October* 26. — Went to Pohick
Church and returned home to dinner—found Dr Stuart at
Mt Vernon who dined there & returned home afterwards."
— *Washington's Diary.*

" *October* 31.—Finished pruning the Weeping Willows & other Trees in
the Serpentine walks front of the House and was on the point of Riding
when Mr William Fitzhugh Junr (of Maryland) came in, about 10 o'clock
—after whom Col^o Henry Lee arrived both stay'd dinner and the latter all
night.—Remained at home all day."—*Washington's Diary.*

SUNDAY, NOVEMBER 2.

At Mount Vernon: " *November* 2.—After dinner word
was bro^t from Alexandria that the Minister of France was
arrived there and intended down here to dinner—Accordingly, a little before Sun setting, he (the Count de Mous-
tiers) * his Sister the Marchioness de Bretan [Brehan]—the
Marquis her Son and Mr du Ponts † came in."— *Washington's Diary.*

" *November* 3.—Remained at home all day.—Col^o Fitzgerald & Doctr.
Craik came down to dinner—& with the copy of an address (which the
Citizens of Alexandria meant to present to the Minister) waited on him to
know when he would receive it. Mr Lear went to Alexandria to invite
some of the Gentlemen and Ladies of the Town to dine with the Count &
Marchioness here tomorrow. *November* 4.—Mr Herbert & his Lady, M^r
Potts & his Lady, Mr Ludwell Lee & his Lady, and Miss Nancy Craik
came here to dinner and returned afterward."—*Washington's Diary.*

---

* Éléonor-François-Élie Comte de Moustier succeeded the Chevalier de la
Luzerne as Minister from France to the United States in 1787. He returned
to France in October, 1789.

† Victor Marie Du Pont, son of Pierre Samuel Du Pont de Nemours, and
elder brother of Eleuthère Irénée Du Pont, who established the well-known
powder-mills on the Brandywine, near Wilmington, Delaware, in 1802.

WEDNESDAY, NOVEMBER 5.

At Mount Vernon : "*November 5.*—The Minister & Madame de Bretan expressing a desire to Walk to the New Barn—we accordingly did so—and from thence through Frenchs Plantation to My Mill and from thence home compleating a tour of at least Seven Miles. Previous to this, in the Morning before breakfast I rid to the Ferry, Frenchs, D: Run and Muddy hole Plantations."— *Washington's Diary.*

" *November 6.*—About Nine Oclock the Minister of France, the Marchioness de Bretan & their Suit left this on their Return for New York I accompanied them as far as Alexandria & returned home to dinner—the Minister proceeded to George Town after having received an Address from the Citizens of the Corporation."— *Washington's Diary.*

SATURDAY, NOVEMBER 8.

At Alexandria : " *November 8.*—Went up to Alexandria, agreeably to a summons, to give testimony in the Suit defending between the Estate of Mr Custis and Mr Robt Alexander—Returned by the New Barn which had got about half the Rafters up."— *Washington's Diary.*

" *November 10.*—The New Barn would *nearly* if not *quite* have the Rafters up to-day."— *Washington's Diary.*

TUESDAY, NOVEMBER 11.

At Mount Vernon : " *November 11.*—All my People, except those in the Neck were on the public Roads Repairing of them to day—attended, in some measure, this business myself—Mr Lund Washington—Overseer of the Roads dined here to day. *November 12.*—The force of yesterday was employed on the Road to day. . . . I rid to the Repairs of the Road and to my New Barn—the Rafters of which were all raised about Noon—Mr Lund Washington dined here again to day."— *Washington's Diary.*

FRIDAY, NOVEMBER 14.

At Mount Vernon : "*November 14.*—Doct^r [George] Logan and Lady of Phila^a and a Monsr —— of Lyons in France came here to dinner and went away afterwards."— *Washington's Diary.*

SATURDAY, NOVEMBER 15.

At Mount Vernon : " *November* 15.—Went with my Compass and finished the line of Stakes from Dogue Run (at the Tumbling dam) to Hunting C^k; for a Road on the border of my land adjoining to Col° Masons—also connected this with the Road leading from the Gum Spring to Alexandria and from the former run the courses and measured the distances to my Mill and from the Mill to the Mansion House.

" On my Return home in the Evening I found Mr Warville and a Mr de Saint Tries here—brought down by Mr Porter who returned again. *November* 16.—Monsⁿ Warville and Saint Tres returned to Alexandria in my Chariot. *November* 17.—It was this day and not yesterday that Mr Warville and Mr Staint trees returned to Alexandria."— *Washington's Diary.*

" I hastened to arrive at Mount Vernon, the seat of General Washington, ten miles below Alexandria on the same river. On this rout you traverse a considerable wood, and after having passed over two hills, you discover a country house of an elegant and majestic simplicity. It is preceded by grass plats ; on one side of the avenue are the stables, on the other a green-house, and houses for a number of negro mechanics. In a spacious back yard are turkies, geese, and other poultry. This house overlooks the Potowmack, enjoys an extensive prospect, has a vast and elevated portico on the front next the river, and a convenient distribution of the apartments within. The General came home in the evening, fatigued with having been to lay out a new road in some part of his plantations. You have often heard him compared to Cincinnatus : the comparison is doubtless just. This celebrated General is nothing more at present than a good farmer, constantly occupied in the care of his farm and the improvement of cultivation. He has lately built a barn, one hundred feet in length and considerably more in breadth, destined to receive the productions of his farm, and to shelter his cattle, horses, asses, and mules. It is built on a plan sent him by that famous English farmer Arthur Young. But the General has much improved the plan. This building is in brick, it cost but three hundred pounds ; I am sure in France it would have cost three thousand.* He planted this year eleven hundred bushels of potatoes. All this is new in Virginia, where they know not the use of barns, and where they lay up no provisions for their cattle. His three hundred negroes are distributed in different log houses, in different parts of his plantation, which in this neighbourhood consists of ten thousand acres. Colonel Humphreys, that poet of whom I have spoken, assured me that the General possesses, in different parts of the country, more than two hundred thousand acres.

" Everything has an air of simplicity in his house ; his table is good, but not ostentatious ; and no deviation is seen from regularity and domestic œconomy. Mrs. Washington superintends the whole, and joins to the qualities of an excellent house-wife, the simple dignity which ought to characterize a woman, whose husband has acted the greatest part on the theatre of human affairs ; while she possesses that amenity, and manifests that attention to strangers, which render hospitality so charming. The same virtues are conspicuous in her interesting niece ; but unhappily she appears not to enjoy good health.

" M. de Chastellux has mingled too much of the brilliant in his portrait of General Washington. His eye bespeaks great goodness of heart, manly sense marks all his answers, and he sometimes animates in conversation, but he has no characteristic features ; which renders it difficult to seize him. He announces a profound discretion, and a great diffidence in himself ; but at the same time, an unshaken firmness of character, when once he has made his decision. His modesty is astonishing to a Frenchman ; he speaks of the American war, and of his victories, as of things in which he had no direction."—J. P. BRISSOT DE WARVILLE, *Nouveau Voyage dans les États Unis de l'Amérique Septentrionale, fait en 1788,* Paris, 1791.

THURSDAY, NOVEMBER 20.

At Alexandria : " *November* 20.—Went to Alexandria with Mrs Washington—Dined with Col^o Henry Lee & Lady at Mr Fendalls and returned home in the Evening—Found Doct^r La Moyeur here."— *Washington's Diary.*

TUESDAY, DECEMBER 2.

At Mount Vernon : " The expensive manner in which I live (contrary to my wishes, but really unavoidable), the bad

---

* " The building of a brick barn has occupied much of my attention this summer. It is constructed according to the plan you had the goodness to send me ; but with some additions. It is now, I believe, the largest and most convenient one in this country."— *Washington to Arthur Young,* December 4, 1788.

years of late, and my consequent short crops, have occasioned me to run in debt, and to feel more sensibly the want of money than I have ever done at any period of my whole life, and obliges me to look forward to every source from whence I have a right to expect relief. Under these circumstances I must ask you what prospect I have, and in what time (after it becomes due) I may expect to receive the present years annuity."— *Washington to David Stuart.*

THURSDAY, DECEMBER 4.

At Mount Vernon: " The more I am acquainted with agricultural affairs, the better I am pleased with them ; insomuch, that I can no where find so great satisfaction as in those innocent and useful pursuits. In indulging these feelings, I am led to reflect how much more delightful to an undebauched mind is the task of making improvements on the earth, than all the vain glory which can be acquired from ravaging it, by the most uninterrupted career of conquests."— *Washington to Arthur Young.*

" I have a prospect of introducing into this country a very excellent race of animals, by means of the liberality of the KING of Spain. One of the jacks which he was pleased to present to me (the other perished at sea) is about 15 hands high, his body and limbs very large in proportion to his height ; and the mules which I have had from him, appear to be extremely well formed for service. I have likewise a jack and two jennetts from Malta, of a very good size, which the Marquis de la FAYETTE sent to me.* The Spanish jack seems calculated to breed for heavy slow draught; and the others for the saddle, or lighter carriages. From these, altogether, I hope to secure a race of extraordinary goodness, which will stock the country."—*Idem.*

FRIDAY, DECEMBER 19.

At Mount Vernon: " *December* 19.—Rid to the Plantations at the Ferry and Frenchs—and to Dogue Run &

---

* The jack presented by Lafayette was called the *Knight of Malta ;* this jack was a superb animal, black in color, with the form of a stag and the ferocity of a tiger.

Muddy hole. . . . Mr Madison came here to dinner. *December* 20.—Remained at home with Mr Madison. *December* 25.—Sent Mr Madison after breakfast as far as Colchester in my Carriage."— *Washington's Diary.*

MONDAY, DECEMBER 29.

At Mount Vernon : " *December* 29.—Rid to the Plantations at the Ferry and Frenchs—and to Dogue Run & Muddy hole. *December* 30.—Rid into the Neck—and to Muddy hole Plantations. *December* 31.—Rid to the Ferry & Frenchs—and to Dogue Run and Muddy hole Plan^a."— *Washington's Diary.*

1789.

THURSDAY, JANUARY 1.

At Mount Vernon: "*January* 1.—Went out after breakfast to lay off or rather measure an old field which is intended to be added to Muddy hole Plantation—after which marked out a line for the New Road across from the Tu[m]bling Dam to little Hunting Creek to begin post and Rail fence on."— *Washington's Diary.*

WEDNESDAY, JANUARY 7.

At Alexandria: "*January* 7.—Went up to the Election of an Elector (for this district) of President & Vice President when the Candidates polled for being Doct^r Stuart and Col^o Blackburn the first rec^d 216 votes from the Freeholders of this County—and the second 16 Votes.—Dined with a large company on Venison at Pages Tav^n and came home in the evening."— *Washington's Diary.*

SUNDAY, JANUARY 18.

At Mount Vernon: "The first wish of my soul is to spend the evening of my days as a private citizen on my farm ; but, if circumstances, which are not yet sufficiently unfolded to form the judgment or the opinion of my friends, will not allow me this last boon of temporal happiness, and I should once more be led into the walks of public life, it is my fixed determination to enter there, not only unfettered by promises, but even unchargeable with creating or feeding the expectation of any man living for my assistance to office."— *Washington to Samuel Hanson.*

116

SATURDAY, JANUARY 24.

At Mount Vernon : "*January 24.*—Went into the Neck —measured some fields there—and laid off 8 acres for Tobacco."— *Washington's Diary.*

"*January 25.*—Colonels Fitzgerald, Lee & Gilpin dined here, and returned to Alexandria in the evening.   *January 28.*—Major Washington set out for Berkley to see his Father [Charles Washington] who had informed him of the low state of health in which he was."— *Washington's Diary.*

THURSDAY, JANUARY 29.

At Mount Vernon : "Nothing but harmony, honesty, industry, and frugality are necessary to make us a great and happy people.   Happily the present posture of affairs, and the prevailing disposition of my countrymen, promise to coöperate in establishing those four great and essential pillars of public felicity."— *Washington to the Marquis de Lafayette.*

MONDAY, FEBRUARY 2.

At Alexandria : "*February 2.*—I went up to the Election of a Representative to Congress for this district.   Voted for Rich⁴ Bland Lee Esqʳ dined at Colonel Hooes & returned home in the afternoon.

"On my way home met Mʳ George Calvert on his way to Abingdon with the Hounds I had lent him—viz. Vulcan & Venus (From France)—Ragman & two other dogs (From England)—Dutchess & Doxey (From Philadelpᵃ)—Tryal, Jupiter & Countess (Descended from the French Hounds)." — *Washington's Diary.*

FRIDAY, FEBRUARY 13.

At Mount Vernon : "I am going on Monday next to visit the works as far as the Seneca Falls."— *Washington to Thomas Jefferson.*

WEDNESDAY, MARCH 4.

At Mount Vernon : "Never till within these two years have I ever experienced the want of money.   Short crops, and other causes not entirely within my control, make me feel it now very sensibly. . . . Under this statement I am inclined to do what I never expected to be driven to—that is, to borrow money on interest. Five hundred pounds would enable me to discharge what I owe in Alexandria, etc.; and to leave the state (if it shall not be in my power to remain at home in retirement) without doing this would be exceedingly disagreeable to me. Having thus fully and candidly explained myself, permit me to ask if it is in your power to supply me with the above, or a smaller sum."— *Washington to Captain Richard Conway.*

" *March 6.*—I am much obliged by your assurance of money. Mr Lear waits upon you for it, and carries a bond, drawn in the manner you requested. . . . Upon collecting my accounts by Mr Lear, the other day, it was found that though five hundred pounds will enable me to discharge them, yet it is incompetent to this and the other purpose, the expenses of my journey to New York, if I go thither. If, therefore, you could add another hundred pounds to the former sum, it would be very acceptable. Mr Lear is provided with a bond for this sum also."— *Washington to Captain Richard Conway.*

SATURDAY, MARCH 7.

At Fredericksburg: " *March* 12.—On Saturday evening last [March 7], His Excellency General Washington arrived in town from Mount Vernon, and early on Monday morning he set out on his return. The object of his Excellency's visit was probably to take leave of his *aged mother*, sister, and friends, previous to his departure for the new Congress, over the councils of which, the united voice of America has called him to preside."—*Fredericksburg paper.*

This was the last visit paid by Washington to his mother. She died on the 25th day of August following, at the age of eighty-two. The following entry in his cash-book refers to this visit: " *March* 11.—By my expenses on a visit to my mother at Fredericksburg £1.8.0. By Mrs Mary Washington advanced her 6 Guineas."

MONDAY, MARCH 9.

At Mount Vernon : " I will therefore declare to you, that, if it should be my inevitable fate to administer the government, (for Heaven knows, that no event can be less desired by me, and that no earthly consideration short of so generall a call, together with a desire to reconcile contending parties as far as in me lies, could again bring me into public life,) I will go to the chair under no preengagement of any kind or nature whatsoever.   But, when in it, I will, to the best of my judgment, discharge the duties of the office with that impartiality and zeal for the public good, which ought never to suffer connexions of blood or friendship to intermingle so as to have the least sway on decisions of a public nature."— *Washington to Benjamin Harrison.*

WEDNESDAY, MARCH 25.

At Mount Vernon : " With very great sensibility I have received the honor of your letter dated the 10th instant, and consider the kind and obliging invitation to your house, until suitable accommodations can be provided for the President, as a testimony of your friendship and politeness, of which I shall ever retain a grateful sense.   But if it should be my lot (for Heaven knows it is not my wish) to appear again in a public station, I shall make it a point to take hired lodgings or rooms in a tavern until some house can be provided."— *Washington to George Clinton*, at New York.

MONDAY, MARCH 30.

At Mount Vernon : " I have been favored with your letter of the 19th, by which it appears that a quorum of Congress was hardly to be expected before the beginning of the next week.   As this delay must be very irksome to the attending members, and every day's continuance of it, before the government is in operation, will be more sensibly felt, I am resolved, that none shall proceed from me that can well be avoided, after notice of the election is announced, and therefore I take the liberty of requesting the favor of you to engage lodgings for me previous to my arrival.

"M'' Lear, who has lived with me three years as a private secretary, will accompany or precede me in the stage; and Colonel Humphreys I presume will be of my party. On the subject of lodgings, I will frankly declare to you, that I mean to go into none but hired ones."— *Washington to James Madison*, at New York.

The day appointed for the assembling of Congress was the 4th of March, but so tardily did the members come together that a quorum of both Houses was not formed till the 6th of April. On that day, in the presence of the Senate and House of Representatives, the votes were opened and counted, when Washington, having received every vote of the sixty-nine cast by the ten States * which took part in the election, was declared President of the United States. John Adams, having received the second highest number of votes (thirty-four), was declared to be Vice-President. He was installed in the chair of the Senate on April 21.

WEDNESDAY, APRIL 1.

At Mount Vernon: " In confidence I tell you, (with the *world* it would obtain little credit) that my movements to the chair of government will be accompanied by feelings not unlike those of a culprit, who is going to the place of his execution; so unwilling am I, in the evening of a life nearly consumed in public cares, to quit a peaceful abode for an ocean of difficulties, without that competency of political skill, abilities, and inclination, which are necessary to manage the helm. I am sensible that I am embarking the voice of the people, and a good name of my own, on this voyage; but what returns will be made for them, Heaven alone can foretell. Integrity and firmness are all I can promise."— *Washington to General Knox.*

---

* The three States not voting were New York, North Carolina, and Rhode Island, New York losing its vote in consequence of a disagreement between the two branches of the Legislature, and North Carolina and Rhode Island not having as yet ratified the Constitution.

"*April* 10.—A combination of circumstances and events seems to have rendered my embarking again on the ocean of public affairs inevitable. How opposite this is to my own desires and inclinations, I need not say. Those who know me are, I trust, convinced of it. For the rectitude of my intentions I appeal to the great Searcher of hearts ; and if I have any knowledge of myself I can declare, that no prospects however flattering, no personal advantage however great, no desire of fame however easily it might be acquired, could induce me to quit the private walks of life at my age and in my situation; but if, by any exertion or services of mine, my country can be benefited, I shall feel more amply compensated for the sacrifices which I make, than I possibly can be by any other means."—*Washington to Hector St.-John de Crèvecœur.*

TUESDAY, APRIL 14.

At Mount Vernon: "I had the honor to receive your Official communication by the hand of M' Secretary Thompson, about one o'clock this day. Having concluded to obey the important & flattering call of my Country, and having been impressed with an idea of the expediency of my being with Congress at as early a period as possible; I propose to commence my journey on Thursday morning which will be the day after to morrow."—*Washington to John Langdon.*

Mr. Langdon was a Senator from New Hampshire, and when the Senate was first organized, on the 6th of April, he was chosen President of that body *pro tempore.* In this capacity it devolved upon him to officially notify General Washington of his having been elected President of the United States. Charles Thomson, who had been since 1774 the sole Secretary of Congress, was selected to bear this official information to Mount Vernon. He left New York on Tuesday morning, April 7, on horseback. The letter was as follows: "*New York*, April 6, 1789.—I have the honor to transmit to your Excellency the information of your unanimous election to the office of President of the United States of America. Suffer me, sir, to indulge the hope that so auspicious a mark of public confidence will meet with your approbation, and be considered as a pledge of the affection and support you are to expect from a free and enlightened people."

THURSDAY, APRIL 16.

Leaves Mount Vernon : "*April* 16.—About ten o'clock I bade adieu to Mount Vernon, to private life, and to domestic felicity, and with a mind oppressed with more anxious and painful sensations than I have words to express, set out for New York in company with M.ʳ Thomson and Col.º Humphreys, with the best disposition to render service to my country in obedience to its calls, but with less hope of answering its expectations."— *Washington's Diary.*

"*Alexandria*, April 23.—Last Thursday [April 16], the great and illustrious Citizen of America, GEORGE WASHINGTON, Esq; passed through this town on his way to New-York accompanied by Mr. CHARLES THOMSON. He was met some miles out of town by a numerous escort of his friends and neighbours, whose attachment to him was such, that not satisfied with attending him to the verge of their own state, they crossed over in numerous crouds to George-Town, where they surrendered him over to the arms of an affectionate sister state. In compliance with their wishes, he partook with them of an early dinner prepared at Mr. Wise's tavern. At his departure, an affectionate address was presented to him by the citizens, to which he made a reply, expressive of his feelings on the occasion." *—Pennsylvania Packet*, April 30.

"*George-Town*, April 23.—Last Thursday, passed through this town, on his way to New-York, the Most Illustrious the President of the United States of America, with Charles Thomson, Esq.; Secretary to Congress. His Excellency arrived at about 2 o'clock, on the banks of the Potowmack, escorted by a respectable corps of gentlemen from Alexandria, where the George-Town ferry boats, properly equipped, received his Excellency and suite, and safely landed them, under the acclamations of a large crowd of their grateful fellow-citizens—who beheld their FABIUS in the evening of his days, bid adieu to the peaceful retreat of Mount Vernon. in order to save his country once more, from confusion and anarchy. From this place his Excellency was escorted by a corps of gentlemen, commanded by Col. William Deakins, jun. to Mr. Spurrier's Tavern, where the escort from Baltimore take charge of him."*—Pennsylvania Packet*, May 5.

FRIDAY, APRIL 17.

At Baltimore: "*Baltimore*, April 21.—The President of the United States arrived in this place on his way to Congress, on Friday afternoon, the 17th instant, with Charles Thomson, Esq; and Colonel Humphries. This great man was met some miles from Town, by a large body of respectable citizens on horseback, and conducted, under a dis-

* For this admirable address and reply, see Sparks, vol. xii. p. 137, etc.

charge of cannon, to Mr. Grant's tavern [the "Fountain
Inn"] through crowds of admiring spectators.

"At six o'clock, a committee chosen in consequence of a
late notification, to adjust the preliminaries for his reception, waited upon him with an address which he answered.
A great number of the citizens were presented to him, and
very graciously received. Having arrived too late for a
public dinner, he accepted an invitation to supper, from
which he retired a little after ten o'clock."—*Pennsylvania
Packet,* April 28.

"*Baltimore*, April 21.—On Saturday morning [April 18] he was in his
carriage at half past five o'clock when he left town, under a discharge of
cannon, and attended as on his entrance, by a body of the citizens on horseback. These gentlemen accompanied him seven miles, when alighting from
his carriage, he would not permit them to proceed any further; but took
leave of them, after thanking them in an affectionate and obliging manner
for their politeness. We shall only add on this occasion, that those who had
often seen him before, and those who never had, were equally anxious to see
him. Such is the rare impression excited by his uncommon character and
virtues."—*Idem.*

SUNDAY, APRIL 19.

At Wilmington, Delaware : "*Wilmington*, April 25.—On
Sunday last [April 19] his Excellency the President-General
arrived in this borough, whither he was accompanied by
a number of gentlemen of this State, who also attended
him next morning to the Pennsylvania line, on his way to
New-York. Before his departure, the corporation of this
borough, attended by many of the inhabitants, waited
upon his Excellency, with an address of congratulation,
which was most graciously received."—*Pennsylvania Packet,*
April 28.

MONDAY, APRIL 20.

At Philadelphia : "*April* 22.—Monday last [April 20]
His Excellency GEORGE WASHINGTON, Esq; the PRESIDENT
ELECT OF THE UNITED STATES, arrived in this city, about
one o'clock, accompanied by the President of the State

[Thomas Mifflin], Governor St. Clair, the Speaker of the
Assembly [Richard Peters], the Chief Justice [Thomas
McKean], the Honorable Mr. Read, the Attorney-General
[William Bradford, Jr.], and Secretary Thomson, the two
city troops of horse, the county troop, a detachment of
artillery, a body of light infantry, and a numerous concourse of citizens on horseback and foot.

"His EXCELLENCY rode in front of the procession, on
horseback. The number of spectators who filled the doors,
windows and streets, which he passed, was greater than on
any other occasion we ever remember.

"The joy of the whole city upon this august spectacle
cannot easily be described. Every countenance seemed to
say, Long, long live GEORGE WASHINGTON, THE FATHER
OF THE PEOPLE! At three o'clock His Excellency sat
down to an elegant Entertainment of 250 covers, at the
City Tavern, prepared for him by the citizens of Philadelphia. A band of music played during the entertainment,
and a discharge of artillery took place at every toast, among
which was *The State of Virginia.* The ship Alliance, and a
Spanish merchant ship, were handsomely decorated with
colours of different nations."—*Pennsylvania Gazette.*

In the approach to the city the Schuylkill was crossed at Gray's Ferry
bridge, which "was highly decorated with laurel and other evergreens, by
Mr. Gray himself, the ingenious Mr. [Charles Willson] Peale and others,
and in such a stile, as to display uncommon taste in these gentlemen.—At
each end there were erected magnificent arches, composed of laurel, emblematic of the ancient triumphal arches used by the Romans, and on each side
of the bridge a laurel shrubbery, which seemed to challenge even Nature
herself for simplicity, ease and elegance. And as our beloved WASHINGTON
passed the bridge, a lad, beautifully ornamented with sprigs of laurel,
assisted by certain machinery, let drop, above the Hero's head, unperceived
by him, a civic crown of laurel."

Washington spent Monday night at the house of Robert Morris, on
Market Street, and on the following morning (April 21) left Philadelphia
on his journey to New York. Previous to his departure he received and
answered addresses from the President and Supreme Executive Council;
from the mayor, aldermen, and Common Council of the city; from the

judges of the Supreme Court of the State; from the trustees and faculty of the University of the State of Pennsylvania; and from the State Society of the Cincinnati.

TUESDAY, APRIL 21.

At Trenton, New Jersey: " *Trenton*, April 21.—This day we were honored with the presence of his Excellency the President of the United States of America on his way to New York. A troop of horse, commanded by Capt. Carle, and a company of infantry, commanded by Capt Halon, compleatly equipped, and in full uniform, with a large concourse of the gentlemen and inhabitants of the town and neighbourhood, lined the Jersey bank of the Delaware, to hail the General's arrival. As soon as he set foot on shore, he was welcomed with three huzzas, which made the shores re-echo the chearful sounds. After being saluted by the horse and infantry, he was escorted to town, in the following order: A detachment of the horse.—The Light Infantry.— His Excellency, on horseback, attended by Charles Thomson, Esq; and Col. Humphreys.—The troop of horse.—The gentlemen of the town and neighbourhood on horseback." —*Pennsylvania Packet*, May 1.

" When the procession arrived at the bridge south of the town, they were presented with a scene to which no description can do justice.

" As Trenton had been rendered twice memorable during the war, once by the capture of the Hessians, and again by the repulse of the whole British army, in their attempt to cross the bridge over the Assanpinck Creek, the evening before the battle of Princeton—a plan was formed by a number of ladies, and carried into execution, solely under their direction, to testify to the General, by the celebration of those eventful actions, the grateful sense they retained of the safety and protection afforded by him to the daughters of New-Jersey. For this purpose, a triumphal arch was raised on the bridge, about 20 feet wide, supported by 13 columns—the height of the arch to the centre was equal to the width. Each column was intwined with wreaths of evergreen. The arch, which extended about twelve feet along the bridge, was covered with laurel, and decorated on the inside with laurel, running-vines, and a variety of evergreens. On the front of the arch the following motto was inscribed in large gilt letters—' *The Defender of the mothers will also protect the daughters.*'—The upper and lower edges of this inscription were ornamented with wreaths of evergreen and artificial flowers of all kinds,

made by the ladies for the occasion, beautifully interspersed. On the centre
of the arch, above the inscription, was a dome, or cupola, of artificial flowers
and evergreens, encircling the dates of the glorious events which the whole
was designed to celebrate, inscribed in large gilt letters.—The summit of the
dome displayed a large sun-flower, which, always pointing to the sun, was
designed to express this sentiment, or motto—' *To you alone*'—as emblematic
of the affections and hopes of the PEOPLE being directed to him, in the
united suffrage of the millions of America.

"A numerous train of ladies, leading their daughters, were assembled at
the arch, thus to thank their Defender and Protector. As the General
passed under the arch, he was addressed in the following SONATA, composed [by Major Richard Howell *] and set to music for the occasion, by a
number of young ladies dressed in white, decked with wreaths and chaplets
of flowers, and holding in their hands baskets filled with flowers :

> "' WELCOME, mighty Chief! once more,
> Welcome to this grateful shore :
> Now no mercenary foe
> Aims again the fatal blow—
> Aims at thee the fatal blow.

> "' Virgins fair, and Matrons grave,
> Those thy conquering arms did save,
> Build for thee triumphal bowers.
> Strew, ye fair, his way with flowers—
> Strew your Hero's way with flowers.'

"*As they sung these lines, they strewed the flowers before the General.*
"When his Excellency came opposite the little female band, he honored
the ladies by stopping until the Sonata was finished. The scene was truly
grand—universal silence prevailed—Nothing was to be heard but the sweet
notes of the songsters—and the mingled sentiments which crouded into the
mind in the moments of solemn stillness during the song, bathed many
cheeks with tears. The General most politely thanked the ladies for their
attention, and the procession moved on to his lodgings." †—*Idem.*

---

* Governor of New Jersey, 1794–1801.

† " At Trenton Washington dined at Samuel Henry's City Tavern, on the
southwest corner of Second and Warren Streets, with the principal citizens
of the place and held a reception in the parlors of the inn. Late in the
afternoon he took carriage for Princeton, the Rev. [James F.] Armstrong
accompanying him that far on his journey. It is generally understood that
they spent that night at the residence of the President of the College, the
Rev. Dr. John Witherspoon."—WILLIAM S. STRYKER, *Washington's Reception by the People of New Jersey in 1789.*

WEDNESDAY, APRIL 22.

At New Brunswick, New Jersey : " *New Brunswick*, April 28.—On Wednesday last [April 22], his Excellency GEORGE WASHINGTON, Esquire, President of the United States of America, passed through this city on his way to the seat of the Federal Government, accompanied by his Excellency [William Livingston] the Governor of the State, Charles Thomson, Esq; Col. Humphreys, and several other gentlemen of distinction. His Excellency was escorted into this city by the Common Council, and other respectable citizens on horseback, and by the companies of artillery and light-infantry under the command of Captains Douglas and Guest. The near approach of his Excellency was announced by the firing of a federal salute from the artillery, and by the ringing of bells."—*Pennsylvania Packet*, May 2.

" The Common Council and other citizens on horseback met his Excellency some miles from the town, and after having congratulated him upon the happy occasion of their meeting, they conducted him into the city, preceded by the companies of artillery and light-infantry, and a detachment of horse from Capt. Carle's cavalry, accompanied with a band of music. At the entrance of the city, the troops formed a line, and saluted his Excellency as he passed them : the street and houses were crowded with many joyful spectators ; among whom were a great number of the fair daughters of Columbia, collected on the occasion with a generous desire of expressing their respect and gratitude to this illustrious friend to mankind, and the great protector of the rights of their country. Joy sparkled in every eye, and perfect satisfaction was demonstrated by the countenance and behaviour of all degrees and conditions of the people, when they beheld the object of their esteem and confidence again coming into public life, from the peaceful retirement of domestic happiness, to preserve by his wisdom, those invaluable privileges which he had defended by his valour.

" The inhabitants, by a committee appointed for the purpose, together with the Reverend Clergy, waited on his Excellency at the house of Major Thomas Egbert, and congratulated him upon his appointment to the office of President of the United States of America, expressed the great happiness they felt on that important occasion, and at the same time assured him that their sincere prayer should be, that he might enjoy in the administration of his office, that felicity which is the just reward of the most exalted and distinguished merit.

" To which his Excellency replied with a politeness particular to himself, and in a manner becoming the dignity of his character.

" About five o'clock in the afternoon his Excellency, accompanied by the Governor of the state, by many citizens of New-Brunswick, and by several gentlemen from the county of Essex, and amidst the joyful acclamations of a large concourse of happy people crossed the river on his way to New-York.

" His Excellency and suite lodged at Woodbridge, and in the morning set out for New-York, and was met in Rahway by the light dragoons from Elizabeth-Town and Newark, and at Elizabeth-Town by the infantry, grenadiers, and artillery, who saluted him as he passed by.'—*Idem.*

" *Elizabeth-Town*, April 29.—Thursday last [April 23], between eight and nine o'clock in the morning, His Excellency General Washington made his entrance into this town, amidst festive throngs of numerous spectators.

" He was met near Bridgetown, by a number of citizens, accompanied by the cavalry, commanded by captains Meeker, Condict, and Wade, which when united with captain Herd's troop. that composed the escort of his Excellency from Brunswick, made a most martial and splendid appearance. —On his Excellency's approaching the town, his arrival was announced by a federal salute from the cannon, and the illustrious hero was received by the grenadiers and light troops under arms. He alighted at the [public] house of Mr. [Samuel] Smith, where he received the congratulations of the town and the committee from New-York. He partook of a repast provided by the gentlemen of the town; and, after that waited on the committee of Congress at Mr. [Elias] Boudinott's, from whence he proceeded, attended by a vast concourse of people, and the cavalry (in order) to the Point, and after reviewing the troops, who were by this time joined by some respectable companies from Newark and its environs, he was conducted on board of the barge prepared for his reception, the beauty of which met his highest approbation ; he was rowed across the bay by thirteen skilful pilots. Thomas Randall, Esq ; acted as cockswain."—*Pennsylvania Packet*, May 5.

THURSDAY, APRIL 23.

At New York : " *New York*, April 24.—Yesterday, about two o'clock, arrived in this city, His Excellency GEORGE WASHINGTON, Esquire, President of the United States of America. A Committee of the honorable the Congress,* a deputation of the State Officers, consisting of his Honor the Chancellor [Robert R. Livingston] and the Adjutant-General [Nicholas Fish], accompanied by a deputation from

IV, ... Few

* John Langdon, Charles Carroll, and William Samuel Johnson of the Senate, Elias Boudinot, Theodoric Bland, Thomas Tudor Tucker, Egbert Benson, and John Lawrence of the House.

the Corporation of this city, consisting of the Recorder [Richard Varick], received His Excellency the President at Elizabethtown, in the elegant barge which was previously constructed for the purpose, and rowed by thirteen pilots, under the superintendence of Captain Randall."—*Pennsylvaniæ Gazette*, April 29.

"On the President's passing the battery, a federal salute was fired, and repeated upon his landing * near the City Coffee-House, where he was received by his Excellency the Governor [George Clinton], the principal officers of the state, his honor the Mayor [James Duane], and the principal officers of the Corporation ; and thence accompanied to the house prepared for his reception,† in the following order, Viz: Troop of Horse.—Artillery and residue of the Legion, under arms.—The military officers in uniform, who were off duty.—The President's Guard, composed of the Grenadiers of the first regiment.—The President, the Governor, and their suites.—The principal officers of the state.—The Mayor and Corporation.—The Clergy.—The Citizens.

"The bells were rung, and colours were displayed from the fort, from the vessels in the harbour, and from the several buildings in the city ; the streets were crowded with citizens, and the windows decorated with the fair daughters of Columbia.

"In the evening ‡ the city was elegantly illuminated. The joy and satisfaction universally expressed on the safe arrival of this Illustrious Personage clearly evince, that patriotism and magnanimity are still held in respect and veneration among our citizens—His Excellency having, in a distinguished manner, displayed those eminent virtues, in a series of important and faithful services, rendered his country, in the most gloomy and distressing periods."—*Idem.*

---

* At Murray's wharf, foot of Wall Street.

† The house prepared for the President, known as the Franklin House, the former residence of Walter Franklin, was at No. 3 Cherry Street. It was owned by Samuel Osgood, one of the Treasury Commissioners, who married the widow of Mr. Franklin, and was until 1856, when the building was taken down, at the junction of Cherry and Pearl Streets, on Franklin Square. Washington retained this house until February 23, 1790, when he removed to the Macomb House, on Broadway near Bowling Green.

‡ On the evening of April 23 Washington dined with a distinguished company at Governor Clinton's house, Queen (now Pearl) Street, opposite Cedar This house was occupied by Washington as head-quarters from April 13 to May 21, 1776.

9

FRIDAY, APRIL 24.

At New York: " *New York*, April 30.—Friday [April 24] the Hon. the Senate and House of Representatives waited on his Excellency the President, to congratulate him on his safe arrival at the seat of government."—*Pennsylvania Packet*, May 5.

" *New York*, April 27.—On Saturday [April 25] the Chamber of Commerce met at the Coffee-House, about half after eleven o'clock, in consequence of a special call from the President. From the Coffee-house they proceeded in form to the house of his Excellency the President of the United States, headed by John Broome, Theophylact Beach and John Murray, Esquires. On their arrival at the President's they were conducted into the audience-room, and upon his Excellency's entering, Mr. Broome, the President of the Chamber, addressed him, and to which he made a reply.

" After his Excellency's reply, he was introduced by the President of the Chamber to every member present."—*Pennsylvania Packet*, April 30.

TUESDAY, APRIL 28.

At New York: " *April* 28.—This day I ought to note with some extraordinary mark. I had dressed and was about to set out, when General Washington, the greatest man in the world, paid me a visit. I met him at the foot of the stairs. Mr. [Henry] Wynkoop just came in. We asked him to take a seat. He excused himself on account of the number of his visits. We accompanied him to the door. He made us complaisant bows—one before he mounted and the other as he went away on horseback."—*Journal of William Maclay*, Senator from Pennsylvania.

William Maclay, of Pennsylvania, was elected September 30, 1788, with Robert Morris, to the United States Senate, and drew the short term, which expired on March 3, 1791. In the Senate, Mr. Maclay advanced democratic principles and led the opposition to Washington, objecting to his presence in the Senate during the transaction of business, assailing the policy of the administration before him, and reprobating the state and ceremony that were observed in his intercourse with Congress. His journal, from which we quote, was published at New York in 1890.

THURSDAY, APRIL 30.

At New York: " *New York*, May 1.—YESTERDAY [April 30] took place according to the resolution of the two houses of Congress, the ceremony of the introduction of his Excellency GEORGE WASHINGTON, to the Presidency of the United States."—*Pennsylvania Packet*, May 4.

" At nine o'clock A.M. the clergy of different denominations assembled their congregations in their respective places of worship, and offered up prayers for the safety of the president.

" About twelve o'clock the procession moved from the house of the president in Cherry-Street, through Dock-Street, and Broad-Street, to Federal Hall [at Wall and Nassau Streets] ; in the following order. Colonel [Morgan] Lewis supported by two officers, Capt. Stakes, with the troop of Horse, Artillery, Major Van Horne, Grenadiers, under Captain Harsin, German Grenadiers, under Capt. Scriba, Major Bicker, The Infantry of the Brigade, Major Chrystie, Sheriff [Robert Boyd] The Committee of the Senate,* The PRESIDENT and suite. The Committee of the Representatives,† The Honorable Mr. Jay, General Knox, Chancellor Livingston, and several other gentlemen of distinction. Then followed a multitude of citizens.

" When they came within a short distance of the Hall, the troops formed a line on both sides of the way, and his Excellency passing through the ranks, was conducted into the building, and in the Senate Chamber introduced to both houses of Congress—immediately afterwards, accompanied by the two houses, he went into the gallery fronting Broad-Street, where, in the presence of an immense concourse of citizens, he took the oath prescribed by the constitution, which was administered to him by the Hon. R. R. Livingston, Esq ; Chancellor of the state of New York.

" Immediately after he had taken the oath, the Chancellor proclaimed him President of the United States.—Was answered by the discharge of 13 guns, and by loud repeated shouts ; on this the President bowed to the people, and the air again rang with their acclamations. His Excellency with the two houses, then retired to the Senate Chamber and delivered his speech.‡

---

* Richard Henry Lee, Ralph Izard, and Tristram Dalton.

† Egbert Benson, Fisher Ames, James Madison, Charles Carroll, and Roger Sherman.

‡ " As the company returned into the Senate chamber, the President took the chair and the Senators and Representatives their seats. He rose, and all arose also, and addressed them. This great man was agitated and embarrassed more than ever he was by the leveled cannon or pointed musket. He trembled, and several times could scarce make out to read, though it

"His excellency accompanied by the Vice President, the Speaker of the House of Representatives [Frederick A. Muhlenberg] and both Houses of Congress went to St. Paul's chapel [Broadway and Vesey Street] where divine Service was performed by Right Reverend Dr. [Samuel] Provost, Bishop of the Episcopal Church in this State and Chaplain in Congress. The religious ceremony being ended, the President was escorted to his house, and the citizens retired to their homes. In the evening was exhibited under the direction of Colonel Bauman, a very ingenious and splendid show of Fireworks." *—*Pennsylvania Packet*, May 4.

FRIDAY, MAY 1.

At New York : " *New York*, May 2.—Yesterday morning The President received the compliments of His Excellency the Vice President, His Excellency the Governor of this State ; the principal Officers of the different Departments ; the foreign Ministers ; and a great number of other persons of distinction."—*Gazette of the United States.*

TUESDAY, MAY 5.

At New York : " *May* 5.—This being a day for receiving company of ceremony, we had a numerous and splendid circle between the hours of two and three in the afternoon.

---

must be supposed he had often read it before. He put part of the fingers of his left hand into the side of what I think the tailors call the fall of the breeches, changing the paper into his left [right] hand. After some time he then did the same with some of the fingers of his right hand. When he came to the words *all the world*, he made a flourish with his right hand, which left rather an ungainly impression. I sincerely, for my part, wished all set ceremony in the hands of the dancing-masters, and that this first of men had read off his address in the plainest manner, without ever taking his eyes from the paper, for I felt hurt that he was not first in every thing. He was dressed in deep brown, with metal buttons, with an eagle on them, white stockings, a bag, and sword."—*Journal of William Maclay.*

* "*April* 30.—In the evening there was a display of most beautiful fireworks and transparent paintings at the Battery. The President, Colonel Humphreys, and myself went in the beginning of the evening in the carriages to Chancellor Livingston's and General Knox's where we had a full view of the fire-works. We returned home on foot, the throng of people being so great as not to permit a carriage to pass through it."—*Diary of Tobias Lear.*

A committee of the House of Representatives * waited on the President with a copy of the address of their House, and a request to know when it would be agreeable to him to receive it."—*Diary of Tobias Lear.*

Soon after the inauguration it became apparent that particular rules should be established for receiving visitors and entertaining company, so that the President might be able to attend to business without interruption. It was therefore decided that he should return no visits, that invitations to dinner should be given only to official characters and strangers of distinction, and that the visits of courtesy should be confined to the afternoon of Tuesday in each week between the hours of three and four. Foreign ministers and strangers were, however, received on other days. On Friday evenings the house was open for visits to Mrs. Washington, which were on a more sociable footing, and at which the President was always present. Mrs. Washington held her first levee on the evening of Friday, the 29th of May, two days after her arrival in New York. Thursday of each week was assigned for the state dinners.

WEDNESDAY, MAY 6.

At New York: " *New York*, May 9.—On Wednesday the 6th inst. was held in *St. Paul's Church*, the annual COM- MENCEMENT of COLUMBIA COLLEGE. . . . THE PRESIDENT—His Excellency the Vice-President—the Senate—the GOVERNOR, and principal officers of the Republic, honored by their presence, this highly useful and important literary Institution."—*Gazette of the United States.*

THURSDAY, MAY 7.

At New York: " *May 9.*—Last Thursday evening [May 7] the subscribers of the Dancing Assembly gave an elegant Ball and Entertainment to his Excellency the President of the United States, who was pleased to honor the company with his presence. His Excellency the Vice President, most of the Members of both Houses of Congress, the Governor of New York, the Chancellor, and Chief Justice of the State [Richard Morris], the Hon. John Jay, and the

---

* Thomas Sinnickson, of New Jersey; Isaac Coles, of Virginia; and William Smith, of South Carolina.

Hon. Gen. Knox, the Commissioners of the Treasury [Samuel Osgood, Walter Livingston, and Arthur Lee], His Worship the Mayor of the city, the late President of Congress [Cyrus Griffin], the Governor of the Western Territory [Arthur St. Clair], the Baron Steuben, the Count de Moustier, Ambassador of his Most Christian Majesty, and many other foreigners of distinction were present. A numerous and brilliant collection of ladies graced the room with their appearance. The whole number of persons was about three hundred. The company retired about two o'clock, after having spent a most agreeable evening. Joy, satisfaction and vivacity was expressive in every countenance — and every pleasure seemed to be heightened by the presence of a Washington."—*New York Packet.*

The ball was held at the Assembly Room, on the east side of Broadway, a little above Wall Street, and it was decorated for the occasion with tasteful and appropriate magnificence. The President danced during the evening in the cotillion with Mrs. Peter Van Brugh Livingston and Mrs. James H. Maxwell, and in a minuet with Mrs. Maxwell's sister, Miss Van Zandt. It is said that an agreeable surprise was prepared by the managers for every woman who attended. A sufficient number of fans had been made for the purpose in Paris, the ivory frames of which displayed, as they were opened, between the hinges and the elegant paper covering, an extremely well executed medallion portrait of Washington, in profile, and a page was appointed to present one, with the compliments of the managers, as each couple passed the receiver of the tickets.

FRIDAY, MAY 8.

At New York: " *New York*, May 8.—Mr. SMITH, of South Carolina, informed the House [of Representatives], that the President was ready to receive their address [in answer to his speech to both Houses]. The House immediately rose, and following the Speaker, attended The President in the room adjoining, where [at twelve o'clock] the Address was presented by the Speaker, in the name of the House."—*Gazette of the United States.*

" *New York*, May 13.—Last Saturday [May 9] the Mayor and Members
of the Corporation of this city, attended by the proper Officers, waited on
THE PRESIDENT of the UNITED STATES. and presented him with an Address."—*Idem.*

MONDAY, MAY 11.

At New York: " *May* 11.—I received a ticket from the
President of the United States to use his box this evening
at the theatre [John Street, near Broadway], being the first
of his appearance at the playhouse since his entering on
his office. The President, Governor of the State, foreign
Ministers, Senators from New Hampshire [John Langdon
and Paine Wingate], Connecticut [William S. Johnson
and Oliver Ellsworth], Pennsylvania [William Maclay and
Robert Morris], M., and South Carolina [Pierce Butler and
Ralph Izard]; and some ladies in the same box. I am old,
and notices or attentions are lost on me. I could have
wished some of my dear children in my place; they are
young and would have enjoyed it. Long might they live
to boast of having been seated in the same box with the
first Character in the world.

" The play was the ' School for Scandal.' I never liked
it; indeed, I think it an indecent representation before
ladies of character and virtue. Farce, the ' Old Soldier.'
The house greatly crowded, and I thought the players
acted well; but I wish we had seen the *Conscious Lovers*, or
some one that inculcated more prudential manners."—
Journal of William Maclay.

THURSDAY, MAY 14.

At New York: " *New York*, May 16.—Last Thursday
evening [May 14], His Excellency THE MINISTER of
FRANCE [Count de Moustier], gave a Ball to THE
PRESIDENT of the UNITED STATES, which was uncommonly elegant, in respect both to the company and the
plan of entertainment. As a compliment to our alliance
with France, there were two sets of *Cotillion Dancers* in

complete uniforms: one set in that of France, and the other in *Blue and Buff:* The ladies were dressed in white, with *Ribbands, Bouquets and Garlands of Flowers,* answering to the uniforms of the Gentlemen.—THE VICE-PRESIDENT—many Members of the Senate, and House of Representatives of the United States—THE GOVERNOR of this State—THE GOVERNOR of the Western Territory, and other characters of distinction were present."—*Gazette of the United States.*

FRIDAY, MAY 15.

At New York: "*New York,* May 16.—Yesterday Mr. F. P. VAN BERCKEL had an audience of THE PRESIDENT of the UNITED STATES of AMERICA, in which he delivered his *Credentials* of RESIDENT from THEIR HIGH MIGHTINESSES THE STATES GENERAL OF THE UNITED NETHERLANDS, having been introduced by the Hon. JOHN JAY, *Secretary of State for the Department of foreign affairs.*"—*Gazette of the United States.*

"*New York,* May 18.—Friday last [May 15], the Vice-President of the United States, the Heads of Departments, the Foreign Ministers, the Judges of the Supreme Court of this State, together with a numerous circle of citizens and foreigners, visited the President at his house."—*Pennsylvania Packet,* May 20.

MONDAY, MAY 18.

At New York: "*New York,* May 20.—Monday last [May 18] the Senate of the United States, with THE VICE-PRESIDENT at their head, went in a body, in carriages, from their Chamber of Congress, to the House of THE PRESIDENT, where the Vice-President read and presented to him an Address, in answer to his Speech, delivered to both Houses of Congress."—*Gazette of the United States.*

TUESDAY, MAY 19.

At New York: "*May 19.*—Had agreed with sundry of our Pennsylvania friends to go to the levee. General Muh-

lenberg came to me and told me they would meet me in
the committee-room. We did so, and went to the levee.
I went foremost, and left them to follow and do as well as
they could. Indeed, they had no great thing of a pattern,
for I am but a poor courtier. The company was large for
the room. The foreign Ministers were there, Van Berkel,
the Dutch Minister (for the first time I suppose), gaudy as a
peacock. Our Pennsylvanians withdrew before me. The
President honored me with a particular *tête-à-tête.* 'How
will this weather suit your farming?' 'Poorly—sir; the
season is the most backward I have ever known. It is remarkably so here, but by letters from Pennsylvania vegeta-
tion is slow in proportion there.' 'The fruit, it is to be
expected, will be safe; backward seasons are in favor of it,
but in Virginia it was lost before I left that place.' 'Much
depends on the exposure of the orchard. Those with a
northern aspect have been found by us [in Pennsylvania]
to be the most certain in producing fruit.' 'Yes, that is a
good observation and should be attended to.' Made my
bow and retired,"—*Journal of William Maclay.*

WEDNESDAY, MAY 27.

At New York: "*New York,* May 27.—This morning at 5
o'clock the President set off in his barge to meet Mrs.
Washington at Elizabeth-Town Point."—*Gazette of the
United States.*

"*New York,* May 30.—Wednesday [May 27] arrived in this city from
Mount Vernon, Mrs. Washington, the amiable consort of The President of
the United States. Mrs. Washington from Philadelphia was accompanied
by the Lady of Mr. Robert Morris. At Elizabethtown-point she was met
by The President, Mr. Morris, and several other gentlemen of distinction,
who had gone there for that purpose.—She was conducted over the bay in
the President's Barge, rowed by 13 eminent pilots, in a handsome white
dress; on passing the Battery a salute was fired; and on her landing [at
Peck's Slip] she was welcomed by crowds of citizens, who had assembled to
testify their joy on this happy occasion.

"The principal ladies of the city have, with the earliest attention and
respect, paid their devoirs to the amiable consort of our beloved PRESIDENT.

viz. The *Lady* of His Excellency the Governor—*Lady Sterling*—*Lady Mary Watts*—*Lady Kitty Duer*—*La Marchioness de Brehan*—the *Ladies* of the Most Hon. Mr. Langdon, and the Most Hon. Mr. Dalton—the *Mayoress*—Mrs. *Livingston* of Clermont—Mrs. *Chancellor Livingston*—the Miss *Livingston's*—*Lady Temple*—*Madam de la Forest*—Mrs. *Montgomery*—Mrs. *Knox*—Mrs. *Thompson*—Mrs. *Gerry*—Mrs. *Edgar*—Mrs. *M·Comb*—Mrs. *Lynch*—Mrs. *Houston*—Mrs. *Griffin*—Mrs. *Provost*—the Miss *Bayards* and a great number of other respectable characters."—*Gazette of the United States.*

THURSDAY, MAY 28.

At New York: "*New York*, May 30.—Although THE PRESIDENT makes no formal invitations, yet the day after the arrival of Mrs. Washington, the following distinguished personages dined at his house, *en famille.*—Their Excellencies the Vice-President—the Governor of this State—the Ministers of France and Spain—and the Governor of the Western Territory—the Hon. Secretary of the United States for Foreign Affairs—the Most Hon. Mr. *Langdon*, Mr. Wingate, Mr. *Izard*, Mr. Few, and Mr. Muhlenberg, Speaker of the Hon. House of Representatives of the United States."—*Gazette of the United States.*

Paine Wingate, Senator from New Hampshire, one of the guests, has left the following description of this dinner: "It was the least showy dinner that I ever saw at the President's. As there was no clergyman present, Washington himself said grace on taking his seat. He dined on a boiled leg of mutton, as it was his custom to eat of only one dish. After the dessert a single glass of wine was offered to each of the guests, when the President rose, the guests following his example, and repaired to the drawing-room, each departing at his option, without ceremony."

FRIDAY, JUNE 5.

At New York: "*New York*, June 8.—THEATRE—JOHN-STREET—Friday evening [June 5] was presented that excellent *Comedy* the CLANDESTINE MARRIAGE. The President of the United States and his Lady—the Most Honourable Robert Morris and Lady—the Gentlemen of the President's Suite—Honourable General Knox and Lady—Baron Steuben—and many other respectable and distinguished

characters honoured the Theatre with their presence."—
Pennsylvania Packet, June 10.

MONDAY, JUNE 8.

At New York: "Although in the present unsettled state
of the executive departments, under the government of the
Union, I do not conceive it expedient to call upon you for
information officially, yet I have supposed, that some informal communications from the office of foreign affairs
might neither be improper nor unprofitable."— *Washington
to John Jay,* Secretary of Foreign Affairs.

The secretaries of the several executive departments under the new government were not appointed till September. In the mean time the usual
business of the departments was transacted by the officers who had charge
of them when the old government expired. Mr. Jay continued to fill the
office of Secretary of Foreign Affairs till Mr. Jefferson (appointed September
26) entered upon his duties in March, 1790. The name of the department
was changed by law to that of the *Department of State,* and its head was
thenceforward called Secretary of State. General Knox acted as Secretary
of War till his new appointment to the same post on the 12th of September.
The affairs of the Treasury were administered by a Board, consisting of
Samuel Osgood, Walter Livingston, and Arthur Lee. These gentlemen
retained their places till September 11, when Alexander Hamilton was
appointed Secretary of the Treasury. Edmund Randolph was appointed
Attorney-General September 26, and Samuel Osgood Postmaster-General on
the same day.

FRIDAY, JUNE 19.

At New York: "*New York,* June 19.—His Excellency
the President of the United States has been much indisposed for several days past, which has caused great anxiety
in the breast of every true friend to America; on Wednesday he was visited by several physicians, and a chain extended across the street to prevent the passing of carriages
before his door; it is however hoped, that this indisposition
will not prove other than incidental, and the cause be soon
removed."—*Pennsylvania Packet,* June 22.

MONDAY, JUNE 22.

At New York: "The President has been confined to his bed for a week past by a fever, and a violent tumor on his thigh;—I have now, however, the pleasure to inform you that the former has left him, and the latter in a fair way of being removed, tho' from its size it will be some time before he will be wholly relieved from the inconvenience of it."—*Tobias Lear to Clement Biddle*, MS. Letter.

"*New York*, June 24.—I informed you in my last, of the 22ᵈ that the President was recovering from his indisposition, and I am now happy to add that he still continues to mend;—his weakness, and the effects of the tumor on his thigh are now his only complaints—these will be removed by time and attention, tho' the latter having been very large & the incision, on opening it, deep, must require some time to be in a state to enable him to take exercise."—*Tobias Lear to Clement Biddle*, MS. Letter.

FRIDAY, JULY 3.

At New York: "I have now the pleasure to inform you, that my health is restored, but a feebleness still hangs upon me, and I am much incommoded by the incision, which was made in a very large and painful tumor on the protuberance of my thigh. This prevents me from walking or sitting. . . . I am able to take exercise in my coach, by having it so contrived as to extend myself the full length of it."—*Washington to James McHenry.*

The cause of the illness of Washington was a case of anthrax so malignant as for several days to threaten mortification. His medical adviser was Dr. Samuel Bard, who attended him with unremitting assiduity. Being alone one day with the doctor, Washington, regarding him steadily, asked his candid opinion as to the probable result of his case. "Do not flatter me with vain hopes," said he, with placid firmness; "I am not afraid to die, and therefore can bear the worst." The doctor expressed hope, but owned that he had apprehensions. "Whether to-night or twenty years hence makes no difference," observed Washington. "I know that I am in the hands of a good Providence." His sufferings were intense and his recovery was slow.

SATURDAY, JULY 4.

At New York: Is waited on by a committee of the Society of the Cincinnati of the State of New York, and addressed by its chairman, Baron Steuben.

The Society afterward marched in procession, attended by Colonel Bauman's artillery and a band of music, to St. Paul's Chapel, where Alexander Hamilton delivered an oration in honor of General Nathanael Greene. William Maclay, Senator from Pennsylvania, referring to this in his journal, says, " The church was crowded. The Cincinnati had seats allotted for themselves; wore their eagles at their button-holes, and were preceded by a flag. The oration was well delivered; the composition appeared good, but I thought he should have given us some account of his virtues as a citizen as well as a warrior, for I supposed he possessed them, and he lived some time after the war, and, I believe, commenced farming."

MONDAY, JULY 6.

At New York: " *New York*, July 6.—With pleasure we announce that the President is considerably recovered from his late indisposition, and has, for these few days past, been able to take an airing in his carriage."—*Pennsylvania Packet, July 8.*

THURSDAY, JULY 23.

At New York: " *New York*, July 25.—On Thursday last [July 23] that venerable patriot CHARLES THOMPSON, Esq. resigned to THE PRESIDENT of the United States his office of Secretary of Congress—a post which he has filled for nearly Fifteen Years, with reputation to himself, and advantage to his country.

" When Heav'n propitious smil'd upon our arms,
Or scenes adverse spread terror and alarms,
Thro' every change the Patriot was the same—
And FAITH and HOPE attended THOMPSON'S NAME."
—*Gazette of the United States.*

The President, in accepting his resignation, wrote to Mr. Thomson under date of July 24, as follows: "The present age does so much justice to the unsullied reputation, with which you have always conducted yourself in the execution of the duties of your office, and posterity will find your name so honorably connected with the verification of such a multitude of astonishing facts, that my single suffrage would add little to the illustration of your merits. Yet I cannot withhold any just testimonial in favor of so old, so faithful, and so able a public officer, which might tend to soothe his mind in the shade of retirement. Accept, then, this serious declaration, that your services have been important, as your patriotism was distinguished; and enjoy that best of all rewards, the consciousness of having done your duty well."

MONDAY, JULY 27.

At New York: "Among the first acts of my recommencing business, after lying six weeks on my right side, is that of writing to you this letter in acknowledgment of yours of the 1st instant. Not being fairly on my seat yet, or, in other words, not being able to sit up without some uneasiness, it must be short."— *Washington to Bushrod Washington.*

"*New York*, July 29.—THE PRESIDENT of the United States was so well as to receive visits of compliment from many official characters and citizens yesterday; but we learn, that, until his strength shall be more fully restored, he proposes to receive them only once a week, and that on Tuesdays. Mrs. Washington, we are informed, will be at home every Friday, at eight o'clock P.M. to see company."—*Gazette of the United States.*

WEDNESDAY, AUGUST 19.

At New York: Receives and answers an address from "The Bishops, the Clergy, and Laity of the Protestant Episcopal Church in the States of *New-York*, *New-Jersey*, *Pennsylvania*, *Delaware*, *Maryland*, *Virginia*, and *South Carolina*, in Convention at Philadelphia, 7th August, 1789."

The address was presented by the Right Rev. Dr. Samuel Provoost, the Rev. Mr. William Smith, Mr. Robert Andrews, Mr. John Cox, Mr. William Brisbane, the Rev. Dr. Abraham Beach, the Rev. Dr. Benjamin Moore, Mr. Moses Rogers, the Rev. Uzal Ogden, the Rev. Mr. George H. Spieren, the Rev. Mr. Henry Waddell, and the Hon. Mr. Duane.

SATURDAY, AUGUST 22.

At New York: "*New York*, August 22.—THE PRESIDENT of the United States will this day, at 11 o'clock, meet the

Senate in their chamber of Congress; to confer with them upon the important subject of the approaching negociations and treaties with the Southern Indians; and to make the necessary previous arrangements of that business. This intention was announced to the Senate by message on Thursday last."—*Gazette of the United States.*

"*August* 22.—Senate met, and went on the Coasting bill. The door-keeper soon told us of the arrival of the President. The President was introduced, and took our Vice-President's chair. He rose and told us bluntly that he had called on us for our advice and consent to some propositions respecting the treaty to be held with the Southern Indians. Said he had brought General Knox with him, who was well acquainted with the business. He then turned to General Knox, who was seated on the left of the chair. General Knox handed him a paper, which he handed to the President of the Senate, who was seated on a chair on the floor to his right. Our Vice-President hurried over the paper. . . . I rose reluctantly. Mr. President: The paper which you have now read to us appears to have for its basis sundry treaties and public transactions between the Southern Indians and the United States and the States of Georgia, North Carolina, and South Carolina. The business is new to the Senate. It is of importance. It is our duty to inform ourselves as well as possible on the subject. I therefore call for the reading of the treaties and other documents alluded to in the paper before us. I cast an eye at the President of the United States. I saw he wore an aspect of stern displeasure. . . .

"I had at an early stage of the business whispered Mr. Morris that I thought the best way to conduct the business was to have all the papers committed. . . . Mr. Morris hastily rose and moved that the papers communicated to the Senate by the President of the United States should be referred to a committee of five, to report as soon as might be on them. . . . I rose and supported the mode of doing business by committees; that committees were used in all public deliberative bodies, etc. I thought I did the subject justice, but concluded the commitment can not be attended with any possible inconvenience. Some articles are already postponed until Monday. Whoever the committee are, if committed, they must make their report on Monday morning. I spoke through the whole in a low tone of voice. Peevishness itself, I think, could not have taken offense at anything I said.

"As I sat down, the President of the United States started up in a violent fret. '*This defeats every purpose of my coming here,*' were the first words that he said. He then went on that he had brought his Secretary of War with him to give every necessary information; that the Secretary knew all about the business, and yet he was delayed and could not go on with the matter. He cooled, however by degrees. Said he had no objection to

putting off this matter until Monday, but declared he did not understand
the matter of commitment. He might be delayed; he could not tell how
long. He rose a second time, and said he had no objection to postponement
until Monday at ten o'clock. By the looks of the Senate this seemed agreed
to. A pause for some time ensued. We waited for him to withdraw. He
did so with a discontented air. Had it been any other man than the man
whom I wish to regard as the first character in the world, I would have said,
with sullen dignity.

"*August* 24.—The Senate met. The President of the United States soon
took his seat, and the business began. The President wore a different aspect
from what he did Saturday. He was placid and serene, and manifested a
spirit of accommodation; declared his consent that his questions should be
amended."—*Journal of William Maclay.*

THURSDAY, AUGUST 27.

At New York: "*August* 27.—Senate adjourned early.
At a little after four I called on Mr. [Richard] Bassett, of
the Delaware State. We went to the President's to dinner.
The company were: President and Mrs. Washington, Vice-
President and Mrs. Adams, the Governor and his wife, Mr.
Jay and wife, Mr. [John] Langdon and wife, Mr. [Tristram]
Dalton and a lady (perhaps his wife), and a Mr. Smith, Mr.
Bassett, myself, [Tobias] Lear, [Robert] Lewis,* the President's secretaries. The President and Mrs. Washington
sat opposite each other in the middle of the table; the two
secretaries, one at each end. It was a great dinner, and the
best of the kind I ever was at. The room, however, was
disagreeably warm.

"First was the soup: fish roasted and boiled; meats,
gammon, fowls, etc. This was the dinner. The middle
of the table was garnished in the usual tasty way, with
small images, flowers (artificial), etc. The dessert was,
first apple-pies, pudding, etc.; then iced creams, jellies,
etc.; then water-melons, musk-melons, apples, peaches,
nuts."—*Journal of William Maclay.*

"It was the most solemn dinner ever I sat at. Not a health drunk;
scarce a word said until the cloth was taken away. Then the President,

---

* A nephew of the President, son of his sister Betty Lewis.

filling a glass of wine, with great formality drank to the health of every individual by name round the table. Everybody imitated him, charged glasses, and such a buzz of 'health, sir,' and 'health, madam,' and 'thank you, sir,' and 'thank you, madam,' never had I heard before. Indeed, I had liked to have been thrown out in the hurry; but I got a little wine in my glass, and passed the ceremony. The ladies sat a good while, and the bottles passed about; but there was a dead silence almost. Mrs. Washington at last withdrew with the ladies.

"I expected the men would now begin, but the same stillness remained. The President told of a New England clergyman who had lost a hat and wig in passing a river called the Brunks. He smiled, and every body else laughed. He now and then said a sentence or two on some common subject, and what he said was not amiss. Mr. Jay tried to make a laugh by mentioning the circumstance of the Duchess of Devonshire leaving no stone unturned to carry Fox's election. There was a Mr. Smith, who mentioned how *Homer* described Æneas leaving his wife and carrying his father out of flaming Troy. He had heard somebody (I suppose) witty on the occasion; but if he had ever read it he would have said *Virgil*. The President kept a fork in his hand when the cloth was taken away, I thought for the purpose of picking nuts. He ate no nuts, however, but played with the fork, striking on the edge of the table with it. We did not sit long after the ladies retired. The President rose, went upstairs to drink coffee; the company followed. I took my hat and came home."—*Idem.*

TUESDAY, SEPTEMBER 1.

At New York : " *September* 1.—Baron Steuben and Governor St. Clair dined with us to day; the Baron was remarkably cheerful and facetious, likewise greatly devoted to the President. In the midst of our mirth my uncle received a letter . . . informing him of the death of my grandmother, an event long expected."—*Diary of Robert Lewis.*

"FREDERICKSBURG [Virginia], August 27, 1789.—On Tuesday, the 25th inst. died at her home in this town, Mrs. MARY WASHINGTON, aged 82 years, the venerable mother of the illustrious President of the United States, after a long and painful indisposition, which she bore with uncommon patience. Though a pious tear of duty, affection and esteem, is due to the memory of so revered a character, yet our grief must be greatly alleviated from the consideration that she is relieved from the pitiable infirmities attendant on an extreme old age.—It is usual when virtuous and conspicuous persons quit this terrestrial abode, to publish an elaborate panegyric on their characters—suffice it to say, she conducted herself through this transitory life with virtue, prudence and christianity, worthy the mother of the greatest Hero that ever adorned the annals of history.

> "*O may kind heaven, propitious to our fate,*
> *Extend* THAT HERO'S *to her lengthen'd date ;*
> *Through the long period,* healthy, active, sage ;
> *Nor know the sad infirmities of age.*"
> —*Gazette of the United States,* September 9.

TUESDAY, SEPTEMBER 8.

At New York: " *New York,* September 12.—On Tuesday last [September 8], being the first public levee at the President's since his mother's decease was known in this city, several gentlemen of the two Houses of Congress, and other respectable persons, attended it, in American mourning. This silent mark of respect, flowing spontaneously from the hearts of freemen sympathizing with him in this domestic misfortune, manifests sentiments and emotions which no language can express in a manner so unequivocal and delicate."—*Gazette of the United States.*

MONDAY, SEPTEMBER 14.

At New York: " *New York,* September 19.—Monday evening last [September 14], the President of the United States, his lady and family, and several other persons of distinction, were pleased to honor Mr. Bowen's exhibition of wax-work, with their company, at No. 74 Water-street, and appeared exceedingly well pleased with the late improvements made by the Proprietor."—*Pennsylvania Packet,* September 24.

" *New York,* September 29.—Yesterday morning the Light Horse, and the other Independent Companies in this city, paraded in the Broadway, under the immediate command of Col. Bauman ; from whence they proceeded to the Race Ground, where they went through a number of manœuvres in a manner that would do credit to regular troops ;—after which they exhibited a sham fight, that afforded the highest entertainment to the President, his Excellency the Governor, and a large concourse of respectable characters."
—*Pennsylvania Packet,* October 2.

THURSDAY, OCTOBER 1.

At New York: " *October* 1.—Exercised in my carriage in
the forenoon. The following company dined here to-day,
viz.: M^r [George] Read of the Senate, Col° [Theodoric]
Bland and M^r [James] Madison of the House of Representatives, M^r [Samuel] Osgood and his lady, Col° [William]
Duer, his lady and Miss Brown, Col° Lewis Morris and
lady, lady Christiana Griffin [wife of Cyrus Griffin] and her
daughter, and Judge [James] Duane and M^{rs} [General
Nathanael] Greene. . . . Mr Thomas Nelson * joined my
family [as a secretary] this day."— *Washington's Diary.*

" *October* 2.—Dispatching Commissions &c. as yesterday, for the Judi-
ciary. The visitors to Mrs Washington this evening were not numerous."—
Washington's Diary.

SATURDAY, OCTOBER 3.

At New York: " *October* 3.—Sat for Mr Rammage near
two hours to-day, who was drawing a miniature Picture of
me for Mrs Washington.

" Walked in the afternoon, and sat about two o'clock for
Madam de Brehan, to complete a miniature profile of me,
which she had begun from memory, and which she had
made exceedingly like the original."— *Washington's Diary.*

A miniature in the possession of Mr. H. S. Stabler, of Baltimore, Maryland, is claimed to be the " miniature Picture," by Ramage, referred to in
the Diary. It represents Washington in uniform, head three-quarters to the
left, the order of the Cincinnati on the left breast, and is beautifully executed. A reproduction of it on wood, with a statement as to its authen-
ticity, will be found in vol. xlvii., p. 545, of *The Century Magazine.* John
Ramage, an Irishman by birth, resided in New York until 1794, when he
went to Canada, where he died.

Madame de Brehan, sister of the French minister, Count de Moustier,
was quite a skilful amateur artist and a great admirer of Washington. On
the evening of the day of the inauguration the front of her brother's residence on Broadway (afterward occupied by the President) was beautifully
decorated with paintings by her own hand. The " miniature profile," re-

---

* Son of General Thomas Nelson, Governor of Virginia, 1781.

ferred to in the Diary as " exceedingly like the original," has been engraved by A. F. Sergent, B. Roger, and Charles Burt. Proofs of the print by Sergent, executed at Paris in 1790, were sent to the President after her return to France. Madame de Brehan left New York with her brother about the middle of October.

SUNDAY, OCTOBER 4.

At New York : " *October* 4.—Went to St. Paul's Chappel in the forenoon. Spent the remainder of the day in writing private letters for to-morrow's Post."— *Washington's Diary.*

" *October* 5.—Exercised on horseback between the hours of 9 and 11 in the forenoon, and between 5 and 6 in the afternoon, on foot. Had conversation with Col⁰ Hamilton on the propriety of my making a tour through the Eastern States during the recess of Congress, to acquire knowledge of the face of the Country, the growth and agriculture thereof—and the temper and disposition of the inhabitants towards the new government, who thought it a very desirable plan, and advised it accordingly. *October* 6.—Exercised in a carriage with Mrs Washington in the forenoon. Conversed with Gen. Knox, Secretary of War, on the above tour, who also recommended it accordingly. *October* 7.—Exercised on horseback, and called on the Vice-President. In the afternoon walked an hour. . . . Upon consulting Mr Jay on the propriety of my intended tour into the Eastern States, he highly approved of it, but observed, a similar visit w'd be expected by those of the Southern."— *Washington's Diary.*

THURSDAY, OCTOBER 8.

At New York : " *October* 8.—Mr Gardoqui took leave, proposing to embark to-morrow for Spain.* The following company dined with me to-day, viz : The Vice-President, his lady and son and her niece, with their son-in-law, Col⁰ [William S.] Smith and his lady—Governor Clinton and his two eldest daughters—Mr [Tristram] Dalton and his

---

* " *New York,* October 14.—On Saturday [October 10] sailed the snow San Nicholas, Melide, for Bilboa. His Excellency Don Diego de Gardoqui, Encargado de Negocios, and Minister of his Catholic Majesty to the United States, went passenger in this vessel, accompanied by his son, and one of his secretaries. Previous to his Excellency's departure, he waited on THE PRESIDENT of the United States, and had his audience of leave in due form : At the same time His Excellency introduced the Hon. Mr. VIAR, as CHARGE DES AFFAIRES from His Most Catholic Majesty."—*Gazette of the United States.*

lady, their son-in-law, M' Dubois, and his lady, and their other three daughters.

" In the evening, the Count de Moustier and Madam de Brehan came in and sat an hour. M' Madison took his leave to-day. He saw no impropriety in my trip to the eastward."— *Washington's Diary.*

" *October* 9.—Exercised on horseback between the hours of 9 and 11. Visited in my route the gardens of M' Perry and M' Williamson.* Received from the French Minister, in person, official notice of his having recd. leave to return to his Court, and intended embarkation. . . . The visiters this evening to M" Washington were respectable, both of gentlemen and ladies. *October* 10.—Pursuant to an engagement formed on Thursday last, I set off about 9 o'clock in my barge to visit M' Prince's fruit gardens and shrubberies at Flushing, on Long Island. The Vice-President, Governor of the State, M' Izard, Col° Smith, and Maj' Jackson accompanied me. These gardens, except in the number of young fruit trees, did not answer my expectations. The shrubs were trifling, and the flowers not numerous. The inhabitants of this place shewed us what respect they could, by making the best use of one cannon to salute. On our return we stopped at the seats of General and M' Gouvern' Morris [Morrisania] and viewed a barn of which 1 have heard the latter speak much belonging to his farm—but it was not of a construction to strike my fancy—nor did the conveniences of it at all answer their cost. From hence we proceeded to Harlaem, where we were met by M" Washington, M" Adams and M" Smith. Dined at the tavern kept by a Capt. Mariner,† and came home in the evening. *October* 11.—At home all day—writing private letters."— *Washington's Diary.*

MONDAY, OCTOBER 12.

At New York : " *October* 12.—Received the compliments of the Count de Penthere, commanding his most Christian Majesty's Squadron in the harbour of Boston—these were

* Perry's garden was on the west side of the Bloomingdale road, west of the present Union Square. Williamson's was a flower and nursery garden, and a place of public resort, on the east side of Greenwich Street, extending about three squares up from Harrison Street.

† Captain William Marriner, who had been associated with Captain Adam Hyler in a whale-boat warfare in the vicinity of New York during a part of the Revolution, lived at Harlem and on Ward's Island for many years after the war, and kept a tavern at each place.

sent by the Marquis de Traversy in the Active Frigate; who, with all his officers were presented by the French Minister at one o'clock."— *Washington's Diary.*

" *October* 13.—At two o'clock received the Address from the People called Quakers.* A good many gentlemen attended the Levee this day. *October* 14.—Wrote several letters to France, and about 7 o'clock in the afternoon made an informal visit with Mrs Washington to the Count de Moustier and Madame de Brehan, to take leave of them. Into the hands of the former I committed these letters, viz: to the Count de Estaing, Count de Rochambeau, the Marqs. de la Fayette and the Marqs. de la Rouirie."—*Washington's Diary.*

THURSDAY, OCTOBER 15.

Leaves New York: " *October* 15.—Commenced my Journey about 9 o'clock for Boston and a tour through the Eastern States.† The Chief Justice, Mr. Jay—and the Secretaries of the Treasury and War Departments accompanied me some distance out of the city. About 10 o'clock it began to Rain, and continued to do so till 11, when we arrived at the house of one Hoyatt, who keeps a Tavern at Kings-bridge, where we, that is, Major Jackson, Mr. Lear and myself with six servants, which composed my Retinue, dined. After dinner, through frequent light showers we proceed'd to the Tavern of a Mrs. Haviland at Rye. . . . The distance of this day's travel was 31 miles, in which we passed through (after leaving the Bridge) East Chester, New Rochelle, and Mamaroneck."—*Washington's Diary.*

" *October* 16.—About 7 o'clock we left the Widow Haviland's, and after passing Horse Neck, six miles distant from Rye, we breakfasted at Stamford, [Connecticut] which is 6 miles further. . . . At Norwalk, which is ten miles further, we made a halt to feed our Horses. . . . From hence to Fair-

---

* For this address and the answer to it, see Penna. Mag., Vol. XIII. p. 245.

† Congress having adjourned from the 29th of September to the 4th of January, 1790, the President resolved to embrace the opportunity to make a tour through the Eastern States, omitting Rhode Island, that State not having, as yet, accepted the Federal Constitution.

field, where we dined and lodged, is 12 miles.   *October* 17.—A little after
sun-rise we left Fairfield, and passing through Et. Fairfield, breakfasted at
Stratford, wch. is ten miles from Fairfield. . . . At this place I was received
with an effort of Military parade; and was attended to the Ferry, which is
near a mile from the center of the Town, by sevl. Gentlemen on horseback. . . . From the Ferry it is abt. 3 miles to Milford. . . . From Milford
we took the lower road through West haven, and arrived at New Haven
before two o'clock; we had time to walk through several parts of the City
before Dinner. . . . The Address [of the Assembly] was presented at 7
o'clock—and at nine I received another address from the Congregational
Clergy of the place. Between the rect. of the two addresses I received the
Compliment of a visit from the Govr. Mr. [Samuel] Huntington—the Lieut.
Govr. Mr. [Oliver] Wolcott—and the Mayor, Mr. Roger Sherman."—*Washington's Diary.*

SUNDAY, OCTOBER 18.

At New Haven, Connecticut: " *October* 18.—Went in the
forenoon to the Episcopal Church, and in the afternoon to
one of the Congregational Meeting-Houses. Attended to
the first by the Speaker of the Assembly, Mr. Edwards,
and a Mr. Ingersoll, and to the latter by the Governor, the
Lieut. Governor, the Mayor, and Speaker.

" These Gentlemen all dined with me, (by invitation,) as
did Genl. [Jedidiah] Huntington, at the House of Mr.
Brown, where I lodged, and who keeps a good Tavern.
Drank Tea at the Mayor's (Mr. Sherman). . . . At 7
o'clock in the evening many Officers of this State, belonging to the late Continental army, called to pay their respects to me."—*Washington's Diary.*

" *October* 19.—Left New-haven at 6 o'clock, and arrived at Wallingford
(13 miles) by half after 8 o'clock, where we breakfasted, and took a walk
through the Town. . . . About 10 o'clock we left this place, and at the distance of 8 miles passed through Durham. At one we arrived at Middletown, on Connecticut River, being met two or three miles from it by the
respectable Citizens of the place, and escorted in by them. While dinner
was getting ready I took a walk round the Town, from the heights of which
the prospect is beautiful. . . . Having dined, we set out with the same
Escort (who conducted us into town) about 3 o'clock for Hartford, and
passing through a Parish of Middletown and Weathersfield, we arrived at
Harfd. about sundown. At Weathersfield we were met by a party of the

Hartford light horse, and a number of Gentlemen from the same place with Col° [Jeremiah] Wadsworth at their head, and escorted to Bull's Tavern where we lodged."—*Washington's Diary.*

TUESDAY, OCTOBER 20.

At Hartford, Connecticut: "*October* 20.—After breakfast, accompanied by Col° Wadsworth, Mr. [Oliver] Ellsworth and Col° Jesse Root, I viewed the Woolen Manufactory at this place, which seems to be going on with spirit. Their Broadcloths are not of the first quality, as yet, but they are good; as are their Coatings, Cassimeres, Serges and Ever-lastings; of the first, that is, broad-cloth, I ordered a suit to be sent to me at New York—and of the latter a whole piece, to make breeches for my servants. All the parts of this business are performed at the Manufactory except the spinning—this is done by the Country people, who are paid by the cut. . . . Dined and drank Tea at Col° Wadsworth's, and about 7 o'clock received from, and answered the Address of, the Town of Hartford."—*Washington's Diary.*

WEDNESDAY, OCTOBER 21.

At Springfield, Massachusetts: "*October* 21.—By promise I was to have Breakfasted at Mr. Ellsworth's at Windsor, on my way to Springfield, but the morning proving very wet, and the rain not ceasing till past 10 o'clock, I did not set out till half after that hour; I called, however, on Mr. Ellsworth and stay'd there near an hour—reached Spring-field by 4 o'clock, and while dinner was getting, examined the Continental Stores at this place. . . . A Col° Worthing-ton, Col° Williams, Adjutant General of the State of Massa-chusetts, Gen. [William] Shepherd [Shepard], Mr. Lyman, and many other Gentlemen sat an hour or two with me in the evening at Parson's Tavern, where I lodged, and which is a good House."—*Washington's Diary.*

"*October* 22.—Set out at 7 o'clock; came to Palmer, at the House of one Scott, where we breakfasted. . . . At Brookland [Brookfield] we fed the Horses and dispatched an Express which was sent to me by Govr. Hancock

—giving notice of the measures he was about to pursue for my reception on
the Road, and in Boston—with a request to lodge at his House. Continued
on to Spencer, 10 miles further, and lodged at the House of one Jenks, who
keeps a pretty good Tavern. *October* 23.—Commenced our course with the
Sun, and passing through Leicester, met some Gentlemen of the Town of
Worcester, on the line between it and the former to escort us. Arrived
about 10 o'clock at the House of —— where we breakfasted—distant from
Spencer 12 miles. Here we were received by a handsome Company of
Militia Artillery in Uniform, who saluted with 13 Guns on our Entry and
departure. At this place also we met a Committee from the Town of
Boston. . . . These matters [entrance into Boston] being settled, the Com-
mittee set forward on their return—and after breakfast I followed. The
same Gentlemen who had escorted me into, conducting me out of Town.
On the Line between Worcester and Middlesex I was met by a Troop of
light Horse belonging to the latter, who Escorted me to Marlborough, (16
miles) where we dined, and thence to Weston (14 more) where we lodged."
— *Washington's Diary.*

SATURDAY, OCTOBER 24.

At Boston : " *October* 24.—Dressed by Seven o'clock, and
set out at eight—at ten we arrived in Cambridge, according
to appointment; but most of the Militia having a distance
to come, were not in line till after eleven; they made however an excellent appearance, with Genl. [John] Brooks at
their Head. At this place the Lieut. Govr. Mr. Saml.
Adams, with the Executive Council, met me and preceeded
my entrance into town—which was in every degree flattering and honorable. To pass over the Minutiæ of the
arrangement for this purpose, it may suffice to say that at
the entrance I was welcomed by the Selectmen in a body.*
Then following the Lieut't. Govr. and Council in the order
we came from Cambridge (preceeded by the Town Corps,
very handsomely dressed,) we passed through the Citizens
classed in their different professions, and under their own

---

* " At one o'clock, The President's approach was announced by federal
discharges from Capt. WARNER's artillery at *Roxbury*—from the *Dorchester*
artillery posted on the celebrated heights of that town—from Capt. Johnson's
artillery at the entrance of the town—and from Castle William ; by a royal
salute from the Ships of his most Christian Majesty's squadron, and by the
ringing of all the bells."—*Massachusetts Magazine*, October, 1789.

banners, till we came to the State House; from which
across the Street an Arch was thrown; in the front of
which was this Inscription—'To the Man who unites all
hearts'—and on the other—'To Columbia's favorite Son'—
and on one side thereof next the State House, in a pannel
decorated with a trophy, composed of the Arms of the
United States—of the Commonwealth of Massachusetts—
and our French Allies, crowned with a wreath of Laurel,
was this Inscription—'Boston relieved March 17th, 1776.'
This Arch was handsomely ornamented, and over the
Center of it a Canopy was erected 20 feet high, with the
American Eagle perched on the top.   After passing through
the Arch, and entering the State House at the S° End and
ascending to the upper floor and returning to a Balcony at
the N° End; three cheers was given by a vast concourse of
people who by this time had assembled at the Arch—then
followed an ode composed in honor of the President; * and
well sung by a band of select singers—after this three
Cheers—followed by the different Professions and Mechanics in the order they were drawn up with their colours
through a lane of the People, which had thronged abt. the
Arch under which they passed.   The Streets, the Doors,
windows and tops of the Houses were crowded with well
dressed Ladies and Gentlemen.   The procession being over,
I was conducted to my lodgings at a Widow Ingersoll's,
(which is a very decent and good house) by the Lieut. Govr.
and Council—accompanied by the Vice President, where
they took leave of me.   Having engaged yesterday to take
an informal dinner with the Govr. [John Hancock] to-day,
but under a full persuasion that he would have waited upon
me so soon as I should have arrived—I excused myself
upon his not doing it, and informing me thro' his Secretary
that he was too much indisposed to do it, being resolved to

---

* This ode, sung by the *Independent Musical Society*, was published in the
October number of the Massachusetts Magazine.

receive the visit. Dined at my Lodgings, where the Vice-President favoured me with his Company."— *Washington's Diary.*

" *October* 25.—Attended Divine Service at the Episcopal Church, whereof Doctor [Samuel] Parker is the Incumbent, in the forenoon, and the Congregational Church of Mr. [Peter] Thatcher in the afternoon.—Dined at my Lodgings with the Vice-President. Mr. [James] Bowdoin accompanied me to both Churches. Between the two I received a visit from the Govr. who assured me that indisposition alone prevented his doing it yesterday, and that he was still indisposed; but as it had been suggested that he expected to *receive* the visit from the President which he knew was improper, he was resolved at all haz'ds to pay his Compliments to-day. *October* 26.—The day being Rainy and Stormy, myself much disordered by a cold, and inflammation in the left eye, I was prevented from visiting Lexington, (where the first blood in the dispute with G. Brit'n was drawn). Rec'd the complim'ts of many visits to-day. Mr. Dalton and Genl. [David] Cobb dined with me, and in the Evening drank Tea with Gov'r Hancock, and called upon Mr. Bowdoin on my return to my lodgings. *October* 27.—At 10 o'clock in the Morning received the visits of the Clergy of the Town. At 11 I went to an Oratorio [at King's Chapel]—and between that and 3 o'clock rec'd the Addresses of the Governor and Council—of the Town of Boston—of the President [Joseph Willard], &c of Harvard College, and of the Cincinnati of the State; after wch. at 3 o'clock, I dined at a large and elegant Dinner at Fanuiel Hall, given by the Gov'r and Council, and spent the evening at my lodgings. *October* 28.—At 11 o'clock I embarked on board the Barge of the Illustrious, Captn. Penthere Gion [commander of the French squadron], and visited his Ship and the Superb, another 74 Gun Ship in the Harbour of Boston, about 4 miles below the Town. Going and coming I was saluted by the two frigates which lye near the wharves, and by the 74s after I had been on board of them; as also by the 40 Gun Ship which lay in the same range with them. I was also saluted going and coming by the fort on Castle Isld. After my return I dined in a large company at Mr. Bowdoin's, and went to the Assembly in the evening, where (it is said) there were upwards of 100 Ladies. Their appearance was elegant, and many of them very handsome; the Room is small but neat, and well ornamented."— *Washington's Diary.*

THURSDAY, OCTOBER 29.

At Salem, Massachusetts: " *October* 29.—Left Boston about 8 o'clock. Passed over the Bridge at Charles-Town, and went to see that at Malden, but proceeded to the College at Cambridge, attended by the Vice-President, Mr.

Bowdoin, and a great number of Gentlemen. . . . From Boston, besides the number of citizens which accompanied me to Cambridge, and many of them from thence to Lynn —the Boston Corps of Horse escorted me to the line between Middlesex and Essex County, where a party of Horse, with Genl. [Jonathan] Titcomb), met me, and conducted me through Marblehead to Salem. . . . At the Bridge, 2 miles from this Town, we were also met by a Committee, who conducted us by a Brigade of the Militia and one or two handsome Corps in Uniform, through several of the Streets to the Town or Court House, where an Ode in honor of the President was sung—an Address presented to him amidst the acclamations of the People; after which he was conducted to his Lodgings. Rec'd the Compliments of many differt. classes of People, and in the evening, between 7 and 8 o'clock, went to an Assembly, where there was at least an hundred handsome and well dressed Ladies. Abt. nine I returned to my Lodgings."— *Washington's Diary.*

FRIDAY, OCTOBER 30.

At Newburyport, Massachusetts : " *October* 30.—A little after 8 o'clock I set out for Newbury-Port ; and in less than 2 miles crossed the Bridge between Salem and Beverly. . . . After passing Beverley, 2 miles, we come to the Cotton Manufactury. . . . From this place, with escorts of Horse, I passed on to Ipswich, about 10 miles : at the entrance of which I was met and welcomed by the Select men, and received by a Regm't of Militia. At this place I was met by Mr. Dalton and some other Gentlemen from Newburyport; partook of a cold collation, and proceeded on to the last mentioned place, where I was received with much respect and parade, about 4 o'clock. In the evening there were rockets and some other fireworks—and every other demonstration to welcome me to the Town."— *Washington's Diary.*

SATURDAY, OCTOBER 31.

At Portsmouth, New Hampshire: " *October* 31.—Left
Newbury-port a little after 8 o'clock (first breakfasting
with Mr. Dalton) . . . and in three miles came to the line
wch. divides the State of Massachusetts from that of New
Hampshire. Here I took leave of Mr. Dalton and many
other private Gentlemen who accompanied me; also of
Gen'l Titcomb, who had met me on the line between Middlesex and Essex Counties—Corps of light Horse, and many
officers of Militia—and was rec'd by the President of the
State of New Hampshire [John Sullivan]—the Vice-President [John Pickering]; some of the Council—Messrs.
Langdon and Wingate of the Senate—Col° [John] Parker,
Marshall of the State, and many other respectable characters; besides several Troops of well cloathed Horse in
handsome Uniforms, and many officers of the Militia also
in handsome (white and red) uniforms of the Manufacture
of the State. With this cavalcade, we proceeded, and
arrived before 3 o'clock at Portsmouth where we were
received with every token of respect and appearance of
cordiality, under a discharge of artillery. The streets,
doors and windows were crowded here, as at all the other
Places; and alighting at the Town House, odes were sung
and played in honor of the President. The same happened
yesterday at my entrance into Newburyport—being stopped
at my entrance to hear it. From the Town House I went
to Colonel Brewster's Ta'n, the place provided for my residence; and asked the President, Vice-President, the two
Senators, the Marshall, and Majr. [Nicholas] Gilman to
dine with me, which they did; after which I drank Tea at
Mr. Langdons."— *Washington's Diary.*

" *November* 1.—Attended by the President of the State (Genl. Sullivan),
Mr. Langdon, and the Marshall, I went in the forenoon to the Episcopal
Church, under the incumbency of a Mr. Ogden; and in the afternoon to one
of the Presbyterian or Congregational Churches, in which a Mr. [Joseph]
Buckminster Preached. Dined at home with the Marshall, and spent the

afternoon in my own room writing letters. *November* 2.—Having made previous preparations for it, about 8 o'clock, attended by the President, Mr. Langdon, and some other Gentlemen, I went in a boat to view the harbour of Portsmouth. . . . In my way to the mouth of the Harbour, I stopped at a place called Kittery, in the Province of Maine. . . . From hence I went by the old Fort (formerly built while under the English government) on an Island which is at the entrance of the harbour, and where the Light House stands. As we passed this Fort we were saluted by 13 Guns. Having Lines, we proceeded to the Fishing banks a little without the Harbour, and fished for Cod; but it not being a proper time of tide, we only caught two, with w'ch, about 1 o'clock, we returned to Town. Dined at Mr. Langdon's and drank Tea there, with a large circle of Ladies, and retired a little after seven o'clock. Before dinner I rec'd an address from the Town, presented by the Vice-President."—*Washington's Diary.*

TUESDAY, NOVEMBER 3.

At Portsmouth: "*November* 3.—Sat two hours in the forenoon for a Mr —— Painter,* of Boston, at the request of Mr. Breck of that place; who wrote Majr. Jackson that it was an earnest desire of many of the Inhabitants of that Town that he might be indulged. . . . About 2 o'clock, I received an Address from the Executive of the State of New Hampshire, and in half an hour after dined with them and a large company, at their assembly room, which is one of the best I have seen anywhere in the United States. At half after seven I went to the assembly, where there were about 75 well dressed, and many of them very handsome ladies—among whom (as was also the case at the Salem and Boston assemblies) were a greater proportion with much blacker hair than are usually seen in the Southern States. About nine I returned to my quarters."—*Washington's Diary.*

---

* The painter, whose name is not mentioned in the Diary, was Christian Gulager, a Dane, who settled in Boston about the year 1781. He left that city in 1791, and after living in New York for some years, went to Philadelphia, where he died in 1827. His portrait of Washington was engraved by William E. Marshall, and published in the "Proceedings of the Massachusetts Historical Society," vol. i., 1855–58.

" *November* 4.—About half after seven I left Portsmouth, quietly, and without any attendance, having earnestly entreated that all parade and ceremony might be avoided on my return.   Before ten I reached Exeter, 14 miles distance. . . . From hence, passing through Kingstown, (6 miles from Exeter) I arrived at Haverhill [Massachusetts] about half-past two, and stayed all night.   Walked through the town, which stands at the head of the tide of Merrimack River, and in a beautiful part of the country."— *Washington's Diary.*

THURSDAY, NOVEMBER 5.

At Watertown, Massachusetts : " *November* 5.—About sunrise I set out, crossing the Merrimack River at the town, over to the township of Bradford, and in nine miles came to Abbot's tavern in Andover, where we breakfasted, and met with much attention from Mr. [Samuel] Phillips, President of the Senate of Massachusetts, who accompanied us through Bellariki [Billerica] to Lexington, where I dined, and viewed the spot on which the first blood was spilt in the dispute with Great Britain, on the 19th of April, 1775.   Here I parted with Mr. Phillips, and proceeded on to Watertown. . . . We lodged in this place at the house of a Widow Coolidge, near the Bridge, and a very indifferent one it is."— *Washington's Diary.*

" *November* 6.—A little after seven o'clock, under great appearances of rain or snow, we left Watertown, and passing through Needham (five miles therefrom) breakfasted at Sherburn, which is 14 miles from the former. Then passing through Holliston, 5 miles, Milford 6 more, Menden 4 more, and Uxbridge 6 more, we lodged at one Taft's, 1 mile further; the whole distance of this day's travel being 36 miles.   *November* 7.—Left Taft's before sunrise, and passing through Douglass wood, breakfasted at one Jacobs' in Thompson [Connecticut], 12 miles distant; not a good house.   Bated the horses in Pomfret, at Col° Grosvenor's distant 11 miles from Jacobs', and lodged at Squire Perkins' in Ashford, (called 10 miles, but must be 12). *November* 8.—It being contrary to law and disagreeable to the People of this State (Connecticut) to travel on the Sabbath day—and my horses, after passing through such intolerable roads, wanting rest, I stayed at Perkins' tavern (which, by the bye, is not a good one,) all day—and a meeting-house being within a few rods of the door, I attended morning and evening service, and heard very lame discourses from a Mr. [Enoch] Pond."— *Washington's Diary.*

MONDAY, NOVEMBER 9.

At Hartford, Connecticut: "*November* 9.—Set out about
7 o'clock, and for the first 24 miles had hilly, rocky, and
disagreeable roads; the remaining 10 was level and good,
but in places sandy. Arrived at Hartford a little before
four. We passed through Mansfield . . . and breakfasted
at one Brigham's, in Coventry."— *Washington's Diary.*

"*November* 10.—Left Hartford about 7 o'clock. . . . Breakfasted at
Worthington, in the township of Berlin, at the house of one Fuller. Bated
at Smith's on the plains of Wallingford, 13 miles from Fuller's which is the
distance Fuller's is from Hartford—and got into New Haven which is 13
miles more, about half an hour before sun-down. At this place I met Mr.
[Elbridge] Gerry, in the stage from New York, who gave me the first cert'n
acct. of the health of Mrs. Washington. *November* 11.—Set out about sun-
rise, and took the upper road to Milford, it being shorter than the lower one
through West Haven. Breakfasted at the former. Baited at Fairfield;
and dined and lodged at a Maj. Marvin's 9 miles further. *November* 12.—
A little before sunrise we left Marvin's, and breakfasting at Stamford, 13
miles distant, reached the Widow Haviland's, 12 miles further; where, on
acct. of some lame horses, we remained all night."— *Washington's Diary.*

FRIDAY, NOVEMBER 13.

At New York: "*November* 13.—Left Mrs. Haviland's as
soon as we could see the road, and breakfasted at Hoyet's
tavern, this side Kings-bridge, and between two and three
o'clock arrived at my house at New York, where I found
Mrs. Washington and the rest of the family all well—and
it being Mrs. Washington's night to receive visits, a pretty
large company of ladies and gentlemen were present."—
Washington's Diary.

"*New York*, November 14.—Yesterday, at one o'clock, THE PRESI-
DENT of the United States returned to this city in perfect health, from his
tour thro the Eastern States. This event was announced by a federal salute
from the Battery."—*Gazette of the United States.*

SATURDAY, NOVEMBER 14.

At New York: "*November* 14.—At home all day—except
taking a walk round the Battery in the afternoon. At 4

o'clock received and answered an Address from the President [John Wheelock] and Corporation of Dartmouth College [Hanover, New Hampshire]—and about noon sundry visits."—*Washington's Diary.*

" *November* 15.—Went to St. Paul's Chapel in the forenoon—and after returning from thence was visited by Majr. Butler, Majr. Meredith and M[r] Smith, So. Car'a. Received an invitation to attend the Funeral of M[rs] [Isaac] Roosevelt (the wife of a Senator of this State), but declined complying with it—first, because the propriety of accepting any invitation of this sort appeared very questionable—and secondly (though to do it in this instance might not be improper), because it might be difficult to discriminate in cases which might thereafter happen. *November* 16.—The Commissioners [General Lincoln, Colonel Humphreys, and David Griffin], who had returned from the proposed treaty with the Creek Indians before me to this city, dined with me to-day, as did their Secretary, Col[o] Franks, and young M[r] Lincoln, who accompanied them. *November* 17.—The visitors at the Levee to-day were numerous. *November* 18.—Took a walk in the forenoon, and called upon M[r] Jay on business, but he was not within. On my return, paid M[r] Vaughan Sen[r] a visit, informal."—*Washington's Diary.*

THURSDAY, NOVEMBER 19.

At New York: " *November* 19.—The following company dined here to-day, viz: M[rs] Adams (lady to the Vice-President) Col[o] [William S.] Smith and lady, and Miss Smith, M[rs] Adam's niece—Gov[r] Clinton and lady, and Miss Cornelia Clinton—and Maj. Butler, his lady and two daughters."—*Washington's Diary.*

" *November* 20.—The visitors of gent'n and ladies to M[rs] Washington this evening were numerous and respectable. *November* 21.—Received in the afternoon the Report from the Commissioners appointed to treat with the Southern Indians—gave it one reading—and shall bestow another and more attentive one on it. *November* 22.—Went to St. Paul's Chapel in the forenoon—heard a charity sermon for the benefit of the Orphan's School of this city. *November* 23.—Rid five or six miles between breakfast and dinner. Called upon M[r] Vanberckel * and M[rs] Adams. *November* 24.—A good deal of company at the Levee to-day. Went to the play in the evening—sent tickets to the following ladies and gentlemen and invited them to seats in

---

* Peter John Van Berckel, of Rotterdam, minister to the United States from the United Netherlands.

my box viz:—Mrs Adams (lady of the Vice-President), Genl. [Philip] Schuyler and lady, M^r [Rufus] King and lady, Maj^r Butler and lady, Col^o Hamilton and lady, Mrs Green—all of whom accepted and came, except Mrs Butler, who was indisposed."—*Washington's Diary.*

WEDNESDAY, NOVEMBER 25.

At New York: " *November* 25.—Exercised on horseback between breakfast and dinner—in which, returning, I called upon Mr Jay and Gen. Knox on business—and made informal visits to the Govr, Mr Izard, Genl Schuyler, and Mrs Dalton. The following company dined with me, viz : Doct^r [William S.] Johnson and lady and daughter (Mrs Neely) Mr Izard and lady and son, M^r [William] Smith (So. Carolina) and lady, Mr Kean and lady, and the Chief Justice, Mr Jay.

" After which I went with Mrs Washington to the dancing assembly, at which I stayed until 10 o'clock."— *Washington's Diary.*

" *November* 26.—Being the day appointed for a thanksgiving,* I went to St. Paul's Chapel, though it was most inclement and stormy—but few people at Church. *November* 27.—Not many visitors this evening to Mrs Washington. *November* 28.—Exercised on horseback. *November* 29.—Went to St. Paul's Chapel in the forenoon. *November* 30 —Went to the Play in the evening, and presented tickets to the following persons, viz : Doct^r Johnson and lady, Mr Dalton and lady, the Chief Justice of the United States and Secretary of War and lady, Baron de Steuben, and Mrs Green. *December* 1.—A pretty full Levee to-day—among the visitors was the Vice-President and all the Senators in town. Exercised on horseback between 10 and 12. *December* 2.—Exercised in the post chaise with Mrs Washing-

---

* On the 29th of September the first session of the first Congress was brought to a close. Before their adjournment the two Houses appointed a joint committee to wait on the President and " request that he would recommend to the people of the United States a day of public thanksgiving and prayer to be observed by acknowledging, with grateful hearts, the many and signal favors of Almighty God, especially by affording them an opportunity peacefully to establish a constitution of government for their safety and happiness." The proclamation recommending Thursday, November 26, for a national thanksgiving was issued on Saturday, October 3.

ton—visited on our return the Vice-President and family—afterwards walked to M⁣ʳ King's—neither he nor his lady were at home, or to be seen."—*Washington's Diary.*

THURSDAY, DECEMBER 3.

At New York : " *December* 3.—The following gentlemen and ladies dined here, viz : Gen. Schuyler, his lady and daughter (Mʳˢ [Stephen Van] Ranselaer) Mʳ Dalton and his lady, the Secretary of the Treasury and his lady, Gen. Knox and lady, and Mʳˢ Greene, Baron de Steuben, Colᵒ Osgood (Post Master Genˡ), and the Treasurer Majʳ [Samuel] Meredith."— *Washington's Diary.*

" *December* 4.—A great number of visiters (gentlemen and ladies) this evening to Mʳˢ Washington. The Governor of New Jersey [William Livingston], and the Speaker of the House of Assembly of that State [John Beatty], presented an Address from the Legislature thereof and received an answer to it, after which they dined with me. *December* 5.—Exercised on horseback between 10 and 12 o'clock. The Vice-President and lady and two sons—Colᵒ Smith and lady, and his sister, and Mʳˢ Adam's niece, dined here. *December* 6.—Went to St. Paul's Chapel in the forenoon. *December* 7.—Walked round the Battery in the afternoon. *December* 8.—Finished my extracts from the Commissioners' Report of their proceedings at the Treaty with the Creek Indians—and from many other papers respecting Indian matters and the Western Territory. A full levee to-day. *December* 9.—Walked round the Battery."— *Washington's Diary.*

THURSDAY, DECEMBER 10.

At New York : " *December* 10.—Exercised on horseback between 10 and 12 o'clock. The following company dined here to-day, viz : Mʳˢ King and Mʳ and Mʳˢ [William] Few, Mʳ and Mʳˢ Harrison, Mʳ and Mʳˢ [Oliver] Wolcott, Mʳ Duer, his lady, and Miss Brown. Mʳ [Samuel] Griffin and lady, and Lady Christiana and her daughter."— *Washington's Diary.*

" *December* 11.—Being rainy and bad, no person except the Vice-President visited Mʳˢ Washington this evening. *December* 12.—Exercised in the coach with Mʳˢ Washington and the two children (Master [George Wash-

ington Parke] and Miss [Nelly] Custis), between breakfast and dinner—
went the 14 miles round. *December* 13.—Went to St. Paul's Chapel in the
forenoon. *December* 14.—Walked round the Battery in the afternoon.
December 15.—Exercised on horseback about 10 o'clock—called on the Secretary for the Department of War, and gave him the heads of many letters
to be written to characters in the Western Country, relative chiefly to Indian
Affairs. Visitors to the levee to-day were not very numerous, though respectable. *December* 16.—Dined with M⁽ʳˢ⁾ Washington and all the family
(except the two children) at Governor Clinton's—where also dined the Vice-
President, his lady, Col° and M⁽ʳˢ⁾ Smith, the Mayor (Col° [Richard] Varick)
and his lady, and old M⁽ʳ⁾ Van Berkel and his daughter."—*Washington's
Diary.*

THURSDAY, DECEMBER 17.

At New York: "*December* 17.—The following company
dined here, viz: The Chief Justice of the U. States and
his lady; M⁽ʳ⁾ King, Col° and M⁽ʳˢ⁾ [John] Lawrence, M⁽ʳˢ⁾
[Elbridge] Gerry, M⁽ʳ⁾ Egbert Benson, Bishop Provost [Pro-
voost], and Doctr. Lynn * and his lady."—*Washington's
Diary.*

"*December* 18.—Read over and digested my thoughts upon the subject
of a National Militia, from the plans of the militia of Europe, those of the
Secretary at War, and the Baron de Steuben. *December* 19.—Committed
the above thoughts to writing, in order to send them to the Secretary for
the Department of War, to be worked into the form of a Bill, with which
to furnish the Committee of Congress which had been appointed to draught
one. *December* 20.—Went to St. Paul's Chapel in the forenoon. *December*
21.—Framed the above thoughts on the subject of a National Militia into
the form of a Letter, and sent it to the Secretary for the Department of
War. Sat from ten to one o'clock for a M⁽ʳ⁾ Savage, to draw my Portrait for
the University of Cambridge, in the State of Massachusetts, at the request
of the President and Governors of the said University." †—*Washington's
Diary.*

---

* William Linn, first chaplain of the United States House of Representatives.

† The bust portrait painted by Edward Savage from this and the subsequent sittings recorded in the Diary is still owned by Harvard College. It
represents Washington in uniform, with the order of the Cincinnati on the
left breast, and has always been considered a faithful likeness of the great
original. Mr. Savage afterward (1792) engraved this portrait in the stipple
manner. Impressions are held in much esteem by good judges of the art.

TUESDAY, DECEMBER 22.

At New York: "*December* 22.—A pretty full and respectable Levee to-day—at which several members of Congress, newly arrived, attended."— *Washington's Diary.*

"*December* 23.—Exercised in the Post-Chaise with M⁷ˢ Washington to-
day. Sent the dispatches which came to me from the Assembly of Virginia,
and from the Representatives of several Counties therein, respecting the state
of the frontiers and depredations of the Indians, to the Secretary for the
Department of War, requesting his attendance to-morrow at 9 o'clock, that
I might converse more fully with him on the subject of the communications.
December 24.—The Secretary of War coming according to appointment, he
was instructed, after conversing fully on the matter, what answers to return
to the Executive of Virginia, and to the Representatives of the frontier
counties. *December* 25.—Went to St. Paul's Chapel in the forenoon. The
visitors to M⁷ˢ Washington this afternoon were not numerous, but respectable."— *Washington's Diary.*

SATURDAY, DECEMBER 26.

At New York: "*December* 26.—Exercised on horseback
in the forenoon. Chief Justice Morris and the Mayor (Col°
Varick), and their ladies, Judge [John Sloss] Hobart, Col°
Cole, Maj⁷ [Nicholas] Gilman, M⁷ˢ Brown, Secretary Otis,*
and M⁷ Beckley,† dined here."— *Washington's Diary.*

"*December* 27.—At home—all day—weather bad. *December* 28.—Sat all
the forenoon for M⁷ Savage, who was taking my portrait. *December* 29.—
Being very snowing, not a single person appeared at the Levee. *December*
30.—Exercised in a carriage. *December* 31.—Bad weather and close house.
The Vice-President and lady, Col° Smith and lady, Chan⁷ Livingston, lady
and sister, Baron Steuben, Messrs. [Alexander] White, [Elbridge] Gerry,
[George] Partridge and [Thomas T.] Tucker, of the House of Representatives, dined here to-day."— *Washington's Diary.*

---

* Samuel Allyne Otis, of Massachusetts, Secretary of the United States
Senate.

† John Beckley, of Virginia, Clerk of the House of Representatives.

1790.

At New York: "*January* 1.—The Vice-President, the Governor, the Senators, Members of the House of Representatives in Town, foreign public characters, and all the respectable citizens, came between the hours of 12 and 3 o'clock, to pay the compliments of the season to me—and in the afternoon a great number of gentlemen and ladies visited Mrs Washington on the same occasion."— *Washington's Diary.*

"*January* 2.—Exercised in the carriage with Mrs Washington. . . . Drank tea at the Chief Justice's of the U. States. *January* 3.—Went to St. Paul's Chapel. *January* 4.—Informed the President of the Senate, and Speaker of the House of Representatives that I had some oral communications to make to Congress when each house had a quorum, and desired to be informed thereof—and of the time and place they would receive them.* Walked round the Battery in the afternoon. *January* 5.—Several Members of Congress called in the forenoon to pay their respects on their arrival in town, but though a respectable Levee, at the usual hour, three o'clock, the visitors were not numerous. *January* 6.—Sat from half after 8 o'clock till 10 for the portrait painter, Mr Savage, to finish the picture of me which he had begun for the University of Cambridge. In the afternoon walked around the Battery. Miss Anne Brown stayed here, on a visit to Mrs Washington, to a family dinner."— *Washington's Diary.*

THURSDAY, JANUARY 7.

At New York: "*January* 7.—About one o'clock rec'd a Committee from both Houses of Congress,† informing me

---

* The second session of the first Congress commenced on the 4th of January, 1790. Ten members only of the Senate having answered to their names, the Senate was adjourned for want of a quorum. A quorum of both houses appeared on the 6th.

† Messrs. Strong and Izard, on the part of the Senate, and Messrs. Gilman, Ames, and Seney, in behalf of the House of Representatives.

166

that each had made a house, and would be ready at any time I should appoint to receive the communications I had to make in the Senate Chamber. Named to-morrow, 11 o'clock, for this purpose.

"The following gentlemen dined here, viz: Messrs. [John] Langdon, [Paine] Wingate, [Caleb] Strong, and [William] Few, of the Senate, the Speaker [Frederick A. Muhlenberg], Gen¹ [Peter] Muhlenberg, and [Thomas] Scott, of Pennsylvania, Judge [Samuel] Livermore and [Abiel] Foster, of New Hampshire, [Fisher] Ames and [George] Thatcher and [Benjamin] Goodhue, of Massachusetts, Mʳ [Ædanus] Burke, of South Carolina, and Mʳ [Abraham] Baldwin, of Georgia."— *Washington's Diary.*

"*January* 8.—According to appointment, at 11 o'clock, I set out for the City Hall in my coach, preceded by Colonel Humphreys and Majʳ Jackson in uniform, (on my two white horses) and followed by Messrs. Lear and Nelson, in my chariot, and Mʳ Lewis, on horseback, following them. In their rear was the Chief Justice of the United States and Secretary of the Treasury and War Departments, in their respective carriages, and in the order they are named. At the outer door of the hall I was met by the door-keepers of the Senate and House, and conducted to the door of the Senate Chamber; and passing from thence to the Chair through the Senate on the right, and House of Representatives on the left, I took my seat. The gentlemen who attended me followed and took their stand behind the Senators; the whole rising as I entered. After being seated, at which time the members of both Houses also sat, I rose, (as they also did) and made my speech; delivering one copy to the President of the Senate, and another to the Speaker of the House of Representatives—after which, and being a few moments seated, I retired, bowing on each side to the assembly (who stood) as I passed, and descending to the lower hall, attended as before, I returned with them to my house. In the evening a *great* number of ladies, and many gentlemen visited Mʳˢ Washington. On this occasion I was dressed in a suit of clothes made at the Woolen Manufactory at Hartford, as the buttons also were."— *Washington's Diary.*

SATURDAY, JANUARY 9.

At New York: "*January* 9.—Exercised with Mʳˢ Washington and the children in the coach the 14 miles round.*

---

* The route was by the old Kings-Bridge road, which passed over Murray Hill, where Lexington Avenue now does, to McGowan's Pass at about One

In the afternoon walked round the Battery."— *Washington's Diary*.

"*January* 10.—Went to St. Paul's Chapel in the forenoon—wrote private letters in the afternoon for the Southern mail.   *January* 11.—Communicated to both Houses, transcripts of the adoption and ratification of the New Constitution by the State of North Carolina.*   *January* 12.—About two o'clock a Committee of the Senate † waited on me with a copy of their address, in answer to my speech, and requesting to know at what time and place it should be presented.   I named my own house, and Thursday next, at 11 o'clock, for the purpose.   Just before Levee hour, a Committee from the House of Representatives ‡ called upon me to know when and where they should deliver their address.   I named 12 o'clock on Thursday. . . . A respectable, though not a full Levee to-day."— *Washington's Diary*.

THURSDAY, JANUARY 14.

At New York: "*January* 14.—At the hours appointed, the Senate and House of Representatives presented their respective addresses—the members of both coming in carriages, and the latter with the Mace preceding the Speaker. The address of the Senate was presented by the Vice-President—and that of the House by the Speaker thereof.

"The following gentlemen dined here to-day, viz : Messrs. [John] Henry and [William] Maclay, of the Senate—and Messrs. [Jeremiah] Wadsworth, [Jonathan] Trumbull, [William] Floyd, [Elias] Boudinot, [Henry] Wynkoop, [Joshua] Seney, [John] Page, [Richard Bland] Lee, and [George] Mathews, of the House of Representatives; and Mʳ John Trumbull."— *Washington's Diary*.

"*January* 14.—Dined this day with the President.   It was a great dinner —all in the taste of high life.   I considered it as a part of my duty as a Senator to submit to it, and am glad it is over.   The President is a cold, formal man ; but I must declare that he treated me with great attention. I was the first person with whom he drank a glass of wine.   I was often

---

Hundred and Eighth Street ; then across on a line with the Harlem River to Bloomingdale, and so down on the westerly side of the island.
* November 21, 1789.
† Messrs. King, Izard, and Paterson.
‡ Messrs. Smith, of South Carolina, Clymer, and Lawrence.

spoken to by him.   Yet he knows how rigid a republican I am."—*Journal of William Maclay.*

FRIDAY, JANUARY 15.

At New York: " *January* 15.—Snowing all day—but few ladies and gentlemen as visitors this evening to M.™ Washington."— *Washington's Diary.*

" *January* 16.—Exercised in the coach with M.™ Washington and the two children, about 12 o'clock.   *January* 17.—At home all day—not well.   *January* 18.—Still indisposed with an aching tooth, and swelled and inflamed gum.   *January* 19.—Not much company at the Levee to-day—but the visitors were respectable.   *January* 20.—A Report from the Secretary at War, on the subject of a National Militia, altered agreeably to the ideas I had communicated to him, was presented to me, in order to be laid before Congress."— *Washington's Diary.*

THURSDAY, JANUARY 21.

At New York: " *January* 21.—The following gentlemen dined here, viz: Messrs. [Oliver] Ellsworth, [William] Paterson, [Jonathan] Elmer, [Richard] Bassett, and [Benjamin] Hawkins, of the Senate—and Messrs. [Roger] Sherman, [Lambert] Cadwalader, [George] Clymer, [Thomas] Hartley, [Daniel] Heister, [William] Smith, (Maryland) and [James] Jackson, of the House of Representatives— and Major [Samuel] Meredith, Treasurer of the United States."— *Washington's Diary.*

" *January* 22.—Exercised on horseback in the forenoon.   Called in my ride on the Baron de Polnitz, to see the operation of his (Winlaw's) threshing machine.* . . . Many and respectable visitors to M.™ Washington this evening.   *January* 23.—Went with M.™ Washington in the forenoon to see the Paintings of M.ʳ Jn° Trumbull.   *January* 24.—Went to St. Paul's Chapel in the forenoon.   Writing private letters in the afternoon.   *January*

---

* The Baron de Poellnitz had a small farm in the vicinity of Murray Hill, where he tried experiments in agriculture.   He wrote a pamphlet on the subject, and also suggested to Washington the propriety of establishing a farm under the patronage of the government.   The baron was the inventor of various agricultural machines and implements, particularly a threshing machine and the horse-hoe.

25.—A M' Francis Bailey [printer of Philadelphia], introduced by Messrs. Scott and Hartley, of Pennsylvania, and M' White, of Virginia, offered a paper, in the nature of a Petition, setting forth a valuable discovery he had made of marginal figures for notes, certificates &c. which could not by the ingenuity of man be counterfeited. *January* 26.—Exercised on horseback in the forenoon. The visitors at the Levee to-day were numerous and respectable—among whom was the Vice-President and the Speaker of the House of Representatives. *January* 27.—Did business with the Secretaries of the Treasury and War."— *Washington's Diary.*

THURSDAY, JANUARY 28.

At New York : " *January* 28.—The following gentlemen dined here, viz : the Vice-President, the Secretary of the Treasury—Messrs. [Philip] Schuyler, [Robert] Morris, [Ralph] Izard, [Tristram] Dalton and [Pierce] Butler, of the Senate ; and Messrs. [William] Smith, (South Carolina,) [Michael] Stone, [James] Schureman, [Thomas] Fitzsimmons, [Theodore] Sedgwick, [Daniel] Huger, and [James] Madison of the House of Representatives."— *Washington's Diary.*

" *January* 29.—Exercised on horseback this forenoon ; during my ride, M' [Samuel] Johnston, one of the Senators from North Carolina, who had just arrived, came to pay his respects, as did M' Cushing, one of the Associate Judges—the latter came again about 3 o'clock, introduced by the Vice-President. . . . The visitors to M' Washington this evening were numerous and respectable. *January* 30.—Exercised with M' Washington and the children in the coach in the forenoon. Walked round the Battery in the afternoon. *January* 31.—Went to St. Paul's Chapel in the forenoon. M' Wilson one of the Associate Judges of the Supreme Court, paid his respects to me after I returned from church. Spent the afternoon in writing letters to Mount Vernon."— *Washington's Diary.*

MONDAY, FEBRUARY 1.

At New York : " *February* 1.—Agreed on Saturday last to take M' McComb's house,* lately occupied by the Minis-

---

* The Macomb house was situated on the west side of Broadway, a little below Trinity Church ; it was subsequently occupied as a hotel, and was called *The Mansion House.* The President moved to this house on the 23d of February.

ter of France, for one year from and after the first day of May next."— *Washington's Diary.*

"*February* 2.—Exercised in the carriage with Mrs Washington. On my return found Mr Blair, one of the Associate Judges, the Attorney-General of the United States [Edmund Randolph], and Col^o Bland here. The Levee to-day was much crowded, and very respectable; among other company, the District Judge and Attorney, with the Marshall and all the Grand Jurors of the Federal District Court, (and a respectable body they were) attended. *February* 3.—Visited the apartments in the house of M^r McComb's —made a disposition of the rooms—fixed on some furniture of the Minister's (which was to be sold, and was well adapted to particular public rooms)— and directed additional stables to be built."— *Washington's Diary.*

THURSDAY, FEBRUARY 4.

At New York: "*February* 4.—The following company dined here, viz: The Vice-President, the Chief Justice of the United States [John Jay], Judges [William] Cushing, [James] Wilson, and [John] Blair, of the Supreme Court; the Attorney-General of the United States (Randolph); the Marshall, Attorney, and Clerk of the District, viz: Smith, Harrison, and Troup; M^r [Samuel] Johnston and M^r [Benjamin] Hawkins, of the Senate, and the Secretaries of the Treasury and War Departments, to wit:—Hamilton and Knox."— *Washington's Diary.*

"*February* 5.—Received from Doct^r [Hugh] Williamson, of North Carolina, a list of names whom he thought would be proper to fill the Revenue offices in that State. Submitted the same to the Senators of that State for their inspection and alteration. *February* 6.—Walked to my newly engaged lodgings to fix on a spot for a new stable which I was about to build. Agreed with —— to erect one 30 feet square, 16 feet pitch, to contain 12 single stalls; a hay loft, racks, mangers, &c; planked floor, and underpinned with stone, with windows between each stall, for £65. *February* 7. —Went to St. Paul's in the forenoon. *February* 8.—Nominated officers for the Revenue department in North Carolina. M^r [James] Iredell as an Associate Judge; . . . likewise Major Samuel Shaw, as Consul for Canton, in China. *February* 9.—A good deal of company at the Levee to-day. Exercised on horseback in the forenoon. *February* 10.—Sat from 9 until 11 o'clock for Mr Trumbull to draw my picture in his historical pieces [the battles of Trenton and Princeton]."— *Washington's Diary.*

THURSDAY, FEBRUARY 11.

At New York: "*February* 11.—Exercised on horseback in the forenoon. The following gentlemen dined here, viz: Messrs. [George] Leonard and Groal [? Grout], of Massachusetts; [Benjamin] Huntington and [Jonathan] Sturges, of Connecticut; [Peter] Silvester, of New York; [Thomas] Sinnickson, of New Jersey; [George] Gale, of Maryland; and [Theodoric] Bland, [Josiah] Parker and [Andrew] Moore, of Virginia."— *Washington's Diary.*

"*February* 12.—Sat from 9 o'clock until 11, for Mʳ John Trumbull, for the purpose of drawing my picture. A good deal of company (gentlemen and ladies) to visit Mⁱˢ Washington this afternoon. *February* 13.—Walked in the forenoon to the house to which I am about to remove. Gave directions for the arrangement of the furniture, &c. and had some of it put up. *February* 14.—At home all day—writing private letters to Virginia. *February* 15.—Sat between 9 and 11, for Mʳ John Trumbull. *February* 16. —Intended to have used exercise on horseback, but the weather prevented my doing it. Rid to my intended habitation, and gave some directions respecting the arrangement of the furniture. The Levee to-day was thin. Received some papers from the Secretary at War respecting a correspondence to be opened between Colᵒ Hawkins, of the Senate, and Mʳ McGillivray,* of the Creek Nation, for the purpose of getting the latter, with some other chiefs of that nation to this place, as an expedient to avert a war with them."— *Washington's Diary.*

THURSDAY, FEBRUARY 18.

At New York: "*February* 18.—Sat for Mʳ Trumbull from 9 o'clock till 10; after which exercised in the post-chaise with Mⁱˢ Washington. On our return home called on Mⁱˢ Adams, lady of the Vice-President. The following company dined here to-day, viz:—Judge Cushing and his lady; the Postmaster General [Samuel Osgood] and his

* Alexander McGillivray was the son of a Scottish trader of that name, who married the daughter of the principal chief of the Creek nation, whose domain originally included the whole of Florida and a greater portion of Alabama and Georgia. He received a liberal education at Charleston, and was also placed for a time in a business house at Savannah. McGillivray was finally chosen by the Creeks for their principal sachem or king.

lady, and Messrs. [Elias] Boudinot, [Samuel] Griffin, [Isaac] Coles, [Elbridge] Gerry, and [Alexander] White, and their ladies."— *Washington's Diary.*

" *February* 19.—Exercised on horseback about 9 o'clock. Walked afterwards to my new house. Received a Cap¹ Drew, Com¹ of a British sloop of war, sent express to Sir John Temple, Consul-General of that nation in the United States. The visitors this evening to M⁻ˢ Washington were numerous and respectable. *February* 20.—Sat from 9 until 11, for M¹ Trumbull. Walked afterwards to my new house—then rode a few miles with M⁻ˢ Washington and the children before dinner; after which I again visited my new house in my coach (because it rained). *February* 21.—Went to St. Paul's Chapel in the forenoon—wrote letters respecting my domestic concerns afterwards. *February* 22.—Set seriously about removing my furniture to my new house. Two of the gentlemen of the family had their beds taken there, and would sleep there to-night."— *Washington's Diary.*

TUESDAY, FEBRUARY 23.

At New York: " *February* 23.—Few or no visitors at the Levee to-day, from the idea of my being on the move. After dinner, M⁻ˢ Washington, myself, and children removed, and lodged at our new habitation."— *Washington's Diary.*

" *February* 24.—Employed in arranging matters about the house and fixing matters. *February* 25.—Engaged as yesterday. In the afternoon a Committee of Congress presented an Act for enumerating the inhabitants of the United States. *February* 26.—A numerous company of gentlemen and ladies were here this afternoon. Exercised on horseback this forenoon. *February* 27.—Sat for M¹ Trumbull this forenoon ; after which exercised in the coach with M⁻ˢ Washington and the children. *February* 28.—Went to St. Paul's Chapel in the forenoon. Wrote letters on private business afterwards."— *Washington's Diary.*

MONDAY, MARCH 1.

At New York : " *March* 1.—Exercised on horseback this forenoon, attended by M¹ John Trumbull, who wanted to see me mounted.

" Informed the House of Representatives (where the Bill

originated) that I had given my assent to the act for taking
a Census of the People," *— *Washington's Diary.*

"*March* 2.—Much and respectable company was at the Levee to-day.
March 3.—Exercised on horseback between 9 and 11 o'clock."— *Washington's Diary.*

THURSDAY, MARCH 4.

At New York: "*March* 4.—Sat from 9 until half after
10 o'clock for Mr Trumbull. The following gentlemen
dined here to-day, viz:—the Vice-President, Messrs. [John]
Langdon, [Paine] Wingate, [Tristram] Dalton, [Caleb]
Strong, [Oliver] Ellsworth, [Philip] Schuyler, [Rufus]
King, [William] Paterson, [Robert] Morris, [William]
McClay, [Richard] Bassett, [John] Henry, [Samuel] John-
ston, [Benjamin] Hawkins, [Ralph] Izard, [Pierce] Butler,
and [William] Few, all of the Senate."— *Washington's
Diary.*

"*March* 4.—Dined with the President of the United States. It was a
dinner of dignity. All the Senators were present and the Vice-President.
I looked often around the company to find the happiest faces. Wisdom,
forgive me if I wrong thee, but I thought folly and happiness most nearly
allied. The President seemed to bear in his countenance a settled aspect of
melancholy. No cheering ray of convivial sunshine broke through the
cloudy gloom of settled seriousness. At every interval of eating or drinking
he played on the table with a fork or knife, like a drumstick."—*Journal of
William Maclay.*

FRIDAY, MARCH 5.

At New York: "*March* 5.—A very numerous company
of ladies and gentlemen here this evening."— *Washington's
Diary.*

"*March* 6.—Exercised in the coach with Mrs Washington and the children, and in the afternoon walked round the Battery. *March* 7.—At home
all day—writing letters on private business. *March* 9 —A good many gen-

* The census directed to be made by the Act of Congress of March 1, 1790,
made the population of the United States to consist of 3,929,326 persons;
this included 697,697 slaves.

tlcmcn attended the Levee to-day—among whom were many members of Congress. *March* 10.—Exercised on horseback between 9 and 11 o'clock. On my return had a long conversation with Col° Willet, who was engaged to go us a private agent, but for public purposes to M^r McGillivray, principal chief of the Creek Nation."—*Washington's Diary.*

THURSDAY, MARCH 11.

At New York: " *March* 11.—The following gentlemen dined here to-day, viz :—M^r [George] Read, of the Senate, the Speaker, and the following gentlemen of the House of Representatives, viz :—Messrs. [Nicholas] Gilman, [Benjamin] Goodhue, [Fisher] Aimes, [Jeremiah] Wadsworth, [Jonathan] Trumbull, [Egbert] Benson, [John] Lawrence, Peter Muhlenberg, [Henry] Wynkoop, [John] Vining, [Daniel] Carroll, [Benjamin] Contee, [James] Madison, [John] Page, and [Thomas] Sumpter—also Judge [Gunning] Bedford and Mr John Trumbull."— *Washington's Diary.*

" *March* 12.—Exercised in the Post chaise with Mrs Washington from 10 o'clock till near 12. Signed the Passport which was to be committed to Col° Willet for Mr Gillivray and other Chiefs of the Creek Nation of Indians, and other papers necessary for his setting out on this business.* A Pretty numerous company of visiters this evening to Mrs Washington's Levee. *March* 13.—Exercised about 11 o'clock with Mrs Washington & the Children, in the coach. *March* 14.—Went to St. Paul's Chapel in the forenoon —wrote letters on private business afterwards. *March* 15.—Received an Address from the Roman Catholics of the United States, presented by M^r [Charles] Carroll of the Senate, M^r [Daniel] Carroll & M^r [Thomas] Fitzsimmons of the House of Representatives and many others, Inhabitants of the City of New York. . . . And Mr Few, Senator from the State of Georgia, presented me with the copy of an Address from that State requiring to know, when it would be convenient for me to receive it in form. *March* 16.—Exercised on horseback between 10 & 12 o'clock: previous to this, I was visited (having given pernisn.) by a Mr. Warner Miflin, one of the People called Quakers; active in pursuit of the Measures laid before Con-

* Colonel Marinus Willett acquitted himself so well of the duty assigned him that the chiefs of the Creek nation, with McGillivray at their head, were induced to repair to New York. Negotiations were immediately entered upon, which terminated in a treaty of peace, signed on the 7th of August and formally ratified on the 13th.

gress for emancipating the Slaves.* . . . The day being bad, not many visiters attended the Levee. At it Mr. Smith of South Carolina, presented the copy of an Address from the Intendant and —— of the City of Charleston, and was told that I would receive it in form on Thursday at 11 o'clock. *March* 17.—Gave Mr. Few notice that I would receive the address of the Legislature of Georgia to morrow at half after ten o'clock."—*Washington's Diary.*

THURSDAY, MARCH 18.

At New York : " *March* 18.—At half past 10 I received the address of the Legislature of Georgia—presented by Mʳ Few the Senator & the 3 Representatives of the State in Congress [Abraham Baldwin, James Jackson, and George Matthews]. At 11 o'clock the address from the Intendant and Wardens of the City of Charleston was presented by Mʳ Smith.

" The following Gentlemen dined here, viz :—Messrs. [Samuel] Livermore, [Abiel] Foster, [George] Partridge, [George] Thatcher, [Roger] Sherman, [Thomas] Fitzsimmons, [Thomas] Hartley, [Joshua] Seney, [Richard H.] See, [Edanus] Burke, [Thomas T.] Tucker, [Abraham] Baldwin, [James] Jackson & [George] Mathews of the Representatives in Congress—and Mʳ Otis, Secretary of the Senate, and Mʳ Beckley, Clerk of the House of Representatives.

" In the Evening (about 8 o'clock) I went with Mʳˢ Washington to the assembly where there were betwn. 60 & 70 Ladies & many Gentlemen."— *Washington's Diary.*

" *March* 19.—Exercised on Horseback betwn. 9 and 11 o'clock. *March* 20.—Exercised in the Coach with Mʳˢ Washington and the Children.

* On February 12 a petition from the Yearly Meeting of Quakers for Pennsylvania, New Jersey, Delaware, and the western parts of Maryland and Virginia, seconded by another from New York, was presented to Congress, praying for the abolition of the slave-trade. Another was presented the next day from the Pennsylvania Society for promoting the Abolition of Slavery, signed by Dr. Franklin as president, on the same subject. These petitions and proceedings thereon produced much agitation in Congress and throughout the country during the spring of 1790.

March 21.—Went to St. Paul's Chappel in the forenoon—wrote private letters in the afternoon. Received Mr Jefferson, Minister of State about one o'clock.* *March* 22.—Sat for Mr Trumbull for my Picture in his Historical pieces—after which conversed for more than an hour with Mr Jefferson on business relative to the duties of his office. *March* 23.—A full & very respectable Levee to day. *March* 24.—Prevented from Riding by the unfavourableness of the weather."—*Washington's Diary.*

THURSDAY, MARCH 25.

At New York: " *March* 25.—Went in the forenoon to the Consecration of Trinity Church, when a Pew was constructed, and set apart for the President of the United Sts.† " The following Company dined here to day, viz:—The Chief Justice Jay & his Lady, Genl. Schuyler & his Lady, the Secretary of the Treasury and his Lady, the Secretary of War & his Lady & Mrs Greene, the Secretary of State (Mr Jefferson) M^r [Charles] Carroll & M^r [John] Henry of Senate, Judge [James] Wilson, Messrs. [James] Madison & [John] Page of the Ho. of Representatives, and Col° [William Stephens] Smith Marshall of the District."— *Washington's Diary.*

" *March* 26.—The company this evening was thin, especially of Ladies. *March* 27.—Exercised in the coach with Mrs Washington and the children. *March* 28.—Went to St. Paul's Chapel in the forenoon. *March* 29.—Exercised on Horseback in the forenoon—and called at Col° [Anthony] Walton White's. *March* 30.—Exercised in the Post Chaise with Mrs Washington. The Company at the Levee to day was numerous & respectable. *March* 31.—Exercised on Horseback."—*Washington's Diary.*

---

* Thomas Jefferson had been called to Washington's cabinet as Secretary of State on his return from France, where he had resided as minister for some time. After a tedious journey of a fortnight from Monticello, Mr. Jefferson reached New York on the 21st of March.

† The original building of Trinity Church, the first Episcopal church organized in the province of New York, was erected in 1696 and enlarged in 1737. It was destroyed in the great fire of September 21, 1776, and the building consecrated this day was erected in 1788 on the same site, Broadway, opposite Wall Street. During the exercises, Washington and his family were seated in the richly ornamented pew, with a canopy over it, set apart by the wardens and vestrymen for the President of the United States.

12

THURSDAY, APRIL 1.

At New York: "*April* 1.—The following Company dined here to day, viz:—Governor Clinton, [Pierre Van Cortlandt] the Speaker of the Senate & [Gulian Verplanck of the] House of Representatives of the State of New York, Judge Duane, Baron de Steuben and Mʳ Arthur Lee. Mʳ [Rufus] King of the Senate, and the following members of the House of Representatives—Mʳ [George] Leonard, Mʳ [Theodore] Sedgwick, Mʳ [Jonathan] Grout, Mʳ [Jeremiah] Van Rensalaer, Mʳ [John] Hathorne, Mʳ [George] Clymer, Mʳ [Daniel] Heister, Mʳ [Michael] Stone, Mʳ [Hugh] Williamson, Mʳ [John B.] Ash, and Mʳ [Daniel] Huger."— *Washington's Diary.*

"*April* 2.—But a thin company this Evening, on acct. of the badness of the weather, & its being good friday. *April* 3.—Exercised in the Coach with Mʳˢ Washington and the Children. *April* 4.—At home all day—unwell. *April* 5.—Exercised with Mʳˢ Washington in the Post Chaise. *April* 6.—Sat for Mʳ Savage, at the request of the Vice President, to have my Portrait drawn for him.* The Company at the Levee to day was thin,—the day was bad. *April* 7.—Exercised with Mʳˢ Washington in the Post-Chaise."—*Washington's Diary.*

THURSDAY, APRIL 8.

At New York: "*April* 8.—The following Company dined here, viz:—of the House of Representatives—Mʳ [Elbridge] Gerry, Mʳ [Benjamin] Huntington, Mʳ [Lambert] Cadwalader, Mʳ [Elias] Boudinot, Mʳ [Thomas] Sinnickson, Mʳ [Thomas] Scott, Mʳ [George] Gale, Mʳ [Josiah] Parker, Mʳ [Andrew] Moore, & Mʳ [John] Browne, of the Treasury Department, the Comptroller (Mʳ [Nicholas] Eveleigh), the Auditor (Mʳ [Oliver] Wolcot) & the Register Mʳ [Joseph] Nourse—and of the Commissioners of Accts. Genl. [William] Irvine, and Mʳ [John] Kean—together with Mʳ [Christopher] Gore, attorney for the District of Massachusetts."— *Washington's Diary.*

---

* This portrait is now owned by Henry Adams, a great-grandson of John Adams.

"*April 9.*—Exercised on Horseback in the forenoon. The company who visited Mᵣˢ Washington this afternoon was very numerous both of Gentlemen & Ladies. *April* 10 —Exercised in the Coach with Mᵣˢ Washington and the Children—walked in the afternoon around the Battery and through some of the principal Streets of the City. In the afternoon the Secretary of State submitted for my approbation Letters of credence for Mᵣ [William] Short as Charge de Affaires, at the Court of Versailles. *April* 11.—Went to Trinity Church in the forenoon—and [wrote] several private letters in the afternoon. *April* 12.—Exercised on Horseback after which did business with the Secretaries of the Treasury and War Departments. *April* 13.—Exercised on Horseback about 10 o'clock. A good deal of Company at the Levee to day. *April* 14.--Exercised in the Post Chaise with Mᵣˢ Washington."— *Washington's Diary.*

THURSDAY, APRIL 15.

At New York : "*April* 15.—The Vice President & Lady, the Chief Justice of the United States & Lady, Mᵣ [Ralph] Izard & Lady, Mᵣ [Tristram] Dalton & Lady, Bishop [Samuel] Provost & Lady, Judge [Cyrus] Griffin & Lady Christina, Colᵒ [Samuel] Griffin & Lady, Colᵒ [William S.] Smith & Lady, the Secretary of State, Mᵣ [John] Langdon, Mᵣ [Rufus] King & Major [Pierce] Butler. Mᵣˢ King was invited but was indisposed."— *Washington's Diary.*

"*April* 16.—Had a long conference with the Secretary of State on the subject of Diplomatic appointments & on the proper places & characters for Consuls or Vice Consuls. After which I exercised on Horseback. The Visiters of Gentlemen and Ladies to Mᵣˢ Washington this evening were very numerous. *April* 17.—Exercised in the coach with Mᵣˢ Washington and the children. *April* 18.—At home all day—the weather being very stormy & bad, wrote private letters. *April* 19.—Prevented from beginning my tour upon Long Island to day from the wet of yesterday and the unfavourableness of the morning."— *Washington's Diary.*

TUESDAY, APRIL 20.

At Long Island : "*April* 20.—About 8 o'clock (having previously sent over my Servants, Horses, and Carriage) I crossed to Brooklyn and proceeded to Flat Bush—thence to Utrich [New Utrecht]—thence to Gravesend—thence through —— Jamaica where we lodged at a Tavern kept by one Warne—a pretty good and decent house,—at the

house of a Mr Barre, at Utrich, we dined,—the man was
obliging but little else to recommend it. . . . From Brooklyn to Flatbush is called 5 miles, thence to Utrich 6—to
Gravesend 2—and from thence to Jamaica 14—in all this
day 27 miles."— *Washington's Diary.*

"*April* 21.—The morning being clear & pleasant we left Jamaica about
eight o'clock, & pursued the Road to South Hempstead, passing along the
South edge of the plain of that name. . . . We baited in South Hempstead, (10 miles from Jamaica) at the House of one Simmonds, formerly a
Tavern, now of private entertainment for money.—From thence turning
off to the right, we fell into the South Rd. at the distance of about five
miles where we came in view of the Sea. . . . We dined at one Ketchum's.
. . . After dinner we proceeded to a Squire Thompson's. *April* 22.—About
8 o'clock we left Mr Thompson's—halted awhile at one Greens distant 11
miles and dined [at] Harts Tavern in Brookhaven township, five miles
farther. . . . From Hart's we struck across the Island for the No. side
passing the East end of the Brushey Plains—and Koram [Corum] 8 miles—
thence to Setukit 7 miles more to the House of a Capt. Roe, which is tolerably dect. with obliging people in it. *April* 23.—About 8 o'clock we left
Roe's, and baited the Horses at Smiths Town at a Widow Blidenberg's a
decent House 10 miles from Setalkat—thence 15 miles to Huntington where
we dined—and afterwards proceeded seven miles to Oyster-Bay. to the House
of a Mr Young (private and very neat and decent) where we lodged.   The
house we dined at in Huntingdon was kept by a Widow Platt, and was
tolerably good.   *April* 24.—Left Mr Young's before 6 o'clock and passing
Musqueto [now Glen] Cove, breakfasted at a Mr Underdunck's [Henry On-
derdonk] at the head of a little bay; where we were kindly received and
well entertained.—This Gentleman works a Grist & two Paper Mills, the
last of which he seems to carry on with spirit, and to profit—distc. from
Oyster-bay 12 miles.—From hence to Flushing where we dined is 12 more—
& from thence to Brooklyne through Newton (the way we travelled and
which is a mile further than to pass through Jamaica) is 18 miles more. . . .
Before sundown we had crossed the Ferry and was at home."— *Washington's
Diary.*

SUNDAY, APRIL 25.

At New York: "*April* 25.—Went to Trinity Church,
and wrote letters home after dinner."— *Washington's Diary.*

"*April* 26.—Appointed a quarter before three to-morrow to receive from
the Senators of the State of Virgna. an address from the Legislature thereof.
April 27.—At the time appointed, Messrs. [Richard Henry] Lee & [John]

Walker (the Senators from Virginia) attended, & presented the Address as mentioned yesterday & and received an answer to it.   A good deal of respectable company was at the Levee to day."— *Washington's Diary.*

THURSDAY, APRIL 29.

At New York: "*April* 29.—The following Gentlemen dined here, viz:—of the Senate, Messrs. [Caleb] Strong, Doctr. [William S.] Johnson, Mʳ [William] Paterson, Mʳ [Robert] Morris, Mʳ [Charles] Carroll, Mʳ [Richard Henry] Lee, Mʳ [John] Walker, Govr. [Samuel] Johnston & Mʳ [James] Gunn—and of the House of Representatives, Mʳ [Jonathan] Sturges, Mʳ [Egbert] Benson, Mʳ [William] Floyd, Mʳ [James] Schureman, Mʳ [John] Vining, Mʳ [William] Smith, Maryland, Mʳ [Theodoric] Bland, and Mʳ [Thomas] Sumpter."— *Washington's Diary.*

"*April* 30.—The Visitors to Mʳˢ Washington this evening were not numerous.   *May* 1.—Exercised in the Coach with Mʳˢ Washington & the children in the forenoon—& on foot in the afternoon.   *May* 2.—Went to Trinity Church in the forenoon—writing letters on private business in the afternoon.   *May* 3.—Exercised on Horseback about 9 o'clock.   *May* 4.— Exercised in the forenoon on Horseback.   A respectable Company at the Levee to-day."— *Washington's Diary.*

THURSDAY, MAY 6.

At New York: " *May* 6.—Exercised on horseback in the forenoon.—The following, out of several others who were invited, but prevented by sickness, dined here, viz:—Mʳ [Paine] Wingate, Mʳ [William] Maclay, Mʳ [John] Walker (of the Senate) and Messrs. [Nicholas] Gilman, [Fisher] Aimes, Genl. Muhlenberg, [Henry] Wynkoop, [John] Page and Lady, [William] Smith So. Carolina & Lady, and Mʳ [Alexander] White & his Lady of the House of Representatives."— *Washington's Diary.*

"*May* 6.—Went to dine with the President agreeably to invitation.   He seemed in more good humor than I ever saw him, though he was so deaf that I believe he heard little of the conversation.   We had ladies, Mrs. Smith, Mrs. Page and Mrs White.   Their husbands all with them."— *Journal of William Maclay.*

FRIDAY, MAY 7.

At New York: "*May* 7.—Exercised in the forenoon.
. . . Much Company—Gentlemen & Ladies—visited M^{rs}
Washington this Evening."— *Washington's Diary.*

"*May* 8.—Exercised in the Coach with Mrs Washington & the Children
in the forenoon. *May* 9.—Indisposed with a bad cold, and at home all day
writing letters on private business."— *Washington's Diary.*

MONDAY, MAY 10.

At New York: "*May* 10.—A severe illness with which
I was siezed the 10th of this month and which left me in
a convalescent state for several weeks after the violence of
it had passed; & little inclination to do more than what
duty to the public required at my hands occasioned the
suspension of this Diary."— *Washington's Diary.*

Incessant application to business made severe inroads upon Washington's
health, and on the 10th of May he was seized with a "severe illness," as he
records in the Diary, which reduced him to the verge of dissolution. He
was confined to his chamber for several weeks. His chief difficulty was
inflammation of the lungs, and he suffered from general debility until the
close of the session of Congress in August.

SATURDAY, MAY 15.

At New York: "*May* 15.—Called to see the President.
Every eye full of tears. His life despaired of. Dr. Mac
Knight told me he would trifle neither with his own character nor the public expectation; his danger was imminent,
and every reason to expect that the event of his disorder
would be unfortunate."—*Journal of William Maclay.*

"*May* 22.—The President has been exceedingly unwell; had the fears of
those acquainted with his situation been verified, the consequences would
have been alarming."—*Oliver Wolcott to Oliver Wolcott, Sen.*

MONDAY, MAY 24.

At New York: "*New York,* May 26.—The President of
the United States is so far recovered that he rode out in his

carriage on Monday last [May 24]."—*Pennsylvania Packet*, May 29.

"*May 25.*—By late accounts from New York, we are informed that the President of the United States has been exceedingly indisposed, but we rejoice at the authentic information of his being much relieved."—*New Brunswick Gazette.*

TUESDAY, JUNE 1.

At New York: "*New York*, June 2.—We have the pleasure to felicitate the public, that the President of the United States has so far recovered his health, that he yesterday saw company at his house, and received the congratulations of many respectable characters on the occasion."—*Pennsylvania Packet*, June 7.

THURSDAY, JUNE 3.

At New York: "I have a few days since had a severe attack of the peripneumony kind; but am now recovered, except in point of strength. My physicians advise me to more exercise and less application to business."—*Washington to the Marquis de Lafayette.*

MONDAY, JUNE 7.

Leaves New York: "*New York*, June 6.—To-morrow I go on a sailing party of three or four days with the President. . . . The President is perfectly reestablished, and looks better than before his illness."—*Thomas Jefferson to William Short.*

"*New York*, June 10.—Yesterday afternoon the PRESIDENT of the UNITED STATES returned from Sandy Hook and the fishing banks, where he had been for the benefit of the sea air, and to amuse himself in the delightful recreation of fishing. We are told he has had excellent sport, having himself caught a great number of sea-bass and black fish—the weather proved remarkably fine, which, together with the salubrity of the air and wholesome exercise, rendered this little voyage extremely agreeable, and cannot fail, we hope, of being very serviceable to a speedy and complete restoration of his health."—*Pennsylvania Packet*, June 12.

THURSDAY, JUNE 24.

At New York: "*June* 24.—Exercised on horseback betwn. 5 & 7 o'clock, A.M. Entertained the following Gentlemen at Dinner, viz:—Messrs. [Elbridge] Gerry, [Benjamin] Goodhue, [Jonathan] Grout, [George] Leonard, [Benjamin] Huntington, [Egbert] Benson, [Elias] Boudinot, [Lambert] Cadwalader, [Thomas] Sinnickson, [Daniel] Heister, [Thomas] Scott, [Benjamin] Contee, [Michael] Stone, [John] Browne, and Morse [?] of the House of Representatives."— *Washington's Diary.*

"*June* 25.—Constant & heavy Rain all day, prevented Company from visiting Mrs Washington this afternoon & all kinds of Exercise. *June* 26.— Exercised in the Coach with Mrs Washington & the Children & by walking in the afternoon. *June* 27.—Went to Trinity Church in the forenoon—and employed myself in writing business [letters] in the afternoon. *June* 28.— Exercised between 5 & 7 o'clock in the morning & drank Tea with Mrs Clinton (the Governors Lady) in the afternoon. *June* 29.—Exercised between 5 & 7 o'clock in the morning on horseback. A good deal of Company, amongst which several strangers and some foreigners at the Levee to day." — *Washington's Diary.*

THURSDAY, JULY 1.

At New York: "*July* 1.—Exercised between 5 and 7 o'clock on Horseback. . . . The following Gentn. & Ladies dined here, to day, viz :—The Secretary of State, Secretary of the Treasury, and Secretary at War & their Ladies— Mr [Tristram] Dalton & Mr [Rufus] King & their Ladies, Mr [Pierce] Butler & his two daughters—Mr [Benjamin] Hawkins, Mr [Joseph] Stanton, & Mr [Theodore] Foster, & Mr [Ralph] Izard.—The Chief Justice & his Lady, Genl. Schuyler & Mrs Izard were also invited but were otherwise engaged."— *Washington's Diary.*

"*July* 2.—Exercised between 5 & 7 on horseback. . . . Much company of both Sexes to visit Mrs Washington this evening. *July* 3.—Exercised between 9 and 11 in the Coach with Mrs Washington and the Children. *July* 4.—Went to Trinity Church in the forenoon. This day [Sunday] being the Anniversary of The declaration of Independency the celebration of it was put of until to morrow."— *Washington's Diary.*

MONDAY, JULY 5.

At New York: " *July* 5.—The members of the Senate, House of Representatives, Public Officers, Foreign Characters &c. The Members of the Cincinnati, Officers of the Militia, &c. came with the compliments of the day to me— about one o'clock a sensible Oration was delivered in St. Paul's Chapel by Mr Brockholst Livingston, on the occasion of the day. . . . In the afternoon many Gentlemen & ladies visited M^m Washington. I was informed this day by General Irvine (who recd. the acct. from Pittsburgh) that the Traitor Arnold was at Detroit & had viewed the Militia in the Neighbourhood of it twice."— *Washington's Diary.*

" *July* 5.—All the town was in arms; grenadiers, light infantry, and artillery passed the Hall, and the firing of cannon and small-arms, with beating of drums, kept all in uproar. The motion [for the Senate to adjourn] was carried, and now all of us repaired to the President's. We got some wine, punch, and cakes. From hence we went to St. Paul's, and heard the anniversary of independence pronounced by a Mr. B. Livingston. The church was crowded. I could not hear him well. Some said it was fine. I could not contradict them. I was in the pew next to General Washington. Part of his family and Senators filled the seats with us."—*Journal of William Maclay.*

TUESDAY, JULY 6.

At New York: " *July* 6.—Exercised on Horseback betwn. 5 & 7 o'clock in the morning,—at 9 o'clock I sat for Mr Trumbull to finish my pictures in some of his historical pieces. Announced to the House of Representatives (where the Bills originated) my Assent to the Acts which were presented to me on Friday last.—One of which Authorizes the President to purchase the whole, or such part of that tract of Land situate in the State of New York, commonly called West-point as shall be by him judged requisite for the purpose of such fortifications & Garrisons as may be necessary for the defence of the same.

" The visitors were few to day, on acct. of the numbers that paid their compliments yesterday. *July* 7.—Exercised between 5 & 7 this morning on Horseback."— *Washington's Diary.*

THURSDAY, JULY 8.

At New York: "*July* 8.—Sat from 9 o'clock till after 10 for Mr John Trumbull who was drawing a Portrait of me at full length which he intended to present to M^n Washington.* . . .

"The following Gentlemen dined here to day—viz—Messrs. [Paine] Wingate, [Caleb] Strong, [William] Maclay, [Richard Henry] Lee, & [Samuel] Johnston (No. Carolina) of the Senate—and Messrs. [Nicholas] Gilman, [Fisher] Aimes, [Jonathan] Sturges, [James] Schureman, [Thomas] Fitzsimmons, [Henry] Wynkoop, [John] Vining, [William] Smith, [James] Madison, [John] Sevier, & [Thomas] Sumpter, of the House of Representatives."— *Washington's Diary.*

"*July* 8.—Stayed at the Hall until four o'clock, and went to dine with the President. It was a great dinner, in the usual style, without any remarkable occurrences. Mrs. Washington was the only woman present."— *Journal of William Maclay.*

FRIDAY, JULY 9.

At New York: "*July* 9.—Exercised on Horseback between 5 & 7 in the morning. . . . Many visitors (male & female) this afternoon to M^n Washington."— *Washington's Diary.*

"*July* 10.—Having formed a Party, consisting of the Vice-President, his lady, Son & Miss Smith; the Secretaries of State, Treasury, & War, and the ladies of the two latter; with all the Gentlemen of my family, Mrs. [Tobias]

---

* This portrait, which represents Washington in uniform, standing by the side of a horse, was bequeathed by Mrs. Washington to Eliza Parke Law, wife of Thomas Law, and daughter of her son, John Parke Custis. The picture is small (twenty by thirty inches) and is exquisitely painted. It is now owned by Mrs. Kirby Flower Smith (Charlotte Rogers), daughter of the late Edmund Law Rogers, of Baltimore, and great-granddaughter of Mrs. Law. This is the original from which the large painting belonging to the city of New York was executed.

Lear & the two Children, we visited the old position of Fort Washington and afterwards dined on a dinner provided by Mʳ Mariner* at the House lately Col° Roger Morris,† but confiscated and in the occupation of a common Farmer. *July* 11.—At home all day—dispatching some business relative to my own private concerns."— *Washington's Diary.*

MONDAY, JULY 12.

At New York : " *July* 12.—Exercised on Horseback between 5 & 6 in the morning. Sat for Mʳ Trumbull from 9 until half after ten.—And about Noon had two Bills presented to me by the joint Committee of Congress—The one ' An Act for Establishing the Temporary & permanent Seat of the Government of the United States.' "— *Washington's Diary.*

The " Act for establishing the Temporary and Permanent Seat of the Government of the United States" was passed by Congress, July 9, 1790, and approved by the President July 16. It was enacted : That a district of territory not exceeding ten miles square, to be located on the river Potomac, at some space between the mouths of the Eastern Branch and Conococheague, be the permanent seat of the government of the United States. That the President be authorized to appoint three Commissioners to survey, define, and limit the district so defined. That prior to the first Monday in December next all offices attached to the seat of government should be removed to and, until the first Monday in December in the year one thousand eight hundred, remain at the city of Philadelphia, at which place the next session of Congress should be held.

TUESDAY, JULY 13.

At New York : " *July* 13.—Again sat for Mʳ Trumbull from 9 until half past 10 o'clock. A good deal of Company at the Levee to day. *July* 14.—Exercised on Horseback from 5 until near 7 o'clock."— *Washington's Diary.*

TUESDAY, JULY 20.

At New York : " *New York*, July 21.—Yesterday the Mayor [Richard Varick] waited on the President of the

---

* See note to October 10, 1789.

† The " Roger Morris House" is still standing on One Hundred and Sixty-first Street, between Ninth and Tenth Avenues. It was occupied by Washington as head-quarters from September 16 to October 19, 1776.

United States, and presented the request of the corporation
that he would honor them with permitting Mr. Trumbull, .
to take his portrait to be placed in the City-Hall, as a mark
of the respect the citizens of New York entertain of his
virtues.

"The President was pleased to express the favorable
impressions occasioned by the application, and chearfully
granted the request."—*Pennsylvania Packet*, July 23.

This life-size portrait (seventy-two by one hundred and eight inches), still
owned by the city of New York, is described by Mr. Trumbull in his autobiography as follows: "I returned in July to New York, where I was
requested to paint for the corporation a full-length portrait of the President.
I represented him in full uniform, standing by a white horse, leaning his arm
upon the saddle ; in the background, a view of Broadway in ruins, as it was
then, the old fort at the termination ; British ships and boats leaving the shore,
with the last of the officers and troops of the evacuating army, and Staten
Island in the distance. . . . Every part of the detail of the dress, horse,
furniture &c., as well as the scenery, was accurately copied from the real
objects."

WEDNESDAY, JULY 21.

At New York : "*New York*, July 22.—Yesterday arrived
in this city Col. Willet, accompanied by Col. M'Gillivray,
with thirty warriors of the Creek and Siminola nations.
They embarked at Elizabeth-town point, about ten o'clock
in the morning, and landed on Murray's wharf about two
P.M. where they were received by the St. Tammany society,
who attended on the occasion, attired in the most splendid
dresses and other emblems of that respectable society."—
Pennsylvania Packet, July 24.

"The society was drawn up in two files, with the grand sachem at the
head, who welcomed Colonel M'Gillivray ashore ; who, with the warriors
marched in the centre of the society, which proceeded through Wall-street.
When they came opposite the Federal Hall, Col. M'Gillivray, and the
warriors saluted the Congress, who were in the front of the balcony, and
returned the compliment—The procession moved on to the Secretary at
War's [in the lower part of Broadway], where the several warriors smoked
the calumet of peace, and next proceeded to the President's, where they

were particularly introduced—after which they waited on Governor Clinton, still accompanied by the society, who afterwards attended them to the city tavern, where they took up their lodgings during their residence in this city."
—*Idem.*

TUESDAY, JULY 27.

At New York: " *New York*, July 30.—Tuesday last [July 27], the legion of General Malcolm's Brigade, and Col. Bauman's Regiment of Artillery, the whole commanded by Col. Rutgers, were reviewed by the President of the United States, and Governor Clinton accompanied by the Kings and Warriors of the Creek nation, who lately arrived in this city.—The troops were compleat in uniform and arms, and performed a variety of firings and manœvres with great precision."—*Pennsylvania Packet*, August 4.

" *New York*, July 30.—We learn, that yesterday there was an entertainment given on board the ship America, Capt. Sarly, lately from Canton—which was honored by the company of the President of the United States, the Secretary of War, several other heads of departments, the Governor of this state—Col. M'Gillivray, with the Kings, Headman, and Warriors of the Creeks, and a very respectable company of officers and soldiers."—*Pennsylvania Packet*, August 5.

TUESDAY, AUGUST 10.

At New York: " I have received in their due order, and have to acknowledge at this time my obligations for your three agreeable letters, in date October 16th 1789, May 1st and May 31st of the present year. With the last I had also the pleasure to receive the key of the Bastille; in acknowledgment of which I write to the Marquis de Lafayette by this conveyance."— *Washington to Thomas Paine.*

Lafayette had intrusted to Thomas Paine for transmission to the President the key of the Bastille and a drawing of that prison after its destruction in July, 1789. In his letter, dated Paris, March 17, the Marquis said, " Give me leave, my dear General, to present you with a picture of the Bastille, just as it looked a few days after I had ordered its demolition, with the main key of the fortress of despotism. It is a tribute, which I owe as a son to my adopted father, as an aid-de-camp to my general, as a missionary of liberty to its patriarch."

The key still remains at Mount Vernon; the drawing was sold at public sale at Philadelphia in April, 1891.

WEDNESDAY, AUGUST 11.

At New York: " Congress, after having been in session ever since last fall, are to adjourn in two or three days.* . . . One of the last acts of the executive has been the conclusion of a treaty of peace and friendship with the Creek nation of Indians, who have been considerably connected with the Spanish provinces, and hostile to the Georgia frontiers since the war with Great Britain. McGillivray and about thirty of the kings and head men are here."— *Washington to the Marquis de Lafayette.*

" *New York,* August 14.—Yesterday the treaty of peace and friendship between the United States and the Creek nation was solemnly ratified by the contracting parties, in Federal Hall, in the presence of a large assembly of citizens.—The vice-president of the United States—the great officers of state —his excellency the governor—and of several members of both houses of Congress.

" At 12 o'clock the President of the United States, and his suite, general Knox, the commissioner; the clerks of the department of the secretary at war; colonel M'Gillivray, and the kings, chiefs, and warriors of the Creek nation being assembled, the treaty was read by the secretary of the president of the United States.

" The president then addressed colonel M'Gillivray the kings, chiefs and warriors. . . . The president then signed the treaty, after which he presented a string of beads as a token of perpetual peace, and a paper of tobacco to smoke in remembrance of it: Mr. M'Gillivray rose, made a short reply to the president, and received the tokens. This was succeeded by the shake of peace, every one of the Creeks passing this friendly salute with the president: a song of peace, performed by the Creeks, concluded this highly interesting, solemn and dignified transaction."—*Pennsylvania Packet*, August 18.

SUNDAY, AUGUST 15.

Leaves New York: " *New York,* August 26.—On Sunday morning, the 15th inst, the President of the United States

---

* The second session of the first Congress under the new Constitution adjourned on August 12, 1790.

embarked for Newport, on a visit to the state of Rhode Island, accompanied by Governor Clinton, Mr. Jefferson, Secretary of State; the Hon. Judge Blair, Mr. Smith of S. Carolina, and three gentlemen of his family [Colonel Humphreys, Major Jackson, and Mr. Nelson]." *—*Pennsylvania Packet*, August 28.

TUESDAY, AUGUST 17.

At Newport, Rhode Island : " *New York*, August 26.— The President arrived at Newport at eight o'clock on Tuesday morning [August 17], at which time he was welcomed to the state by a salute from the fort. From the landing place he was attended to his lodgings by the principal inhabitants of the town, who were severally presented to him. He then walked round the town, and surveyed the various beautiful prospects from the eminences above it. At four o'clock he was waited on by the most respectable citizens of the place, who conducted him to the Town Hall, where a very elegant dinner was provided, and several toasts drank. After dinner he took another walk, accompanied by a large number of gentlemen.†

" On Wednesday morning at nine o'clock the President and his company embarked for Providence."—*Pennsylvania Packet*, August 28.

WEDNESDAY, AUGUST 18.

At Providence, Rhode Island : " *Providence*, August 19.— Yesterday about four o'clock P.M. arrived from New York,

---

* Rhode Island having ratified the Constitution on May 29, 1790, was now included in the new order of things, and the President, having already visited the other Eastern States, determined before leaving New York to make a short tour through the State which was the last to come into the Federal Union.

† On this day the President received addresses from the clergy of Newport, from the Hebrew congregation of Newport, and from the master, wardens, and brethren of King David's Lodge in Newport, Rhode Island ; all of which he answered.

in the Packet Hancock, Capt. Brown, the President of the
United States, with his suite, accompanied by his excellency
Governor Clinton of New York; the hon. Thomas Jefferson, Esq. secretary of state; the hon. Theodore Foster,
Esq. one of the senators from this state; Judge Blair;
Mr. Smith of South Carolina; and Mr. Gorman of New
Hampshire, member of Congress."—*Pennsylvania Packet,*
August 30.

"A procession [civil and military] was formed agreeable to a previous
arrangement, and the President escorted to his lodgings at Mr. Daggett's.
On the President's landing a Federal Salute was fired, and the bells in town
rang a joyful peal. The salute was reiterated on his arrival at Mr. Daggett's.
The general attendance of almost every inhabitant of the town in the procession, together with the brilliant appearance of the ladies at the windows
and doors of the houses, evinced in the most sensible manner their pleasure
on this happy occasion. In the evening the college edifice was splendidly
illuminated."—*Idem.*

THURSDAY, AUGUST 19.

At Providence: "*Providence,* August 21.—On Thursday
[August 19], in the forenoon, the President, accompanied
by the gentlemen who came passengers with him, and
many of the citizens, walked thro' the principal streets, to
view the town, in the course of which they were escorted
to the college by the students, and by Dr. [James] Manning
introduced into the college library and museum, and afterwards went on board a large Indiaman on the stocks
belonging to Messrs. Browne and Francis."—*Pennsylvania
Packet,* August 31.

"At three o'clock an elegant entertainment was served in the Courthouse, for upwards of two hundred persons. Thirteen toasts were drank
under discharges of cannon. At the close of the toasts, the President gave
'The Town of Providence,'—rose from the table, and went immediately on
board Capt. Brown's Packet for departure. He was attended by a very
numerous procession—which returned to Governor [Arthur] Fenner's, and
after three cheers dispersed in good order. It may be proper to remark,
that no untoward accident took place—that every countenance indicated the

most heart felt joy, and that we have reason to believe the President was perfectly satisfied with his reception."*—*Idem*.

SUNDAY, AUGUST 22.

At New York: " *New York*, August 26.—The President of the United States arrived in this city on Sunday [August 22], after a short and agreeable passage of 24 hours."— *Pennsylvania Packet*, August 28.

"The visit [to Rhode Island] was gratifying to the citizens as it was unexpected. All classes vied with each other in demonstrations of joy, respect and admiration :—The pleasing affability and gracious manners of the President, and his polite attention to the great number of citizens who were successfully presented to him, added if possible, to that love which was felt before. When he withdrew from table at Newport, the company rising, drank the following toast—*The man we love*—and never was a toast drank with more severity.—When, ' *The President of the United States*' was given at Providence, the huzzas, plaudits, and shouts of the company within and without the Town Hall, continued for some time. There never was, per-haps, a greater exhibition of sincere public happiness than upon this occa-sion ; every individual thought he beheld a friend and patron ; a father or a brother after a long absence ; and on his part, the President seemed to feel the joy of a father on the return of the prodigal son.† We have little room to doubt that his visit to the state of Rhode Island will be productive of happy effects, for whatever aversion the citizens of that state may have hitherto had to the new government, they must now feel a confidence in the administration of one who possesses their universal esteem, and of whose virtues and patriotism they have, upon numerous occasions, had the strongest pledges."—*Idem*.

SATURDAY, AUGUST 28.

At New York: " *New York*, August 31.—On Saturday last [August 28] the governor of this state, the mayor of the city, and the corporation, were regaled at the festive board of the President of the United States.

" We are informed, that on this occasion the President

---

* On this day the President was waited upon by the Society of the Cin-cinnati of Rhode Island, and received addresses from the inhabitants of Providence and from the Corporation of Rhode Island College, both of which he answered.

† In allusion to the delay of Rhode Island in ratifying the National Con-stitution.

took an opportunity to express his great reluctance at leaving the city, and those who had taken so much pains to treat him, not only with dignified respect, but with reverence and esteem, as the Father and Patron of the United States. Mrs. Washington, also, seemed hurt at the idea of bidding adieu to these hospitable shores."—*Pennsylvania Packet*, September 2.

MONDAY, AUGUST 30.

Leaves New York:* "*New York*, August 31.—Yesterday, about nine o'clock the corporation attended at the Presidency in Broadway, where the governor of this state, the executive officers of government, several other officers, gentlemen of the clergy, and others, had already assembled to take their leave."—*Pennsylvania Packet*, September 2.

"About ten o'clock the procession moved for the President's barge which was laying at M'Comb's wharf on the North River, in the following order: Sheriff with his insignia of office—Marshals and Constables, with insignias—Gov. Clinton—PRESIDENT—Chief Justice Jay—The Executive Officers of Government—Corporation of New-York—Several Officers—Clergy—Citizens. At the wharf the escort opened to the right and left, when the President, his Lady, &c accompanied, marched forward and entered on board the barge, under the discharge of a salute of 13 guns from the battery. . . . The barge was manned with 13 men, in a uniform of white jackets and black caps; the weather was serene and beautiful, and a few minutes landed them at Powles Hook ferry [Jersey City], where the carriages of the President and suite were waiting."—*Idem*.

THURSDAY, SEPTEMBER 2.

At Philadelphia: "*September* 4.—Thursday last [September 2] about 2 o'clock arrived in town from New-York, the President of the United States—his Lady, and their suite.†

---

* "*New York*, August 26.—The President will leave this place on Monday [August 30]—reach Elizabeth Town that night—Brunswick on Tuesday night—Trenton on Wednesday night—Breakfast at Bristol on Thursday morning, and proceed from thence to Philadelphia."—*Tobias Lear to Clement Biddle*, MS. Letter.

† Besides the President and Mrs. Washington, the travelling party comprised Eleanor Parke and George Washington Parke Custis, the two grand-

They were joined on their approach by a number of respectable citizens—the city troops of horse, artillery, and companies of light infantry, who on this occasion, as well as others, *all* testified their affection for the BENEFACTOR OF MANKIND."—*Pennsylvania Packet.*

"Every public demonstration of joy was manifested;—the bells announced his welcome—a *feue de joye* was exhibited—and as he rode through town, to the City Tavern, *age* bowed with respect, and *youth* repeated, in acclamations, the applauses of the *Hero* of the Western World. At 4 o'clock he partook of a repast (provided by the Corporation at the City Tavern) accompanied by the members of our Legislature and of the state Convention—by the President [Thomas Mifflin] and other executive officers of Pennsylvania, at which REASON, VALOR and HOSPITALITY presided. After dinner thirteen toasts were drunk. In the evening there was a brilliant display of fire works in Market street."—*Idem.*

FRIDAY, SEPEMBER 3.

At Philadelphia : Dines with the members of the Convention for revising the Constitution of Pennsylvania, who, having finished their business the day before, had adjourned with an understanding that they should come together as a body the next day to meet President Washington.

SATURDAY, SEPTEMBER 4.

At Philadelphia : "*September* 8.—The President of the United States during his short stay in this city, received every mark of respect, attention and affection to his person, which the public or individuals could demonstrate : of the latter we cannot omit mentioning an elegant *Fête Champêtre* that was given to this illustrious personage, his amiable consort and family, on Saturday last [September 4] on the banks of the Schuylkill, in the highly improved grounds of the Messrs. Gray, by a number of respectable private citizens."—*Pennsylvania Packet.*

---

children of Mrs. Washington, Major William Jackson, Thomas Nelson, two maids, four white and four black servants, and sixteen horses.

" The company amounting to near two hundred ladies and gentlemen, assembled at two o'clock, and at three sat down to a sumptuous and splendid cold collation in which (though only 24 hours were given for the preparation) all viands and fruits of the season were assembled and elegantly arranged. A band of music played during the repast, and at the close several excellent songs were sung, and toasts were given. The President and Ladies then withdrew; when the following toast was drank with loud applause. *The* ILLUSTRIOUS TRAVELLERS."—*Idem.*

SUNDAY, SEPTEMBER 5.

At Philadelphia: " After a pleasant journey we arrived in this city on Thursday last, and to-morrow we proceed (if Mrs. Washington's health will permit, for she has been much indisposed since we came here) toward Mount Vernon."—*Washington to Tobias Lear.*

MONDAY, SEPTEMBER 6.

Leaves Philadelphia : " *September* 7.—Yesterday morning the President of the United States proceeded on his journey to his seat in Virginia."—*Pennsylvania Packet.*

WEDNESDAY, SEPTEMBER 8.

At Baltimore: *Baltimore,* September 10.—On Wednesday last [September 8] at Six o'clock in the afternoon, the President of the United States and his Lady, attended by their suite, arrived here from Philadelphia, on their way to Mount Vernon. On their entrance into town they were received and saluted by a Federal discharge from Capt. Stodder's company of artillery ; and such other public demonstrations were manifested by the citizens as shewed the most unfeigned affection and veneration for the ILLUSTRIOUS TRAVELLERS."—*Pennsylvania Packet,* September 16.

" *Baltimore,* September 10.—Thursday forenoon [September 9], the President was waited on by a number of the citizens, whom he received with his usual politeness and attention, and, at four o'clock he honored the merchants with his company at an elegant entertainment, prepared at Mr. Grant's tavern, at which his suite and several other gentlemen were present. Thirteen toasts were drank on this occasion."—*Idem.*

FRIDAY, SEPTEMBER 10.

Leaves Baltimore: "*Baltimore*, September 10.—This morning at six o'clock, the President, his Lady and suite, set out on their journey. Captain Stodder saluted them on their departure, with a Federal Discharge from his Artillery Park."—*Pennsylvania Packet*, September 16.

"*George-Town*, September 15.—Last Saturday [September 11] about eight o'clock in the morning arrived here from Bladensburg, where they lodged the preceding night, the PRESIDENT of the United States, his Lady and suite, on their way to Mount Vernon. The members of the Patowmack Company of Alexandria, and this place, met their illustrious President at Mr. John Suter's, notwithstanding the fatigue of a long journey, his Excellency proceeded to business respecting the navigation of the Patowmack."— *The Pennsylvania Mercury*, September 21.

SATURDAY, SEPTEMBER 11.

At Mount Vernon : "*September 23.*—The President of the United States arrived at Mount Vernon on Saturday, the 11th instant."—*Pennsylvania Packet.*

"*Mount Vernon*, 16 Sept. 1790.—I have been here two days, and have seen most of the improvements which do honour at once to the taste and industry of our Washington. I have been treated as usual with every most distinguished mark of kindness and attention. Hospitality indeed seems to have spread over the whole its happiest, kindest influence. The President exercises it in a superlative degree, from the greatest of its duties to the most trifling minutiæ, and Mrs. Washington is the very essence of kindness. Her soul seems to overflow with it like the most abundant fountain and her happiness is in exact proportion to the number of objects upon which she can dispense her benefits."—*Thomas Lee Shippen to Dr. William Shippen, Jr.*

SUNDAY, OCTOBER 3.

At Mount Vernon: In a letter of this date to Tobias Lear, Washington requests that a transcript be made of one from Count d'Estaing, referring to a bust of M. Necker, which had been sent to him by the Count.

This small Parian bust of M. Necker, the famous French Minister of Finance, which stood for many years on a bracket in the library at Mount Vernon, is now in the possession of The Historical Society of Pennsylvania, having been purchased (April, 1891) from Lawrence Washington, son of Colonel John Augustine Washington, the last private owner of Mount Vernon. It bears upon a brass plate on the pedestal the following inscription: " Presented to GEORGE WASHINGTON President of the UNITED STATES of AMERICA by his most dutiful, most obedient and most humble servant, Estaing, a Citizen of the state of Georgia, by an act of 22ᵈ feb. 1785, and a Citizen of France in 1790."

SUNDAY, OCTOBER 10.

At Mount Vernon : " We are approaching the first Monday in December by hasty strides. I pray you, therefore, to revolve in your mind such matters as may be proper for me to lay before Congress, not only in your department, if any there be, but such others of a general nature, as may happen to occur to you, that I may be prepared to open the session with such communications as shall appear to merit attention."— *Washington to Alexander Hamilton.*

Congress had adjourned at New York on the 12th day of August, to meet at Philadelphia the first Monday of December, in pursuance of the act of July 9, fixing the seat of government in that city until the first Monday in December, 1800.

WEDNESDAY, OCTOBER 27.

At Mount Vernon : In a letter of this date written to Tobias Lear at Philadelphia, Washington states that he had just returned from a twelve days' excursion up the Potomac.

MONDAY, NOVEMBER 1.

At Mount Vernon : " I have had the pleasure to receive your letters of the 11th of May and 12th of July last, together with the flattering mark of your and Madame de Brehan's regard, which accompanied the former ; for which, and the obliging satisfaction you express on the restoration of my health, I beg you and her to accept my grateful acknowledgments."— *Washington to the Count de Moustier.*

The flattering mark of regard on the part of the Count de Moustier and his sister, referred to in the above-quoted letter, consisted of some proof impressions of the engraving by A. F. Sergent, after the profile of the

President executed by Madame de Brehan from the sitting recorded in the Diary of October 3, 1789. One of these impressions, presented to Mrs. Robert Morris with the compliments of the President, was in turn presented by a granddaughter of Mrs. Morris to General George B. McClellan shortly after the battle of Antietam. An admirable copy of this print was made by Charles Burt; it is described in Baker's "Engraved Portraits of Washington," page 70.

WEDNESDAY, NOVEMBER 17.

At Alexandria: Present at a dinner given to him by the citizens of Alexandria.

FRIDAY, NOVEMBER 19.

At Mount Vernon : " I expect to commence my journey for Philadelphia on Monday [November 22]—but from the state of the Roads after the incessant and heavy rains which have fallen, my progress must be slow."— *Washington to General Knox.*

November 23.—Washington, writing to Tobias Lear under this date, from Spurrier's Tavern, ten miles south of Baltimore, says, "The roads are infamous—no hope of reaching Baltimore to night; we have not yet gone to dinner, but are waiting for it."

SATURDAY, NOVEMBER 27.

At Philadelphia: " *November* 27.—This forenoon [at eleven o'clock] the President of the United States, George Washington, arrived here from his seat in Virginia [with his lady and family], and proceeded to the house of Robert Morris on Market Street, provided for him by the city corporation."— *Diary of Jacob Hiltzheimer.*

The house owned by Robert Morris, and occupied by the President during his residence in Philadelphia, was on the south side of Market, sixty feet east of Sixth Street. The original building erected by Mary Masters (widow of William Masters), prior to 1772, was successively occupied by Richard Penn, who married Mary the daughter of Mrs. Masters; by General Howe as head-quarters during the possession of the city by the British; by Benedict Arnold, after the evacuation; and by John Holker, Consul-General of France. During the occupancy of the latter the house was partially consumed by fire (January 2, 1780) and rendered uninhabitable.* After this date, Robert Morris contracted for the purchase of the ground with the ruins, and caused the mansion to be "rebuilt and repaired," and finally obtained a deed for the same from Mrs. Masters, Richard Penn and wife, and Sarah Masters, dated August 25, 1785. Mr. Morris was living in the house at this time.

Richard Rush, in his "Reminiscences," speaking of the house as it appeared in his boyhood, when Washington lived in it, says, "It was a large double house. To the east a brick wall six or seven feet high ran well on toward Fifth street, until it met other houses; the wall enclosed a garden, which was shaded by lofty old trees, and ran back to what is now Minor street, where the stables stood. To the west no building adjoined it, the nearest house in that direction being at the corner of Sixth and Market, where lived Robert Morris."

The house was taken down in 1833 and three stores erected upon the site, now known as Nos. 526, 528, and 530 Market Street.†

TUESDAY, DECEMBER 7.

At Philadelphia: "*December* 8.—Yesterday, at the levee of the President of the United States, IGNATIUS PALYRAT, Esq; as Consul-General from her most faithful Majesty the Queen of Portugal to the United States of America, was presented by the Hon. Thomas Jefferson, Secretary of State, and most graciously received."‡—*Pennsylvania Packet.*

The Presidential levees at Philadelphia were held every Tuesday between three and four o'clock in the afternoon, at which Washington understood that he was visited as the *President* of the United States, and not on his own account. The visitors were either introduced by his secretary or by some gentleman whom he knew himself. The place of reception was the dining-room on the first floor, in the rear of the house.

"At three o'clock, or at any time within a quarter of an hour afterward, the visitor was conducted to this dining room, from which all seats had been removed for the time. On entering, he saw the tall manly figure of Wash-

* "*January* 2, 1780.—Early this morning a fire broke out in Mr. Penn's house on Market Street, occupied by Mr. Holker, the French Consul, which was consumed to the first floor."—*Diary of Jacob Hiltzheimer.*

† The site has lately (May 8, 1897) been marked by a tablet erected by The Pennsylvania Society of Sons of the Revolution on No. 528, the middle building.

‡ "*December,* 7, 1790.—The first levee was held this day, at which I attended."—*Journal of William Maclay.*

ington clad in black velvet; his hair in full dress, powdered and gathered behind in a large silk bag; yellow gloves on his hands; holding a cocked hat with a cockade in it, and the edges adorned with a black feather about an inch deep. He wore knee and shoe buckles; and a long sword, with a finely wrought and polished steel hilt, which appeared at the left hip; the coat worn over the sword, so that the hilt, and the part below the coat behind, were in view. The scabbard was white polished leather. He stood always in front of the fire-place, with his face towards the door of entrance. The visitor was conducted to him, and he required to have the name so distinctly pronounced that he could hear it. He had the very uncommon faculty of associating a man's name, and personal appearance, so durably in his memory, as to be able to call one by name, who made him a second visit. He received his visitor with a dignified bow, while his hands were so disposed of as to indicate, that the salutation was not to be accompanied with shaking hands. This ceremony never occurred in these visits, even with his most near friends, that no distinction might be made.

" As visitors came in, they formed a circle around the room. At a quarter past three, the door was closed, and the circle was formed for that day. He then began on the right, and spoke to each visitor, calling him by name, and exchanging a few words with him. When he had completed his circuit, he resumed his first position, and the visitors approached him in succession, bowed and retired. By four o'clock this ceremony was over."—WILLIAM SULLIVAN, *Public Men of the Revolution*, page 120.

WEDNESDAY, DECEMBER 8.

At Philadelphia: At twelve o'clock addresses both Houses of Congress in the Senate Chamber.*

The sessions of Congress at Philadelphia were held in the two-story brick building at the southeast corner of Sixth and Chestnut Streets, erected 1787–89 for a county building, and still standing. As originally constructed the building was sixty-five feet in depth along Sixth Street, the Senate Chamber being in the second story back room, the front being occupied as committee rooms. In 1793, however, an addition was made to the rear of about thirty-seven feet, and the Senate Chamber moved to the addition. The Hall of the House of Representatives was on the first floor, the whole of which (including the addition) was in one chamber, with the exception of a vestibule running along the full front on Chestnut Street, and containing on the left of the main entrance the staircase leading to the chambers above.

---

* " *December* 8.—This was the day assigned for the President to deliver his speech, and was attended with all the bustle and hurry usual on such occasions. The President was dressed in black, and read his speech well enough, or at least tolerably."—*Journal of William Maclay.*

MONDAY, DECEMBER 13.

At Philadelphia: " *December* 14.—At 12 o'clock yesterday, the Senate of the United States attended the President at his own house, and delivered their [answer to his] address. At 2 o'clock [December 14] the House, preceded by the Sergeant at arms, waited upon the President, and delivered their answer, to which they received a reply."— *Pennsylvania Packet.*

TUESDAY, DECEMBER 14.

At Philadelphia: " *December* 14.—This was levee day, and I accordingly dressed and did the needful. It is an idle thing, but what is the life of men but folly?—and this is perhaps as innocent as any of them, so far as respects the persons acting. The practice, however, considered as a feature of royalty, is certainly anti-republican. This certainly escapes nobody. The royalists glory in it as a point gained. Republicans are borne down by fashion and a fear of being charged with a want of respect to General Washington. If there is treason in the wish I retract it, but would to God this same General Washington were in heaven! We would not then have him brought forward as the constant cover to every unconstitutional and irrepublican act."—*Journal of William Maclay.*

WEDNESDAY, DECEMBER 15.

At Philadelphia: " *December* 25.—Wednesday evening, the 15th. inst. the Hon. Judge [James] Wilson, law professor in the College of Philadelphia, delivered his introductory lecture in the College-hall [Fourth, below Arch Street]. The President of the United States, with his lady—also the Vice-President, and both houses of Congress, the President [Thomas Mifflin] and both houses of the Legislature of Pennsylvania, together with a great number of ladies and gentlemen, were present; the whole composing a most brilliant and respectable audience."—*Pennsylvania Packet.*

FRIDAY, DECEMBER 24.

At Philadelphia: " *December* 26.—On Friday evening last [December 24], I went with Charles* to the drawing-room, being the first of my appearance in public. The room became full before I left it, and the circle very brilliant. How could it be otherwise, when the dazzling Mrs. Bingham and her beautiful sisters [the Misses Willing] were there; the Misses Allen, and Misses Chew; in short, a constellation of beauties?"—*Mrs. John Adams to Mrs. William S. Smith.*

Miss Sally McKean, daughter of Thomas McKean, Chief-Justice of Pennsylvania, who was present at this levee or drawing-room, writing to a friend in New York, said, " You never could have had such a drawing-room; it was brilliant beyond any thing you could imagine; and though there was a good deal of extravagance, there was so much of Philadelphia taste in every thing that it must be confessed the most delightful occasion of the kind ever known in this country."

At the levees of Mrs. Washington, which were held every Friday evening, the President did not consider *himself* as visited. On these occasions he appeared as a private gentleman, with neither hat nor sword, conversing without restraint, generally with women, who rarely had other opportunities of meeting him.

TUESDAY, DECEMBER 28.

At Philadelphia: " *December* 28.—This being levee day, I attended in a new suit. This piece of duty I have not omitted since I came to town and if there is little harm in it there can not be much good."—*Journal of William Maclay.*

---

* The third child of John and Abigail Adams. The other children were Abigail, who married Colonel William Stephens Smith, John Quincy, and Thomas Boylston.

1791.

SATURDAY, JANUARY 1.

At Philadelphia: This being New Year's Day, the President was visited by members of Congress, citizens, and others, to pay him the compliments of the season.

"*January* 1.—Just as I passed the President's house Griffin called to me and asked whether I would not pay my respects to the President. I was in boots and had on my worst clothes. I could not prevail on myself to go with him. I had, however, passed him but a little way when Osgood, Postmaster-General, attacked me warmly to go with him. I was pushed forward by him; bolted into his presence; made the President the compliments of the season; had a hearty shake by the hand. I was asked to partake of the punch and cakes, but declined. I sat down, and we had some chat. But the diplomatic gentry and foreigners coming in, I embraced the first vacancy to make my bow and wish him good morning."—*Journal of William Maclay.*

TUESDAY, JANUARY 4.

At Philadelphia: "*January* 4.—It was levee day. I dressed and did the duty of it."—*Journal of William Maclay.*

WEDNESDAY, JANUARY 5.

At Philadelphia: "*January* 5.—We hear that the President of the United States will honour the Theatre with his presence, this evening."—*Pennsylvania Journal.*

The advertisement for the evening's performance was as follows: "By Particular Desire. By the OLD AMERICAN COMPANY, At the THEATRE, in Southwark,* *This Evening*, January 5 A COMEDY— Called The School for Scandal. DANCING by Mr. [John] Durang. To which will be added, a Comedy in two acts, Called, The Poor Soldier."

---

* The Southwark Theatre was at the corner of South and Apollo (now Charles) Streets, between Fourth and Fifth Streets.

Charles Durang, in his "History of the Philadelphia Stage," partly compiled from the papers of his father, John Durang, says, "'The School for Scandal,' and the 'Poor Soldier,' were the favorite pieces of General George Washington, such was his revolutionary designation, whenever he was spoken of in those days. These pieces were often acted at his desire, whenever he visited the theatre. His suite was generally very large, and filled nearly the whole of the first tier of boxes. It may be recollected that the auditory was of limited size. The presence of that virtuous and pure patriot, that model of a national executive, at any public place, was the harbinger of enthusiastic pleasure to all. His attendance on the play was the unfailing magnet that attracted the entire circles of fashion, and of all classes of the sovereign people, to do homage to the defender and founder of their national institutions."

SATURDAY, JANUARY 8.

At Philadelphia: "*January* 8.—At 11 o'clock, the members of Congress and the [Pennsylvania] Assembly attended a concert in the Lutheran Church on Fourth Street [corner of Cherry]. The President of the United States with his lady were present."—*Diary of Jacob Hiltzheimer.*

Jacob Hiltzheimer, a German by birth, settled at Philadelphia in the latter part of 1748. He was a member of the State Assembly from 1786 to 1797, and was quite a prominent citizen. Mr. Hiltzheimer kept a diary from 1768 to 1798, extracts from which were first published in Volume XVI. of the *Pennsylvania Magazine*. It was subsequently privately printed at Philadelphia in 1893. He died of yellow fever September 14, 1798. Mr. Hiltzheimer became the owner, in July, 1777, of the house at the southwest corner of Seventh and Market Streets, in which Thomas Jefferson wrote the Declaration of Independence.

THURSDAY, JANUARY 20.

At Philadelphia: "*January* 20.—Dined with the President this day. . . . I have now seen him for the last time, perhaps. Let me take a review of him as he really is. In stature about six feet, with an unexceptionable make, but lax appearance. His frame would seem to want filling up. His motions rather slow than lively, though he showed no signs of having suffered by gout or rheumatism. His complexion pale, nay, almost cadaverous. His voice hollow and indistinct, owing as I believe to artificial teeth before his upper jaw, which occasioned a flatness of . . ."—*Journal of William Maclay.*

The above extract from the Journal of William Maclay, published in 1890, is, unfortunately, but a fragment, the editor, Edgar S. Maclay, stating in a note that "the leaf on which the rest of the description was written had been torn out and lost."

MONDAY, JANUARY 24.

At Philadelphia: Issues a proclamation directing the commissioners appointed under the act of July 16, 1790, to run four lines of experiment for the purpose of determining, for immediate acceptance, the locality of the ten miles square on the Potomac for the seat of government of the United States.

WEDNESDAY, JANUARY 26.

At Philadelphia: "*January* 25.—To-morrow the President dines with us, the Governor, the Ministers of State, and some Senators."—*Mrs. John Adams to Mrs. William S. Smith.*

THURSDAY, FEBRUARY 17.

At Philadelphia: "*February* 21.—On Thursday last [February 17] I dined with the President, in company with the ministers and ladies of the court. He was more than usually social. . . . He asked very affectionately after you and the children, and at table picked the sugar-plums from a cake, and requested me to take them for Master John."
—*Mrs. John Adams to Mrs. William S. Smith.*

TUESDAY, FEBRUARY 22.

At Philadelphia: "*February* 23.—Yesterday being the Anniversary of the Birth-Day of THE PRESIDENT OF THE UNITED STATES, when he attained to the 59th year of his age—the same was celebrated here with every demonstration of public joy. The Artillery and Light-Infantry corps of the city were paraded, and at 12 O'clock a federal Salute was fired. The congratulatory Compliments of the Members of the Legislature of the Union—the Heads of the Departments of State—Foreign Ministers —Officers, civil and military of the State—the Reverend Clergy—and Strangers and Citizens of distinction, were presented to the President on this auspicious occasion."— *Gazette of the United States.*

WEDNESDAY, MARCH 2.

At Philadelphia : " *March* 2.—The American Philosophical Society held in this city, for promoting useful knowledge, having directed that an eulogium to the memory of their late worthy President Doctor Benjamin Franklin,* should be prepared ; the society met this morning, at their hall [Fifth Street below Chestnut], and proceeded in a body to the German Lutheran Church in Fourth street, when the Rev. Dr. [William] Smith pronounced an elegant oration on the important occasion.

" The Society invited and were honored with the attendance of—The President of the United States † and his Lady. —The Vice President and his Lady.—The Senate and House of Representatives of the United States.—Both Houses of the Legislature of this State.—Foreign Ministers and consuls &c &c."—*Dunlap's American Daily Advertiser.*

WEDNESDAY, MARCH 16.

At Philadelphia : " Congress finished their session on the 3d of March.‡ . . . They made provision for the interest on

---

* Benjamin Franklin died in Philadelphia April 17, 1790.

† George Washington was elected a member of the American Philosophical Society in January, 1780.

‡ The first Congress elected under the new Constitution terminated on the third day of March, 1791. This Congress held three sessions : the first from March 4, 1789, to September 29, 1789 ; the second from January 4, 1790, to August 12, 1790 ; the third from December 6, 1790, to March 3, 1791. The first and second sessions were held in New York, and the third and last in Philadelphia.

the national debt, by laying a higher duty than that which
hitherto existed on spirituous liquors, imported or manufactured; they established a national bank; they passed
[March 3, 1791] a law for certain measures to be taken
towards establishing a mint;* and finished much other
business of less importance, conducting on all occasions
with great harmony and cordiality. . . .

"The remarks of a foreign Count [Andriani] are such as
do no credit to his judgment, and as little to his heart.
They are the superficial observations of a few months' residence, and an insult to the inhabitants of a country, where
he has received more attention and civility than he seems
to merit."— *Washington to David Humphreys.*

Count Andriani, of Milan, visited the United States in 1790. He was the
bearer of an ode addressed to Washington by Alfieri, the celebrated Italian
poet, who also in 1788 had dedicated his tragedy of "The First Brutus" to
the "most illustrious and free citizen, General Washington." After his
return to Europe, Andriani published an abusive account of American
politics and manners, to which Colonel Humphreys, under date of London,
October 31, 1790, had drawn the attention of the President.

SATURDAY, MARCH 19.

At Philadelphia: "The tender concern, which you express on my late illness, awakens emotions, which words
will not explain, and to which your own sensibility can
best do justice. My health is now quite restored, and I
flatter myself with the hope of a long exemption from sickness. On Monday next I shall enter on the practice of
your friendly prescription of exercise, intending at that
time to begin a journey to the southward, during which I
propose visiting all the Southern States."— *Washington to
the Marquis de Lafayette.*

---

* The act of Congress establishing the mint and regulating the coins of
the United States was passed March 26, 1792, and approved by the President
on April 2.

MONDAY, MARCH 21.

Leaves Philadelphia: " *March* 21.—Left Philadelphia
about 11 o'clock to make a tour through the Southern
States—Reached Chester about 3 o'clock—dined and lodged
at Mr. Wythes. . . . In this tour I was accompanied by
Majr. Jackson.—My equipage & attendance consisted of a
Charriot & four horses drove in hand—a light baggage
Waggon & two horses—four saddle horses besides a led
one for myself—and five—to wit—my Valet de Chambre,
two footmen, Coachman & postillion."— *Washington's Diary.*

" *March* 22.—At half past 6 o'clock we left Chester, & breakfasted at
Wilmington . . . crossing Christiana Creek proceeded through Newcastle
& by the Red Lyon to the Buck tavern 13 miles from Newcastle, and 19
from Wilmington where we dined and lodged   *March* 23.—Set off at 6
o'clock—breakfasted at Warwick—bated with hay 9 miles farther—and
dined and lodged at the House of one Worrell's in Chester[town].   *March*
24.—Left Chestertown about 6 o'clock—before nine I arrived at Rock-Hall
[on the Chesapeake Bay] where we breakfasted and immediately; after
which we began to embark. . . . After 8 o'clock P.M. we made the Mouth
of Severn River (leading up to Annapolis) but the ignorance of the People
on board, with respect to the navigation of it run us aground first on Green-
bury point from whence with much exertion and difficulty we got off; &
then, having no knowledge of the Channel and the night being immensely
dark with heavy and variable squals of wind—constant lightning & tremen-
dous thunder—we soon got aground again on what is called Horne's point—
where finding all efforts in vain, & not knowing where we were we remained, not knowing what might happen, till morning."— *Washington's
Diary.*

FRIDAY, MARCH 25.

At Annapolis: " *March* 25.—Having lain all night in my
Great Coat & Boots, in a birth not long enough for me by
the head, & much cramped; we found ourselves in the
morning within about one mile of Annapolis, & still fast
aground.   Whilst we were preparing our small Boat in
order to land in it, a sailing Boat came of to our assistance
in wch. with the Baggage I had on board I landed. . . .

" Was informed upon my arrival (when 15 Guns were

fired) that all my other horses arrived safe that embarked at the same time I did, about 8 o'clock last night.

"Was waited upon by the Governor [John Eager Howard] as soon as I arrived at Man's tavern & was engaged by him to dine with the Citizens of Annapolis this day at Mann's tavern, and at his House to-morrow—the first I accordingly did."— *Washington's Diary.*

"*March* 26.—Dined at the Governors—and went to the Assembly in the Evening where I stayed till half past ten o'clock. *March* 27.—About 9 o'clock this morning I left Annapolis, under a discharge of Artillery, and being accompanied by the Governor a Mr. Kilty of the Council and Mr. Charles Stuart proceeded on my Journey for George-Town. Bated at Queen Ann, 13 miles distant and dined and lodged at Bladensburgh."— *Washington's Diary.*

MONDAY, MARCH 28.

At George Town: "*March* 28.—Left Bladensburgh at half after six, & breakfasted at George Town about 8; where, having appointed the Commissioners under the Residence Law to meet me, I found Mr. [Thomas] Johnson one of them (& who is Chief Justice of the State) in waiting—& soon after came in David Stuart & Danl. Carroll Esqrs. the other two.—A few miles out of Town I was met by the principal Citizens of the place and escorted in by them; and dined at Suter's tavern (where I also lodged) at a public dinner given by the Mayor & Corporation—previous to which I examined the Surveys of Mr. [Andrew] Ellicot who had been sent on to lay out the district of ten miles square for the federal seat; and also the works of Majr. L'Enfant who had been engaged to examine & make a draught of the grds. in the vicinity of George Town and Carrollsburg on the Eastern branch."— *Washington's Diary.*

"*March* 29.—Finding the interests of the Landholders about Georgetown and those about Carrollsburgh much at variance and that their fears and jealousies of each were counteracting the public purposes & might prove injurious to its best interests whilst if properly managed they might be made to subserve it—I requested them to meet me at six o'clock this afternoon at my lodgings, which they accordingly did. . . . Dined at Col° Forrest's to day with the Commissioners & others. *March* 30.—The parties to whom I addressed myself yesterday evening, having taken the matter into consideration saw the propriety of my observations; and that whilst they were contending for the shadow they might loose the substance; and therefore mutually agreed and entered into articles to surrender for public purposes, one half of the land they severally possessed within bounds which were designated as necessary for the City to stand. . . .

"This business being thus happily finished & some directions given to the Commissioners, the Surveyor and Engineer with respect to the mode of laying out the district—Surveying the grounds for the City & forming them into lots—I left Georgetown—dined in Alexandria & reached Mount Vernon in the evening."—*Washington's Diary.*

THURSDAY, MARCH 31.*

At Mount Vernon: "Having been so fortunate as to reconcile the contending interests of Georgetown and Carrollsburg, and to unite them in such an agreement as permits the public purposes to be carried into effect on an extensive and proper scale, I have the pleasure to transmit to you the enclosed proclamation, which, after annexing the seal of the United States, and your countersignature, you will cause to be published."—*Washington to Thomas Jefferson.*

The proclamation alluded to in the above letter was issued for the purpose of publicly defining the lines of the territory selected for the permanent seat of government of the United States. It is dated Georgetown, March 30. The descriptive clause is as follows: "Beginning at Jones' Point, being the upper cape of Hunting Creek in Virginia, and at an angle in the outset of forty-five degrees west of the north, and running in a direct line ten miles for the first line; then beginning again at the same Jones' Point and running another direct line at a right angle with the first across the Potomac, ten miles, for the second line; then, from the termination of the said first and second lines, running two other direct lines of ten miles each, the one crossing the Eastern Branch aforesaid, and the other the Potomac, and meeting each other in a point."

MONDAY, APRIL 4.

At Mount Vernon: "I shall be on the 8th of April at Fredericksburg, the 11th at Richmond, the 14th at Peters-

---

* "*March* 31.—From this time, until the 7th of April, I remained at Mount Vernon—visiting my Plantations every day."—*Washington's Diary.*

burg, the 16th at Halifax, the 18th at Tarborough, the 20th at Newbern, the 24th at Wilmington, the 29th at Georgetown, South Carolina; on the 2d of May at Charleston, halting there five days; on the 11th at Savannah, halting there two days. Thence leaving the line of the mail, I shall proceed to Augusta; and according to the information which I may receive there, my return by an upper road will be regulated."— *Washington to the Secretaries of State, Treasury, and War.*

With a single exception, that of the stay in Charleston being prolonged one day beyond the time allowed, this itinerary for the early part of the southern tour was accurately fulfilled, and forms an interesting example of the methodical care observed by Washington in all the affairs of his life.

THURSDAY, APRIL 7.

Leaves Mount Vernon : " *April* 7.—Recommenced my journey with Horses apparently much refreshed and in good spirits. . . . Proceeded to Dumfries where I dined—after which I visited & drank Tea with my Niece Mrs. Thos. Lee." *— *Washington's Diary.*

" *April* 8—Set out about 6 o'clock—breakfasted at Stafford Court House—and dined and lodged at my Sister Lewis's in Fredericksburgh."— *Washington's Diary.*

SATURDAY, APRIL 9.

At Fredericksburg : " *April* 9.—Dined at an entertained given by the Citizens of the town.—Received and answered an address from the Corporation."— *Washington's Diary.*

" *April* 10.—Left Fredericksburgh about 6 o'clock,—myself Majr. Jackson and one Servant breakfasted at General Spotswood's—the rest of my Servants continued on to Todd's Ordinary where they also breakfasted.—Dined at the Bowling Green—and lodged at Kenner's Tavern 14 miles farther—in all 35 m."— *Washington's Diary.*

---

* Mildred, daughter of John Augustine Washington. She married (October, 1788) Thomas, the eldest son of Richard Henry Lee.

MONDAY, APRIL 11.

At Richmond: "*April* 11.—Took an early breakfast at Kinner's—bated at one Rawling's half way between that & Richmd. and dined at the latter about 3 o'clock.—On my arrival was saluted by the Cannon of the place—waited on by the Governor [Henry Lee] and other gentlemen—and saw the City illuminated at night."— *Washington's Diary.*

"*April* 12.—In company with the Governor,—The Directors of the James River Navigation Company—the Manager & many other Gentlemen—I viewed the Canal, Sluces, Locks, & other works between the City of Richmond & Westham. . . . Received an Address from the Mayor, Aldermen & Common Council of the City of Richmond at three o'clock, & dined with the Governor at 4 o'clock. *April* 13.—Dined at a public entertainment given by the Corporation of Richmond."— *Washington's Diary.*

THURSDAY, APRIL 14.

At Petersburg, Virginia: "*April* 14.—Left Richmond after an early breakfast—& passing through Manchester received a Salute from cannon & an Escort of Horse under the command of Captn. David Meade Randolph as far as Osbornes where I was met by the Petersburgh horse & escorted to that place & partook of a Public dinner given by the Mayor & Corporation and went to an Assembly in the evening for the occasion at which there were between 60 & 70 ladies."— *Washington's Diary.*

"*April* 15.—Set out a little after five. . . . I came twelve miles to break-fast, at one Jesse Lee's, and 15 miles farther to dinner; and where I lodged, at the House of one Oliver, which is a good one for horses, and where there are tolerable clean beds. . . . *April* 16.—Got into my Carriage a little after 5 o'clock, and travelled thro' a cloud of dust until I came within two or three miles of Hix's ford when it began to Rain.—Breakfasted at one Andrew's about a mile after passing the ford (or rather the bridge) over Meherrin River. . . . The only Inn short of Hallifax having no stables in wch. the horses could be comfortable & no Rooms or beds which appeared tolerable & every thing else having a dirty appearance, I was compelled to keep on to Hallifax; 27 miles from Andrews—48 from Olivers—and 75 from Petersburgh—At this place (i.e., Hallifax) I arrived about six o'clock, after crossing the Roanoke; on the South bank of which it stands."— *Washington's Diary.*

SUNDAY, APRIL 17.

At Halifax, North Carolina: "*April 17.*—Col° [John B.] Ashe the Representative of the district in which this town stands, and several other Gentlemen called upon, and invited me to partake of a dinner which the Inhabitants were desirous of seeing me at & excepting it dined with them accordingly."— *Washington's Diary.*

"*April 18.*—Set out by six o'clock—dined at a small house kept by one Slaughter, 22 Miles from Hallifax and lodged at Tarborough. *April 19.*— At 6 o'clock I left Tarborough accompanied by some of the most respectable people of the place for a few miles—dined at a trifling place called Greenville 25 miles distant—and lodged at one Allan's 14 miles further a very indifferent house without stabling which for the first time since I commenced my Journey were obliged to stand without a cover."— *Washington's Diary.*

WEDNESDAY, APRIL 20.

At Newbern, North Carolina: "*April 20.*—Left Allans before breakfast, & under a misapprehension went to a Col° Allans, supposing it to be a public house; where we were very kindly & well entertained without knowing it was at his expence, until it was too late to rectify the mistake. After breakfasting, & feeding our horses here, we proceeded on & crossing the River Neuse 11 miles further arrived in Newbern to dinner. At this ferry which is 10 miles from Newbern, we were met by a small party of Horse; the district Judge (Mr. [John] Sitgreave) and many of the principal Inhabitants of Newbern, who conducted us into town to exceeding good lodgings."— *Washington's Diary.*

"*April 21.*—Dined with the Citizens at a public dinner given by them: and went to a dancing assembly in the evening—both of which was at what they call the Pallace—formerly the Government House & a good brick building but now hastening to Ruins.—The Company at both was numerous at the latter there was abt. 70 ladies. *April 22.*—Under an Escort of horse, and many of the principal Gentlemen of Newbern I recommenced my journey—dined at a place called Trenton which is the head of the boat navigation of the River Trent, wch. is crossed at this place on a bridge—and lodged at one Shrine's 10 m. farther—both indifferent Houses. *April 23.*—Breakfasted at one Everets 12 miles bated at a Mr. Foy's 12 miles farther and lodged at one Sage's 20 miles beyd. it—all indifferent Houses."—*Washington's Diary.*

SUNDAY, APRIL 24.

At Wilmington, North Carolina: "*April* 24.—Breakfasted at an indifferent House about 13 miles from Sage's— and three miles further met a party of Light Horse from Wilmington; and after these a Commee. & other Gentlemen of the Town; who came out to escort me into it, and at which I arrived under a federal salute at very good lodgings prepared for me, about two o'clock—at these I dined with the Commee. whose company I asked."—*Washington's Diary.*

"*April* 25.—Dined with the Citizens of the place at a public dinner given by them—Went to a Ball in the evening at which there were 62 ladies— illuminations, Bonfires, &c. *April* 26.—Having sent my Carriage across the day before, I left Wilmington about 6 o'clock, accompanied by most of the Gentlemen of the Town, and breakfasting at Mr. Ben. Smith's lodged at one Russ' 25 miles from Wilmington.—An indifferent House. *April* 27.— Breakfasted at Willm. Gause's a little out of the direct Road 14 miles— crossed the boundary line between No. & South Carolina abt. half after 12 o'clock which is about 10 miles from Gause's—dined at a private house (one Cochran's) about 2 miles farther—and lodged at Mr. Vareen's 14 miles more. *April* 28.—Mr. Vareen piloted us across the Swash . . . and it being at a proper time of the tide we passed along it with ease and celerity to the place of quitting it, which is estimated 16 miles,—five miles farther we got dinner & fed our horses at a Mr. Pauley's a private house, no public one being on the Road;—and being met on the Road, & kindly invited by a Doctor Flagg to his house, we lodged there; it being about 10 miles from Pauley's & 33 from Vareen's. *April* 29.—We left Doctr. Flagg's about 6 o'clock, and arrived at Captn. Wm. Alston's on the Waggamau [Waccamaw] to Breakfast. At Captn. Alston's we were met by General Moultree, Colo [William] Washington & Mr. Rutledge (son of the present Chief Justice of So. Carolina) who had come out that far to escort me to town.—We dined and lodged at this Gentlemans."—*Washington's Diary.*

SATURDAY, APRIL 30.

At Georgetown, South Carolina: "*April* 30.—Boats being provided we crossed the Waggamau to Georgetown by descending the River three miles—at this place we were recd.

under a salute of Cannon, & by a Company of Infantry handsomely uniformed.—I dined with the Citizens in public; and in the afternoon, was introduced to upwards of 50 ladies who had assembled (at a Tea party) on the occasion." — *Washington's Diary.*

"*May* 1.—Left Georgetown about 6 o'clock and crossing the Santee Creek at the Town, and the Santee River 12 miles from it at Lynch's Island, we breakfasted and dined at Mrs. Horry's about 15 miles from Georgetown & lodged at the Plantation of Mr. Manigold [Manigault] about 19 miles further.— *Washington's Diary.*

MONDAY, MAY 2.

At Charleston, South Carolina : "*May* 2.—Breakfasted at the Country seat of Govr. [Charles] Pinckney about 18 miles from our lodging place, & then came to the ferry at Haddrel's point, 6 miles further, where I was met by the Recorder of the City, Genl. [Charles Cotesworth] Pinckney & Edward Rutledge, Esqr. in a 12 oared barge rowed by 12 American Captains of Ships, most elegantly dressed.— There were a great number of other Boats with Gentlemen and ladies in them :—and two Boats with Music : all of them attended me across, and on the passage were met by a number of others.—As we approached the town a salute with artillery commenced, and at the Wharf I was met by the Governor, the Lt. Governor, the Intendt. of the city; —the two Senators of the State [Pierce Butler and Ralph Izard], Wardens of the City—Cincinnati. &c &c. and conducted to the Exchange where they passed by in procession —from thence I was conducted in like manner to my lodgings —after which I dined at the Governors (in what he called a private way) with 15 or 18 Gentlemen."— *Washington's Diary.*

"*May* 3.—Breakfasted with Mrs. [John] Rutledge (the Lady of the Chief-Justice of the State who was on the Circuits) and dined with the Citizens at a public dinr. given by them at the Exchange. Was visited about 2 o'clock, by a great number of the most respectable ladies of Charleston— the first honor of the kind I had ever experienced and it was as flattering as

it was singular. *May* 4.—Dined with the Members of the Cincinnati, and
in the evening went to a very elegant dancing Assembly at the Exchange—
At which were 256 elegantly dressed & handsome ladies. In the forenoon
(indeed before breakfast to day) I visited and examined the lines of attack
& defence of the City and was satisfied that the defence was noble & honorable altho' the measure was undertaken upon wrong principles and im-
politic. *May* 5.—Visited the works of Fort Johnson James' Island, and
Fort Moultree on Sullivan's Island; both of which are in Ruins. . . .
Dined with a very large Company at the Governor's & in the evening went
to a Concert at the Exchange at weh. there were at least 400 ladies the
number & appearance of weh. exceeded any thing of the kind I had ever
seen. *May* 6.—Viewed the town on horseback by riding through most of
the principal Streets Dined at Majr. [Pierce] Butler's and went to a Ball
in the evening at the Governor's where there was a select Company of
ladies. *May* 7.—Before break[fast] I visited the Orphan House at which
there were one hundred & seven boys & girls—This appears to be a chari-
table institution and under good management. *May* 8.—Went to crowded
Churches in the morning and afternoon. . . . Dined with General Moultree ''—*Washington's Diary.*

MONDAY, MAY 9.

Leaves Charleston : " *May* 9.—At six o'clock I recommenced my journey for Savanna; attended by a Corps of
the Cincinnati and most of the principal Gentlemen of the
City as far as the bridge over Ashley River, where we
breakfasted, and proceeded to Col° W. Washington's at
Sandy-hill with a select party of particular friends—distant
from Charleston 28 miles."— *Washington's Diary.*

" *May* 10.—Took leave of all my friends and attendants at this place (except General Moultree & Majr. Butler the last of whom intended to accompany me to Savanna and the other to Purisburgh, at which I was to be met
by Boats,) & breakfasting at Judge Bee's 12 miles from Sandy Hill, lodged
at Mr. Obrian Smith's 18 or 20 further on. *May* 11.—After an early breakfast at Mr. Smith's we road 20 miles to a place called Pokitellico [Pocotaligo]
where a dinner was provided by the Parishoners of Prince William for my
reception, and an address from them was presented and answered. After
dinner we proceeded 16 miles farther to Judge Hayward's where we lodged.''
— *Washington's Diary.*

THURSDAY, MAY 12.

At Savannah, Georgia : " *May* 12.—By five o'clock we
set out from Judge Hayward's, and rode to Purisburgh 22

miles to breakfast. At that place I was met by Messrs.
[Noble Wimberly] Jones, Col° [Joseph] Habersham, Mr.
Jno. Houston, Genl. [Lachlin] McIntosh and Mr. [Joseph]
Clay, a Comee. from the City of Savanna to conduct me
thither.—Boats also were ordered there by them for my
accommodation; among which a handsome 8 oared barge
rowed by 8 American Captns. attended.—In my way down
the River I called upon Mrs. Green the Widow of the
deceased Genl. [Nathanael] Green, (at a place called Mulberry Grove) & asked her how she did. . . . We were
seven hours making the passage which is often performed
in 4 tho' the computed distance is 25 miles—Illumns. at
night.

"I was conducted by the Mayor & Wardens to very good
lodging which had been provided for the occasion, and partook of a public dinner given by the Citizens at the Coffee
Room.—At Purisburgh I parted with Genl. Moultree."—
Washington's Diary.

"*May* 13.—Dined with the Members of the Cincinnati at a public dinner
given at the same place—and in the evening went to a dancing Assembly at
which there was about 100 well dressed and handsome ladies. *May* 14.—A
little after 6 o'clock, in Company with Genl. McIntosh, Genl. [Anthony]
Wayne, the Mayor and many others (principal Gentlemen of the City.) I
visited the City, and the attack & defence of it in the year 1779, under the
combined forces of France and the United States, commanded by the Court
de Estaing & Genl. Lincoln. . . . Dined to day with a number of the Citizens (not less than 200) in an elegant Bower erected for the occasion on the
Bank of the River below the Town.—In the evening there was a tolerable
good display of fireworks."—*Washington's Diary.*

SUNDAY, MAY 15.

Leaves Savannah: "*May* 15.—After morning Service,
and receiving a number of visits from the most respectable
ladies of the place (as was the case yesterday) I set out for
Augusta, Escorted beyd. the limits of the City by most of
the Gentlemen in it, and dining at Mulberry Grove the
Seat of Mrs. Green,—lodged at one Spencers—distant 15
miles."— *Washington's Diary.*

" *May* 16.—Breakfasted at Russells—15 miles from Spencer's—dined at Garnets 19 further & lodged at Pierces 8 miles more, in all—42 miles to day. *May* 17.—Breakfasted at Spinner's 17 miles—dined at Lamberts 13—and lodged at Waynesborough (wch. was coming 6 miles out of the way) 14, in all 43 miles."— *Washington's Diary.*

WEDNESDAY, MAY 18.

At Augusta, Georgia: "*May* 18.—Breakfasted at Tulcher's 15 miles from Waynesborough; and within 4 miles of Augusta met the Govor. [Edward Telfair], Judge [George] Walton, the Attorney Genl. & most of the principal Gentlemen of the place; by whom I was escorted into the Town, & recd. under a discharge of Artillery,—the distance I came to day was about 32 miles—Dined with a large Company at the Governors, & drank Tea there with many well dressed Ladies."— *Washington's Diary.*

" *May* 19.—Received & answered an Address from the Citizens of Augusta; dined with a large Company of them at their Court Ho.—and went to an Assembly in the evening at the Acendamy; at which there were between 60 & 70 well dressed ladies.   *May* 20.—Viewed the Ruins, or rather small Remns. of the Works which had been erected by the British during the War and taken by the Americans.—Also the falls, which are about 2 miles above the Town;—and the Town itself. . . . Dined at a private dinner with Govr. Telfair to day.   *May* 21.—Left Augusta about 6 o'clock, and takg. leave of the Governor & principal Gentlemen of the place at the bridge over Savanna River, where they had assembled for the purpose, I proceeded in Company with Col^o^ [Wade] Hampton & Taylor, & Mr. Lithgow a committee from Columbia, (who had come on to meet & conduct me to that place) & a Mr. Jameson from the Village of Granby on my Rout. Dined at a house about 20 miles from Augusta and lodged at one Odem about 20 miles farther."— *Washington's Diary.*

SUNDAY, MAY 22.

At Columbia, South Carolina: " *May* 22.—Rode about 21 miles to breakfast, and passing through the village of Granby just below the first falls in the Congaree (which was passed in a flat bottomed boat at a Rope ferry,) I lodged at Columbia, the newly adopted Seat of the Government of South Carolina about 3 miles from it, on the

No. side of the River, and 27 from my breakfasting stage."
— *Washington's Diary.*

" *May 23.*—Dined at a public dinner in the State house with a number of Gentlemen & Ladies of the Town of Columbia, & Country round about to the amt. of more than 150, of which 50 or 60 were of the latter. *May 24.*— The condition of my foundered horse obliged me to remain at this place, contrary to my intention, this day also."—*Washington's Diary.*

WEDNESDAY, MAY 25.

At Camden, South Carolina: " *May 25.*—Set out at 4 o'clock for Camden—(the foundered horse being led slowly on)—breakfasted at an indifferent house 22 miles from the town, (the first we came to) and reached Camden about two o'clock, 14 miles further, when an address was recd. & answered.—Dined late with a number of Gentlemen & Ladies at a public dinner."— *Washington's Diary.*

" *May 26.*—After viewing the british works about Camden I set out for Charlotte—on my way—two miles from Town—I examined the ground on wch. Genl. Green & Lord Rawdon had their action [Hobkirk's Hill, April 25, 1781] . . . Six miles further on I came to the ground where Genl. Gates & Lord Cornwallis had their Engagement [August 16, 1780] wch. terminated so unfavourably for the former. . . . After Halting at one Sutton's 14 m. from Camden I lodged at James Ingrams 12 miles father. *May 27.*—Left Ingrams about 4 o'clock, and breakfasting at one Barr's 18 miles distant lodged at Majr. Crawford's 8 miles farther."—*Washington's Diary.*

SATURDAY, MAY 28.

At Charlotte, North Carolina: " *May 28.*—Set off from Crawford's by 4 o'clock and breakfasting at one Harrison's 18 miles from it got into Charlotte 13 miles further, before 3 o'clock,—dined with Genl. [Thomas] Polk and a small party invited by him, at a Table prepared for the purpose."
— *Washington's Diary.*

" *May 29.*—Left Charlotte about 7 o'clock, dined at Colo Smiths 15 miles off, and lodged at Majr. Fifers [Phifer] 7 miles farther."—*Washington's Diary.*

MONDAY, MAY 30.

At Salisbury, North Carolina: "*May* 30.—At 4 o'clock I was out from Majr. Fifers; and in about 10 miles at the line which divides Mecklenburgh from Rowan Counties; I met a party of horse belonging to the latter who came from Salisbury to escort me on. . . . I was also met 5 miles from Salisbury by the Mayor of the Corporation, Judge McKoy, & many others. . . . We arrived at Salisbury about 8 o'clock, to breakfast,—20 miles from Captn. Fifers. . . . Dined at a public dinner givn. by the Citizens of Salisbury; & in the afternoon drank Tea at the same place with about 20 ladies, who had been assembled for the occasion."—*Washington's Diary.*

TUESDAY, MAY 31.

At Salem, North Carolina: "*May* 31.—Left Salisbury about 4 o'clock; at 5 miles crossed the Yadkin, the principal stream of the Pedee, and breakfasted on the No. Bank, (while my Carriages & horses were crossing) at a Mr. Youngs' fed my horses 10 miles farther at one Reeds—and about 3 o'clock (after another halt) arrived at Salem, one of the Moravian towns 20 miles farther—In all 35 from Salisbury. . . . Salem is a small but neat village; & like all the rest of the Moravian settlements, is governed by an excellent police—having within itself all kinds of artizans— The number of Souls does not exceed 200."—*Washington's Diary.*

"June 1.—Spent the forenoon in visiting the Shops of the different Tradesmen—The houses of accomodation for the single men & Sisters of the Fraternity—& their place of worship.—Invited six of their principal people to dine with me—and in the evening went to hear them sing, & perform on a variety of instruments Church music. In the Afternoon Governor [Alexander] Martin as was expected (with his Secretary) arrived."— *Washington's Diary.*

THURSDAY, JUNE 2.

At Guilford, North Carolina: "*June* 2.—In company with the Govʳ I set out by 4 Oclock for Guilford.—Breakfasted at one Dobsons at the distance of eleven Miles from Salem and dined at Guilford 16 miles farther; where there was a considerable gathering of people who had receiv'd Notice of my intention to be there to-day & came to satisfy their curiosity. . . . On my approach to this place (Guilford) I was met by a party of light horse which I prevailed on the Governor to dismiss, and to countermand his orders for others to attend me through the State."— *Washington's Diary.*

"*June* 3.—Took my leave of the Govern' whose intention was to have attend me to the line, but for my request that he would not; and about 4 Oclock proceeded on my journey.—Breakfasted at troublesome Ironworks (called 15, but which is at least) 17 Miles from Guilford partly in Rain and from my information or for want of it was obliged to travel 12 miles further than I intended to day—to one Gatewoods within two Miles of Dix' ferry over the Dan, at least 30 Miles from the Iron works. *June* 4.—Left M' Gatewoods about half after Six oclock—and between his house & the Ferry passed the line which divides the States of Virginia and N° Carolina & dining at one Wisoms 16 Miles from the Ferry lodged at Hallifax old Town. *June* 5.—Left the old Town about 4 oclock A. M. & breakfasting at one Pridie's (after crossing Banister River 1½ Miles) ab' 11 Miles from it, came to Staunton River about 12; where meeting Col° Isaac Coles (formerly a Member of Congress for this district &) who pressing me to it, I went to his house about one Mile off to dine and to halt a day, for the Refreshment of myself and horses; leaving my Servants and them at one of the usually in-different Taverns at the Ferry that they might give no trouble, or be incon-venient to a private family. *June* 6.—Dined at this Gentlemans to day also. *June* 7.—Left Col° Coles by day break, and breakfasted at Charlotte C' H° 15 Miles where I was detained some time to get Shoes put on such horses as had lost them—proceeded afterwards to Prince Edward Court House 20 Miles further. *June* 8.—Left Prince Edward Court H° as soon as it was well light & breakfasted at one Treadways 13 Miles off,—dined at Cumberland C' H° 14 Miles further—and lodged at Moores Tavern within 2 miles from Carter's ferry over James River. *June* 9.—Set off very early from Moores—but the proper ferry boat being hauled up we were a tedious while crossing in one of the Boats used in the navigation of the River; being obliged to carry one carriage at a time without horses & crossways the Boat on planks.—Break-fasted at a Widow pains 17 Miles on the N° side of the River, and lodged at a M" Jordans a private house where we were kindly entertained and to which we were driven by necessity having Rode not less than 25 miles from our breakfasting stage through very bad Roads in a very sultry day with' any re-freshment & by missing the right Road had got to it."— *Washington's Diary.*

FRIDAY, JUNE 10.

At Fredericksburg, Virginia : " *June* 10.—Left M" Jordans early & breakfasting at one Johnston's 7 miles off reached Fredericksburgh after another (short) halt about 3 oclock & dined and lodged at my Sister Lewis's."— *Washington's Diary.*

" *June* 11.—After a dinner with several Gentlemen whom my Sister had envited to dine with me I crossed the Rappahannock & proceeded to Stafford C¹ House where I lodged. *June* 12.—About Sunrise we were off—breakfasted at Dumfries and arrived at M¹ Vⁿ to Dine."— *Washington's Diary.*

MONDAY, JUNE 13.

At Mount Vernon : "From Monday 13ᵗʰ until Monday the 27ᵗʰ (being the day I had appointed to meet the Commissioners under the Residence Act, at Georgetown) I remained at home; and spent my time in daily Rides to my sever¹ farms—and in receiving many visits."— *Washington's Diary.*

" *June* 27.—Left Mount Vernon for Georgetown before Six o'clock ;—and according to appointment met the Commissioners at that place by 9—then calling together the Proprietors of those Lands on which the federal City was proposed to be built who had agreed to cede them on certain conditions at the last meeting I had with them at this place but from some misconception with respect to the extension of their grants had refused to make conveyances and recapitulating the principles upon which my comⁿˢ to them at the former meeting were made and giving some explanations of the present State of matters & the consequences of delay in this business they readily waved their objections & ag⁴ to convey to the utmost extent of what was required. *June* 28.—Whilst the Commissioners were engaged in preparing the Deeds to be signed by the Subscribers this afternoon, I went out with Maj" L'Enfant and Ellicot to take a more perfect view of the ground, in order to decide finally on the Spots on which to place the public buildings— and to direct how a line which was to leave out a Spring (commonly known by the name of the Cool Spring) belonging to Maj" Stoddart should be run. *June* 29.—The Deeds which remained unexecuted yesterday were signed to day and the Dowers of their respective wives acknowledged according to Law. This being accomplished, I called the Several Subscribers together and made known to them the spots on which I meant to place the buildings for the P: & Executive departments of the Government—and for the Legislature of D°—A Plan was also laid before them of the City in order to convey to them general ideas of the City—but they were told that some deviations from it would take place—particularly in the diagonal Streets or avenues, which would not be so numerous; and in the removal of the Presidents house more westerly for the advantage of higher ground—they were also told that a Town house, or exchange w⁴ be placed on some convenient ground between the spots designed for the public build⁵ before mentioned.— And it was with much pleasure that a general approbation of the measure seemed to pervade the whole."— *Washington's Diary.*

THURSDAY, JUNE 30.

At Frederick Town, Maryland : "*June* 30.—The business which bro⁵ me to Georgetown being finished & the Com⁹ instructed with respect to the mode of carrying the plan into effect I set off this morning a little after 4 oclock in the prosecution of my journey towards Philadelphia: and being desirous of seeing the nature of the Country North of Georgetown, and along the upper Road, I resolved to pass through Fredericktown in Maryland—& York & Lancaster in Pennsylvania & accordingly—Breakfasted at a small Village called Williamsburgh in which stands the C⁵ House of Montgomerie County 14 M from George Town— dined at one Peter's tavern 20 Miles further—and arrived at Frederick town about sundown—the whole distance 43 miles."— Washington's Diary.

"*Frederick-Town* July 5.—On Thursday evening last [June 30], at twenty-five minutes past seven o'clock, the President of the United States, accompanied by his secretary Major Jackson, arrived in this town from Mount Vernon, on his way to Philadelphia.—So sudden and unexpected was the visit of this amiable and illustrious character, as to leave it entirely out of the power of the citizens to make the necessary preparations for his reception.—On notice being given of his arrival, the bells of the Lutheran and Calvinist churches were rung—fifteen rounds from Cannon-Hill were discharged—and a band of music serenaded him in the evening. He was politely invited to spend the succeeding day in town ; but answered (as an apology for not accepting the invitation), that public business obliged him to hasten to Philadelphia. The next morning, at ten o'clock, he proceeded on his journey, escorted by several gentlemen, over the Monocosy, on his route to York. Previous to his departure, an address, drawn in great haste, was presented to him : to which he was pleased to return an answer ; exhibiting as usual, fresh proofs of his greatness and goodness."—*Claypoole's Daily Advertiser*, July 9.

FRIDAY, JULY 1.

At Taneytown, Maryland: "*July* 1.—Received an address from the Inhabitants of Frederick town and about 7 o'clock left it—dined at one Cookerlys 13 miles off & lodged at Tawny town only 12 Miles farther—being detained at the first stage by Rain and to answer the address wch had been presented to me in the Morning. Tawny town is but a small place with only the Street through wch the Road passes, built on—the buildings are principally of wood."— *Washington's Diary.*

SATURDAY, JULY 2.

At Yorktown, Pennsylvania: "*July* 2.—Set out a little after 4 o'clock and in ab^t 6 Miles crossed the line wch divides the States of Maryland & Pennsylvania—the Trees in wch are so grown up th^t I could not perceive the opening though I kept a lookout for it.—9 Miles from Tawny town, Littletown is past, they are of similar app^e but ye latter is more insignificant than the former.—Seven Miles farther we came to Hanover (commonly called McAlister's town) a very pretty village with a number of good brick Houses & Mechanics in it. At this place, in a good Inn, we breakfasted—and in 18 Miles more reached York Town where we dined and lodged. . . . After dinner in company with Col^o [Thomas] Hartley & other Gentlemen I walked through the principal Streets of the Town and drank Tea at Col. Hartleys.—The C^t H^o was illuminated." *—Washington's Diary.*

---

* "Saturday last [July 2] the President of the United States arrived here [Yorktown] from Mount Vernon on his way to Philadelphia. His arrival which was about 2 o'clock was announced by the ringing of bells. The Independent Light Infantry, commanded by Capt. George Hay, paraded, and being drawn up before his Excellency's lodging fired fifteen

15

"On the 2nd. of July, 1791, in the afternoon, at 2 o'clk came the Honorable President Washington to York town ; all the bells of the town rang in honor of the event as if the voices of the Archangels sounding in harmony commanded attention. I could not repress my tears at the thought of all this, indeed I cried aloud, not from a sense of sadness, but from a feeling of very joyfulness. In the evening, there was a general illumination, and in the Court House in each pane was set a light."—Rev. John Roth, *Diary of the Moravian Congregation of Yorktown, Pennsylvania*, MS.

SUNDAY, JULY 3.

At Lancaster, Pennsylvania : " *July* 3.—Received and answered an address from the Inhabitants of Yorktown— & there being no Episcopal Minister *present* in the place, I went to hear morning Service performed in the Dutch reformed Church—which, being in that language not a word of which I understood I was in no danger of becoming a proselyte to its religion by the eloquence of the Preacher.—

" After Service, accompanied by Col° Hartley & half a dozen other Gentlemen, I set off for Lancaster—Dined at Wrights Ferry [Columbia] where I was met by Gen¹ [Edward] Hand & many of the principal characters of Lancaster & escorted to the town by them, arriving ab' 6 o'clock."— *Washington's Diary.*

" *Lancaster*, July 3.—This evening at 6 o'clock, arrived here, on his return from his Southern Tour, his Excellency the President of the United States, accompanied by Major Jackson. He was escorted from Wright's Ferry by a respectable number of the inhabitants of this borough."—*Claypoole's Daily Advertiser*, July 12.

MONDAY, JULY 4.

At Lancaster : " *July* 4.—This being the Anniversary of American Independence and being kindly requested to do it, I agreed to halt here this day and partake of the entertainment which was preparing for the celebration of it.—In

rounds. At night there were illuminations and every other demonstration of joy."—*The Pennsylvania Herald and York General Advertiser*, July 6, 1791.

the forenoon I walked about the town—At half passed 2
oclock I received, and answered an address from the Corporation and the Complim" of the Clergy of different denominations—dined between 3 & 4 oclock—drank Tea with
M" Hand."— *Washington's Diary.*

"*July* 12.—On Monday, July 4, being the Anniversary of American
Independence, the Corporation [of Lancaster], at the particular request of
the inhabitants, waited on him [the President] with an address : At three
o'clock the President, and a very large number of citizens, set down to an
elegant entertainment, provided for the occasion, in the court-house."—
Claypoole's Daily Advertiser.

WEDNESDAY, JULY 6.

At Philadelphia : "*July* 7.—Yesterday the President of
the United States arrived in this city, on his return from
his southern tour. His approach was announced to the
citizens, by the firing of cannon and the ringing of bells."
—*Dunlap's American Daily Advertiser.*

WEDNESDAY, JULY 20.

At Philadelphia : "I yesterday had Mr. Jaudenes,* who
was in this country with Mr. Gardoqui, and is now come
over in a public character, presented to me for the first
time by Mr. Jefferson. Colonel Ternant is expected here
every day as minister from France."— *Washington to David
Humphreys.*

Colonel Humphreys was at this time in Lisbon, having been appointed
minister to Portugal on February 21. At the time of the appointment he
was in London, having left the United States in August, 1790. Mr. Humphreys revisited this country in 1794, returned the following year, and soon
afterward married Miss Bulkly, an English woman of fortune. He was
transferred (May 20, 1796) from Lisbon to the court of Madrid, where he
remained until succeeded by Charles Pinckney in 1802.

---

* Don Joseph De Jaudennes was associated with Don Joseph De Viar, the
Spanish minister, in the management of Spanish interests in the United
States. He subsequently acted as commissioner and envoy from Spain.

TUESDAY, AUGUST 9.

At Philadelphia: "A slight indisposition, since my return, (occasioned by a tumor, not much unlike the one I had at New York in 1789), of which I am now recovered, does not forbid the expectation, that my health may be ultimately improved by my tour through the southern States."—*Washington to William Moultrie.*

THURSDAY, AUGUST 18.

At Philadelphia: "*August* 20.—Thursday [August 18], the French and Spanish Ambassadors, together with several other distinguished personages dined with the President of the United States, and in the evening there was a small display of fire works exhibited nearly opposite the President's house, given by a few citizens in compliment to the Company."—*Dunlap's American Daily Advertiser.*

"*August* 10.—Yesterday arrived in this city Mons. DE TERNANT, Minister Plenipotentiary from his Most Christian Majesty to the United States of America, after a passage of 45 days from Rochefort, on board the frigate La Favorite. In his suite came Messieurs Dupont and Kellerman." *—*Idem.*

MONDAY, SEPTEMBER 5.

At Philadelphia: "*September* 5.—This afternoon went to the President's house on Market Street and there dined with him and his lady, and four members of his family, besides the following members of the [Pennsylvania] House [of Representatives]: Hon. William Bingham, Speaker, Messrs. [Richard] Wells, [Francis] Gurney, [Lawrence] Seckel from the city: [William] Macpherson, [Thomas] Lilly, [Philip] Gardner, [Henry] Tyson, [Joseph] Reed,

* Jean Baptiste Ternant served as major in the Revolutionary War under Baron Steuben (whom he accompanied to this country) until September 25, 1778, when he was made lieutenant-colonel and inspector of the armies in Georgia and South Carolina. He was taken prisoner at Charleston in 1780, but was soon exchanged, and returned to France after the conclusion of peace.

[David] Stewart, [Jonathan] Hoge, [John] Montgomery, [Samuel] Maclay, [John] White, [William] Findlay, [John] Baird, [Jacob] Eyerly, [Anthony] Lerch, [John] Mulhollan, [Adamson] Tannehill, and Peter Lloyd, our clerk. I cannot help remarking that President Washington is an unassuming, easy and sociable man, beloved by every person."—*Diary of Jacob Hiltzheimer.*

THURSDAY, SEPTEMBER 15.

Leaves Philadelphia: "*September* 19.—Thursday afternoon [September 15], the PRESIDENT left this city on a tour to Mount Vernon."—*Claypoole's Daily Advertiser.*

The Viscount de Châteaubriand, who dined with the President the day before his departure for Mount Vernon, after describing in his "Travels in America and Italy," published in 1828, his first interview * with Washington, refers to the dinner in the following words: "The conversation turned almost entirely on the French revolution. The general showed us a key of the Bastille: those keys of the Bastille were but silly playthings which were about that time distributed over the two worlds. Had Washington seen like me the *conquerors of the Bastille* in the kennels of Paris, he would have had less faith in the relic. The gravity and the energy of the revolution were not in those sanguinary orgies. At the time of the revocation of the edict of Nantes, in 1685, the same populace of the Faubourg Saint-Antoine demolished the Protestant church at Charenton with as much zeal as it despoiled the church of St Denis in 1793.

"I left my host at ten in the evening, and never saw him again: he set out for the country the following day, and I continued my journey.

"Such was my interview with that man who gave liberty to a whole world. Washington sunk into the tomb before any little celebrity had attached to my name. I passed before him as the most unknown of beings; he was in all his glory, I in the depth of my obscurity, my name probably dwelt not a whole day in his memory. Happy, however, that his looks were cast upon me! I have felt myself warmed for it all the rest of my life. There is a virtue in the looks of a great man."

---

* At this interview, upon perceiving the astonishment of the President when he stated that the object of his voyage was to discover the passage to the northwest by penetrating to the polar sea, Châteaubriand said, "But it is less difficult to discover the northwest passage than to create a nation as you have done."

MONDAY, SEPTEMBER 19.

At George Town : " *George-Town*, September 24.—MON-
DAY evening last [September 19] the PRESIDENT of
the United States, his Lady, and Suite, arrived in this town
from the Seat of Government, and on Tuesday took their
departure for Mount Vernon."—*Claypoole's Daily Advertiser*, September 30.

SATURDAY, OCTOBER 15.

At Mount Vernon : " From long experience I have laid
it down as an unerring maxim, that to exact rents with
punctuality is not only the *right* of the landlord, but that it
is also for the benefit of the tenant that it should be so,
unless by uncontrollable events and providential strokes
the latter is rendered unable to pay them."— *Washington to
Robert Lewis.*

FRIDAY, OCTOBER 21.

At Philadelphia : " *October* 22.—The President of the
United States arrived in town yesterday, from Mount
Vernon."—*Claypoole's Daily Advertiser.*

TUESDAY, OCTOBER 25.

At Philadelphia : " *October* 25.—At noon President Wash-
ington went to the Congress at the corner of Chestnut and
Sixth Streets, and delivered his address [in the Senate
Chamber]—yesterday being the first day of meeting of the
Second Congress."—*Diary of Jacob Hiltzheimer.*

SATURDAY, OCTOBER 29.

At Philadelphia : " *October* 29.—The Speaker of the House
of Representatives [Jonathan Trumbull] attended by the
Members repaired to the President's house, and presented
him with an answer to his address."—*Dunlap's American
Daily Advertiser.*

" November 1.—Yesterday [Monday, October 31] at twelve o'clock, the Vice-President attended by the Senate, repaired to the President's House, and presented him with an answer to his address."—*Idem.*

FRIDAY, NOVEMBER 11.

At Philadelphia: " *November* 15.—On Friday last [November 11] Mr. Hammond was introduced to the President, by the Secretary of State, and presented his credentials as his Britannic Majesty's Minister Plenipotentiary to the United States."—*Dunlap's American Daily Advertiser.*

George Hammond was the first minister from Great Britain to the United States. He married (May 20, 1793) Margaret Allen, daughter of Andrew Allen, of Philadelphia, a girl of remarkable beauty. Mr. Hammond remained in this country until 1795, when he returned to England to become under-secretary at the foreign office in London.

THURSDAY, DECEMBER 8.

At Philadelphia: " This afternoon accounts received, which are believed, that General St. Clair's army has been defeated by the Indians. The action happened November 4th, within fifteen miles of the Miami towns. Six hundred of our men killed and wounded. General [Richard] Butler and many officers among the slain."—*Timothy Pickering to Mrs. Pickering.*

When the President received the news of the surprise and defeat of General St. Clair, it is said, on the authority of Colonel Lear,* who was present, that for a few moments he lost all control of himself, and with great violence of manner vehemently denounced the action of St. Clair in allowing himself to be surprised,—an event which he had been expressly cautioned against. The paroxysm of passion, however, lasted but a short time, when he regained his habitual composure.

FRIDAY, DECEMBER 30.

At Philadelphia: " *January* 3, 1792.—On Friday morning [December 30, 1791] was presented to the President of the United States, a BOX elegantly mounted with silver,

---

* " Washington in Domestic Life," by Richard Rush, p. 65.

and made of the celebrated oak tree that sheltered the
WASHINGTON of Scotland, the brave and patriotic Sir
William Wallace, after his defeat at the battle of Falkirk,
in the beginning of the fourteenth century, by Edward the
1st. This magnificent and truly characteristic present is
from the Earl of Buchan, by the hands of Mr. Archibald
Robertson, a Scotch gentleman, and portrait painter who
arrived in America some months ago."—*Claypoole's Daily
Advertiser.*

At the request of the Earl of Buchan, Washington sat to Mr. Robertson
for his portrait, to be placed among those most honored by the earl. The
portrait obtained at these sittings was taken in miniature; it was retained
by the artist, and a large painting executed from it was sent to the earl in
May, 1792.

A family dinner to which Mr. Robertson was invited is thus described by
him : "The dinner, served at three o'clock in the afternoon, was plain, but
suitable for a family in genteel and comfortable circumstances. There was
nothing specially remarkable at the table, but that the General and Mrs.
Washington sat side by side, he on the right of his lady ; the gentlemen on
his right hand and the ladies on her left. It being on Saturday, the first
course was mostly of eastern cod and fresh fish. A few glasses of wine were
drunk during dinner, with other beverage ; the whole closed with a few
glasses of sparkling champagne, in about three quarters of an hour, when
the General and Colonel Lear retired, leaving the ladies in high glee about
Lord Buchan and the ' Wallace box.' "

1792.

MONDAY, JANUARY 2.

At Philadelphia: Receives and answers an address from the "Right Worshipful Grand Officers of the Grand Lodge of Pennsylvania."

TUESDAY, FEBRUARY 21.

At Philadelphia: "*February* 24.—On Tuesday evening the 21st. inst. the city dancing assembly,* gave a ball in honor of the birth day of the President of the United States. They were honored on this occasion with the company of the President and Mrs. Washington, the Vice-President, the foreign Ministers, Mr. Speaker [Jonathan Trumbull] and most of the members of the two houses of Congress, the governor of the state [Thomas Mifflin], and of the Western Territory [Arthur St. Clair], together with many of the most respectable officers of the United States and of this state; and to crown the whole with one of the most brilliant displays of beauty ever exhibited in this city."—*Dunlap's American Daily Advertiser.*

WEDNESDAY, FEBRUARY 22.

At Philadelphia: "*February* 23.—Yesterday both Houses of Congress walked in Procession to wait on the President of the United States to congratulate him on the anniversary of his Birth Day. . . . The officers of the militia of the

---

* This social organization, which dates back to 1748, is still in existence, its members meeting twice during the winter for the enjoyment of dancing. In the early days the balls were given every Thursday evening from January to May, beginning at six and ending at twelve o'clock. Now they *begin* at twelve.

City, Liberties and Districts of Philadelphia paid their respects in a body and there was also a military parade, with
firing of guns and ringing of bells."—*Dunlap's American
Daily Advertiser.*

" *February* 25.—The entertainment given last Wednesday evening [Feb-
ruary 22], by the New City Dancing Assembly,* in honor of the President's
birth day, was remarkable, we hear, for a brilliant display of beauty, taste
and elegance. The President and a number of officers of the government
attended "—*Idem.*

" *February* 25.—On Tuesday and Wednesday evenings, the 21st and 22d
instants, the two Dancing assemblies gave each, successively, a Ball, in
honor of this anniversary—at both of which were present, the President of
the United States, his Lady and Family—the Vice-President of the United
States—the Heads of Departments—the Foreign Ministers—the Speaker,
and most of the Members of the two Houses of Congress—the Governor of
the State—the Governor of the Western Territory—and many other respectable Officers of the United States, and of this Commonwealth—and to crown
all, there was as brilliant a display of Beauty as was ever exhibited in this
city.   Elegant entertainments succeeded, when a variety of sentimental and
patriotic Toasts were given."—*Gazette of the United States.*

FRIDAY, MARCH 23.

At Philadelphia : " *March* 26.—Friday last [March 23]
the Indian Warriors lately arrived in this city [March 15],
had an audience of the President of the United States."—
Dunlap's American Daily Advertiser.

The Indian warriors received by the President consisted of fifty chiefs
from the Northern tribes of the Six Nations,† among whom was the celebrated orator Sa-go-ya-wat-ha (He keeps them awake), better known as
Red Jacket. In his address to them the President said, " You have been
invited to this place by Colonel Pickering, at my special request, in order
to remove all causes of discontent; to devise and adopt plans to promote
your welfare, and firmly to cement the peace between the United States
and you, so that in future we shall consider ourselves brethren indeed.   I
assure you that I am desirous that a firm peace should exist not only between the United States and the Five Nations, but also between the United

---

* A distinct and separate association from the one of a similar character
referred to under date of February 21, and probably of short duration.

† The Mohawks, Oneidas, Onondagas, Cayugas, Senecas, and Tuscaroras.

States and all the Nations of this land—and that this peace should be
founded upon the principles of justice and humanity, as upon an immovable
rock, that you may partake of all the comforts of this earth, which can be
derived from civilized life, enriched by the possession of industry, virtue
and knowledge."

It was during this visit to Philadelphia that the President presented to
Red Jacket a large silver medal, on the principal side of which was engraved
a design representing Washington in uniform and standing, having just
given the calumet of peace to an Indian chief, who is smoking it. The re-
verse bore the United States shield on the breast of the American eagle displayed, and over his head a glory breaking through a cloud and surrounding
thirteen stars. This silver memento, known as the " Red Jacket Medal,"
which is still in existence, is interesting as being the first presentation of the
kind on the part of the Federal government that we are aware of.

MONDAY, APRIL 2.

At Philadelphia : Under this date, Edward Thornton,
secretary to Mr. George Hammond, the British minister,
in writing to Sir James Bland Burges, drew the following
character of Washington.

" *Philadelphia*, April 2, 1792.—I promised you in a former letter a description of the President of the United States, General Washington. Conscious as I am of the difficulty and danger of describing again what has
been so often described before, I will yet attempt to convey to you my idea
of him. His person is tall and sufficiently graceful ; his face well-formed,
his complexion rather pale, with a mild philosophic gravity in the expression of it. In his air and manner he displays much *natural* dignity ; in his
address he is cold, reserved, and even phlegmatic, though without the least
appearance of haughtiness or ill-nature ; it is the effect, I imagine, of constitutional diffidence. That caution and circumspection which form so striking
and well-known a feature in his military, and indeed in his political character, is very strongly marked in his countenance, for his eyes retire inward
(do you understand me ?) and have nothing of fire of animation or openness
in their expression. If this circumspection is accompanied by discernment
and penetration, as I am informed it is, and as I should be inclined to believe from the judicious choice he has generally made of persons to fill public
stations, he possesses the two great requisites of a statesman, the faculty of
concealing his own sentiments and of discovering those of other men. A
certain degree of indecision, however, a want of vigour and energy, may be
observed in some of his actions, and are indeed the obvious result of too re-
fined caution. He is a man of great but secret ambition, and has sometimes,
I think, condescended to use little arts, and those, too, very shallow ones, to
secure the object of that ambition. He is, I am told, indefatigable in busi-

ness, and extremely clear and systematic in the arrangement of it; his time is regularly divided into certain portions, and the business allotted to any one portion rigidly attended to. Of his private character I can say little positive. I have never heard of any truly noble, generous, or disinterested action of his; he has very few who are on terms of intimate and unreserved friendship; and what is worse he is less beloved in his own State (Virginia) than in any part of the United States. After all, he is a great man, circumstances have made him so; but I cannot help thinking that the misconduct of our commanders has given him a principal part of that greatness." *

SATURDAY, MAY 5.

At Philadelphia: "I am much pleased to hear, that the picture by Colonel Trumbull gives so much satisfaction. The merit of this artist cannot fail to give much pleasure to those of his countrymen, who possess a taste for the fine arts; and I know of no part of the United States, where it would be put to a stronger test than in South Carolina."— *Washington to William Moultrie.*

"The picture by Colonel Trumbull," referred to in the above-quoted letter, was a full-length portrait of Washington in military costume, standing by a horse, painted from life at Philadelphia, in 1792, for the city of Charleston, South Carolina. The picture is still owned by the city. The resolution of the City Council requesting the President to sit to Colonel Trumbull was passed May 7, 1791, at the time he was in Charleston, during his southern tour. The resolution is as follows: "*Resolved* unanimously, that his Honor the Intendant in behalf of the City Council and their constituents, be desired to request of George Washington, Esquire, President of the United States, that he will be pleased, when it is convenient to him, to permit his portrait to be taken by Colonel Trumbull, in order that it may be placed in the City Hall, as the most lasting testimony of their attachment to his person, to commemorate his arrival in the Metropolis of this State, and to hand down to posterity the resemblance of the man to whom they are indebted for the blessings of Peace, Liberty and Independence."

THURSDAY, MAY 10.

Leaves Philadelphia: "*May* 11.—The PRESIDENT of the UNITED STATES, yesterday left this city, on a journey to the Southward."— *The Aurora.*

---

* Selections from the "Letters and Correspondence of Sir James Bland Burges, Bart., sometime Under-Secretary of State for Foreign Affairs," edited by James Hutton. London, 1885.

SATURDAY, MAY 19.

At Mount Vernon: "My family now Howell* is admitted into it, will be *more* than full, and in truth than is
convenient for the House, as Mr. [Bartholomew] Dandridge † (a nephew of Mrs. Washington) is already one of
it, and but one room for him, Howell and another person
to sleep in, all the others being appropriated to public or
private uses."— *Washington to Charles Carter.*

FRIDAY, JUNE 1.

At Philadelphia: "*June* 1.—The President of the United
States has arrived in this city from the Southward."—*Dunlap's American Daily Advertiser.*

"Since his [the President's] return from Virginia, prior to which journey
he had desired me to forward a packet for Sir Isaac Heard ‡ which I addressed to you, or to Mr. Boyd for you, by the ship *George Barclay*, since
that time I have been honoured by an invitation to dine with him. Except
in the honour, believe me there is nothing pleasant in the circumstance, for
it is of all others the most dull and unentertaining. The President's reserve,
the effect partly I think of pride, partly of constitutional diffidence, throws
a restraint on the whole party. The conversation was in consequence uncommonly phlegmatic and trivial, though as the party contracted into a
smaller circle, the Secretary of State's strictures on monarchs began to throw
a certain portion of animation into it. This gentleman (Thomas Jefferson)
is, or affects to be, a most rigid republican; a warm admirer of Thomas
Paine, and a vigorous stickler for revolutions and for the downfall of all
aristocracy. The death of the King of Sweden [Gustavus III.] made it
extremely probable, he said, that there would be a revolution in that country
during the minority of his successor.

"The most dignified character in this country (Washington) has a good
deal of (I cannot call it republicanism, for he affects state, he loves to be
treated with great respect, and (by the by) is not a little flattered, I conceive, by the particular attention of Mr. Hammond not to visit him but in

---

* Howell Lewis, son of Washington's sister Betty.

† Son of Judge Bartholomew Dandridge, a brother of Mrs. Washington.
He died in 1802, while consul at San Domingo.

‡ This packet, under date of May 2, 1792, contained particulars respecting
the Washington family in Virginia, for which Sir Isaac Heard, Garter
Principal King of Arms, had written to the President. This history of the
American branch will be found in Sparks, vol. i. p. 547.

full dress, but of) a certain dislike to monarchy. If Kings were Presidents, or if the President were a King, I believe that aversion would cease. At present he cannot but conceive himself much inferior in dignity and importance to any of them. When he travels, it is in a very *kingly* style; for on his last journey he foundered five horses, and I am informed that his secretaries are not admitted into his carriage, but stand with their horses' bridles in their hands till he is seated, and then mount and ride before his carriage."—*Edward Thornton to Sir James Bland Burges, Bart.*, June 11, 1792.

TUESDAY, JUNE 5.

At Philadelphia : "*June* 5.—We have authority to inform the Public, that the PRESIDENT of the UNITED STATES intends to honor the Theatre with his Presence this Evening." *—*Dunlap's American Daily Advertiser.*

"*June* 8.—We hear, that on Tuesday last [June 5], the President of the United States and his Lady, attended by the Secretary of State, and the Secretary of the Treasury and his Lady, honoured Mr. Pearce with a visit to his Cotton Manufactory [No. 13 Penn Street].—The President attentively viewed the Machinery &c. and saw the business performed in its different branches, which met with his warmest approbation."—*Idem.*

THURSDAY, JUNE 21.

At Philadelphia : "In the course of last winter, I had some of the chiefs of the Cherokees in this city, and in the spring I obtained, with some difficulty indeed, a full representation of the Six Nations to come hither. I have sent all of them away well satisfied, and fully convinced of the justice and good dispositions of this government towards the Indian nations generally. . . . With difficulty still greater, I have brought the celebrated Joseph Brant [Thayendanegea] to this city, with a view to impress him also with the equitable intentions of this government towards all the nations of his color. He only arrived last

* " For the Benefit of Mons. Placide. BY AUTHORITY. By the Old American Company, *at the Theatre in Southwark.* This Evening, June 5, Will be presented a COMEDY, Called—The Beaux Stratagem. End of the Play, DANCING on the TIGHT ROPE, By Monsieur PLACIDE and the LITTLE DEVIL."—*Dunlap's American Daily Advertiser*, June 5.

night,* and I am to give him an audience at twelve this day."—*Washington to Gouverneur Morris.*

The policy of the first President toward the Indians was, if possible, to attach them to the interests of the United States, and at the same time to persuade them to exchange the savage state for one of civilization. To carry out this design it was thought that no better plan could be adopted than to impress upon them the habits of industry and the cultivation of their lands. In concluding an address (January 19, 1791) to Cornplanter, Halftown, and Great-Tree, three chiefs of the Seneca Nation, at that time on a visit to the seat of government, Washington said. " You may, when you return from this city to your own country, mention to your nation my desire to promote their prosperity, by teaching them the use of domestic animals, and the manner that the white people plough and raise so much corn ; and if, upon consideration, it would be agreeable to the nation at large to learn these arts, I will find some means of teaching them at such places within their country as shall be agreed upon."

TUESDAY, JULY 3.

At Philadelphia : " Your letter of the 20th ultimo was presented to me by Mr. Williams, who as a professional man may or may not be, for aught I know, a luminary of the first magnitude. But to be frank, and I hope you will not be displeased with me for being so, I am so heartily tired of the attendance, which, from one cause or another has been given to these people, that it is now more than two years since I have resolved to sit no more for any of them, and have adhered to it, except in instances where it has been requested by public bodies, or for a particular purpose (not of the painters), and could not without offence be refused."—*Washington to Henry Lee.*

Notwithstanding this refusal, Mr. Williams persevered in his purpose, and, acting upon the hint conveyed in the above-quoted letter, offered to compliment the Alexandria Washington Lodge, No. 22, with a portrait of the President, provided the Lodge would apply to him for that purpose.

---

* " *June* 21.—Arrived yesterday Evening in this City, Escorted by Colonel Thomas Proctor, and Major Stagg, Col. Joseph Brandt, the celebrated Chief of the Six Nations of the Northern Indians."—*Dunlap's American Daily Advertiser.*

This offer was brought before the Lodge at a meeting held August 29, 1793, and, being received with favor, the application was ordered to be made.

Being thus armed, Mr. Williams met with better success, and obtained a sitting from the President in September, 1794.* This portrait, a half-length, is still in the possession of the Alexandria Lodge ; it represents Washington as a Mason, with the collar and jewel of a Past Master, and amounts so nearly to a caricature (judging from the print after it by O'Neill) † that it would seem the President, in refusing the original application, must have had some inkling as to the lack of artistic powers on the part of Mr. Williams.

WEDNESDAY, JULY 4.

At Philadelphia : "*July* 5.—Yesterday, being the anniversary of the political birth-day of our country, was ushered in with every demonstration of joy due to the occasion, which gave freedom to a world—Congratulations, becoming freemen governed by equal laws, were expressed with a cordiality, which freemen only can feel—Bells and cannon but feebly proclaimed the sentiments of citizens, who, conscious of the advantages which result from political and religious liberty, revere the return of that day, on which they emerged from the horrors of servitude to the blessings of INDEPENDENCE."—*Dunlap's American Daily Advertiser.*

"Among the offerings to the altar of Freedom—we beheld with sincere satisfaction the homage paid by all orders of men to the Military Defender, and Civil Guardian of his country. Congratulations were offered to the President of the United States by the foreign Ministers—the officers of the militia, and many respectable citizens. The Society of the Cincinnati headed by their President [Thomas Mifflin] and Vice President [Thomas McKean] (the Governor and Chief Justice of the State) went in procession to pay their respects to the President of the United States."—*Idem.*

WEDNESDAY, JULY 11.

Leaves Philadelphia : "*July* 18.—This day se'nnight the President of the United States and his Lady, left this

---

* On the back of the portrait is the following inscription : "His Excellency George Washington Esquire President of the United States, aged 64 —Williams Pinxit ad vivum in Philadelphia, September 18, 1794."

† See Baker's "Engraved Portraits of Washington," p. 101

city, on a tour to Mount Vernon."—*Dunlap's American Daily Advertiser.*

SUNDAY, JULY 29.

At Mount Vernon: "At present all my business public and private is on my own shoulders; the two young gentlemen [Howell Lewis and Bartholomew Dandridge], who came home with me, being on visits to their friends, and my nephew, the Major [George Augustine Washington], too much indisposed to afford me any aid."— *Washington to Alexander Hamilton.*

SUNDAY, AUGUST 5.

At Mount Vernon: "Since the date of my last despatch to you of the 1ˢᵗ instant, I have received your letters of the 26ᵗʰ and 30ᵗʰ ultimo."— *Washington to Alexander Hamilton.*

From Alexander Hamilton's Letter.—" I received the most sincere pleasure at finding in our last conversation, that there was some relaxation in the disposition you had before discovered to decline a reëlection. Since your departure, I have lost no opportunity of sounding the opinions of persons, whose opinions were worth knowing, on these two points; first, the effect of your declining upon the public affairs, and upon your own reputation; secondly, the effect of your continuing, in reference to the declarations you have made of your disinclination to public life. And I can truly say, that I have not found the least difference of sentiment on either point. The impression is uniform, that your declining would be to be deplored as the greatest evil that could befall the country at the present juncture, and as critically hazardous to your own reputation; that your continuance will be justified in the mind of every friend to his country by the evident necessity for it. . . . I trust, Sir, and I pray God, that you will determine to make a further sacrifice of your tranquility and happiness to the public good. I trust, that it need not continue above a year or two more. And I think, that it will be more eligible to retire from office before the expiration of the term of election, than to decline a reëlection."—*Philadelphia,* July 30.

Thomas Jefferson also, in writing to Washington on the same subject, under date of May 23, said, " The confidence of the whole Union is centred in you. Your being at the helm will be more than an answer to every argument which can be used to alarm and lead the people in any quarter into violence or secession. North and south will hang together, if they have you to hang on; and, if the first corrective of a numerous representa-

16

tion should fail in its effect, your presence will give time for trying others not inconsistent with the union and peace of the States."

SUNDAY, AUGUST 26.

At Mount Vernon: "With respect, however, to the interesting subject treated in your letter of the 5th instant, I can express but one sentiment at this time, and that is a wish, a devout one, that, whatever my ultimate determination shall be, it may be for the best. The subject never recurs to my mind but with additional poignancy; and, from the declining state of the health of my nephew, to whom my concerns of a domestic and private nature are entrusted, it comes with aggravated force. But as the All-wise Disposer of events has hitherto watched over my steps, I trust, that, in the important one I may soon be called upon to take, he will mark the course so plainly, as that I cannot mistake the way."— *Washington to Edmund Randolph.*

From Edmund Randolph's Letter.—"Permit me, then, in the fervor of a dutiful and affectionate attachment to you, to beseech you to penetrate the consequences of a dereliction of the reins. The constitution would never have been adopted, but from a knowledge that you had once sanctioned it, and an expectation that you would execute it. It is in a state of probation. The most inauspicious struggles are past, but the public deliberations need stability. You alone can give them stability. You suffered yourself to yield when the voice of your country summoned you to the administration. Should a civil war arise, you cannot stay at home. And how much easier will it be to disperse the factions, which are rushing to this catastrophe, than to subdue them after they shall appear in arms? It is the fixed opinion of the world, that you surrender nothing incomplete."—*Philadelphia, August 5.*

SATURDAY, SEPTEMBER 15.

At Mount Vernon: Issues a proclamation respecting the opposition to the excise laws imposing a tax on domestic distilled spirits.*

---

* The proclamation was sent to Thomas Jefferson, at Monticello, for his signature, and then published at Philadelphia, September 27.

The excise law of the 3d of March, 1791, was extremely offensive to the people in many parts of the country, but especially to the inhabitants of Pennsylvania west of the Alleghany Mountains, whiskey at that time being their most important item of trade. Soon after the publication of the law public meetings were held in the counties of Fayette, Alleghany, Westmoreland, and Washington, at which the law was denounced as inimical to the interests of the country, and at a meeting in Pittsburgh, August 21, 1792, resolutions were passed recommending that no intercourse or dealings should be held with any one who had accepted or might accept an office to carry out the provisions of the act; and that all aid, support, or comfort should be withheld from them. In course of time this movement assumed an organized form, which finally culminated in armed opposition and violence.

The proclamation earnestly admonished and exhorted all persons to refrain and desist from combinations to obstruct the operation of the law, "inasmuch as all lawful ways and means will be strictly put in execution for bringing to justice the infractors thereof and securing obedience thereto."

MONDAY, OCTOBER 1.

At Mount Vernon: "*Georgetown*, October 1.—I called at Gunstonhall, the proprietor [George Mason] just recovering from a dreadful attack of the colic. . . . I proceeded to Mount Vernon & had a full free & confidential conversation with the President. . . . He declares himself quite undecided about retiring, desirous to do so, yet not decided if strong motives against it exist."—*Thomas Jefferson to James Madison.*

SUNDAY, OCTOBER 7.

At Mount Vernon: "As Mrs. Washington and myself expect to set out to-morrow for Philadelphia, I have taken advantage of the good opportunity afforded by Mr. Robert Lewis of sending Harriot [Washington] to Fredericksburg."—*Washington to Mrs. Betty Lewis.*

SATURDAY, OCTOBER 13.

At Philadelphia: "*October* 15.—The President of the United States, his Lady, and Family, arrived here on Saturday afternoon [October 13], from Mount Vernon."—*Dunlap's American Daily Advertiser.*

" In the year 1790, the Federal Government removed from New York to Philadelphia, for a ten years residence, and to give time to prepare the City of Washington for a permanent location. I came two years after, with my father's family, to fix myself for life in Philadelphia. Living in the same town, I had frequent opportunities of seeing the President, and attending his reception days in the morning, and those of Mrs. Washington in the evening: a pleasure of which I availed myself for several years; and, at the opening of Congress, which the President did in person, I was always a spectator. On these occasions he went in state, drawn in a coach by four horses; and taking the Vice President's chair in the Senate Chamber, where the House of Representatives was assembled, he read his Speech His successor, John Adams, followed this custom. But Jefferson, dispensing with personal attendance, sent his speech, in the form of a Message, to both houses; a mode which has been in use ever since; and is, no doubt an improvement, because it has put an end to long and angry speeches in each house, when the answer to the President was under debate. A message requiring no answer, that cause of contention, often protracted for days, was happily laid aside.

" Washington's stables in Minor Street,* contained some of the finest horses in the Union, both for carriage and saddle. The sixteen stalls were generally filled. He inspected them every morning, and thus insured good grooming and care. Those stables were shown by me to all strangers under my guidance; being, as I always thought, one of the most attractive sights in the City. I have seen the President in his large white coach start from his door, with six of those splendid horses, driven by a coachman and two postillions, suitably dressed in livery. His rides for health and recreation were very often to Belmont, the country seat of Judge Richard Peters, who had been his friend and intimate acquaintance during the long war of the Revolution. The gardens at Belmont, on the right bank of the Schuylkill about five miles from town, are remarkable for their umbrageous and retired walks; where the Fir-trees, Hemlocs and Pines, cast their deep shades, from trees of one hundred years growth. There it was the great man sought relaxation from the cares of Government. A tree must still stand in those grounds which he planted with his own hands; it was pointed out to me by one of the family. . . .

" Washington's personal presence was majestic. Six feet high and finely proportioned; no individual of his day was so remarkable for dignity and grace in deportment when in public. At the receptions, his manners were so engaging and affable, yet exercised with discrimination, that it pleased and contented every one. Sir Robert Liston, the British Minister, was so surprized, that he said to his friends: 'I have read much about this great man; but no passage in his history prepared me to see such commanding

---

* A small street extending from Fifth to Sixth Street, directly in the rear of the President's house.

dignity in person and behavior.' Beloved Man! Can the bosom of an American suppress its pride when your story is told? Can it calm the glowing,—the tender affection, the heart-felt gratitude, which the recollection of your services awakens? No, Never! Never!" *—*MS. of Samuel Breck.*

TUESDAY, NOVEMBER 6.

At Philadelphia: "*November* 7.—Yesterday the President of the United States met both Houses of the National Legislature in the Senate Chamber and delivered his speech." †—*Dunlap's American Daily Advertiser.*

Dr. Ashbel Green, chaplain of Congress from November 5, 1792, until the seat of government was removed from Philadelphia to Washington City, has left us in his "Reminiscences" the following description of Washington's manner of delivering his speech at the opening of Congress:

"There was more of the indefinable quality called *presence* in President Washington than any other person I have ever known. In his general manners he was eminently courteous and kind; and yet to the last, I could never speak to him without feeling a degree of embarrassment such as I have never felt in the presence of any other individual, man or woman, with whom I was well acquainted. In his observance of appointments he was punctiliously exact. After I was chaplain, I believe I was present at all his speeches on the opening of a session of congress; for the custom of sending a message to congress, which was introduced by Mr. Jefferson, was then unknown. Twelve o'clock at noon, was the usual hour agreed on for his opening speech, and in no instance did he fail in a punctual attendance at that hour; indeed, he commonly crossed the threshold of the door where the congress sat, exactly when the clock was striking the hour of twelve. The two houses always assembled to receive him in the senate chamber.‡

* From a "Sketch of General George Washington," by Samuel Breck, of Philadelphia, forming part of the contents of a manuscript volume entitled "Sketches of Members of the American Philosophical Society personally known to the Writer." The sketches, twenty in number, were written by Mr. Breck in the summer of 1862. Samuel Breck was born in Boston, July 17, 1771, and died at Philadelphia, September 1, 1862. He was a member of the Pennsylvania Legislature for many years, and a member of Congress 1823-25.

† "*November* 6, 1792.—About noon fifteen guns were fired at corner of Ninth and Market Streets because the President delivered his address to Congress, which met yesterday."—*Diary of Jacob Hiltzheimer.*

‡ This is an error. On three occasions—November 19, 1794, December 8, 1795, and December 7, 1796—the President read his speech to Congress in the hall of the House of Representatives.

When he entered, all the members of both houses rose from their seats, and stood up until he had taken his seat, which he did immediately after bowing to his audience. When he was seated, he looked around on the audience for a minute or two, and then took out his spectacles from a common red morocco case, and laid them on his knee, and then took from his side-pocket his written speech. After putting on his spectacles he rose and began his address, which he read closely. He read distinctly and audibly, but in no other respect was his reading excellent. Dr. Witherspoon had heard George the Third deliver one of his speeches to the British parliament, which he said was in the very best style of elocution. This could not be said of the speeches of Washington; his elocution had no glaring fault, and no high excellence."

FRIDAY, NOVEMBER 9.

At Philadelphia: "*November* 10.—Yesterday (Friday) the Members of the Senate waited on the President of the United States, at his own house, with an answer to his speech to both Houses of Congress."—*Dunlap's American Daily Advertiser.*

SUNDAY, NOVEMBER 11.

At Philadelphia: "The mulberry trees may be planted about in clumps, as mentioned in my letter by last post to the gardener. They are not trimmed, because, as I am informed, these trees may be propagated by cuttings from them, and save me the trouble and expense of sending more from this place. With respect to the shrubs from Mr. Bartram's botanical garden, directions at the foot of the list are given so fully, as to render it unnecessary to add aught concerning them in this letter: but the grapes the gardener must take particular care of, as they are of a very fine kind."— *Washington to Anthony Whiting.*

While Washington was absent from home, discharging the duties of President of the United States, it was his custom to exact from the manager at Mount Vernon, once in each week, a full report of the proceedings on all the farms. These were regularly answered each week by the President, and sometimes oftener. His letters frequently filled two or three sheets closely written. The importance he attached to these letters, and his diligence in preparing them, may be understood from the fact that he first made rough drafts, which were copied out by himself in a fair hand before they were sent off. Press copies were then taken, which he preserved.

MONDAY, NOVEMBER 12.

At Philadelphia: On this day the Speaker (Jonathan Trumbull), preceded by the Sergeant-at-Arms and attended by the members of the House of Representatives, waited on the President with an answer to his speech to both Houses of Congress.

THURSDAY, DECEMBER 13.

At Philadelphia: " *December* 13.—The President called on me to see the model and drawings of some mills for sawing stone. After showing them, he in the course of a subsequent conversation asked me if there was not some good manufactories of porcelain in Germany; that he was in want of table china, and had been speaking to Mr. Shaw, who was going to the East Indies to bring him a set, but he found that it would not come till *he should no longer be in a situation to want it.* He took occasion a second time to ob- serve that Shaw said it would be two years at least before he could have the china here, before which time he said he should be where he should not want it. I think he asked the question about the manufactories in Germany merely to have an indirect opportunity of telling me he meant to retire, and within the limits of two years."—*Jefferson Anas.*

1793.

At Philadelphia: "*January* 9.—With three of my daughters and some of their friends, went on the roof of the small building Southwest corner Ninth and Market Streets and saw Mr. Blanchard take his aerial flight out of the prison yard [Sixth and Walnut Streets]. Cannon fired from daylight to the time of his departure, between ten and eleven o'clock A.M."—*Diary of Jacob Hiltzheimer.*

"*January* 10.—Mr. BLANCHARD, the bold AERONAUT, agreeably to his advertisement, at five minutes past ten o'clock yesterday morning rose with a BALOON from the Prison Court in this city, in presence of an immense concourse of spectators, there assembled on the occasion. . . . As soon as the clock had struck 10 everything being punctually ready, Mr. Blanchard took a respectful leave of all the spectators, and received from the hands of the President a paper,* at the same time the President spoke a few words to this bold adventurer, who immediately leap'd into his boat which was painted blue and spangled; the baloon was of a yellowish color'd-silk highly varnished, over which there was a strong net work—Mr. Blanchard was dressed in a plain blue suit, a cock'd hat and white feathers. . . .

"About half after 6 o'clock last evening we were happy to meet Mr. Blanchard again in this city going to pay his respects to the President of the United States.—He informed us, that his aerial voyage lasted forty-six minutes, in which time he ran over a space of more than 15 miles and then descended a little to the eastward of Woodbury in the state of New Jersey—where he took a carriage and returned to Cooper's ferry—and was at the President's, as we have already mentioned at half past six o'clock last evening."—*Dunlap's American Daily Advertiser.*

* The paper received from the President was in the nature of an endorsement or protection, with a request that the residents of the locality in which Mr. Blanchard might land from his aerial flight would render him such assistance as was in their power.

248

SATURDAY, JANUARY 19.

At Philadelphia: "*January 19.*—Dined with the President of the United States on Market Street, with our Speaker [Gerardus Wynkoop] and eighteen members of the [Pennsylvania] House [of Representatives]. I cannot help remarking the ease and great sociability shown to all by the President."—*Diary of Jacob Hiltzheimer.*

SUNDAY, JANUARY 20.

At Philadelphia: " I have been favored with your letter of the 6th instant, congratulatory on my reëlection to the chair of government. A mind must be insensible indeed, not to be gratefully impressed by so distinguished and honorable a testimony of public approbation and confidence; and as I suffered my name to be contemplated on this occasion, it is more than probable that I should, for a moment, have experienced chagrin, if my reëlection had not been by a pretty respectable vote. But to say I feel pleasure from the prospect of commencing another tour of duty would be a departure from truth."—*Washington to Henry Lee.*

At the second election for President and Vice-President under the Constitution, fifteen States chose electors, Vermont and Kentucky having been admitted into the Union,—the former on March 4, 1791, and the latter on June 1, 1792. Washington received one hundred and thirty-two votes, the full vote of the college. John Adams, having received the second highest number of votes (seventy-seven), was declared to be Vice-President.

THURSDAY, JANUARY 31.

At Philadelphia: " If I had words that could convey to you an adequate idea of my feelings on the present situation of the Marquis de Lafayette, this letter would appear to you in a different garb. The sole object in writing to you now is, to inform you that I have deposited in the hands of Mr. Nicholas Van Staphorst, of Amsterdam, two thousand three hundred and ten guilders, Holland currency, equal to two hundred guineas, subject to your orders.

"This sum is, I am certain, the least I am indebted for services rendered to me by the Marquis de Lafayette, of which I never yet have received the account."— *Washington to the Marchioness de Lafayette.*

The Marquis de Lafayette, who on the declaration of war by France against Austria (April 20, 1792) was in command of the Army of the Centre, fifty-two thousand strong, was at his camp at Maubeuge at the time of the insurrection of June 20, 1792. Having denounced the dangerous policy of the Jacobins, and refusing, after the revolution of August 10, to obey the orders of the Assembly, he was removed from the command and his impeachment decided upon. He fled into Belgium, was taken prisoner by the Austrians, and handed over by them to the Prussians, by whom he was imprisoned first at Wesel, and afterward (March, 1793) at Magdeburg. The marchioness was retained a prisoner at Paris, but was subsequently permitted to live on the family estate in Auvergne (Chavaniac), under the responsibility of the municipality of the village.

After a year's incarceration at Magdeburg, Lafayette was transferred to Austria (May, 1794) for safe-keeping, and passed three years and more in a loathsome dungeon at Olmutz, where he was treated with barbarous cruelty. With much difficulty, his wife and two daughters, Anastasie and Virginia, got permission in October, 1795, to share his captivity. Much sympathy was felt for him in the United States and in England. In Parliament, Fox, Wilberforce, and Sheridan were active in his behalf, and Washington wrote (May 15, 1796) to the emperor, Francis II., asking that he might be allowed to come on parole to the United States. He was at length set free, September 19, 1797, by the victories of Bonaparte.

FRIDAY, FEBRUARY 15.

At Philadelphia: Is waited upon by a joint committee of both Houses of Congress and notified of his unanimous re-election to the office of PRESIDENT OF THE UNITED STATES.

The committee was composed of Rufus King, of New York; Ralph Izard, of South Carolina; and Caleb Strong, of Massachusetts, on the part of the Senate; and William Smith, of South Carolina; James Madison, of Virginia; and John Lawrence, of New York, on the part of the House of Representatives.

FRIDAY, FEBRUARY 22.

At Philadelphia: " *February* 23.— *Yesterday* (February 22) being the Anniversary of the *Birth-Day* of our beloved fellow citizen, GEORGE WASHINGTON, *President of the United States of America,* who was born on the 11th of February 1732, old stile: Capt. Fisher's volunteer company of Artillery & three companies of Light Infantry, paraded at the State house, from whence they marched to the Artillery ground, and proceeded to the corner of Ninth and Market streets where they fired 15 rounds, and gave three cheers; afterwards, they marched down Market street, and gave a salute as they passed the President's house; from whence proceeding down Market to Third street, they returned to the State House."—*Dunlap's American Daily Advertiser.*

"All the shipping in the Harbour had their colours hoisted out, and the bells of Christ church rang peals every half hour, during the day. Most of the Members of both houses of Congress, and many hundreds of respectable citizens, waited on the President, to pay him a visit of personal respect, & offer their sincere congratulations on the occasion. Indeed every possible testimony of joy was expressed throughout the city of Philadelphia; and the beauty of the weather added greatly to the scene, by seeming to welcome the day on which our trusty Patriot, Victorious General, and excellent Chief Magistrate, entered his SIXTY SECOND YEAR. In the evening there was an elegant ball at Oeller's Hotel; and in many other places the day was closed with conviviality and heart-felt rejoicings.

"Disclaiming as we do, all pretensions to adulation, it was impossible for us, it is impossible for any American, or perhaps for the people of any nation upon earth, to refrain from expressing a degree of satisfaction at the return of every revolving year that prolongs the life of a man, whose virtues have raised him to the very highest pitch of esteem.

"'Oft as this auspicious day,
Sacred to mem'ry, shall return,
Let Freedom pour the grateful lay,
And haughty Tyrants mourn!'"—*Idem.*

MONDAY, MARCH 4.

At Philadelphia: "*March* 5.—Yesterday, our beloved and venerable GEORGE WASHINGTON, came to the Senate Chamber of Congress, and took the usual oath of office, which was administered to him by Judge Cushing, at noon, in presence of an immense concourse of his fellow citizens, members of both Houses of the United States, Legislature,

and several foreign ministers, consuls, &c.—There was likewise an assemblage of ladies, attending on this solemn occasion, and the day was extremely serene; for, Providence
has always smiled on the day of this man, and on the
glorious cause which he has ever espoused, of LIBERTY and
EQUALITY.

" After taking the oath, the President retired, as he had
come, without pomp or ceremony; but on his departure
from the House, the people could no longer refrain obeying
the genuine dictates of their hearts, and they saluted him
with three cheers."—*Dunlap's American Daily Advertiser.*

" *March* 5, 1793.—I was present yesterday at the ceremony of adminis-
tering the oath of office to Mr. Washington on his re-election for the next
four years as President of the United States. It was administered by one
of the Judges of the Supreme Court in the Senate Chamber, in the presence
of the Senators and as many individuals as could be crowded into the room.
The President first made a short speech, expressive of his sense of the high
honour conferred on him by his re-election. There was nothing particular
in the ceremony itself. . . .

" There was one thing, which I observed yesterday in the Senate Chamber, which, if not accidental, will serve to mark the character of the people,
though it was trifling in itself. The portraits of the King and Queen of
France, which were presented, I believe during the war, were covered with a
curtain, a circumstance which was not the case most certainly when I have
been there on former occasions. Alas! poor Louis!

<blockquote>
"' Deserted at his utmost need
By those his former bounty fed!'
</blockquote>

" The French, those murderous imitators will, I fear, supply the rest of
this passage, and in the very spirit, too, which actuated the assassins of the
unfortunate Darius. I don't know whether I mentioned to you formerly
that the key of the Bastile, given to a certain great man here by La Fayette, is hung up in a glass frame in the principal room of the great man's
house, with an engraving of Louis XVI., *le patriote Roi des Français,* opposite to it. In the drawing-room of Mr. Jefferson there are three busts.—
of Franklin, Paul Jones, and La Fayette, three gentlemen, the first of
whom had talents without virtue, the second *deserved* hanging, and the last,
not improbably, may meet with that fate. The French principles are gaining ground fast in this country; you will have heard of their rejoicings at
the late successes of the French; you will have heard of the attacks upon
the President himself for his levees and other *appendages of monarchy and*

aristocracy; the name of 'citizen' is bandied about, and in the course of last
month a motion was made in the House of Representatives, in the very
spirit of Cromwell and democracy, that the mace of that House should be
broken up as a useless bauble, and the silver, of which part of it is composed, sent to the public mint.   The mace is somewhat in the form of the
ancient Roman Fasces; it consists of thirteen arrows bound together, and an
eagle on the top."—*Edward Thornton to Sir James Bland Burges, Bart.*

SATURDAY, MARCH 23.

At Philadelphia: "If it can be esteemed a happiness to
live in an age productive of great and interesting events,
we of the present age are very highly favored.   The ra-
pidity of national revolutions appears no less astonishing,
than their magnitude.   In what they will terminate is
known only to the Great Ruler of events; and, confiding
in his wisdom and goodness, we may safely trust the issue
to him, without perplexing ourselves to seek for that, which
is beyond human ken; only taking care to perform the parts
assigned to us, in a way that reason and our own consciences
approve."— *Washington to David Humphreys.*

SUNDAY, MARCH 24.

At Philadelphia: "I shall leave this on Wednesday next,
so as to be at Georgetown on the Monday following (the
first of April); and if not detained there by business, shall
be at Mount Vernon the day after.   I shall take Osborne
and the two postillions with me, and eight horses."—
Washington to Anthony Whiting.

WEDNESDAY, MARCH 27.

Leaves Philadelphia: "*April* 1.—The President of the
United States left town last Wednesday afternoon [March
27], on a visit to Mount Vernon."—*Dunlap's American Daily
Advertiser.*

TUESDAY, APRIL 9.

At Mount Vernon: "On Thursday next [April 11] at
one o'clock, I mean to pay the last respect to the remains

of my deceased Nephew—by having the funeral obsequies
performed. . . . The funeral will be in the presence of a
few friends only."— *Washington to David Stuart.*

The nephew whose death is referred to was Major George Augustine
Washington, son of the President's brother Charles, who had been living
at Mount Vernon since 1784, and had taken charge of the estate as manager
in April, 1789. His health had been failing for some time from a pul-
monary affection. Major Washington served in the Revolution as an aide
to General Lafayette in his Virginia campaign.

FRIDAY, APRIL 12.

At Mount Vernon: " War having actually commenced
between France and Great Britain, it behoves the government of this country to use every means in its power to
prevent the citizens thereof from embroiling us with either
of those powers, by endeavouring to maintain a strict neutrality. I therefore require, that you will give the subject
mature consideration, that such measures as shall be deemed
most likely to effect this desirable purpose may be adopted
without delay; for I have understood, that vessels are
already designated as privateers, and are preparing accordingly. . . . I shall set out to-morrow [for Philadelphia]
but will leave it to the advices, which I may receive to-night
by the post, to determine whether it is to be by the most
direct route, or by the one I proposed to come, that is, by
Reading &c."— *Washington to Thomas Jefferson.*

WEDNESDAY, APRIL 17.

At Philadelphia: " *April* 19.—The *President* of the
United States arrived in town, from his southern tour last
Wednesday [April 17] in good health."—*Dunlap's American
Daily Advertiser.*

" My visit to Mount Vernon, intended to be short when I set out, was
curtailed by the declaration of war by France against Great Britain and
Holland; for I foresaw, in the moment information of that event came to
me at that place, the necessity for announcing the disposition of this country towards the belligerent powers, and the propriety of restraining, as far

as a proclamation would do it, our citizens from taking part in the contest."
— *Washington to Henry Lee*, May 6.

FRIDAY, APRIL 19.

At Philadelphia : A Cabinet meeting at the President's house. Present, Thomas Jefferson, Alexander Hamilton, General Knox, and Edmund Randolph, Attorney-General. It was agreed unanimously, " That a proclamation shall issue forbidding our citizens to take part in any hostilities on the seas, with or against any of the belligerent powers ; and warning them against carrying to any such powers any of those articles deemed contraband, according to the modern usage of nations ; and enjoining them from all acts and proceedings inconsistent with the duties of a friendly nation towards those at war." It was also unanimously agreed that a minister from the Republic of France should be received.

MONDAY, APRIL 22.

At Philadelphia : Issues a proclamation, reciting " that a state of war exists between Austria, Prussia, Sardinia, Great Britain, and the United Netherlands, on the one part, and France on the other ; and the duty and interest of the United States require, that they should with sincerity and good faith adopt and pursue a conduct friendly and impartial towards the belligerent powers ;

" I have therefore thought fit by these presents to declare the disposition of the United States to observe the conduct aforesaid towards those powers respectively, and to exhort and warn the citizens of the United States carefully to avoid all acts and proceedings whatsoever, which may in any manner tend to contravene such disposition," etc.

The proclamation of neutrality may be considered, in regard to its character and consequences, one of the most important measures of Washington's administration. It was the commencement of that system to which the American government afterward inflexibly adhered, and to which much of the national prosperity is to be ascribed. But this act, founded on the clearest principles of justice and policy, was at variance with the prejudices, the feelings, and the passions of a large portion of the citizens, blinded for the time by their partiality for republican France and antipathy for their ancient enemy. It also presented the first occasion which was thought a fit one for openly assaulting a character around which the affections of the people had thrown an armor heretofore deemed sacred, and for directly criminating the conduct of the President himself. It was stigmatized as a royal edict, an unwarrantable and daring assumption of executive power, and an open manifestation by the President and his political friends of partiality for England and hostility to France.

Washington saw that a deadly blow was aimed at his influence and his administration, and that both were at hazard; but he was convinced that neutrality was the true national policy, and he resolved to maintain it whatever might be his immediate loss of popular favor. Under date of July 21 he wrote to Henry Lee, "But in what will this abuse terminate? For the result. as it respects myself, I care not; for I have a consolation within, that no earthly efforts can deprive me of, and that is, that neither ambitious nor interested motives have influenced my conduct. The arrows of malevolence, therefore, however barbed and well pointed, never can reach the most vulnerable part of me; though, whilst I am *up* as a *mark*, they will be continually aimed. The publications in Freneau's and Bache's papers* are outrages on common decency; and they progress in that style, in proportion as their pieces are treated with contempt, and are passed by in silence, by those at whom they are aimed."

WEDNESDAY, APRIL 24.

At Philadelphia: "*April 24.—*After dinner Mr. and Mrs. Barge and my three daughters went to Rickett's circus [Market and Twelfth Streets]. General Washington and family were present."—*Diary of Jacob Hiltzheimer.*

"*April 30.—*Took two men down to the meadow [below the city] to repair fence and gate-posts, and while there President Washington came to see his mare [on pasture]."—*Diary of Jacob Hiltzheimer.*

SUNDAY, MAY 5.

At Philadelphia: "In the conversation you may have with a certain gentleman [Viscount de Noailles] to-day, I pray you to intimate to him gently and delicately, that, if the letters or papers, which he has to present, are, know-

---

* *The National Gazette* and *The Aurora.*

ingly to him, of a nature which relates to public matters, and not particularly addressed to me, or if he has any verbal communications to make of a similar kind, I had rather they should come through the proper channel. Add thereto, generally, that the peculiar situation of European affairs at this moment, my good wishes for his nation aggregately, my regard for those of it in particular, with whom I have had the honor of an acquaintance, my anxious desire to keep this country in peace, and the delicacy of my situation, render a circumspect conduct indispensably necessary on my part."— *Washington to Alexander Hamilton.*

The Viscount de Nouilles, who married a sister of the Marchioness de Lafayette, had served with distinction in the United States during the Revolution, and at Yorktown was appointed, in conjunction with Colonel John Laurens, to arrange with Lord Cornwallis the details of the capitulation. Having engaged with enthusiasm in the early movements of the French Revolution, and acted a conspicuous part, he at length found himself in a proscribed party, and was obliged to flee from his country to escape the rage of the contending factions. He passed by way of England to this country, and arrived at Philadelphia on May 3, 1793. The President exercised much caution in receiving any of the French refugees, as is indicated by the above-quoted letter, and De Nouilles with others never saw him but in public. Louis Marie, Viscount de Noailles, resided for some time in Philadelphia. He died at Havana, Cuba, January 9, 1804.

FRIDAY, MAY 17.

At Philadelphia: Receives an address from the merchants and traders of Philadelphia, expressing the high sense they entertained of the wisdom and goodness which dictated the late proclamation of neutrality, and their determination to pay the strictest regard to it.

To this address, which was signed by about three hundred of the principal merchants and traders of the city of Philadelphia, the President made the following reply : " Fully persuaded that the happiness and best interests of the people of the United States will be promoted by observing a strict neutrality in the present contest among the powers of Europe, it gives me pleasure to learn that the measures which I have taken to declare to the world, their disposition on this head, has given general satisfaction to the citizens of Pennsylvania. The friends of humanity will deprecate war

17

wherever it may appear: and we have experienced enough of its evils in this country, to know, that it should not be wantonly or unnecessarily entered upon. I trust, therefore, that the good citizens of the United States will shew to the world, that they have as much wisdom in preserving peace at this critical juncture as they have heretofore displayed valour in defending their just rights."

SATURDAY, MAY 18.

At Philadelphia: "*May* 20.—Last Saturday afternoon [May 18] at two o'clock Mr. Genet, being introduced by Mr. Jefferson, Secretary of State, produced his credentials to the President; he was received and acknowledged as Minister Plenipotentiary from the Republic of France to the United States of America."—*Dunlap's American Daily Advertiser.*

Edmund Charles Genet, "Citizen Genet," who succeeded M. Ternant as minister from France to the United States, arrived at Charleston, South Carolina, in the French frigate "L'Embuscade," April 8, 1793, and was received with open arms by the citizens. Bearing secret instructions to foment a war between this country and Great Britain, he began at once to fit out privateers to prey on British commerce, and gave authority to every French consul in America to constitute a Court of Admiralty to dispose of prizes brought into American ports by French cruisers. Genet travelled by land to Philadelphia, where, as well as on his route, his reception was of the most enthusiastic character; and although momentarily subdued by the calmness and dignity of the President, when presenting his credentials, he soon resumed his former attitude, and continued his violation of the sovereignty of the United States by commissioning privateers. When reminded of this offence by the Secretary of State, Genet denied the doctrine of neutrality as contrary to right, justice, and the laws of nations, and threatened to appeal from the President to the people, and actually undertook in July to fit out a privateer at Philadelphia in defiance of the government. It was a vessel captured by "L'Embuscade," the "Little Sarah," named by him "Le Petit Démocrat." Matters having thus reached a point where forbearance toward the insolent French minister was no longer required by the most exacting courtesy, the President called the Cabinet together on the first day of August, when it was decided that the French government should be requested to recall its minister, because he was offensive to that of the United States. This was acceded to, and M. Fauchet was appointed in his place, who arrived in February, 1794. Mr. Genet did not return to France, and, marrying the daughter of Governor George Clinton, became a naturalized citizen of the United States. He was twice married, his second wife being a daughter of Samuel Osgood, the first Postmaster-General under the Constitution.

MONDAY, JUNE 24.

Leaves Philadelphia: "*June* 25.—Yesterday the President of the United States left this city on a visit to his seat in Mount Vernon."—*Dunlap's American Daily Advertiser.*

SUNDAY, JUNE 30.

At Mount Vernon: "I expect to return to the seat of government about the 10th of next month."—*Washington to Thomas Jefferson.*

MONDAY, JULY 1.

At Mount Vernon: "The very polite invitation which you have given me, in the name of the citizens of Alexandria, to celebrate with them the approaching anniversary of American Independence, is received by me as a mark of attention meriting my warmest thanks; and as the best proof I can give of my feelings on the occasion will be to accept the invitation, I shall accordingly have the pleasure of meeting them at Alexandria on the 4th inst."—*Washington to the Committee on Celebration.*

THURSDAY, JULY 4.

At Alexandria: Participates in the celebration of the day, and dines with the citizens of Alexandria.

"*Alexandria*, July 11.—On a signal-gun from the camp of captain Hannah, the day was ushered in by 15 rounds from two 12 pounders under the direction of Mr. Isaac Roberdeau—these were returned by 15 from the camp. At noon 15 from a six-pounder, commanded by captain Hannah, were answered by 15 from the 12 pounders. Then divine service began in the Protestant Episcopal Church, where the President of the United States attended, and a discourse suited to the occasion was delivered by the Rev. Mr. Davis.

"At 3 o'clock the company, to the number of one hundred and ten, sat down to an elegant dinner in Mr. Wise's long room. . . . The President gave the toast ' Prosperity to the town of Alexandria;' and, after drinking the health of the company, retired. . . .

" Words cannot express the happiness of the company; which was increased by beholding the pleasure that beamed on the countenance of their illustrious and revered neighbour. His extraordinary talents and virtues had contributed, in a signal manner, to the attainment of that blessing which they were now assembled to commemorate. Him, therefore they could not but contemplate, in some sort, as the Father of the Feast—'The feast of Reason and the flow of Soul.' "—*Dunlap's American Daily Advertiser*, July 18.

THURSDAY, JULY 11.

At Philadelphia: "*July* 12.—Yesterday forenoon the President of the United States arrived in town from the Southward."—*Dunlap's American Daily Advertiser.*

" My journey to and from Mount Vernon, was rapid, and as short as I could make it. It was occasioned by the unexpected death of Mr. Whiting, my manager, at a critical season for the business with which he was intrusted." *—Washington to Henry Lee*, July 21.

SATURDAY, JULY 13.

At Philadelphia: "*July* 13.—Went to see Mr. Ricketts ride, and saw there the President and his lady."—*Diary of Jacob Hiltzheimer.*

" *July* 16.—The benefit to the poor, last Saturday [July 13], by Mr. Ricketts, produced 430 dollars, which is intended as a beginning for establishing a *Fund*, to be placed in the hands of the Corporation, for the purpose of laying in *Fire-Wood*, to be distributed in the winter to such poor families as may require it.† The appearance of the President of the United States, with his family, amongst his fellow-citizens, always adds to the satisfaction we receive from those innocent public amusements, and it was rendered particularly agreeable by a handsome compliment, very genteely

* Anthony Whiting died in the early part of June. He was succeeded as manager of the Mount Vernon farms by William Pearce, who took charge in October.

† The amount realized on this occasion, with an additional sum of two hundred and one dollars derived from a performance of a like character by Mr. Ricketts, on the 19th of May, 1796, now forms, together with other donations, what is known as the *City Fuel Fund* of six thousand seven hundred dollars principal, the interest of which is used for supplying the deserving poor with coal during the winter.

tho' indirectly, paid by Mr. Ricketts, who being obliged in the middle of the performance to drink a glass of wine, was required by one of his people to give a toast; He instantly drank off a bumper to the health of *The Man of the People.* This operated like electricity, in producing a general clap of applause, accompanied by a huzza from every part of the Circus."
—*Dunlap's American Daily Advertiser.*

SUNDAY, JULY 21.

At Philadelphia: "I should have thanked you at an earlier period for your obliging letter of the 14th ultimo, had it not come to my hands a day or two only before I set out for Mount Vernon, and at a time when I was much hurried, and indeed, very much perplexed with the disputes, memorials, and what not, with which the government were pestered by one or the other of the petulant representatives of the powers at war, and because, since my return to this city, nine days ago, I have been more than ever overwhelmed with their complaints. In a word, the trouble they give is hardly to be described."— *Washington to Henry Lee.*

MONDAY, JULY 29.

At Philadelphia: "*July* 31.—Died on Sunday last [July 28], after a short but severe illness, universally lamented, Mrs. Mary Lear—the amiable and accomplished wife of TOBIAS LEAR, Esq. Secretary to the President of the United States—and on Monday her Funeral was attended by a train of unaffected mourners, to Christ Church burying ground, where her remains were entombed!

"Youth, Beauty, Virtue, Loveliness and Grace, in vain would soothe 'the dull cold ear of Death.'"—*Dunlap's American Daily Advertiser.*

"*July* 30.—We have lately had a very affecting death in this city. Mrs. Lear, the wife of Mr. Lear, the President's Secretary, died on Sunday last, after a short but very severe illness. She was only 23, and beloved and respected by all who knew her, and she and her husband had been fond of each other from infancy. He attended the funeral himself, and so did the President and Mrs. Washington. Mr. Hamilton, Mr. Jefferson, General

Knox, Judge Wilson, Judge Peters, and myself were pall-bearers."—*James Iredell* * *to Mrs. Tredwell.*

THURSDAY, AUGUST 1.

At Philadelphia: A Cabinet meeting to take into consideration the conduct of M. Genet, and what course should be pursued in reference thereto. It was unanimously agreed that a full statement of his actions should be made in a letter to Gouverneur Morris (minister to France), that in the letter his recall should be required, and that his correspondence with the Secretary of State should be communicated through Mr. Morris to the Executive Council of France. It was also taken into consideration whether a publication of the whole correspondence and a statement of the proceedings should not be made by way of appeal to the people. The meeting adjourned without coming to any conclusion on the latter proposition.

August 2.—An adjourned meeting of the Cabinet. On the question of the appeal to the people coming up, Mr. Jefferson, after referring to the discussion thereon, and giving his reasons for opposing such action, makes the following statement in his *Anas:* "The President manifestly inclined to the appeal to the people. Knox, in a foolish incoherent sort of a speech, introduced the pasquinade lately printed, called the funeral of George W——n, and James W——n [Judge Wilson, of the Supreme Court], King and Judge, &c., where the President was placed on a guillotine. The President was much inflamed; got into one of those passions when he cannot command himself; ran on much on the personal abuse which had been bestowed on him; defied any man on earth to produce one single act of his since he had been in the government which was not done on the purest motives; that he had never repented but once the having slipped the moment of resigning his office, and that was every moment since; that *by God* he had rather be in his grave than in his present situation; that he had rather be on his farm than to be made *Emperor of the world;* and yet that they were charging him with wanting to be a King. That that *rascal Freneau* sent him three of his papers every day, as if he thought he would become the distributor of his papers; that he could see in this nothing but an impudent design to insult him: he ended in this high tone. There was

---

* Associate Justice of the Supreme Court of the United States from February 10, 1790, until his death, October 20, 1799.

a pause. Some difficulty in resuming our question; it was, however, after a little while, presented again, and he said there seemed to be no necessity for deciding it now; the propositions before agreed on might be put into a train of execution, and perhaps events would show whether the appeal would be necessary or not."

MONDAY, AUGUST 26.

At Philadelphia: "I expect to be at Mount Vernon about the 20th of next Month for a stay of 8 or 10 days." — *Washington to William Pearce.*

MONDAY, SEPTEMBER 9.

At Philadelphia: "I think it would not be prudent either for you, or the clerks in your office, or the office itself, to be too much exposed to the malignant fever, which, by well authenticated report, is spreading through the city. The means to avoid it, your own judgment under existing circumstances must dictate."— *Washington to Henry Knox.*

TUESDAY, SEPTEMBER 10.

Leaves Philadelphia: "*September* 11.—Yesterday morning the President of the United States set off from this city for Mount Vernon."—*Dunlap's American Daily Advertiser.*

SATURDAY, SEPTEMBER 14.

At Mount Vernon: "We remained in Philadelphia until the 10th instant.—It was my wish to have continued there longer; but as Mrs. Washington was unwilling to leave me surrounded by the malignant fever which prevailed, I could not think of hazarding her, and the Children any longer by *my* continuance in the City, the house in which we lived being, in a manner blockaded, by the disorder, and was becoming every day more and more fatal; I therefore came off with them on the above day and arrived at this place the 14th, without incountering the least accident on the road."— *Washington to Tobias Lear,* September 25.

At Washington City: Takes part as a Mason in the ceremonies of laying the corner-stone of the Capitol of the United States. The stone was laid at the southeast corner of the edifice.

"The President of the United States, the Grand Master P. T. and the Worshipful Master of [Alexandria Lodge] No. 22 taking their stand to the east of a large stone, and all the Craft forming a circle westward, stood a short time in awful order. The artillery discharged. The Grand Marshal delivered the commissioners [Thomas Johnson, David Stuart, and Daniel Carroll] a large silver plate with an inscription thereon, which the commissioners ordered to be read, and was as follows:

"'This Southeast corner-stone of the Capitol of the United States of America, in the City of Washington, was laid on the 18th day of September, 1793, in the thirteenth year of American independence, in the first year of the second term of the presidency of GEORGE WASHINGTON, whose virtues in the civil administration of his country have been as conspicuous and beneficial, as his military valor and prudence have been useful in establishing her liberties, and in the year of Masonry, 5793, by the President of the United States, in concert with the Grand Lodge of Maryland, several lodges under its jurisdiction, and Lodge No. 22 from Alexandria, Virginia.'

"The artillery discharged a volley. The plate was then delivered to the President, who, attended by the Grand Master P. T. and three most Worshipful Masters, descended to the cavazion trench and deposed the plate, and laid it on the corner-stone of the Capitol of the United States of America, on which was deposed Corn, Wine, and Oil, when the whole congregation joined in reverential prayer, which was succeeded by Masonic chanting honors, and a volley from the artillery. The President of the United States and his attendant brethren ascended from the cavazion to the east of the corner-stone; and there the Grand Master P. T., elevated on a triple rostrum, delivered an oration fitting the occasion, which was received with brotherly love and commendation. At intervals, during the delivery of the oration, several volleys were discharged by the artillery. The ceremony ended in prayer, Masonic chanting honors, and a 15-volley from the artillery.

"The whole company retired to an extensive booth, where an ox of 500 lbs. weight was barbecued, of which the company generally partook, with every abundance of other recreation. The festival concluded with fifteen successive volleys from the artillery, whose military discipline and manoeuvres merit every commendation. Before dark the whole company departed with joyful hopes of the production of their labor."—*Georgetown*, September 21, 1793.

MONDAY, SEPTEMBER 30.

At Mount Vernon : " The continuation and spreading of the malignant fever, with which the city of Philadelphia is visited, together with the absence of the heads of departments therefrom, will prolong my abode at this place until about the 25th of October ; at or about which time, I shall myself, if the then state of things should render it improper for me to take my family, set out for that city, or the vicinity, say Germantown."— *Washington to Edmund Randolph.*

SUNDAY, OCTOBER 6.

At Mount Vernon : " It appearing to me that the public business will require the executive officers to be together sometime before the meeting of Congress, I have written to the Secretaries of the Treasury and War to meet me at Philadelphia or vicinity, say Germantown, by the first of November, and should be glad to see you there at the same time."— *Washington to Thomas Jefferson.*

MONDAY, OCTOBER 14.

At Mount Vernon : " The accounts from the city [of Philadelphia] are really affecting. Two gentlemen now here from New York (Colonels Platt and Sergeant) say, that they were told at the Swedes' Ford of Schuylkill, by a person who had it from the Governor (Mifflin), that, by an official report from the mayor of the city [Matthew Clarkson], upwards of three thousand and five hundred had died, and the disorder was raging more violently than ever." — *Washington to James Madison.*

The yellow fever of 1793, the spread of which was due to the neglect of sanitary precautions in its early stages, was most disastrous in its consequences. The fever first made its appearance in a lodging-house in the eastern part of the city in July, but it was not until the middle of August that its progress began to attract attention, and about the 25th of the month a general exodus of the population commenced. The epidemic lasted from the 1st of August to the 9th of November, during which period the number of deaths was over four thousand.

WEDNESDAY, OCTOBER 23.

At Mount Vernon : " I shall set out, so as to be in Germantown or thereabouts on the 1st of November, if no difficulties should be encountered on the road. . . . It is not in my power to despatch a servant before me. I shall have but two, neither of whom can be spared for such a purpose. These, with five horses, Mr. Dandridge, and myself, form the total of my family and equipage."— *Washington to Edmund Randolph.*

SUNDAY, OCTOBER 27.

At Mount Vernon : " Tomorrow I leave this for Philadelp* or the vicinity of it ; where, when you have occasion to write to me, direct your letters."— *Washington to William Pearce.*

FRIDAY, NOVEMBER 1.

At Germantown : " *Germantown*, November 2.—I overtook the President at Baltimore, and we arrived here yesterday. . . . The fever in Philadelphia has so much abated as to have almost disappeared. The inhabitants are about returning." ·*Thomas Jefferson to James Madison.*

SUNDAY, NOVEMBER 3.

At Germantown : " I will mention a proverb to you which you will find worthy of attention all the days of your life ; under any circumstances, or in any situation you may happen to be placed :—and that is, to put nothing off 'till the Morrow, that you can do to day."— *Washington to Howell Lewis.*

WEDNESDAY, NOVEMBER 6.

At Germantown : Receives a communication from Henry Hill and others, Trustees of " The Public School at Germantown," tendering the school buildings for the accommodation of Congress should it convene at that place.

"The Public School at Germantown," incorporated in 1784, was on the south side of School Lane, a short distance west of the main street. The building, erected in 1760–61 is still standing and used for its original purposes. It is now known as the *Germantown Academy*, and is in good repute as an educational institution. The plan of education embraces all the studies necessary to prepare young men to enter the sophomore class at college. Congress did not accept the offer of the Trustees, but convened at Philadelphia on Monday, December 2, all danger from the yellow fever having by that time been dispelled.

SUNDAY, NOVEMBER 24.

At Germantown: "The malady with which Philadelphia has been sorely afflicted, has, it is said, entirely ceased;— and all the Citizens are returning to their old habitations again.—I took a house in this town when I first arrived here, and shall retain it until Congress get themselves fixed; * although I spend part of my time in the city."— *Washington to Colonel Burgess Ball.*

The house in Germantown at which the President lived in the month of November, 1793,† is still standing, on the west side of the main street, now known as Germantown Avenue, in the Twenty-second Ward of the city of Philadelphia, and about six miles northwest of Independence Hall. The house—a substantial stone structure about forty feet square, with considerable back buildings, and numbered 5442—is directly opposite Mill Street (formerly Church Lane), and faces an open area which until recent years was known as Market Square. It was erected in 1772, and at the time of its being occupied by Washington was owned by Colonel Isaac Franks, of

---

* "*Germantown*, November 27.—The President will be established [in Philadelphia] in about a week, at which time Congress is to meet."— *Thomas Jefferson to Mr. Pinckney.*

† In Rupp's History of Berks County, Pennsylvania, it is stated that General Washington stayed all night, the 13th of November, 1793, at Womelsdorf (fourteen miles west of Reading), and that the inhabitants delivered him an address, which he answered. "A company of volunteers assembled, and amidst repeated firing of guns, near the door of the house in which he lodged, exclaimed, 'Lang lebe George Washington! Lang lebe George Washington!!'"

the Army of the Revolution. It is now owned and occupied by Elliston Perot Morris, a great-grand-son of Samuel Morris, captain of the First City Troop, 1776–86. Mr. Morris is the fortunate owner of the letter written by General Washington to Captain Morris, dated Morristown, January 23, 1777, in which he thanks the "Captain and Gentlemen" of the Troop for the many essential services which they had rendered to their country and to him personally during the course of the campaign which ended at Princeton on January 3.

TUESDAY, DECEMBER 3.

At Philadelphia: Addresses both Houses of Congress in the Senate Chamber. "Exactly at 12 o'clock the President arrived, accompanied by the Secretary of State, the Secretary of the Treasury, the Secretary at War, and the Attorney General &c and in the presence of a large assemblage of citizens and foreigners delivered to both Houses his address." *

The state of affairs, both external and internal, was largely explained in the President's speech and in a separate message accompanied with many documents. In these were comprised the reasons for the course he had pursued respecting foreign powers, and suggestions for additional legislative enactments to protect the rights of American citizens and maintain the dignity of the country. It was in allusion to these communications to Congress that Mr. Fox made the following remarks in the British Parliament, January 31, 1794: "And here, Sir, I cannot help alluding to the President of the United States, General Washington, a character whose conduct has been so different from that which has been pursued by the ministers of this country. How infinitely wiser must appear the spirit and principles manifested in his late address to Congress, than the policy of modern European courts! Illustrious man, deriving honor less from the splendor of his situation than from the dignity of his mind; before whom all borrowed greatness sinks into insignificance, and all the potentates of Europe (excepting the members of our own royal family) become little and contemptible! He has had no occasion to have recourse to any tricks of policy or arts of alarm; his authority has been sufficiently supported by the same means by which it was acquired, and his conduct has uniformly been characterized by wisdom, moderation, and firmness. Feeling gratitude to France for the assistance received from her in that great contest, which secured the independence of America, he did not choose to give up the system of neutrality. Having once laid down that line of conduct,

---

* *Dunlap's American Daily Advertiser*, December 4.

which both gratitude and policy pointed out as most proper to be pursued, not all the insults and provocation of the French minister Genet could turn him from his purpose. Intrusted with the welfare of a great people, he did not allow the misconduct of another, with respect to himself, for one moment to withdraw his attention from their interest. He had no fear of the Jacobins, he felt no alarm from their principles, and considered no precaution as necessary in order to stop their progress.''

SATURDAY, DECEMBER 7.

At Philadelphia : Receives from the House of Representatives, through the committee, Messrs. Madison, Sedgwick, and Hartley, an answer to his address of December 3.

TUESDAY, DECEMBER 10.

At Philadelphia : Is waited on by the Senate, and the Vice-President, in its name, presents him with an answer to his address.

THURSDAY, DECEMBER 12.

At Philadelphia : "All my landed property, east of the Apalachian mountains, is under Rent, except the estate called Mount Vernon. This, hitherto, I have kept in my own hands : but from my present situation, from my advanced time of life, from a wish to live free from care, and as much at my ease as possible, during the remainder of it, and from other causes, which are not necessary to detail, I have, latterly, entertained serious thoughts of letting this estate also, reserving the mansion-house farm for my own residence, occupation, and amusement in agriculture ; provided I can obtain what, in my own judgment, and in the opinion of others whom I have consulted, the low rent which I shall mention hereafter ; and provided also I can settle it with *good* farmers."— *Washington to Arthur Young.*

Extract from the above-quoted letter : "No estate in United America is more pleasantly situated than this. It lies in a high, dry and healthy country, 300 miles by water from the sea, and, as you will see by the plan, on one of the finest rivers in the world. Its margin is washed by more than ten miles of tide-water; from the bed of which and the innumerable coves, inlets, and small marshes, with which it abounds, an inexaustible fund of rich mud may be drawn, as a manure, either to be used separately, or in a compost, according to the judgment of the farmer.   It is situated in a latitude between the extremes of heat and cold, and is the same distance by land and water, with good roads, and the best navigation (to and) from the Federal City, Alexandria, and George-Town ; distant from the first, twelve, from the second nine, and from the last sixteen miles.   The Federal City, in the year 1800, will become the seat of the general government of the United States.   It is increasing fast in buildings, and rising into consequence ; and will I have no doubt, from the advantages given to it by Nature, and its proximity to a rich interior country, and the western territory, become the emporium of the United States. . . . This river, which encompasses the land the distance above-mentioned, is well supplied with various kinds of fish, at all seasons of the year ; and, in the spring, with the greatest profusion of shad, herrings, bass, carp, perch, sturgeon &c.   Several valuable fisheries appertain to the estate ; the whole shore, in short, is one entire fishery.   There are, as you will perceive by the plan, four farms besides that at the mansion-house : these four contain 3260 acres of cultivable land."

TUESDAY, DECEMBER 31.

At Philadelphia : " It has been my intention ever since my return to the city, to contribute my mite towards the relief of the *most* needy inhabitants of it.   The pressure of public business hitherto has suspended, but not altered my resolution.   I am at a loss, however, for whose benefit to apply the little I can give and in whose hands to place it . . . and therefore have taken the liberty of asking your advice."— *Washington to William White*, Bishop of Pennsylvania.

1794.

At Philadelphia: "*January* 6.—On Wednesday last [January 1], New Year's day—Members of both Houses of Congress—Heads of Departments—Foreign Ministers—Members of the Society of the Cincinnati—Officers of the Militia, &c., waited on the President of the United States, to offer him the compliments of the Season."—*Dunlap and Claypoole's American Daily Advertiser.*

THURSDAY, JANUARY 9.

At Philadelphia: "The news of this evening is, that the Queen of France is no more.* When will the savages be satiated with blood? No prospect of peace in Europe, and therefore none of internal harmony in America. We cannot well be in a more disagreeable situation than we are with all Europe, with all Indians, and with all Barbary rovers. Nearly one half the continent is in constant opposition to the other, and the President's situation, which is highly responsible, is very distressing. He made me a very friendly visit yesterday, which I returned to-day, and had two hours' conversation with him alone in his cabinet."—*John Adams to Mrs. Adams*, January 9.

SATURDAY, FEBRUARY 22.

At Philadelphia: "*February* 24.—Saturday [February 22], being the anniversary of that auspicious event the birth of the President of the United States, the same was observed here with unusual demonstrations of joy."—*Dunlap and Claypoole's American Daily Advertiser.*

---

* Marie Antoinette was executed October 16, 1793.

271

"A Federal Salute ushered in the dawn, and the bells of Christ Church rang peals at intervals through the day. At noon the Members of both Houses of Congress—the Heads of Departments—the Foreign Ministers— his brother veterans, the Society of the Cincinnati—the Governor, Civil and Military Officers of this Commonwealth—the Reverend Clergy—the Faculty of the University of Pennsylvania—and a great assemblage of other citizens, waited on the President at his house to pay him their respects and congratulations.

"The Light Horse, Artillery, & Light Infantry, which paraded in honor of the day, were more numerous than on any recent occasion—and their truly soldier-like appearance merits the highest approbation. Repeated federal salutes were fired in the course of the day, by the artillery in High Street. The field officers of the militia were dressed in new and elegant uniforms on this occasion. The general joy and hilarity evinced this day, indicate that the purest republican principles actuate the public mind. The President enters into the 63d year of his age.

"The Managers of the City Dancing Assembly gave a Ball in the evening. They were honored with the company of the President and Mrs. Washington, several of the Foreign Ministers, a number of the members of Congress, the Secretaries of the treasury and of war, the Governors of the State and of the Western Territory, and the most brilliant display of beauty, perhaps, ever exhibited in this city. The countenances of all present appeared perfectly congenial with the happy occasion."—*Idem.*

"Saturday last [February 22] M. Fauchet, the new Minister from France, was introduced to the President of the United States, by Mr. Randolph, Secretary of State." *—Idem.*

MONDAY, FEBRUARY 24.

At Philadelphia: "Enclosed you will find three Bank notes for one hundred dollars each; out of which pay the Rev^d. Mr. Muir of Alexandria Fifty pounds, and take his signature to the enclosed receipt."— *Washington to William Pearce.*

This was an annual subscription to the Orphan School under the care of the Rev. James Muir, pastor of the Presbyterian Church in Alexandria. The following item in Washington's will refers to this school: "To the Trustees (Governors or by whatsoever other name they may be designated) of the Academy in the Town of Alexandria, I give and bequeath, in Trust,

* Edmund Randolph was appointed Secretary of State on the second of January as successor to Thomas Jefferson, who had resigned from the office December 31, 1793. The place of Mr. Randolph as Attorney-General was supplied by William Bradford, of Pennsylvania.

Four thousand dollars, or in other words twenty of the shares which I hold in the Bank of Alexandria toward the support of a Free School, established at, and annexed to the said Academy for the purpose of educating such orphan children, or the children of such other poor and indigent persons as are unable to accomplish it with their own means, and who in the judgment of the trustees of the said Seminary, are best entitled to the benefit of this donation. . . . And to prevent misconception, my meaning is, and is hereby declared to be that, these twenty shares are in lieu of and not in addition to the Thousand pounds given by a missive letter some years ago [December 17, 1785] in consequence whereof an annuity of fifty pounds has since been paid toward the support of that institution."

SUNDAY, MARCH 2.

At Philadelphia: "The Price of Midlings and Ship stuff in Alexandria is greatly below the selling price in this market; especially the first, which is 5½ dollars the barrel of 196 lbs—and the latter, from a dollar and half to two dollars pʳ. hundred—but as these articles never are so high there as here, you must enquire the most favorable season to dispose of them, and do it to the best advantage.—Keep me informed from time to time of the prices of Superfine and fine flour, that I may know when to strike for mine;—and ask the Miller why he does not, as usual, note in his weekly returns the number of barrels he has packed of *all* the different kinds."— *Washington to William Pearce.*

SUNDAY, MARCH 23.

At Philadelphia: "Mr. Smith has, I believe, been furnished with fish from my landing, and if he will give as much as another, ought to have the preference;—but before you positively engage, enquire what the other fisheries are disposed to sell at.—4/. pʳ. thousand for Herrings, and 10/. pʳ. hundred for shad is very low.—I am, at this moment, paying 6/. a piece for every shad I buy."— *Washington to William Pearce.*

SUNDAY, MARCH 30.

At Philadelphia: "I am sorry to hear your drilled and other wheat, makes but an indifferent appearance. — I

was in hopes such extreame fine weather as we have had
during the whole month of March would have occasioned
a pleasing change in both.—As grain puts on different
looks at this season, according as the weather, while growing, happens to be, let me know from time to time how
mine comes on.—If it stands thick enough on the ground,
such uncommon mildness and warmth as we have had
since February, must have recovered that Crop greatly.
as well as the Winter Barley."—*Washington to William
Pearce*.

The letters from which the last three quotations are made form part of a
series of one hundred and sixteen, written by Washington to William Pearce,
manager of the Mount Vernon farms from October, 1793, to January, 1797.
The originals are in the possession of the Long Island Historical Society, and
were published in 1889, with an historical and genealogical introduction and
notes by Moncure Daniel Conway, being volume iv. of the Memoirs of that
society. The letters quoted, it will be perceived, were all written on Sunday,
and, with but few exceptions, this is the case with the entire series, it having
been the custom of the President to devote the afternoon of that day to his
private correspondence.

Upon a careful perusal of the letters comprising the series, we find that
the smallest as well as the most important matters connected with his Mount
Vernon interests are noted with a detail almost painfully minute. Letter
after letter, many of them of considerable length, devoted to instructions as
to building, labor, crops, and, in brief, everything pertaining to the management of a large landed estate; disclosing an ability for the supervision of
business by an absentee that would be remarkable had the writer been
entirely free from responsibility other than the proper conduct of his own
affairs. And when we reflect that these letters were written during the most
trying and exacting period of Washington's life, we may well be impressed
with the extraordinary qualities of a mind which could thus calmly withdraw from the engrossing consideration of matters of state, the harassing
care of great office, to devote itself, with unfailing regularity, to the accurate and voluminous direction of private affairs, of which these letters are a
most striking proof.

Truly a remarkable record of a remarkable mind!

SUNDAY, APRIL 6.

At Philadelphia: "I had no doubt but that the late capture of our Vessels by the British Cruisers, followed by the

Embargo * which had been laid on the Shipping in our Ports, w^d naturally occasion a temporary fall in the article of provisions;—yet, as there are the same mouths to feed as before;—as the demand, consequently, will be as great; and as the Crops in other parts of the world will not be increased by these means, I have no doubt at all, but that, as soon as the present impediments are removed the prices of flour will rise to what it has been (at least) for which reason hold mine up to the prices mentioned in my last; and if they are offered, make a provisory agreement, to be ratified, or not, by me;—an answer to which can be obtained in a week."— *Washington to William Pearce.*

TUESDAY, APRIL 8.

At Philadelphia: "*April 9.*—I arrived here [Philadelphia] on Monday evening; and yesterday dined with the President. The question of war or peace seems to be as much in suspense here as in New York when I left you. I am rather inclined to think that peace will continue, but should not be surprised if war should take place. In the present state of things, it will be best to be ready for the *latter* event in every respect."—*John Jay to Mrs. Jay.*

TUESDAY, APRIL 15.

At Philadelphia: "Let me know whether the message, which in the evening of yesterday I requested you to draw, will be ready by eleven o'clock this forenoon?"— *Washington to Edmund Randolph.*

This message was the one in which Mr. Jay was nominated to the Senate as envoy extraordinary to England. The message, which was sent

---

* Congress, in retaliation for the "Provision Order" of the British Council of November 6, 1793, which directed the seizure of all vessels carrying food products to France, passed (March 26, 1794) a joint resolution laying an embargo on commerce for thirty days. The measure seemed to have chiefly in view the obstructing the supply of provisions for the British fleet and army in the West Indies. It operated quite as much against the French.

in the next day, April 16, is as follows: "Gentlemen of the Senate; The communications which I have made to you during your present session, from the despatches of our minister in London [Thomas Pinckney], contain a serious aspect of our affairs with Great Britain. But, as peace ought to be pursued with unremitted zeal, before the last resource, which has so often been the scourge of nations, and cannot fail to check the advanced prosperity of the United States, is contemplated; I have thought proper to nominate, and do hereby nominate, John Jay, as envoy extraordinary of the United States to his Britannic Majesty."

The nomination of Mr. Jay, which was confirmed April 19, was made in consequence of a motion introduced in the House of Representatives (April 7) that all commercial intercourse with Great Britain and her subjects be suspended so far as respected all articles of the growth or manufacture of Great Britain or Ireland, until the surrender of the frontier posts, etc. This motion, if adopted, would have led directly to war.

FRIDAY, APRIL 25.

At Philadelphia: "*April 26.*—Yesterday about 11 o'clock, the President, accompanied by the Governor, the Secretary of State, the Secretary of War, and a number of respectable citizens, went down the river in one of the New Castle packets, to Fort Mifflin and other places on the banks of the Delaware."—*Dunlap and Claypoole's American Daily Advertiser.*

TUESDAY, MAY 6.

At Philadelphia: "To tell you that the order of his Britannic Majesty in council, of the 8th of June last, respecting neutral vessels, had given much discontent in the United States, and that that of the 6th of November and its result had thrown them into a flame, will hardly be news to you when you shall receive this letter. The subsequent order of the 8th of January has in a degree allayed the violence of the heat, but will by no means satisfy them without reparation for the spoliations on our trade, and the injuries we sustain from the non-performance of the treaty of peace. To effect these if possible by temperate means, by fair and firm negotiations, an envoy extraordinary is appointed, and will, I expect, sail in a few days. Mr. Jay is chosen for the

trust.   Mr. John Trumbull goes as his private Secretary."
— *Washington to Tobias Lear.*

The order of the British Council of the 8th of June, 1793, directed that
armed vessels should arrest and send into port vessels loaded with corn or
meal or flour destined for France, and all neutral vessels, save those of
Denmark and Sweden, which should attempt to enter any blockaded port.
The order of the 6th of November, which was partially revoked by that of
the 8th of January, 1794, directed English vessels to seize and bring to
British ports "all ships laden with goods the produce of any colony belonging to France, or carrying provisions or other supplies for the use of any
such colony."

FRIDAY, JUNE 6.

At Philadelphia : " *June 6.*—I had the honor of an interview with the President of the United States, to whom I
was introduced by Mr. Dandridge, his secretary.   He received me very politely, and after reading my letters, I
was asked to breakfast."—HENRY WANSEY, *Excursion to the
United States in 1794.*

" The President, in his person, is tall and thin, but erect; rather of an
engaging than a dignified presence.   He appears very thoughtful, is slow
in delivering himself, which occasions some to conclude him reserved, but
it is rather, I apprehend, the effect of much thinking and reflection, for
there is great appearance to me of affability and accommodation.   He was
at this time in his sixty-third year, being born February 11, 1732, O.S.,
but he has very little the appearance of age, having been all his life-time so
exceeding temperate.   There is a certain anxiety visible in his countenance
with marks of extreme sensibility. . . .

" Mrs. Washington herself made tea and coffee for us.   On the table were
two small plates of sliced tongue, dry toast, bread and butter, &c. but no
broiled fish, as is the general custom.   Miss Custis her grand-daughter, a
very pleasing young lady, of about sixteen, sat next to her, and her brother
George Washington Custis, about two years older than herself.*   There was
but little appearance of form : one servant only attended, who had no
livery; a silver urn for hot water, was the only article of expence on the
table.   She appears something older than the President, though, I under-

---

* This is an error.   George Washington Parke Custis was two years *younger*
than his sister Nelly.

stand, they were both born in the same year ;* short in stature, rather robust; very plain in her dress, wearing a very plain cap, with her grey hair closely turned up under it. She has routs or levees (whichever the people chuses to call them) every Wednesday and Saturday at Philadelphia, during the sitting of Congress.† But the Anti-federalists object even to these, as tending to give a super-eminency, and introductory to the paraphernalia of courts."—WANSEY.

SUNDAY, JUNE 15.

At Philadelphia : " If nothing, unforseen by me at present, intervenes to prevent it, I shall leave this city for Mount Vernon the day after tomorrow; (tuesday) but as the weather is warm, my horses fat and out of exercise, and I may have occasion to stop a day on the road, it is not probable I shall reach home before Sunday or Monday next."— *Washington to William Pearce.*

TUESDAY, JUNE 17.

Leaves Philadelphia : " *June* 19.—The President left this city on Tuesday [June 17], on a visit to his seat in Virginia."—*Dunlap and Claypoole's American Daily Advertiser.*

" *Baltimore*, June 19.—At five o'clock this afternoon I reached this place, and shall proceed in the morning."—*Washington to Edmund Randolph.*

WEDNESDAY, JUNE 25.

At Mount Vernon: "I shall endeavour to be back by the time I allotted before I left Philadelphia, if I am able; but an exertion to save myself and horse from falling among the rocks at the Lower Falls of the Potomac, whither I went on Sunday morning [June 22] to see the canal and locks, has wrenched my back in such a manner as to prevent my riding; and hitherto has defeated the purposes for which I came home. My stay here will only be until I can ride with ease and safety, whether I accomplish my own business or not."— *Washington to Edmund Randolph.*

---

* Mrs. Washington was born June 21, 1731. (" Martha Washington," by Anne H. Wharton, page 3.)

† The levees of Mrs. Washington were held every Friday evening.

MONDAY, JUNE 30.

At Mount Vernon: "I expect to leave this place on Thursday [July 3] for Philadelphia; and if, upon inquiry at Georgetown, I should find the upper road the smoothest and best, I shall proceed by it."—*Washington to Edmund Randolph.*

MONDAY, JULY 7.

At Philadelphia: "*July 9.*—Monday afternoon [July 7] the President of the United States arrived in town from the southward."—*Dunlap and Claypoole's American Daily Advertiser.*

"*Philadelphia,* July 13.—I arrived in this City myself on Monday; made rather worse by my journey, and a wetting I got on the Road on Saturday; having travelled all day through a constant Rain. . . . P.S. Mrs. Washington desires you will send her by the first Vessel to this place one doz^n of the best Hams, and half a doz^n Midlings of Bacon.—Weigh the whole and send me the Account of it."—*Washington to William Pearce.*

THURSDAY, JULY 10.

At Philadelphia: "*July* 10.—I waited on Mr. Randolph, who immediately accompanied me and introduced me to the President of the United States. He said little or nothing to me upon the subject of the business on which I am to be sent [as resident minister to the United Netherlands]. All his directions and intentions on this head I am to receive through the medium of his Ministers. I dined with him General and Mrs. Knox, Mr. Randolph and Mr. Bradford were there, and also Mrs. R. Morris."—*Diary of John Quincy Adams.*

"*July* 11.—By the invitation of the President, I attended the reception he gave to *Piomingo* and a number of other Chickasaw Indians. Five Chiefs, seven Warriors, four boys and an interpreter constituted the Company. As soon as the whole were seated the ceremony of smoking began. A large East Indian pipe was placed in the middle of the Hall. The tube which appeared to be of leather, was twelve to fifteen feet in length. The President began and after two or three whiffs, passed the tube to Piomingo; he to the next chief, and so all round. . . . When it was finished, the President addressed them in a speech which he read, stopping at the close of every sentence for the interpreter to translate it. . . . Piomingo then desired he might be excused from giving his talks at this time, being very unwell, but promised to give them in a few days. They then made several inquiries respecting the Cherokees who have recently been here.* Their questions discovered a mixture of curiosity and animosity. These two nations are at war, and the Chickasaws spoke of the others as perfidious people. The *fides punica* it seems is not confined to civilized nations. " The informal conversation was held while wine, punch and cake were carrying round. . . . These formalities employed about an hour; after which they rose, shook hands with us all, and departed."—*Diary of John Quincy Adams.*

SUNDAY, JULY 20.

At Philadelphia: "I know of no pursuit in which more real & important service can be rendered to any Country, than by improving its agriculture—its breed of useful animals—and other branches of a husband-mans cares."— *Washington to Sir John Sinclair.*

Sir John Sinclair, a Scottish nobleman distinguished for his statistical publications and philanthropy, was a frequent correspondent of Washington on agricultural matters, in which he took great interest of a practical nature. He was the founder of the Board of Agriculture in Scotland (1793) and its first president. Sinclair published at London in 1800, in fac-simile, the letters addressed to him by Washington on " agriculture and other interesting topics," to which was appended a brief sketch of the character of the writer.

WEDNESDAY, JULY 30.

At Germantown : " *August* 8.—I removed to this place on Wednesday last [July 30], in order to avoid the heat of the City of Philadelphia.—It is probable I shall remain here until about the middle of September."— *Washington to William Pearce.*

---

* " *June* 7.—Yesterday arrived here in the brig Fame, Capt. Hunt, eight days from Charleston, twenty-one Indian Chiefs, or head warriors, of the Cherokee nation, deputised by that nation to treat with the President of the United States. They were conducted from the place of landing to the accommodations provided for them by the directions of the Governor of this State."- *Dunlap and Claypoole's American Daily Advertiser.*

THURSDAY, AUGUST 7.

At Germantown : Issues a proclamation warning the insurgents in the western parts of Pennsylvania to desist from their opposition to the laws laying duties upon spirits distilled within the United States, and upon stills.

In this proclamation, after briefly stating the doings of the insurgents, the measures thus far pursued by the government, and the principal points of the law which authorized force to be employed against insurrectionary movements, the President expressed the opinion that the time had come when it was necessary to call out the militia for this purpose; and the insurgents were warned that, unless they should disperse before the 1st of September, the law would be put in execution. In pursuance thereof a requisition was issued for raising 12,950 of the militia,* to be held in readiness to march at a moment's warning: Pennsylvania, 5200; New Jersey, 2100; Maryland, 2350; Virginia, 3300   The militia were called out on the 2d of September, and the President, in a proclamation of the 25th of the month, expressed his satisfaction at learning of their patriotic alacrity in obeying the call, and that a force, which, according to every reasonable expectation, was adequate to the exigency, was already in motion to the scene of disaffection.

SATURDAY, AUGUST 30.

At Germantown : " I will undertake without the gift of prophecy, to predict, that it will be impossible to keep this country in a state of amity with Great Britain long, if the posts are not surrendered. A knowledge of these being my sentiments would have little weight, I am persuaded, with the British administration, and perhaps not with the nation in effecting the measure ; but both may rest satisfied that, if they want to be in peace with this country, and to enjoy the benefits of its trade, to give up the posts is the only road to it. Withholding them, and consequences we feel at present continuing, war will be inevitable."— *Washington to John Jay*, at London.

It was stipulated in Article VII. of the definitive treaty of peace of September 3, 1783, that the British government should with all convenient speed withdraw its armies from every post, place, and harbor within the

---

* This requisition was afterward augmented to fifteen thousand.

United States. The troops, however, had not as yet been withdrawn from the posts of Mackinaw, Detroit, Fort Erie, Niagara, Oswego, Oswegatchie (on the St. Lawrence), and Port-au-fer and Dutchman's Point on Lake Champlain. It was the opinion of the President that all the difficulties with the Indians were the result of the conduct of the British agents protected by these frontier posts. They endeavored to remove friendly tribes over the line, and also to keep those who were hostile to the United States in a state of irritation; and they also furnished the whole with arms, ammunition, clothing, and even provisions to carry on the war. From these facts came the positive conviction (expressed in the above-quoted letter) that without their surrender a state of amity with Great Britain could not long be continued. The surrender of these posts, thus urged by Washington, was incorporated in Article II. of the "Jay Treaty," concluded at London, October 25, 1795, it being stipulated that His Majesty should withdraw all his troops and garrisons from all posts and places within the boundary lines assigned by the treaty of peace with the United States; this evacuation was to take place on or before the first day of June, 1796.

SUNDAY, SEPTEMBER 14.

At Germantown: "Love is a mighty pretty thing, but like all other delicious things it is cloying; and when the first transport of the passion begins to subside, which it assuredly will do, and yield—oftentimes too late—to more sober reflections, it serves to evince, that love is too dainty a food to live upon *alone*, and ought not to be considered further than as a necessary ingredient for that matrimonial happiness which results from a combination of causes; none of which are of greater importance than that the object on whom it is placed should possess good sense,—good dispositions,—and the means of supporting you in the way you have been brought up, and who, at the same time, has a claim to the respect of the circle in which he moves."— *Washington to Eliza Parke Custis.*

Eliza Parke Custis, to whom this letter was addressed, was the eldest child of John Parke Custis, the son of Mrs. Washington, who died in November, 1781. At the date of the letter she was living at Hope Park, Fairfax County, Virginia, with her mother, who had married Dr. David Stuart, their former residence having been at Abingdon. Miss Custis married (March 21, 1796) Thomas Law, who had been chief of a large district in Bengal. In England his family was opulent and distinguished. Her sister

Martha Parke Custis married (January 6, 1795), at the age of seventeen, Thomas Peter, son of Richard Peter, of Georgetown, Maryland. The two younger children, Eleanor Parke and George Washington Parke Custis, were brought up at Mount Vernon, as has been previously stated.

SATURDAY, SEPTEMBER 20.

At Philadelphia : " *September* 21.—We left our Quarters at German Town yesterday, and are again fixed in this City."— *Washington to William Pearce.*

The President occupied the same house at Germantown in 1794 as in the previous year. Under date of September 24, 1794, the following entry occurs in his Cash-Book : " Isaac Franks in Full for House rent &c at Germ town p^r rect.—201.60."

SUNDAY, SEPTEMBER 28.

At Philadelphia : " I leave this on Tuesday for Carlisle, where I shall (from the information I expect to receive from the Insurgent Counties of this state) be better enabled to determine whether I shall proceed on with the Troops, than I can do here."— *Washington to William Pearce.*

" *September* 29.—The insurgents in the back country have carried matters so high that the President has been obliged to send a large body of men to settle the matter, and is to go himself tomorrow to Carlyle to meet the troops. God knows when he will return again. I shall be left quite alone with the children."—*Mrs. Washington to Mrs. George Augustine Washington.*

TUESDAY, SEPTEMBER 30.

Leaves Philadelphia : " *September* 30.—Having determined from the Report of the Commissioners, who were appointed to meet the Insurgents in the Western Counties in the State of Pennsylvania, and from other circumstances—to repair to the places appointed for the Rendezvous, of the Militia of New Jersey Pennsylvania Maryland & Virginia ; I left the City of Philadelphia about half past ten o'clock this forenoon accompanied by Col° Hamilton (Secretary of the Treasury) and my private Secretary [Bartholomew Dandridge].* Dined at Norris Town and lodged at a place called the Trap—the first 17, and the latter 25 miles from Philadelphia."— *Washington's Diary.*

" At Norris Town we passed a detachment of Militia who were preparing to March for the Rendezvous at Carlisle—and at the Trap late in the evening, we were overtaken by Major [John] Stagg principal Clerk in the Department of War with letters from Gen¹ Wayne & the Western Army containing official & pleasing accounts of his engagement [August 20th] with the Indians near the British Post at the Rapids of the Miami of the Lake—and of his having destroyed all the Indian Settlements on that River in the Vicinity of the said Post quite up to the grand Glaize—the quantity not less than 5000 Acres—and the Stores &c of Col° McGlee [M'Kee] the British Agent of Indian Affairs a mile or two from the Garrison."—*Washington's Diary.*

WEDNESDAY, OCTOBER 1.

At Reading, Pennsylvania: " *October* 1.—Left the Trap early, and breakfasting at Pottsgrove 11 Miles we reached Reading to Dinner 19 miles farther where we found several detachm⁺ˢ of Infantry & Cavalry preparing for their March to Carlisle."— *Washington's Diary.*

" *October* 2.—An accident happening to one of my horses, occasion⁴ my setting out later than was intended—I got off in time, however, to make a halt (to bait my horses) at Womelsdorps [Womelsdorf] 14 miles and to view the Canal from Myerstown towards Lebanon—and the Locks between the two places; which (four adjoining each other, in the dissent from the Summit ground along the Tulpihockin; built of Brick;) appeared admirably constructed.—Reached Lebanon at Night, 28 miles."— *Washington's Diary.*

FRIDAY, OCTOBER 3.

At Harrisburg, Pennsylvania: " *October* 3.—Breakfasted at Humels T[own]. 14 M and dined and lodged at Harris-

---

* " *September* 30.—That great and good man General Washington, President of the United States, set out from his house on Market Street, with Secretary Hamilton on his left and his Private Secretary on his right, to head the troops called out to quell the insurrection to the westward."— *Diary of Jacob Hiltzheimer.*

burgh on the Banks of the Susquehanna 23 miles from
Lebanon.

" At Harrisburgh we found the first Regiment of New
Jersey (about 560 strong) comm^d by Col^o Turner drawn out
to receive me—passed along the line, to my Quarters—and
after dinner walked through and round the Town which is
considerable for its age (of about 8 or 9 years)—The Susquehanna at this place abounds in the Rock fish of 12 or 15
Inches in length & a fish which they call Salmon."—*Washington's Diary.*

" *Harrisburgh*, October 6.—On Friday last [October 3], the president of
the United States arrived in this town.   The pleasure excited, in beholding,
for the first time, our beloved chief, in this borough, is not easily described.
An address was delivered to him, by the burgesses, in behalf of the inhabitants of the town, which he was pleased to answer."—*Dunlap and Claypoole's American Daily Advertiser*, October 16.

SATURDAY, OCTOBER 4.

At Carlisle, Pennsylvania: " *October* 4.—Forded the Susquehanna; nearly a mile wide, including the Island.   At
the lower end of wch the road crosses it.   On the Cumberland side I found a detachment of the Philadelphia light
horse ready to receive, and escort me to Carlisle 17 miles;
where I arrived about 11 Oclock.—two miles short of it, I
met the Governors of Pennsylvania [Thomas Mifflin] &
New Jersey [Richard Howell] with all the Cavalry that had
Rendezvoused at that place drawn up—passed them—and
the Infantry of Pennsylvania before I alighted at my
quarters."—*Washington's Diary.*

" *Carlisle*, October 8.—On Saturday last [October 4] the President of the
United States arrived here.   Every exertion was made by the respectable
army now encamped, and by the inhabitants of this place to receive him
with that respect correspondent to those sentiments of attachment and
veneration, with which every good man and patriot had been long impressed.
The Governors of Pennsylvania and Jersey, at the head of their respective
squadrons of horse, and the friends of government inhabitants of this town,
met him at some distance from the borough.   The President was escorted

by a detachment of Philadelphia horse, who left the camp at three o'clock in the morning of that day, and who arrived at the river as he had just passed it. He was accompanied by Secretary Hamilton, and his private secretary Mr. Dandridge. This grand procession passed through the borough to the camp. Here the horse formed on the right and left wings of the army, drawn up in martial order, and forming a line the most respectable ever perhaps before displayed. Besides the great mass of respectable yeomanry, there might be seen as private troopers some of the principal officers of the state government, members of the senate and house of representatives of Pennsylvania, officers who had commanded regiments in the continental service, merchants of the most respectable characters and fortunes, lawyers of eminent talents and property. Amongst the infantry as volunteer soldiers, there are young gentlemen of the first families in the respective states. Some of them men of great opulence, and a number of them of consequence in the commercial world.

" The line was composed of the cavalry before mentioned, a regiment of artillery with 16 pieces, with the infantry from various parts of Pennsylvania, amounting in the whole to near three thousand men beautifully equipped, and all in handsome uniforms. The army was reviewed by the President who appeared to enjoy the utmost satisfaction at the illustrious display of patriotic exertion ; he remarked, as we are informed, that he had never beheld a more respectable body of troops, and some gentlemen who had been American officers in the late war with Great Britain, admitted that they had never seen at any period of the war so strong and fine a body of cavalry. In the evening the court house in this borough was illuminated by the federal citizens, and a transparency exhibited with the following inscriptions in large illuminated characters—in the front of the transparency, 'WASHINGTON IS EVER TRIUMPHANT.' On one side 'THE REIGN OF THE LAWS;' on the other side, 'WOE TO ANARCHISTS.' "—*Dunlap and Claypoole's American Daily Advertiser*, October 17.

SUNDAY, OCTOBER 5.

At Carlisle : " *October 5.*—Went to the Presbiterian Meeting and heard Doct⸢r⸣ Davidson Preach a political Sermon, recommendatory of order & good government ; and the excellence of that of the United States."— *Washington's Diary.*

" *October 6th** to *October 12.*—Employed in organizing the several detachments, which had come in from different Counties of this State, in a very disjointed & loose manner ;—or rather I ought to have said in urging

---

* On Monday, October 6, a number of the principal inhabitants of Carlisle presented the President with an address, which he answered.

& assisting Gen¹ Mifflin to do it; as I no otherwise took the command of the Troops than to press them forward, and to provide them with necessaries for their March, as well, & as far, as our means would admit.—To effect these purposes, I appointed General [Edward] Hand adjutant General on the 7th. On the 9th William Findlay and David Redick—deputed by the Committee of Safety (as it is dissignated) which met on the 2d of this month at Parkinson's Ferry [now Monongahela City] arrived in Camp with the Resolutions of the said Committee;—and to give information of the State of things in the four Western Counties of Pennsylvania to wit—Washington Fayette West^d [Westmoreland] & Allegany in order to see if it would prevent the March of the Army into them.—At 10 o'clock I had a meeting with these persons in the presence of Govr Howell (of New Jersey) the Secretary of the Treasury, Col° Hamilton, & Mr Dandridge :—Govr Mifflin was invited to be present, but excused himself on Acc^t of business. . . . On the 10th the light & legionary Corps under the immediate Command of Maj^r [William] McPherson—The Jersey Regiment & Guirneys [Colonel Francis Gurney] from Philadelphia, commenced their March under the orders of Governor Howell; and the day following the whole body of Cavalry (except the three Troops of Phil^a Horse commanded by Captn [John] Dunlap, as part of the legion above mentioned) under Genl White *—a new formed Corp of Independant uniform Companies under & several other Corps under the Command of Govr Mifflin Marched all for the Rendezvous at Bedford."—*Washington's Diary.*

SUNDAY, OCTOBER 12.

At Chambersburg, Pennsylvania: " *October* 12.—Having settled these matters; seen the Troops off, as before mentioned; given them their Rout & days Marching; and left Maj^r Gen¹ [William] Irvine to organize the remainder of the Pennsylvania detachments as they might come in, & to March them & the Jersey Troops on when refreshed,—I set out from Carlisle about 7 o'clock this Morning—dined at Shippensburgh 21 miles & lodged at Chambersburgh 11 m. further where I was joined by the Adg^t Gen¹ Hand."— *Washington's Diary.*

MONDAY, OCTOBER 13.

At Williamsport, Maryland : " *October* 13.—Breakfasted at Greencastle [Pennsylvania] 10 Miles, & lodged at Williamsport, 14 Miles further."— *Washington's Diary.*

---

* Anthony W. White, Adjutant-General of New Jersey.

" *Williamsport*, October 14.—With pleasure we announce to the public, that the President of the United States arrived here last evening, in good health—his presence made every heart rejoice, and beat high with affection and gratitude—last night every window was illuminated—Early this morning he set out for Cumberland "—*Dunlap and Claypoole's American Daily Advertiser*, October 25.

TUESDAY, OCTOBER 14.

At Bath, Virginia : " *October* 14.—About Seven o'clock, or half after it, we left Williamsport; and travelling up, on the Maryland side of the River, we breakfasted at one ——— 13 miles on our way—& crossing the Potomac a mile or two below Hancock Town lodged at the Warm Springs; or Bath [now Berkeley Springs, Morgan County, West Virginia]; 16 miles, from our breakfasting stage—and 29 from Williamsport."— *Washington's Diary.*

" *October* 15.—Left Bath by seven oclock; & crossing the Cacapehon Mountain, and the Potomack River by a very rough Road, we breakfasted at one Goldens—distant about 7 Miles—Bated our horses at a very indifferent place abt 13 Miles further on—and lodged at the old Town 33 or 34 Miles—This distance from the extreme badness of the Road, more than half of it being very hilly, & great part of it Stoney, was a severe days journey for the Carriage horses; they performed it however well."—*Washington's Diary.*

THURSDAY, OCTOBER 16.

At Cumberland, Maryland : " *October* 16.—After an early breakfast we set out for Cumberland—and about 11 o'clock arrived there.—Three Miles from the Town I was met by a party of Horse under the command of Major [George] Lewis (my Nephew) and by Brigr Genl [Samuel] Smith of the Maryland line, who Escorted me to the Camp; where, finding all the Troops under Arms, I passed along the line of the Army: & was conducted to a house the Residence of Major Lynn of the Maryland line (an old Continental Officer) where I was well lodged & civily entertained."— *Washington's Diary.*

" *October* 17th & 18th.—Remained at Cumberland, in order to acquire a
true knowledge of the strength condition &c of the Troops;—and to see
how they were provided, and when they could be got in readiness to proceed.—I found upward of 3200 men (Officers included) in this encampment;
Understood that about 500 more were at a little Village on the Virginia
side, 11 Miles distant, called Frankfort, under the command of Maj⁴ Gen¹
[Daniel] Morgan ; that 700 more had arrived at that place the evening of
the 18ᵗʰ und⁴ Brig⁴ Mathews—and 500 More were expected in the course of
a few days under Col⁰ Page—and That the whole were well supplied with
Prov⁴⁴ Forage & Straw.—Having requested that every thing might be
speedily arranged for a forward movement, and a light Corps to be organized for the advance under the command of Major Gen¹ Morgan, I resolved
to proceed to Bedford next morn⁵."—*Washington's Diary.*

SUNDAY, OCTOBER 19.

At Bedford, Pennsylvania : " *October* 19.—In company
with Gen¹ Lee, who I requested to attend me, that all the
arrangements necessary for the Army's crossing the Mount⁴⁴
in two columns might be made;—Their Routs & days
Marches fixed, that the whole might move in Unison—and
accompanied by the Adjutant General and my own family
we set out, ab⁴ eight oclock, for Bedford, and making one
halt at the distance of 12 Miles, reached it a little after 4
oclock in the afternoon being met a little out of the Encampment by Gov⁴ Mifflin Gov⁴ Howell—& several other
Officers of distinction.—

" Quarters were provided for me at the House of a M⁴
[David] Espy, Prothonotary of the County of Bedford—
to which I was carried & lodged very comfortably."—*Washington's Diary.*

" *October* 19.—The Cavalry this morning escorted the President about
five miles from [the Cumberland] camp when he requested the Troops to
return & taking leave spoke to Major George Lewis as follows : ' George,
You are the eldest of five nephews that I have in this Army, let your conduct be an example to them and do not turn your back untill you are ordered.' . . . The Presidents 5 nephews are Major George Lewis, Commandant
of the Cavalry. Major Lawrence Lewis Aid de Camp to Major Genl Morgan. Mr. Howell Lewis in Capt. Mercer's troop and Mr. Sam¹ Washington
(son of Col. Ch's Washington), and Mr. Lawrence Washington (son of

19

Col. Sam'l Washington) both of whom are light horsemen in the troop lately commanded by Capt. Lewis."—*Diary of Robert Wellford, Surgeon-General.*

MONDAY, OCTOBER 20.

At Bedford : " *October* 20.—Called the Quarter Master General, Adjutant General, Contractor, & others of the Staff departmᵗ before me, & the Commander in chief [Henry Lee], at 9 oclock this morning, in order to fix on the Routs of the two columns & their stages;—and when they wᵈ be able to put the Army in motion.—Also to obtain a correct return of the strength—and to press the commanding Officers of Corps to prepare with all the Celerity in their power for a forward movement.—Upon comparing accᵗˢ it was found that the army could be put in motion [on the] 23ᵈ—and it was so ordered. . . . Matters being thus arranged I wrote a farewell address to the Army through the Commander in chief Govʳ Lee—to be published in orders—and having prepared his Instructions and made every arrangement that occurred, as necessary I prepared for my return to Philadelphia in order to meet Congress, and to attend to the Civil duties of my Office."—*Washington's Diary.*

TUESDAY, OCTOBER 21.

Leaves Bedford : " *Bedford,* October 23.—We understand the President of the United States left Bedford, on his return to Philadelphia, on Tuesday last [October 21]."—*Dunlap and Claypoole's American Daily Advertiser,* October 28.

" From Cumberland and Bedford, the army marched in two divisions into the country of the insurgents. As had been foreseen, the greatness of the force prevented the effusion of blood. The disaffected did not venture to assemble in arms. Several of the leaders who had refused to give assurances of future submission to the laws were seized, and some of them detained for legal prosecution. A Mr. Bradford, who, in the latter stages of the insurrection, had manifested a peculiar degree of violence, and had openly advocated the appeal to arms, made his escape into the territories of Spain.

" But although no direct and open opposition was made, the spirit of insurrection was by no means subdued. A sour and malignant temper displayed itself, which indicated but too plainly that the disposition to resist had only sunk under the pressure of the great military force brought into the country, but would rise again should that force be suddenly removed. It was, therefore, thought advisable to station for the winter, a detachment, to be commanded by major general Morgan, in the centre of the disaffected country.

"Thus, without shedding a drop of blood, did the prudent vigour of the executive terminate an insurrection which, at one time, threatened to shake the government of the United States to its foundation."—*Marshall's Washington*, vol. v. p. 589.

SUNDAY, OCTOBER 26.

At Wright's Ferry : * " Thus far I have proceeded without accident to man horse or carriage, altho' the latter has had wherewith to try its goodness ; especially in ascending the North Mountain from Skinners by a wrong road ; that is,—by the old road which never was good and is rendered next to impassible by neglect. . . .

" I rode yesterday afternoon thro' the rain from York Town to this place, and got twice in the height of it hung (and delayed by that means) on the rocks in the middle of the Susquehanna. . . . I do not intend further than Lancaster to-day.—But on Tuesday, if no accident happens I expect to be landed in the City of Philadelphia."—*Washington to Alexander Hamilton.*

TUESDAY, OCTOBER 28.

At Philadelphia: " *October* 29.—Yesterday morning the President of the United States, and his suite arrived in town from Bedford."—*Dunlap and Claypoole's American Daily Advertiser.*

" *Philadelphia,* 31 October.—By pushing through the rain, which fell more or less on Saturday, Sunday, and Monday, I arrived in this city before noon on Tuesday, without encountering any accident on the road, or anything more unpleasant than the badness of the ways, after the rains had

---

* On the Susquehanna, now Columbia, Lancaster County, Pennsylvania.

softened the earth and made them susceptible of a deep impression of the wheels."—*Washington to Alexander Hamilton.*

THURSDAY, OCTOBER 30.

At Philadelphia : " *November* 1.—The Chevalier DE FREIRE was on Thursday [October 30] presented by the Secretary of State, to the President, as Minister Resident of Her Most Faithful Majesty [Maria-Frances-Isabella, Queen of Portugal], to the United States of America, and was received as such.

" We also hear that Madam FREIRE was yesterday [October 31,] introduced to the President and Mrs. Washington."—*Dunlap and Claypoole's American Daily Advertiser.*

WEDNESDAY, NOVEMBER 19.

At Philadelphia: " *November* 19.—This Day at twelve o'Clock the President of the United States met both Houses of the Legislature, in the Chamber of the House of Representatives, and delivered his Address."—*Dunlap and Claypoole's American Daily Advertiser.*

SATURDAY, NOVEMBER 22.

At Philadelphia: " *November* 22.—This day the Senate waited on the President of the United States, and the Vice President in their name presented him with an answer to his speech to both Houses of Congress."—*Dunlap and Claypoole's American Daily Advertiser.*

" *December* 1.—Last Saturday [November 29] at twelve o'clock the House of Representatives of the United States waited on the President with their answer to his speech."—*Idem.*

THURSDAY, DECEMBER 4.

At Philadelphia: " *December* 4.—We are happy in announcing to the public that the President of the United States means to honor the OLD AMERICAN COMPANY with his presence at the THEATRE this evening."—*The Aurora.*

"Old American Company.—THEATRE.—CEDAR [or South] Street.
—LAST NIGHT THIS SEASON.—FOR THE BENEFIT of Mr. and
Mrs. HALLAM.—*This Evening, Thursday, December* 4.—Will be presented, a Comedy, called THE YOUNG QUAKER; or The Fair Phila-
delphian. Written by O'Keefe, and performed in London with the most
unbounded applause.—End of the Play (by particular desire) the Panto-
mime Ballet of the TWO PHILOSOPHERS.—To which will be added, a
new Musical Piece, called The CHILDREN in the Wood.—The MUSIC
by Dr. Arnold, with additional SONGS by Mr. Carr.—End of the Farce,
Mr. Martin will recite Dr. Goldsmith's celebrated Epilogue in the character
of Harlequin.—The whole to conclude with a LEAP through A Barrel of
FIRE."—*Idem.*

WEDNESDAY, DECEMBER 10.

At Philadelphia: "*December* 11.—Yesterday returned
from the western expedition MACPHERSON's volunteer battalion of blues,* headed by their friend general [Frederick]
Frelinghuysen, who commanded the legion. At Broad-
Street they were received under a discharge of artillery by
a detachment which went out for that purpose—from Schuylkill they were escorted into the city by Captains [John]
Dunlap, [Abraham] Singer, and [Matthew] M'Connell's
Horse, in full uniform—their companions in the late truly
glorious, successful, and bloodless expedition. . . . As they
passed the President's House who was at the door, the band
played ; the Father of his country, expressed in his countenance, more than can be described."—*Dunlap and Claypoole's American Daily Advertiser.*

TUESDAY, DECEMBER 30.

At Philadelphia: "The considerations, which you have
often suggested to me, and which are repeated in your
letter of the 28th instant, as requiring your departure from
your present office, are such as to preclude the possibility

---

* A special body of volunteers formed for the purpose of assisting in quell-
ing the "Whiskey Insurrection." They were organized into a battalion,
and in compliment to their commander, Major William Macpherson, styled
themselves "Macpherson Blues." On the threatened war with France in
1798 the "Blues" were reorganized.

of my urging your continuance in it.   This being the case,
I can only wish that it was otherwise.

   " I cannot suffer you, however, to close your public service, without uniting with the satisfaction, which must
arise in your own mind from a conscious rectitude, my
most perfect persuasion, that you have deserved well of
your country."— *Washington to Henry Knox.*

   Timothy Pickering, at this time Postmaster-General, was appointed to
succeed General Knox as Secretary of War on January 2, 1795.

1795.

THURSDAY, JANUARY 1.

At Philadelphia : Issues a proclamation appointing Thursday, the nineteenth day of February, as a "Day of Public Thanksgiving and Prayer."

THURSDAY, JANUARY 22.

At Philadelphia: "A month from this day, if I should live to see the completion of it, will place me on the wrong (perhaps it would be better to say on the advanced) side of my grand climacteric; and although I have no cause to complain of the want of health, I can religiously aver, that no man was ever more tired of public life, or more devoutly wished for retirement than I do."— *Washington to Edmund Pendleton.*

WEDNESDAY, JANUARY 28.

At Philadelphia: "A plan for the establishment of a university in the Federal City has frequently been the subject of conversation ; but, in what manner it is proposed to commence this important institution, on how extensive a scale, the means by which it is to be affected, how it is to be supported, or what progress is made in it, are matters altogether unknown to me."— *Washington to the Commissioners of the Federal District.*

In continuing this letter, Washington wrote, "It has always been a source of serious reflection and sincere regret with me, that the youth of the United States, should be sent to foreign countries for the purpose of education. Although there are doubtless many, under these circumstances, who escape the danger of contracting principles unfavorable to republican government, yet we ought to deprecate the hazard attending ardent and susceptible minds, from being too strongly and too early prepossessed in favor of other political systems, before they are capable of appreciating their own.

"For this reason I have greatly wished to see a plan adopted, by which the arts, sciences, and belles-lettres could be taught in their fullest extent, thereby embracing all the advantages of European tuition, with the means of acquiring the liberal knowledge, which is necessary to qualify our citizens for the exigencies of public as well as private life; and (which with me is a consideration of great magnitude) by assembling the youth from the different parts of this rising republic, contributing from their intercourse and interchange of information to the removal of prejudices, which might perhaps sometimes arise from local circumstances." *

MONDAY, FEBRUARY 2.

At Philadelphia: "After so long an experience of your public services, I am naturally led at this moment of your departure from office (which it has always been my wish to prevent), to review them. In every relation, which you have borne to me, I have found that my confidence in your talents, exertions, and integrity has been well placed. I the more freely render this testimony of my approbation, because I speak from opportunities of information, which cannot deceive me, and which furnish satisfactory proof of your title to public regard. My most earnest wishes for your happiness will attend you in your retirement."— *Washington to Alexander Hamilton.*

Mr. Hamilton resigned the office of Secretary of the Treasury on the 31st of January. Oliver Wolcott, Jr., was appointed his successor on the 3d of February.

---

* The national university in which the first President took so much interest, and towards the endowment of which he bequeathed the fifty shares of the Potomac Company donated to him by the State of Virginia, has not as yet been established. Several attempts, however, have been made to procure the proper legislation, but no positive action by Congress has been taken. The site selected by Washington is now occupied by the National Observatory.

THURSDAY, FEBRUARY 19.

At Philadelphia: Thanksgiving Day. Attends Christ Church, Second Street above Market.*

"On a thanksgiving day appointed by the President for the suppression of the western insurrection,† I preached a sermon in his presence. The subject was the Connection between Religion and Civil Happiness. It was misrepresented in one of our newspapers. This induced the publishing of the sermon,‡ with a dedication to the President, pointedly pleading his proclamation in favour of the connection affirmed. . . .

"The father of our country, whenever in this city, as well during the revolutionary war as in his Presidency, attended divine service in Christ Church of this city; except during one winter [1781-82]; when, being here for the taking of measures with Congress towards the opening of the next campaign, he rented a house ₰ near St. Peter's Church [Third and Pine Streets], then in parochial union with Christ Church. During that season, he attended regularly at St. Peter's. His behaviour was always serious and attentive; but as your letter seems to intend an inquiry on the point of kneeling during the service, I owe it to truth to declare, that I never saw him in the said attitude. During his Presidency, our vestry provided him with a pew, ten yards in front of the reading desk. It was habitually occupied by himself, by Mrs. Washington, who was regularly a communicant, and by his secretaries."—*William White to the Rev. B. B. C. Parker*, November 28, 1832.

---

* This building, erected 1727–44, is still standing in perfect preservation; present rector, Rev. Charles Ellis Stevens.

† This was not a thanksgiving day appointed especially for the suppression of the Western or Whiskey Insurrection. but was the date named in the President's proclamation of January 1, for a "Day of Public Thanksgiving and Prayer," in which mention was made of the "seasonable controul which has been given to a spirit of disorder in the suppression of the late insurrection."

‡ "A Sermon on the Reciprocal Influences of Civil Policy and Religious Duty. Delivered in Christ Church, in the City of Philadelphia, on Thursday, the 19th of February, 1795, Being a day of General Thanksgiving. By William White, D.D., Bishop of the Protestant Episcopal Church in the Commonwealth of Pennsylvania. Philadelphia: March 2, 1795." 8vo, pp. 36.

₰ No. 110 South Third Street, between Walnut and Spruce Streets. This house, which at the time was the property of Benjamin Chew, was taken down about 1830. The house which now stands on the site is known as No. 242 South Third Street.

FRIDAY, FEBRUARY 20.

At Philadelphia: "*February* 20.—Cash paid Mr John Greenwood of the City of New York in full for his services as Dentist to the present date, viz. 60 Dollars, sent by Post in B. Notes."—*Washington's Cash-Book.*

This early practitioner of dentistry in America was the son of Isaac Greenwood, of Boston, the first to follow the profession in that city. He enlisted at the early age of fifteen in the Revolutionary army, was in the battle of Bunker Hill, and served in the expedition to Canada under General Arnold. He was also at the battle of Trenton, and afterward entered the naval privateer service, in which he remained until the close of the war. Mr. Greenwood then settled in New York, and became known as a successful dentist; he has the reputation of being the first in the United States to strike up a gold plate to serve as a base for artificial teeth, without a knowledge of it ever having been done before that time, 1799.

John Greenwood, however, is best known as being the dentist of the first President, his services beginning at New York in 1789, at which time he constructed for him a complete set of teeth, including both upper and lower jaws. The entire upper portion was carved from a piece of sea-horse or hippopotamus tusk; into the lower portion, worked out of the same material, human teeth were inserted and fixed permanently by means of gold pivots. He afterward constructed other sets for the President.

MONDAY, FEBRUARY 23.

At Philadelphia: "*February* 24.—Sunday last was the Birth-day of the President of the United States, when he entered into the *Sixty-Fourth* year of his age. The Auspicious Anniversary was yesterday celebrated with every expression of respect becoming the Members of a Free Republic towards the Father of his Country. The Members of both Houses of Congress—Foreign Ministers—the Reverend Clergy, and other Citizens, and respectable Foreigners, assembled at the House of the President, to offer their congratulations.

"At noon, a Federal salute was fired by a detachment of the Artillery—immediately after both Branches of the Legislature of this Commonwealth, preceded by the Governor, the President of the Senate [William Bingham], and Speaker of the House of Representatives [George Latimer], the Offi-

cers of the Militia—and the Members of the Cincinnati,
went in procession from the State House, escorted by a
Military Corps, to the House of the President of the United
States—to present their felicitations on the occasion."—
Dunlap and Claypoole's American Daily Advertiser.

" *February* 26.—On Monday last [February 23] the anniversary of the
President's birth was celebrated. The artillery announced the dawning of
the day by a federal salute. In the morning the President was waited on
by Congress, the Cincinnati, and a vast number of citizens. In the evening
he attended at a ball and supper given in honour of the day, by the City
Dancing Assembly. The rooms were crowded by a brilliant assemblage of
the Fair of the metropolis. Near 150 ladies, and nearly twice the number of
citizens were present. A greater display of beauty and elegance no country,
we believe, could ever boast of. Most of the foreign Ministers attended
with their ladies.

" After the supper the President gave the following toast : ' The Dancing
Assembly of Philadelphia—May the members thereof, and the Fair who
honour it with their presence, long continue in the enjoyment of an amusement so innocent and agreeable.' "—*Idem.*

" The President's birth-day was celebrated with uncommon zeal and
attachment, and I never saw him in better health and spirits. The crowds
of gentlemen that waited on him in the day were innumerable, and in the
Assembly at night it was scarcely possible to move. I came off a little
after eight, having business of great importance to attend to, and indeed
the room was much too crowded to be comfortable."—*James Iredell to Mrs.
Iredell,* February 26.

FRIDAY, FEBRUARY 27.

At Philadelphia : " *February* 28, 1795.—I received [Feb-
ruary 24] an invitation by my father from Mrs. Washington
to visit her, and Col. [Thomas] Hartley politely offered to
accompany me to the next drawing-room levee.

" On this evening my dress was white brocade silk,
trimmed with silver, and white silk, high-heeled shoes, embroidered with silver, and a light blue sash, with silver cord
and tassel tied at the left side. My watch was suspended
at the right, and my hair was in its natural curls. Sur-
mounting all was a small white hat and white ostrich-
feather, confined by brilliant band and buckle. Punctual
to the moment, Col. Hartley, in his chariot, arrived. He

brought with him Dr. Price, from England, who has sought America as an asylum, having given some political umbrage to his own government.

"The hall, stairs, and drawing-room of the President's house were lighted by lamps and chandeliers. Mrs. Washington, with Mrs. Knox, sat near the fire-place. Other ladies were seated on sofas, and gentlemen stood in the centre of the room conversing. On our approach, Mrs. Washington arose and made a courtesy—the gentlemen bowed most profoundly—and I calculated my declension to her own with critical exactness. The President soon after, with that benignity peculiarly his own, advanced, and I arose to receive and return his compliments with the respect and love my heart dictated. He seated himself beside me, and inquired for my father, a severe cold having detained him at home."—*Charlotte Chambers to Mrs. James Chambers.*

Charlotte Chambers, the writer of the above-quoted letter, was the daughter of General James Chambers, of the Pennsylvania line, and granddaughter of Benjamin Chambers, the founder of Chambersburg, Pennsylvania. She married Israel Ludlow in November, 1796. In a subsequent letter, dated March 11, also to her mother, referring to a visit paid her by Mrs. Washington, she writes, "On taking leave, she observed a portrait of the President hanging over the fire-place, and said 'she had never seen a correct likeness of General Washington. The only merit the numerous portraits of him possessed was their resemblance to each other.'"

Miss Chambers was also present at the birthnight ball, February 23, of which, in a letter dated the 25th, she gives her mother the following description : * "Dr. Rodman, master of ceremonies, met us at the door, and conducted us to Mrs. Washington. She half arose as we made our passing compliments. She was dressed in a rich silk, but entirely without ornament, except the animation her amiable heart gives to her countenance. Next her were seated the wives of the foreign ambassadors, glittering from the floor to the summit of their headdress. One of the ladies wore three large ostrich-feathers. Her brow was encircled by a sparkling fillet of diamonds ; her neck and arms were almost covered with jewels, and two watches were suspended from her girdle, and all reflecting the light from a

---

* These letters are printed in a volume published at Philadelphia in 1856, entitled "Memoir of Charlotte Chambers, by her Grandson Louis H. Garrard."

hundred directions. Such superabundance of ornament struck me as injudicious; we look too much at the gold and pearls to do justice to the lady. However, it may not be in conformity to their individual taste thus decorating themselves, but to honor the country they represent.

"The seats were arranged like those of an amphitheatre, and cords were stretched on each side of the room, about three feet from the floor, to preserve sufficient space for the dancers. We were not long seated when General Washington entered, and bowed to the ladies as he passed round the room. 'He comes, he comes, the hero comes!' * I involuntarily but softly exclaimed. When he bowed to me, I could scarcely resist the impulse of my heart, that almost burst through my bosom, to meet him. The dancing soon after commenced."

MONDAY, MARCH 9.†

At Philadelphia: "I am directed by the President of the United States to acknowledge the receipt of your letter of the 7th inst., and that of the present day;—and to express to you his regret at your despair of bringing your plan of a national monument to a fortunate issue."—*Bartholomew Dandridge to Giuseppe Ceracchi.*

Giuseppe Ceracchi, an Italian sculptor, a pupil of Canova, came to this country in 1791. He sought the aid of Congress in the erection of a monument to the American Revolution, but that body did not favor the design. Ceracchi modelled a bust of Washington from life in 1792, which, although rather severe in style, is claimed to be an admirable representation of the man. The mouth is particularly remarkable for its fidelity of expression. This bust is owned by the estate of the late Gouverneur Kemble, of New York. He also repeated it in colossal size. Ceracchi returned to Europe in 1795, and was executed in 1802 for a supposed connection with an attempt to assassinate Napoleon.

SUNDAY, MARCH 29.

At Philadelphia: "*March* 30.—I dined yesterday with the President. He was in fine health and spirits, and so

---

* The first line of a song written by Henry Carey, an English musician and poet, who died in 1743. His poems were first published at London in 1713.

† "*March* 9.—At four o'clock with the Speaker and twenty-two members of the [Pennsylvania] House [of Representatives], dined with President Washington. He was exceedingly affable to all."— *Diary of Jacob Hiltzheimer.*

were Mrs. Washington and the whole family. There is now there an elderly sister of Miss Custis's [Eliza Parke Custis] not so handsome as herself, but she seems to be very agreeable."—*James Iredell to Mrs. Iredell.*

THURSDAY, APRIL 2.

At Philadelphia : " *April* 2.—We dined to-day with the President and Mrs. Washington, in company with Mr. and Mrs. Hammond, the Chevalier and Madame Frere (who is truly an elegant woman) Don Philip [Joseph De] Jaudennes and his lady, Mr. and Mrs. Van Berckel, Mr. and Mrs. Randolph, Mr. and Mrs. Wolcott, Mr. and Mrs. Pinckney, and Mr. and Mrs. Coxe. Madame Frere and Madame Jaudennes were brilliant with diamonds."—*Mrs. William Cushing to* ——.

TUESDAY, APRIL 14.

Leaves Philadelphia: "*April* 16.—On Tuesday [April 14] the President of the United States set out from this city for his seat at Mount Vernon."—*Dunlap and Claypoole's American Daily Advertiser.*

" *Tuesday, April* 14.—Left Phil[a] for Mt. V. reached Wilmington. *April* 15.—Reached Rogers Susq[a]. *April* 16.—Baltimore. *April* 17.— Bladensburgh. *April* 18.—George Town. *April* 19.—Mount Vernon and remained there until the 26th."— *Washington's Diary.*

SUNDAY, APRIL 26.

Leaves Mount Vernon: " *April* 26.—Came to George Town. *April* 27.—In the federal city. *April* 28.—Arrived at Bladensburgh. *April* 29.—Baltimore. *April* 30.— Rogers's—Susquehanna. *May* 1.—Came to Wilmington. *May* 2.—Arrived at Philadelphia."— *Washington's Diary.*

" *Philadelphia*, 4th May.—I arrived in this city on Saturday [May 2] at noon."— *Washington to William Pearce.*

MONDAY, MAY 4.

At Philadelphia: "I intended, but forgot when I was at Mount Vernon, to measure the size of the picture frames in the parlour; which contains my picture *—Mrs. Washington—and the two child^r. I wish you to do it, and send me the account in your next letter. Measure the frames (I believe they are all of a size) from out to out; and then on the inside, where they show the Canvas, or picture."— *Washington to William Pearce.*

SUNDAY, MAY 10.

At Philadelphia: " I am sorry to find by your last reports that there has been two deaths in the family since I left Mount Vernon; and one of them a young fellow.—I hope every necessary care and attention was afforded him.—I expect little of this from McKoy [an overseer],—or indeed from most of his class; for they seem to consider a Negro much in the same light as they do the brute beasts, on the farms; and often treat them as inhumanly."— *Washington to William Pearce.*

MONDAY, JUNE 8.

At Philadelphia: "*June* 9.—I dined yesterday in the family way with the President. . . . The whole family made the usual inquiries concerning you and sent you the usual compliments."—*John Adams to Mrs. Adams.*

TUESDAY, JUNE 16.

At Philadelphia: "*June* 18.—Mr. Adet was presented to the President on Tuesday [June 16], and, accompanied by

---

* The three-quarter-length representing Washington in the costume of a colonel in the Virginia militia, painted by Charles Willson Peale at Mount Vernon, in May, 1772, the first original portrait of the Pater Patriæ. George Washington Parke Custis, referring to this portrait in his " Recollections," says, " This splendid and most interesting picture formed the principal ornament of the parlor at Mount Vernon for twenty-seven years." The picture is now owned by General George W. C. Lee; the original study for the head is in the possession of the Historical Society of Pennsylvania.

the Secretary of State made me a visit immediately after his
audience. I was not at home, but in Senate. On Wednesday morning I returned his visit at Oeller's hotel."—*John
Adams to Mrs. Adams.*

Pierre Auguste Adet succeeded M. Fauchet as minister from France to
the United States. In 1797 he broke off diplomatic relations, presenting
the note of the Directory declaring that France would treat neutrals as they
allowed themselves to be treated by the English. Before returning to his
own country he issued an address to the American people intended to inflame
them against the policy of their government.

FRIDAY, JULY 3.

At Philadelphia: "The treaty of Amity, Commerce and
Navigation, which has lately been before the Senate, has, as
you will perceive, made its public entry into the Gazettes of
this City.—Of course the merits, and demerits of it will
(especially in its unfinished state), be freely discussed."—
Washington to Alexander Hamilton.

Mr. Jay closed his English mission by signing a treaty on November 19,
1794. The treaty, in which, for the sake of peace, more was yielded than
gained, was long on its passage, for it was not received by the President till
March 7, a few days after the adjournment of Congress. Washington
summoned the Senate to convene on Monday the 8th of June, and on that
day laid before it the treaty and accompanying documents; and on the 24th
of the month, after a minute and laborious investigation, the Senate, by
precisely a constitutional majority (twenty to ten), advised and consented to
its conditional ratification. A sketch of the document appeared in the
Aurora (June 29), and led Senator Stevens Thomson Mason, of Virginia, a
strong opponent of the treaty, to send to that paper his copy, and on July 1
it was issued by Bache in a pamphlet. The ratification of the treaty was
signed by the President on the 18th of August.

SATURDAY, JULY 4.

At Philadelphia: "*July 6.*—Saturday last being the Anniversary of Independence, the same was celebrated by every
friend to the United States. The Day was ushered in with
ringing of bells, which continued thro' the Day—The military paraded. Federal Salutes were fired. Public Bodies
dined together—Congratulations were mutual, and the

Father of his Country, received the Felicitations of every class of Citizens, civil, clerical and military."—*Gazette of the United States.*

FRIDAY, JULY 10.

At Philadelphia : Issues a proclamation granting a full, free, and entire pardon to all persons concerned in the "Whiskey Insurrection," in Western Pennsylvania, who had given assurance of submission to the laws of the United States. The proclamation was not published till the 6th of August.

WEDNESDAY, JULY 15.

Leaves Philadelphia : "*July* 15.—President Washington about eight o'clock this morning set out for Mount Vernon in a two-horse phaeton for one person, his family in a coach and four horses, and two servants on horseback leading his saddle horse."—*Diary of Jacob Hiltzheimer.*

"*July* 15.—Left Phila^a with Mrs Washington & my family for Mt Vernon —Dined at Chester & lodged at Wilmington. *July* 16.—Breakfasted at Christ^a dined at Elkton—& lodged at Susquehanna—One of my horses overcome with heat. *July* 17.—Breakfasted before I set out dined at Hartford & lodged at Websters.—bro^t on the sick horse led. *July* 18.—Breakfasted in Baltim^e—dined & lodged at Spurriers where my sick horse died. *July* 19.—Breakfasted at Vanhornes—dined at Bladensburgh & lodged in Geo: Town. *July* 20.—After doing business with the Com^rs of the fed^l City I proceeded on my journey & got home to dinner."—*Washington's Diary.*

SATURDAY, JULY 18.

At Baltimore : Receives the resolutions, denouncing the *Jay Treaty*, passed by a meeting of the citizens of Boston, held on the 10th of the month. The resolutions were enclosed to him in a letter from the selectmen of that town dated the 13th.

As any negotiation or amicable arrangements with Great Britain were extremely unpopular, the consent of the Senate to the ratification of the treaty was met with virulent opposition, and meetings in Boston, New York,

Philadelphia, Baltimore, Charleston, and other parts of the country were held and addresses and resolutions against the measure forwarded to the President. The first meeting of this character was the one held in Boston. Addresses to the chief magistrate and resolutions of town and country meetings were not the only means which were employed on this occasion to enlist the American people against the measures which had been advised by the Senate. An immense number of essays in opposition were written, which the friends of the instrument met by counter-efforts, and the gazettes of the day are replete with appeals to the passions and to the reason of those who are the ultimate arbiters of every political question.

FRIDAY, JULY 24.

At Mount Vernon: "I have not, as I mentioned to you in my last, heard much respecting the treaty since I left Philadelphia. At Baltimore I remained no longer than to breakfast. In Georgetown my whole time was spent in business with the commissioners; and in Alexandria I did not stop. Yet the same leaven, that fermented the town of Boston, is at work, I am informed, in other places; but whether it will produce the same fruit remains to be decided."—*Washington to Edmund Randolph.*

WEDNESDAY, JULY 29.

At Mount Vernon : "The contents of your letters of the 21st and 24th instant, which I received by Monday's post, the importance of some of their enclosures, and the perturbed state of men's minds respecting the late treaty with Great Britain, together with the proceedings in some of the principal towns to embarrass the business, have determined me to repair to the seat of government."—*Washington to Edmund Randolph.*

A meeting of the citizens of Philadelphia, for the purpose of passing resolutions against the treaty, was held at the State-House on July 25. After the business of the meeting was closed, a copy of the treaty was suspended on a pole and carried about the streets by a company of people, who at length stopped in front of the British minister's house (Mr. Hammond) and there burnt the treaty, and also before the door of the British consul (Phineas Bond), amidst the huzzas and acclamations of the populace.

THURSDAY, AUGUST 6.

Leaves Mount Vernon: "*August* 6.—Left home on my return to Philadelphia—met the Poto^k C° at Geo : Town & lodged there. *August* 7.—Breakfasted at Bladensburgh—din^d at Vanhornes & lodged at Spur^{rs}. *August* 8.—Breakfasted at Baltimore—and dined and loged at Websters. *August* 9.—Breakfasted at Hartford dined at Susquehanna and lodged at Charles town. *August* 10.—Breakfasted at Elkton—Dined at Newcastle and lodged at Wilmington. *August* 11.—Breakfasted at Chester and dined in Phil^a."— *Washington's Diary.*

"Expenses of my Journey to Philadelphia.—*August* 6.—At Wise's 3.9. Turnpike 1.8. Ferriage Geo : Town 7.6; *August* 7.—Bill at Suters 2.6.7. Servants Do 3.9. Bill at Bladensb'g 8.9. Servants at Do 3.10. Bill at Vanhornes 15.6. Servants Do. 1.10½. Getting horses out of the Mire 1.7.6; *August* 8.—Bill at Spurriers 1.14.0. Servants Do 11.7½. Ferriage Elkridge 2.8. Bill at Baltimore 14.1. Servants at Do 3.9; *August* 9.—Bill at Websters 1.10.6. Servants at Do 2.0. Bill at Hartford 8.9. Servants Do 3.0. Bill at Susquehanna 14.8. Servants at Do 1.10½; *August* 10.—Bill at Charlestown 1.1.8. Servants at D 1.10½. Bill at Elkton 14.6. Servants at Do 1.10½. Porter at Mitchells 3.c. Bill at the Bear 3.10½. Ditto at Newcastle 11.10. Ferry over Christa 2.10; *August* 11.—Bill at Wilmington 1.2.10. Servants Do 11.7½. Ferry over Brandy-Wine 2.10. Bill at Chester 10.9. Servants Do 2.0. Ferry over Schuylkill 1.6. Sundries pd for besides the above 1.10.11."— *Washington's Memorandum-Book.*

TUESDAY, AUGUST 11.

At Philadelphia : "*August* 12.—The President of the United States arrived in town yesterday at noon."—*Dunlap and Claypoole's American Daily Advertiser.*

On the day after the arrival of the President at Philadelphia (August 12) the question respecting the immediate ratification of the treaty was brought before the Cabinet. "The secretary of state maintained singly the opinion, that during the existence of the provision order, and during the war between Britain and France, this step ought not to be taken. This opinion did not prevail. The resolution was adopted to ratify the treaty immediately, and to accompany the ratification with a strong memorial against the provision order, which should convey in explicit terms the sense of the American government on that subject. By this course, the views of the executive were happily accomplished. The order was revoked, and the ratifications of the treaty were exchanged."—MARSHALL's *Life of Washington*, vol. v. p. 633.

THURSDAY, AUGUST 20.

At Philadelphia : " Your resignation of the office of State is received. Candor induces me to give you in a few words the following narrative of facts. The letter from M. Fauchet, with the contents of which you were made acquainted yesterday, was, as you supposed, an intercepted one. It was sent by Lord Grenville to Mr. Hammond, by him put into the hands of the Secretary of the Treasury, by him shown to the Secretary of War and the Attorney-General ; and a translation thereof was made by the former for me."— *Washington to Edmund Randolph.*

Late in March, 1795, a French corvette was captured by a British man-of-war off Penmarch, and some of M. Fauchet's despatches to his government were taken. These despatches were sent to the British minister, Mr. Hammond, and by him given to Mr. Wolcott, Secretary of the Treasury, July 28. The intercepted despatch was No. 10, dated 10 Brumaire (October 31, 1794), and purported to give some "*précieuses confessions*" of Mr. Randolph on the Western insurrection. The inference from the general tenor of the despatch was, that the Secretary of State had shown himself accessible to a bribe from the French minister, and that he was at heart favorable to the Western insurrection, either from party motives or from others not known. The suspicion thus excited was strengthened by the fact that he had changed his mind respecting the ratification of the " Jay treaty," and had suggested difficulties and promoted delay.

M. Fauchet wrote a declaration, however, as soon as it was known to him that his letter had been intercepted, and when he was on the point of leaving the country to return to France, denying in the most positive terms that Mr. Randolph had ever indicated to him a willingness to receive money for personal objects, and affirming that in his letter he had no intention of saying anything to the disadvantage of Mr. Randolph's character.

On August 19, in the presence of Messrs. Wolcott and Pickering, Washington gave to Mr. Randolph the intercepted despatch, and the Secretary requested an opportunity to throw his ideas on paper. Instead of so doing, he sent in his resignation that evening.

SATURDAY, AUGUST 22.

At Philadelphia : " The seaport towns, or rather parts of them, are involved, and are endeavouring as much as in them lies to involve the community at large, in a violent opposition to the treaty with Great Britain, which is ratified as far as the measure depends upon me. The general opinion, however, as far as I am able to come at it is, that the current is turning."— *Washington to James Ross.*

TUESDAY, SEPTEMBER 8.

Leaves Philadelphia: " *September* 10.—Tuesday last [September 8] the President of the United States set out from this city for Mount Vernon."—*Dunlap and Claypoole's American Daily Advertiser.*

" *September* 8.—Left Phil* for M* Vernon dined at Chester—& lodged at Wilmington. *September* 9.—Breakfasted at Christiana dined at Elkton—& lodged at Charlestown. *September* 10.—Breakfasted at Susquehanna (M** Rogers's) dined at Harford—& loged at Websters. *September* 11.—Breakfasted at Baltimore dined & lodged at Spurriers. *September* 12.—Breakfasted at Van Horns Dined at Bladensburgh—& lodged at George Town. *September* 13.—Breakfasted in George Town and reached M* Vernon to dinner."—*Washington's Diary.*

SUNDAY, SEPTEMBER 20

At Mount Vernon: "If any power on earth could, or the Great Power above would, erect the standard of infallibility in political opinions, there is no being that inhabits this terrestrial globe, that would resort to it with more eagerness than myself, so long as I remain a servant of the public. But as I have found no better guide hitherto, than upright intentions and close investigation, I shall adhere to those maxims, while I keep the watch; leaving it to those, who will come after me, to explore new ways, if they like or think them better."— *Washington to Henry Knox.*

FRIDAY, SEPTEMBER 25.

At Alexandria: " *September* 25.—Went to Alexandria— dined with M* & M** Lear.* *September* 26.—Returned home to dinner."— *Washington's Diary.*

* Tobias Lear married Fanny Washington, widow of George Augustine Washington, early in August, 1795. His first wife, who died at Philadel-

SUNDAY, SEPTEMBER 27.

At Mount Vernon : "I shall not, whilst I have the honor to administer the government, bring a man into any office of consequence knowingly, whose political tenets are adverse to the measures, which the general government are pursuing; for this, in my opinion, would be a sort of political suicide. That it would embarrass its movements is most certain. But of two men equally well affected to the true interests of their country, of equal abilities, and equally disposed to lend their support, it is the part of prudence to give the preference to him, against whom the least clamor can be excited."— *Washington to Timothy Pickering.*

FRIDAY, OCTOBER 9.

At Mount Vernon : "I can most religiously aver I have no wish, that is incompatible with the dignity, happiness, and true interest of the people of this country. My ardent desire is, and my aim has been, as far as depended upon the executive department, to comply strictly with all our engagements, foreign and domestic; but to keep the United States free from political connexions with every other country, to see them independent of all and under the influence of none. In a word, I want an *American* character, that the powers of Europe may be convinced we act for *ourselves*, and not for others."— *Washington to Patrick Henry.*

MONDAY, OCTOBER 12.

Leaves Mount Vernon : "I shall set out for Philadelphia this day; but business with the commissioners of the Federal City will detain me in George Town to-morrow, and of course keep me a day longer from the seat of government, than I expected."— *Washington to Timothy Pickering.*

---

phia July 28, 1793, was Mary Long, of Portsmouth, New Hampshire, his native place.

" *October* 12.—Set out for Phil*ᵃ*. *October* 13.—Stayed at Geo: Town.
October 14.—Lodged at Spurriers. *October* 16.*—Lodged at Websters.
October 17.—Lodged at Hartford. *October* 18.—Lodged at Elkton. *October*
19.—Lodged at Wilmington. *October* 20.—Arrived at Phil."—*Washington's Diary.*

TUESDAY, OCTOBER 20.

At Philadelphia : " *October* 21.—Yesterday afternoon THE
PRESIDENT arrived in town from the Southward."—
Gazette of the United States.

SUNDAY, OCTOBER 25.

At Philadelphia : " I want a Green Pocket book, w*ᶜʰ* is
to be found in the hair trunk, which is usually put on my
writing Table in the Study, with my Land papers.—The
key of this trunk is under the lid of the writing Table.—it
is tied to a bunch of other keys by a twine.—This Pocket
book is of green parchment, and contains the courses, and
distances of many surveys of the grounds &c in, and about
my farms."—*Washington to William Pearce.*

This book, which contains seventy-eight closely written pages in the
handwriting of Washington, was sold at public sale in Philadelphia, December, 1890, for two hundred and fifty dollars. The sale was made by
order of the administrator of the estate of the widow of Lorenzo Lewis,
who was the son of Lawrence Lewis and Nelly Custis. The sale included
many articles from the household at Mount Vernon which were inherited
by Mr. and Mrs. Lawrence Lewis.

WEDNESDAY, NOVEMBER 11.

At Philadelphia : "*November* 13.—MARRIED. On Wed-
nesday last [November 11], by the Rev. Dr. [Robert] BLACK-
WELL, Major WILLIAM JACKSON, to Miss ELIZA
WILLING, daughter of Thomas Willing, Esq. President
of the Bank of the United States."—*Gazette of the United
States.*

---

* " *Baltimore.* October 17.—Yesterday morning the President of the
United States passed through this town on his way to the seat of government. We with pleasure add, that this venerable patriot appeared in perfect health."—*Gazette of the United States*, October 20.

"The ceremony was performed by Bishop White, assisted by his associate, Dr. Blackwell. Among those present were General and Mrs. Washington, Robert Morris and his wife, Hamilton, Lincoln, Knox, Vicomte de Noailles, the brother-in-law of Lafayette, and many others who then added so much to the attraction of Philadelphia society." —*Pennsylvania Magazine,* vol. ii. p. 366.

THURSDAY, NOVEMBER 19.

At Philadelphia: "The office of Attorney-General of the United States is not yet filled. The reason why it is not, General Lee at my request, will frankly relate to you. If you could make it convenient, and agreeable to yourself to accept it, I should derive pleasure therefrom, both from public and private considerations."— *Washington to Charles Lee.*

Charles Lee, of Virginia, brother of General Henry Lee, was appointed Attorney-General on December 10, succeeding William Bradford, who died August 23, and on the same day Timothy Pickering was appointed Secretary of State in the place of Edmund Randolph. The office of Secretary of War was filled January 27, 1796, by the appointment of James McHenry, of Maryland.

SUNDAY, NOVEMBER 22.

At Philadelphia: "It was with sincere pleasure I received your letter from Boston; and, with the heart of affection, I welcome you to this country."— *Washington to George Washington Lafayette.*

George Washington Lafayette, only son of the Marquis de Lafayette, came to the United States late in the summer of 1795, accompanied by his preceptor M. Frestel. He landed at Boston, and immediately informed Washington of the fact, but reasons of state prevented the President from inviting him to his house, which was his first impulse. After leaving Boston, young Lafayette (he was barely sixteen years of age) lived with his tutor for a while in the vicinity of New York, in comparative seclusion. Congress at length took cognizance of his presence in the country, and on the 18th of March, 1796, the House of Representatives passed a resolution directing a committee to inquire into the matter, and to report such measures as would be proper " to evince the grateful sense entertained by this country for the services of his father." This committee, through its chairman Edward Livingston, advised him to come to the seat of government, which he did, remaining in Philadelphia until the following spring, avoiding society as much as possible, when Washington, on becoming a private citizen, received him into his family as if he had been his own child. He remained with the family until early in October, 1797, when news of the release of his father from prison caused him to leave for the seaboard to depart for France. In 1824 he accompanied his father on his visit to the United States.

SUNDAY, DECEMBER 6.

At Philadelphia: "By Thursday's post I was favored with your letter of the 27th ultimo, enclosing a Declaration of the General Assembly of Maryland. At any time the expression of such a sentiment would have been considered as highly honorable and flattering. At the present, when the voice of malignancy is so high-toned, and no attempts are left unessayed to destroy all confidence in the constituted authorities of this country, it is peculiarly grateful to my sensibility; and, coming spontaneously, and with the unanimity it has done from so respectable a representation of the people, it adds weight as well as pleasure to the act."—*Washington to John H. Stone*, Governor of Maryland.

The Declaration of the General Assembly of Maryland, referred to in this letter, was expressed in the following language, and was unanimously adopted by the House of Delegates and the Senate.

"Resolved unanimously, that the General Assembly of Maryland, impressed with the liveliest sense of the important and disinterested services rendered to his country by the President of the United States; convinced that the prosperity of every free government is promoted by the existence of rational confidence between the people and their trustees, and is injured by misplaced suspicion and ill-founded jealousy; considering that public virtue receives its best reward in the approving voice of a grateful people, and that, when this reward is denied to it, the noblest incentive to great and honorable actions, to generous zeal and magnanimous perseverance, is destroyed; observing, with deep concern, a series of efforts, by indirect insinuation, or open invective to detach from the first magistrate of the Union the well-earned confidence of his fellow citizens; think it their duty to declare, and they do hereby declare, their unabated reliance on the *integrity, judgment*, and *patriotism* of the President of the United States."

TUESDAY, DECEMBER 8.

At Philadelphia: "*December* 8.—The House [Pennsylvania Legislature] adjourned at noon and proceeded to

Congress Hall, where President Washington delivered [in the Hall of the House] his address to the Senate and House."—*Diary of Jacob Hiltzheimer.*

William Cobbett (Peter Porcupine), who was present on this occasion, says in his pamphlet entitled "A Prospect from the Congress-Gallery," published at Philadelphia in 1796, "When the President arrived at the House this day, he found it in that state of composed gravity, of respectful silence, for which the Congress is so remarkable, and which, whatever witlings may say, is the surest mark of sound understanding.—The gallery was crowded with anxious spectators, whose orderly behaviour was not the least pleasing part of the scene.

"The President is a timid speaker: he is a proof, among thousands, that superior genius, wisdom, and courage, are ever accompanied with excessive modesty. His situation was at this time almost entirely new. Never, till a few months preceding this session, had the tongue of the most factious slander dared to make a public attack on his character. This was the first time he had ever entered the walls of Congress without a full assurance of meeting a welcome from every heart. He now saw, even among those to whom he addressed himself, numbers who, to repay all his labours, all his anxious cares for their welfare, were ready to thwart his measures, and present him the cup of humiliation, filled to the brim. When he came to that part of his speech, where he mentions the treaty with His Britannic Majesty, he cast his eyes towards the gallery.—It was not the look of indignation and reproach, but of injured virtue, which is ever ready to forgive. I was pleased to observe, that not a single murmur of disapprobation was heard from the spectators that surrounded me; and, if there were some amongst them, who had assisted at the turbulent town-meetings, I am persuaded, they were sincerely penitent When he departed, every look seemed to say: God prolong his precious life."

SATURDAY, DECEMBER 12.

At Philadelphia: Is waited on by the Senate, and the Vice-President, in its name, presents him with an answer to his address.

SUNDAY, DECEMBER 13.

At Philadelphia: "When you receive the money for my last years flour and Corn, I wish that every demand, of whatsoever nature or kind, may be discharged.—I never like to owe anything, lest I might be called upon for payment when I am not possessed of the means.—A Dun,

would not be agreeable to me, at any time;—and not to pay
money when it is due, and might really be wanting, would
hurt my feelings."—*Washington to William Pearce.*

THURSDAY, DECEMBER 17.

At Philadelphia: Is waited on by the House of Representatives of the United States, with an answer to his
address.

TUESDAY, DECEMBER 22.

At Philadelphia: "It is wellknown, that peace has been
(to borrow a modern phrase) the order of the day with me
since the disturbances in Europe first commenced. My policy has been, and will continue to be, while I have the honor
to remain in the administration, to maintain friendly terms
with, but be independent of, all the nations of the earth;
to share in the broils of none; to fulfil our own engagements; to supply the wants and be carriers for them all;
being thoroughly convinced, that it is our policy and interest to do so. Nothing short of self-respect, and that justice
which is essential to a national character, ought to involve
us in war; for sure I am, if this country is preserved in
tranquility twenty years longer, it may bid defiance in a
just cause to any power whatever; such in that time will
be its population, wealth, and resources."—*Washington to
Gouverneur Morris.*

THURSDAY, DECEMBER 24.

At Philadelphia: "*December* 26.—Last Thursday [Decem-
ber 24] I had the honor of dining with the President, in
company with the Vice-President, the Senators and Delegates of Massachusetts, and some other members of Congress, about 20 in all."—*Theophilus Bradbury to Mrs. Thomas
Hooper.*

In continuing this letter to his daughter Harriet, wife of Major Thomas
Hooper, the writer, who was a member of Congress from Essex County,

Massachusetts, says, " In the middle of the table was placed a piece of table furniture about six feet long and two feet wide, rounded at the ends. It was either of wood gilded, or polished metal, raised only about an inch, with a silver rim round it like that round a tea board ; in the centre was a pedestal of plaster of Paris with images upon it, and on each end figures, male and female, of the same. It was very elegant and used for ornament only. The dishes were placed all around, and there was an elegant variety of roast beef, veal, turkeys, ducks, fowls, hams, &c.; puddings, jellies, oranges, apples, nuts, almonds, figs, raisins, and a variety of wines and punch. We took our leave at six, more than an hour after the candles were introduced. No lady but Mrs. Washington dined with us. We were waited on by four or five men servants dressed in livery."

1796.

FRIDAY, JANUARY 1.

At Philadelphia: Receives from M. Adet, the minister from France, the colors of France, sent by the Committee of Public Safety of the National Convention as a token of friendship to the United States.*

The flag, which was directed to be placed in the archives of the government, is described as follows in the papers of the day: "The flag is tricolor, made of the richest silk and highly ornamented with allegorical paintings. In the middle, a cock is represented, the emblem of France standing on a thunderbolt. At two corners diagonally opposite are represented two bomb-shells bursting, at the other two corners, other military emblems. Round the whole is a rich border of oak leaves, alternately yellow and green, the first shaded with brown and heightened with gold; the latter shaded with black and relieved with silver; in this border are entwined warlike musical instruments. The edge is ornamented with a rich gold fringe. The staff is covered with black velvet crowned with a golden pike and enriched with the tricolor *cravatte* and a pair of tassels worked in gold and the three national colors."

SUNDAY, JANUARY 3.

At Philadelphia: "I am not disposed to take any thing less for my flour than it sells at here (allowing for freight and Insurance) for if it is well manufactured, it will pass Inspection in this Market, and of course command the price of other flour, without the credit which is required in Alexandria and would be for my interest to bring it hither, rather than sell at an under rate."— *Washington to William Pearce.*

---

* "*Jany.* 1, 1796.—Remarkably mild and pleasant—perfectly clear. Received the National Colours from Mr Adet the Minister Plenipo. to day: Much company visited."— *Washington's Diary.*

SUNDAY, JANUARY 17.

At Philadelphia: "I am under no concern for the fall which has taken place in the price of flour—that it will be up again, and higher than ever in the spring there is but little doubt—indeed some well informed Merchants declare they should not be surprized to find it at twenty dollars p^r Barrel at that season.

"There can be no question in my mind that herrings will be at 10*l.* p^r Thousand and Shads at three dollars at least p^r hundred for which reason, my advice to you is, not to take less from Mr Smith, or any other who may offer to contract, beforehand."—*Washington to William Pearce.*

MONDAY, FEBRUARY 1.

At Philadelphia: "I feel obliged by the expression of your concern for the attacks, which have been made upon my administration. If the enlightened and virtuous part of the community will make allowances for my involuntary errors, I will promise, that they shall have no cause to accuse me of wilful ones. Hoping for the former, I feel no concern on account of the latter."—*Washington to Oliver Wolcott,* Governor of Connecticut.

THURSDAY, FEBRUARY 11.

At Philadelphia: "*February* 13.—Dr. Priestly is here. I drank tea with him at the President's on Thursday evening [February 11]. He says he always maintained against Dr. Price, that old age was the pleasantest part of life, and he finds it so."—*John Adams to Mrs. Adams.*

Joseph Priestley, LL.D., scientist and dissenting minister, came to America in June, 1794, and settled at Northumberland, Pennsylvania, making his home with his sons who had preceded him. Dr. Priestley often preached at Philadelphia, and in the spring of 1796 delivered in that city a series of "Discourses relating to the Evidences of Revealed Religion," which were published the same year. His friend Richard Price, D.D., LL.D., to whom allusion is made, was the author of a pamphlet entitled

" Observations on the Nature of Civil Liberty, Principles of Government, and the Justice and Policy of the War with America," published at London and Boston in 1776, and of which sixty thousand copies were distributed. Dr. Price also published, in 1785, " Observations on the Importance of the American Revolution and the Means of making it a Benefit to the World." He died in London, England, March 19, 1791.

FRIDAY, FEBRUARY 12.

At Philadelphia : " *February* 13.—I went with Charles last night to the drawing room. As the evening was fair and mild, there was a great circle of ladies and a greater of gentlemen. General Wayne was there in glory.* This man's feelings must be worth a guinea a minute. The Pennsylvanians claim him as theirs, and show him a marked respect."—*John Adams to Mrs. Adams.*

" *Philadelphia,* February 8.—On Saturday last [February 6], about five o'clock in the afternoon, arrived in this city, after an absence of more than three years, on an expedition against the Western Indians, in which he proved so happily successful, MAJOR GENERAL WAYNE. Four miles from the city, he was met by the three Troops of Philadelphia Light Horse, and escorted by them to town. On his crossing the Schuylkill, a salute of fifteen cannon was fired from the Centre-square, by a party of Artillery. He was ushered into the city by ringing of bells and other demonstrations of joy, and thousands of citizens crowded to see and welcome the return of their brave General, whom they attended to the City Tavern, where he alighted. In the evening, a display of Fire-Works was exhibited, in celebration of the Peace lately concluded with the Western Indians, and the Algerines ; and also, on account of the Peace concluded by France with several European Powers."—*Claypoole's American Daily Advertiser.*

MONDAY, FEBRUARY 22.

At Philadelphia : " *February* 23.—Yesterday being the anniversary of the birth-day of the President of the United States, when he entered into the 64th [65th] year of his age, it was ushered in here by the firing of cannon, ringing of bells, and other demonstrations of joy. In the course of

---

* Gained by his victory over the Indians on the banks of the Miami, August 20, 1794.

the day, the members of both houses of Congress, the Senate and representatives of this state,* the heads of departments, foreign ministers, the clergy of every denomination, the Cincinnati, civil and military officers of the United States, several other public bodies, and many respectable citizens and foreigners, waited upon the President according to annual custom to congratulate him on the occasion. Detachments of artillery and infantry paraded in honor of the day, and in the evening there was perhaps one of the most splendid balls at Rickett's amphitheatre ever given in America."—*Claypoole's American Daily Advertiser.*

"*Philadelphia,* February, 1796.—On General Washington's birth-day, which was a few days ago, this city was unusually gay; every person of consequence in it, Quakers alone excepted, made it a point to visit the General on this day. As early as eleven o'clock in the morning he was prepared to receive them, and the audience lasted till three in the afternoon. The society of the Cincinnati, the clergy, the officers of the militia, and several others, who formed a distinct body of citizens, came by themselves separately. The foreign ministers attended in their richest dresses and most splendid equipages. Two large parlours were open for the reception of gentlemen, the windows of one of which towards the street were crowded with spectators on the outside. The sideboard was furnished with cake and wines, whereof the visitors partook. I never observed so much cheerfulness before in the countenance of General Washington; but it was impossible for him to remain insensible to the attention and compliments paid to him on this occasion.

"The ladies of the city, equally attentive paid their respects to Mrs. Washington, who received them in the drawing-room up stairs. After having visited the General, most of the gentlemen also waited upon her. A public ball and supper terminated the rejoicings of the day."—ISAAC WELD, JUNIOR, *Travels through the States of North America during the Years 1795, 1796, and 1797.* London, 1799.

* "*February* 22.—At noon Speaker [Robert] Hare of the Senate, and Speaker [George] Latimer of the House, with their members, called on President Washington to congratulate him on his birthday. He stood in the centre of the back room, where he bowed to each member as he passed into the front room, where wine and cake were served. At night the ladies and gentlemen had a dance at Rickett's riding place, southwest corner Sixth and Chestnut Streets."—*Diary of Jacob Hiltzheimer.*

MONDAY, FEBRUARY 29.

At Philadelphia : " *February 29.*—We are informed THE PRESIDENT OF THE UNITED STATES intends visiting the Theatre this Evening; and, the Entertainments are by his particular desire." *—Gazette of the United States.*

" *March* 1.—Yesterday [February 29] the President sent his carriage for me to go with the family to the theatre. The Rage and the Spoiled Child were the two pieces. It rained and the house was not full. I thought I perceived a little mortification. Mr. George Washington and his fair lady were with us. † . . . After all, persuasion may overcome the inclination of the chief to retire. But, if it should, it will shorten his days, I am convinced. His heart is set upon it, and the turpitude of the Jacobins touches him more nearly than he owns in words. All the studied efforts of the federalists to counterbalance abuse by compliment don't answer the end." —*John Adams to Mrs. Adams.*

FRIDAY, MARCH 4.

At Philadelphia : " If the people of this country have not abundant cause to rejoice at the happiness they enjoy, I know of no country that has. We have settled all our disputes, and are at peace with all nations. We supply their wants with our superfluities, and are well paid for doing so.—The earth generally, for years past, has yielded its fruits bountifully. No City, Town, Village, or even farm but what exhibits evidences of increasing wealth and prosperity; while Taxes are hardly known but in name. Yet by the second sight,—extraordinary foresight, or some other sight attainable by a few only, evils afar off are discovered

---

* "NEW THEATRE [north side of Chestnut, above Sixth Street]— *By Particular Desire.* On MONDAY EVENING, February 29, Will be presented, A celebrated COMEDY (written by the Author of the Dramatist) called THE RAGE! To which will be added, A FARCE in two acts, called THE SPOIL'D CHILD. The Public are respectfully informed, that the Doors of the Theatre will open at a quarter after FIVE o'clock, and the Curtain rise precisely at a quarter after SIX—until further notice." —*Gazette of the United States,* February 27.

† George Steptoe Washington, a nephew of the President, son of his brother Samuel. He had recently married Lucy Payne, daughter of John Payne, of Virginia, and a sister of Mrs. James Madison.

by these, alarming to themselves; and as far as they are
able to render them so, disquieting to others."— *Washington
to Gouverneur Morris.*

THURSDAY, MARCH 24.

At Philadelphia : " *March* 25.—Yesterday I dined at the
President's, with ministers of state and their ladies, foreign
and domestic.   After dinner the gentlemen drew off after
the ladies, and left me alone with the President in close
conversation.   He detained me there till nine o'clock, and
was never more frank and open upon politics.   I find his
opinions and sentiments are more exactly like mine than I
ever knew before, respecting England, France, and our
American parties.   He gave me intimations enough that
his reign would be very short.   He repeated it three times
at least, that this and that was of no consequence to him
personally, as he had but a very little while to stay in his
present situation."—*John Adams to Mrs. Adams.*

FRIDAY, MARCH 25.

At Philadelphia : " The resolution moved in the House
of Representatives, for the papers relative to the negotiation
of the treaty with Great Britain, having passed in the
affirmative, I request your opinion,

" 1. Whether that branch of Congress has or has not a
right, by the constitution, to call for those papers ?

" 2. Whether, if it does not possess the right, it would be
expedient under the circumstances of this particular case to
furnish them ?

" 3. And, in either case, in what terms would it be most
proper to comply with, or to refuse, the request of the
House?"— *Washington to Timothy Pickering,* Secretary of
State.*

The treaty with Great Britain, commonly called *Jay's Treaty*, having
been ratified in London on the 28th day of October, 1795, and returned to

* Sent as a circular to the other members of the Cabinet.

the United States, a copy of it was laid before Congress, by the President, on the 1st of March. It now became the duty of the House of Representatives to make appropriations for carrying the treaty into effect. The party in the House opposed to the treaty was not satisfied with the course pursued by the President in promulgating it by a proclamation (February 29) before the sense of the House of Representatives had been in any manner obtained upon the subject. A resolution was brought forward by Mr. Livingston (March 2), which, after an amendment by the original mover, assumed the following shape:

" *Resolved,* That the President of the United States be requested to lay before this House a copy of the instructions given to the minister of the United States, who negotiated the treaty with Great Britain communicated by his message of the 1st instant, together with the correspondence and documents relating to the said treaty, excepting such of said papers as any existing negotiation may render improper to be disclosed."

A debate arose which did not terminate till the 24th of March, when the resolution passed in the affirmative by a vote of sixty-two to thirty-seven, and it was accordingly sent to the President by a committee of the House.* The President replied to the committee " that he would take the request of the House into consideration."

The members of the Cabinet were unanimous in advising the President not to comply with the resolution. Each of them stated the grounds of his opinion in writing. During the progress of the debate, Chief-Justice Ellsworth drew up an argument, showing that the papers could not be constitutionally demanded by the House of Representatives. A message was therefore framed and sent to the House on the 30th of March, at the conclusion of which the President said, " A just regard to the constitution, and to the duty of my office, under all the circumstances of this case, forbid a compliance with your request."

A motion to refer the message to a committee of the whole House was carried by a large majority; and on the 29th of April,† after a debate which had lasted for two weeks, the question was taken in committee, and determined by the casting vote of the chairman (Frederick A. Muhlenberg) in favor of the expediency of making the necessary laws for carrying out the treaty. The resolution was finally carried (April 30), fifty-one voting in the affirmative and forty-eight in the negative.

---

* Edward Livingston, of New York, and Albert Gallatin, of Pennsylvania.

† The speech of Fisher Ames, made on the 28th of April, advocating the appropriation required for the execution of the treaty, was such a remarkable effort that a member of the opposition objected to the taking of a vote at that time, on the ground that the House was too excited to come to a decision.

THURSDAY, MARCH 31.

At Philadelphia : " I do not know how to thank you sufficiently for the trouble you have taken to dilate on the
request of the House of Representatives for the papers
relative to the British treaty. . . . I had, from the first
moment, and from the fullest conviction in my own mind,
resolved to *resist the principle*, which was evidently intended
to be established by the call of the House of Representatives; * and only deliberated on the manner, in which this
could be done with the least bad consequences."— *Washington to Alexander Hamilton.*

MONDAY, APRIL 11.†

At Philadelphia : " I am under promise to Mrs. Bingham
to sit for you to-morrow, at nine o'clock, and wishing to
know if it be convenient to you that I should do so, and
whether it shall be at your own house (as she talked of the
State House) I send this note to ask information."— *Washington to Gilbert Stuart.*

The full-length portrait of Washington, as President, painted by Gilbert
Stuart in compliance with the above-mentioned request of Mrs. William
Bingham, and known as the " Lansdowne Portrait," was executed for the
purpose of presentation to the Marquis of Lansdowne (Lord Shelburne), a
great admirer of Washington, and who, during the Revolution, was an active
opponent of the policy of Lord North. At this date Stuart had a studio in
a house at the southeast corner of Fifth and Chestnut Streets (now included
in the Drexel Building), and in this room, in all probability, the sittings were
had. The portrait, which will always retain the name of the original owner,
is now in the possession of Lord Rosebery, late Prime Minister of England.
It is well known through numerous engravings, the first of which, executed
by James Heath, was published at London, February 1, 1800.

In a letter to Major William Jackson (who married a sister of Mrs. Bing-

---

* That the assent of the House was necessary to the validity of a treaty.

† " *April* 13.—I dined on Monday [April 11] at the President's with
young La Fayette and his preceptor, tutor or friend, whatever they call
him, whose name is Frestel. . . . There is a resemblance of father and
mother in the young man. He is said to be studious and discreet."—*John
Adams to Mrs. Adams.*

ham), dated London, March 5, 1797, the marquis writes, "I have received the picture, which is in every respect worthy of the original. I consider it a very magnificent compliment, and the respect I have for both Mr. and Mrs. Bingham will always enhance the value of it to me and my family. . . . General Washington's conduct is above all praise. He has left a noble example to sovereigns and nations present and to come. I beg you will mention both me and my sons * to him in the most respectful terms possible. If I was not too old, I would go to Virginia to do him homage."

The "Lansdowne Portrait" was brought to this country in 1876, and exhibited at Philadelphia in the Centennial International Exhibition of that year. At that time it belonged to John Delaware Lewis. A replica of this portrait, executed for Mr. Bingham, is owned by the Pennsylvania Academy of the Fine Arts.

SUNDAY, MAY 8.

At Philadelphia: "We are an Independent Nation, and act for ourselves—Having fulfilled, and being willing to fulfil, (as far as we are able) our engagements with other nations,—and having decided on, and strictly observed a Neutral conduct towards the Belligerent Powers, from an unwillingness to involve ourselves in War. . . . We will not be dictated to by the Politics of any Nation under Heaven, farther than Treaties require of us.

"Whether the *present*, or any circumstances should do more than *soften* this language, may merit consideration.— But if we are to be told by a foreign Power (if our engagements with it are not infracted) what we *shall do*, and what we shall *not do*, we have Independence yet to seek & have contended hitherto for very little."—*Washington to Alexander Hamilton.*

FRIDAY, MAY 13.

At Philadelphia: "*May* 13.—At one o'clock to-day I called at General Washington's with the picture and letter I had for him. He lived in a small red brick house on the left side of High Street, not much higher up than Fourth

---

* Lord Wycombe, the eldest son of the Marquis of Lansdowne, visited the United States in the latter part of 1791. He was entertained by the President when in Philadelphia.

Street. There was nothing in the exterior of the house that denoted the rank of the possessor. Next door was a hair-dresser."—*Diary of Thomas Twining.**

In continuing the above entry in his diary, Mr. Twining says, "Having stated my object to a servant who came to the door, I was conducted up a neat but rather narrow staircase, carpeted in the middle, and was shown into a middling-sized well-furnished drawing-room on the left of the passage. Nearly opposite the door was the fire-place, with a wood-fire in it. The floor was carpeted. On the left of the fire-place was a sofa, which sloped across the room. There were no pictures on the walls, no ornaments on the chimney-piece. Two windows on the right of the entrance looked into the street. There was nobody in the room, but in a minute Mrs. Washington came in, when I repeated the object of my calling, and put into her hands the letter for General Washington, and his miniature. She said she would deliver them to the President, and, inviting me to sit down, retired for that purpose. She soon returned, and said the President would come presently. Mrs. Washington was a middle-sized lady, rather stout; her manner extremely kind and unaffected. She sat down on the sofa, and invited me to sit by her. I spoke of the pleasant days I had passed at Washington, and of the attentions I had received from her grand-daughter, Mrs. Law.

"While engaged in this conversation, but with my thoughts turned to the expected arrival of the General, the door opened, and Mrs. Washington and myself rising, she said, 'The President,' and introduced me to him. Never did I feel more interest than at this moment, when I saw the tall, upright, venerable figure of this great man advancing towards me to take me by the hand. There was a seriousness in his manner which seemed to contribute to the impressive dignity of his person, without diminishing the confidence and ease which the benevolence of his countenance and the kindness of his address inspired. There are persons in whose appearance one looks in vain for the qualities they are known to possess, but the appearance of General Washington harmonized in a singular manner with the dignity and modesty of his public life. So completely did he *look* the great and good man he really was, that I felt rather respect than awe in his presence, and experienced neither the surprise nor disappointment with which a personal introduction to distinguished individuals is often accompanied.

* Thomas Twining, an Englishman by birth, who occupied a prominent position under the British government in the East Indies, made a short visit to the United States in 1796. When at Washington City he called upon Tobias Lear, then residing near Georgetown, who gave him a letter of introduction, and also intrusted him with a miniature picture of the President, to be delivered to him. We have no means of ascertaining what portrait this was. Mr. Twining's diary was published at New York in 1894.

"The General having thanked me for the picture, requested me to sit down next the fire, Mrs. Washington being on the sofa on the other side, and himself taking a chair in the middle. . . . In the course of the conversation I mentioned the particular regard and respect with which Lord Cornwallis always spoke of him. He received this communication in the most courteous manner, inquired about his lordship, and expressed for him much esteem. . . . After sitting about three quarters of an hour, I rose to take leave, when the General invited me to drink tea with him that evening. I regret to say I declined this honor on account of some other engagement—a wrong and injudicious decision, for which I have since reproached myself. . . . The General's age was rather more than sixty-four. In person he was tall, well-proportioned, and upright. His hair was powdered and tied behind. Although his deportment was that of a general, the expression of his features had rather the calm dignity of a legislator than the severity of a soldier."—THOMAS TWINING.

MONDAY, MAY 16.

At Philadelphia: "*May* 18.—On Monday last [May 16] ROBERT LISTON, Esq. was received by the President of the United States, as Envoy Extraordinary and Minister Plenipotentiary from his Britannic Majesty to the United States of America."—*Gazette of the United States.*

TUESDAY, MAY 17.

At Philadelphia: "*May* 21.—EDWARD THORNTON Esq. was presented to the President of the United States on Tuesday last [May 17] by the British Ambassador, as his Britannick Majesty's secretary of legation to the United States."—*Gazette of the United States.*

SUNDAY, MAY 29.

At Philadelphia: "Congress talk of rising about the middle of this week; but there is no dependance on it.—In about ten or twelve days after the session closes, it is likely I shall commence my journey homewards :—as soon as I can fix the day, I will advise you of it. . . . During my stay at Mount Vernon I expect much company there, and of the most respectable sort, it would be pleasing to us therefore to find everything in nice order."— *Washington to William Pearce.*

SATURDAY, JUNE 4.

At Philadelphia : "*June* 4.—On our return [to the city] we met, just below the stone bridge in the meadows, our President, Washington, and lady in a coach and four, two postillions, and only one servant on horseback. In old countries a man of his rank and dignity would not be seen without a retinue of twenty or more persons."—*Diary of Jacob Hiltzheimer.*

SUNDAY, JUNE 5.

At Philadelphia : "On Wednesday last [June 1] Congress closed their Session : but there is yet a good deal for me to do, before I can leave the Seat of the Government.—My present expectation however is, that I shall be able to do this tomorrow week : but as this is not certain, and as I shall travel slow, to avoid what usually happens to me at this season—that is—killing or knocking up a horse : and as we shall, moreover, stay a day or two at the Federal City, it is not likely we shall be at Mount Vernon before the 20th or 21st of this month.—

"In a few days after *we* get there, we shall be visited, I expect, by characters of distinction ; I could wish therefore that the Gardens, Lawns, and every thing else, in, and about the Houses, may be got in clean and nice order."— *Washington to William Pearce.*

MONDAY, JUNE 13.

Leaves Philadelphia : "*June* 13.—The President and family left town this morning for Mount Vernon."—*Gazette of the United States.*

SUNDAY, JUNE 19.

At George Town : " *George-Town*, June 21.—The President of the United States arrived in the City of Washington on the 18th instant, and at this place on the 19th. He is accompanied by the Son of his illustrious friend,

Fayette."—*Dunlap and Claypoole's American Daily Advertiser*, June 27.

MONDAY, JUNE 20.

At Mount Vernon : *" June 26.*—We arrived at this place
on Monday last [June 20], where it is probable I shall remain till the middle of August, when public business will
require *my* attendance in Philadelphia, until towards the
end of September.   I shall then return to this place again
for Mrs Washington, with whom, in the latter part of October, I shall make my last journey, to close my public life
the 4th of March; after which no consideration under
heaven, that I can foresee, shall again withdraw me from
the walks of private life.

" My house, I expect, will be crowded with company all
the while we shall be at it, this summer, as the ministers of
France, Great Britain, and Portugal, in succession, intend
to be here—besides other strangers."— *Washington to Robert
Lewis.*

MONDAY, JULY 4.

At Mount Vernon : " The Spanish minister M. de Yrujo,
spent two days with me, and is just gone."— *Washington to
Timothy Pickering.*

Don Carlos Martinez, Marquis de Casa Yrujo, succeeded Don Joseph
Jaudennes as Spanish minister to the United States, but was not formally
presented to the President until August 25.   He married (April 10, 1798)
Sally McKean, a daughter of Thomas McKean, Chief-Justice of Pennsylvania 1777-99.   Their son, the Duke of Sotomayer, born in Philadelphia,
became Prime Minister of Spain.

WEDNESDAY, JULY 6.

At Mount Vernon : " Until within the last year or two, I
had no conception that parties would or even could go the
length I have been witness to; nor did I believe until lately,
that it was within the bounds of probability, hardly within
those of possibility, that, while I was using my utmost

exertions to establish a national character of our own, independent, as far as our obligations and justice would permit, of every nation of the earth, and wished, by steering a steady course, to preserve this country from the horrors of a desolating war, I should be accused of being the enemy of one nation, and subject to the influence of another; and, to prove it, that every act of my administration would be tortured, and the grossest and most insidious misrepresentations of them be made, by giving one side only of a subject, and that too in such exaggerated and indecent terms as could scarcely be applied to a Nero, a notorious defaulter, or even to a common pickpocket."— *Washington to Thomas Jefferson.*

MONDAY, JULY 18.

At Mount Vernon: "I hope and expect, that the proposed visit from the Cherokee chiefs will be so managed, as not to take place before the month of November. I have already been incommoded at this place by a visit of several days from a party of a dozen Catawbas, and should wish, while I am in this retreat, to avoid a repetition of such guests."— *Washington to James McHenry.*

WEDNESDAY, AUGUST 10.

At Mount Vernon: "In the course of next week, probably about the middle of it, I expect to commence my journey for Philadelphia; but, as I shall be obliged to halt a day at the Federal City, and from the heat of the season and other circumstances must travel slowly, it is not likely I shall arrive there before the middle of the following week."— *Washington to Timothy Pickering.*

TUESDAY, AUGUST 16.

At Mount Vernon: "I propose to enter upon my journey to Philadelphia to morrow."— *Washington to James McHenry*, MS. Letter.

THURSDAY, AUGUST 18.

At Washington City: "*August* 18.—In passing through Alexandria yesterday, on my way to Philadelphia, I saw Col° Fitzgerald, who informed me of a letter he had received from you."—*Washington to James Anderson.*

James Anderson, to whom the above letter was addressed, succeeded William Pearce as superintendent at Mount Vernon in December. He was acting in that capacity at the time of the decease of Washington, and the last letter written by him, dated December 13, 1799, was to Mr. Anderson. This letter is now in the Ferdinand J. Dreer Autograph Collection of the Historical Society of Pennsylvania.

SUNDAY, AUGUST 21.

At Philadelphia: "*August* 22.—The President of the United States arrived in town last evening."—*Gazette of the United States.*

THURSDAY, AUGUST 25.

At Philadelphia: "My conduct in public and private life as it relates to the important struggle in which the latter nation [France] is engaged, has been uniform from the commencement of it, and may be summed up in a few words; that I have always wished well to the French revolution; that I have always given it as my decided opinion, that no nation had a right to intermeddle in the internal concerns of another; that every one had a right to form and adopt whatever government they liked best to live under themselves; and that, if this country could, consistently with its engagements, maintain a strict neutrality and thereby preserve peace, it was bound to do so by motives of policy, interest, and every other consideration, that ought to actuate a people situated as we are, already deeply in debt, and in a convalescent state from the struggle we have been engaged in ourselves."—*Washington to James Monroe.*

"*August* 26.—The President of the United States yesterday received the *Chevalier Martinez De Yrujo*, as Envoy Extraordinary and Minister Plenipotentiary from his Catholic Majesty [Charles IV., King of Spain], to the United States of America."—*Gazette of the United States.*

TUESDAY, AUGUST 30.

At Philadelphia: "*August* 31.—The President yesterday received R. G. VAN POLANEN, Esq. as Minister Resident of the Batavian Republic."—*Gazette of the United States.*

MONDAY, SEPTEMBER 5.

At Philadelphia: "Write me by the first Post (fridays) after you get this letter, how every thing is, and going on; for if I can accomplish the business which bro' me here, I hope by Wednesday, or thursday in next week, to leave this, on my return to Mount Vernon."—*Washington to William Pearce.*

SUNDAY, SEPTEMBER 11.

At Philadelphia: "I recollect a year or two ago to have sent some rape Seed to Mount Vernon, but do not recollect what has been the result of it:—but particular care ought always to be paid to these kind of Seeds as they are, generally, given to me, because they are valuable—rare—or curious."—*Washington to William Pearce.*

SATURDAY, SEPTEMBER 17.

At Philadelphia: Issues his Farewell Address to the people of the United States.*

"The end of the same year [1796] witnessed the resignation of the presidency of the United States of America by General Washington, and his voluntary retirement into private life. Modern history has not a more spotless character to commemorate. Invincible in resolution, firm in conduct, incorruptible in integrity, he brought to the helm of a victorious republic the simplicity and innocence of rural life; he was forced into greatness by circumstances rather than led into it by inclination, and prevailed over his enemies rather by the wisdom of his designs, and the perseverance of his character, than by any extraordinary genius for the art of

---

* The Farewell Address first appeared in *Claypoole's American Daily Advertiser* for September 19, 1796.

war. A soldier from necessity and patriotism rather than disposition, he was the first to recommend a return to pacific counsels when the independence of his country was secured; and bequeathed to his countrymen an address on leaving their government, to which there are few compositions of uninspired wisdom which can bear a comparison. He was modest without diffidence; sensible to the voice of fame without vanity; independent and dignified without either asperity or pride. He was a friend to liberty, but not to licentiousness—not to the dreams of enthusiasts, but to those practical ideas which America had inherited from her British descent, and which were opposed to nothing so much as the extravagant love of power in the French democracy. Accordingly, after having signalized his life by a successful resistance to English oppression, he closed it by the warmest advice to cultivate the friendship of Great Britain; and exerted his whole influence, shortly before his resignation, to effect the conclusion of a treaty of friendly and commercial intercourse between the mother country and its emancipated offspring. He was a Cromwell without his ambition; a Sylla without his crimes; and after having raised his country, by his exertions, to the rank of an independent state, he closed his career by a voluntary relinquishment of the power which a grateful people had bestowed."—ARCHIBALD ALISON.

MONDAY, SEPTEMBER 19.

Leaves Philadelphia: " *September* 21.—Monday last [September 19] the President of the United States left this city, on his journey to Mount Vernon."—*Pennsylvania Gazette.*

TUESDAY, SEPTEMBER 20.

At Lancaster, Pennsylvania: " *September* 23.—The President of the United States arrived here [Lancaster] on Tuesday afternoon last [September 20], and on Wednesday morning at 6 o'clock proceeded on his way to Mount Vernon."—*Lancaster Journal.*

MONDAY, OCTOBER 17.

At Mount Vernon: " A few months will put an end to my political existence, and place me in the shades of Mount Vernon under my Vine and Fig Tree; where at all times I should be glad to see you."— *Washington to Landon Carter.*

WEDNESDAY, OCTOBER 26.

At Washington City: " Mrs. Washington desires me to inform you that there was some Butter left in the Cellar, and some Beef in a Tub which (after supplying James) may be applied to any uses you think proper."—*Washington to William Pearce.*

MONDAY, OCTOBER 31.

At Philadelphia: " *November* 2.—On Monday last [October 31] the President of the United States arrived in town from Mount Vernon."—*Claypoole's American Daily Advertiser.*

THURSDAY, NOVEMBER 3.

At Philadelphia: " *November* 3.—Gave Geo. W. Fayette for the purpose of getting himself such small articles of clothing as he might want, and not chuse to ask for, 100 Dollars."—*Washington's Cash-Book.*

SATURDAY, DECEMBER 3.

At Philadelphia: " *December* 4.—Yesterday I dined with the President, in company with John Watts, the King of the Cherokees, with a large number of his chiefs and their wives; among the rest the widow and children of Hanging Maw, a famous friend of our's who was basely murdered by some white people. The President dined four sets of Indians on four several days the last week."—*John Adams to Mrs. Adams.*

WEDNESDAY, DECEMBER 7.

At Philadelphia: " *December* 7.—This day precisely at 12 o'clock the President of the United States met both Houses of Congress in the Hall of the Representatives, where he addressed them in a speech. The President was accompanied by his Secretary [George Washington Craik], the Secretaries of State, the Treasury and War Departments, and the Attorney-General, &c. The hall was filled at an early hour with the largest assemblage of citizens, ladies and gentlemen ever collected on a similar occasion. The

English, Spanish, and Portuguese Ministers had Seats assigned them, and were present."—*Gazette of the United States.*

SATURDAY, DECEMBER 10.

At Philadelphia: "A few months more, say the 3d of March next (1797), and the scenes of my political life will close, and leave me in the shades of retirement; when if a few years are allowed me to enjoy it (many I cannot expect, being upon the verge of sixty-five), and health is continued to me, I shall peruse with pleasure and edification, the fruits of the exertions of the Board [of Agriculture, England] for the improvement of Agriculture; and shall have leisure, I trust, to realise some of the useful discoveries which have been made in the science of husbandry."— *Washington to Sir John Sinclair.*

MONDAY, DECEMBER 12.

At Philadelphia: "*December* 12.—At 12 o'clock this day, the Senate in a body, waited on the President of the United States, at his house, when the Vice President presented an answer to his speech to both Houses at the opening of the Session."—*Gazette of the United States.*

FRIDAY, DECEMBER 16.

At Philadelphia: "*December* 16.—At 2 o'clock this day, the members of the House of Representatives in a body, waited upon the President at his house, and the Speaker [Jonathan Dayton] presented an answer to his address to both Houses."—*Gazette of the United States.*

SATURDAY, DECEMBER 17.

At Philadelphia: "*December* 17.—At noon the [Pennsylvania] Assembly went to the Presbyterian Church on Market Street [between Second and Third Streets], where Dr. [Benjamin] Rush, a member of the Philosophical Society, pronounced an eulogium in memory of their late president, David Rittenhouse. The church was crowded,

President Washington and lady, with members of Congress being present."—*Diary of Jacob Hiltzheimer.*

"On Saturday [December 17], at twelve o'clock agreeably to appointment, Dr. Rush delivered his Eulogium in the Presbyterian Church in High street, on the late Mr. RITTENHOUSE. The Doctor commenced his Oration with an account of the birth of the great philosopher whose eulogy he was about to make, and proceeded to give an account of all the material transactions of his life, till he came to the awful period of his death, in all which he found occasion to pay the highest tribute of praise to the deceased. Indeed, we believe, we shall be joined in sentiment by all who heard it, in pronouncing the Oration a most masterly composition, and that it was pronounced with all the ability of an Orator and with all the feeling of a Friend. The Church was exceedingly full, but very attentive. The President of the United States, the Members of Congress, and of the Legislature of this State, the foreign Ministers, the Philosophical Society, Medical Students, &c. were a part of the auditory on this solemn and affecting occasion."—*Gazette of the United States*, December 20.

SUNDAY, DECEMBER 18.

At Philadelphia: "I had a letter from Mr. Anderson by the last Post, who informs me that it was not in his power to leave the concern he was engaged in at the time I wished him to be at Mount Vernon;—but that he certainly would be there by the 27ᵗʰ or 28ᵗʰ of this month, if he was alive and well.—I wish it may be convenient for you to stay a few days after he comes to give him a thorough insight into the business, and then transfer the directions I have given concerning it to him." — *Washington to William Pearce.*

FRIDAY, DECEMBER 23.

At Philadelphia: "Yesterday I received your letter of the 16th instant, covering the resolutions of the Senate and House of Delegates of the State of Maryland, passed on the 13th and 14th. The very obliging and friendly terms, in which you have made this communication, merit my sincere thanks."— *Washington to John H. Stone*, Governor of Maryland.

Resolutions had been unanimously adopted by the Legislature of Maryland, approving in the highest terms the public services of the President. and particularly the sentiments advanced by him in the *Farewell Address*. It was "resolved, that, to perpetuate this valuable present in the most striking view to posterity, it be printed and published with the laws of this session, as an evidence of our approbation of its political axioms, and a small testimony of the affection we bear to the precepts of him, to whom, under Divine Providence, we are principally indebted for our greatest political blessings."

From the time the President published his *Farewell Address* till the term of the presidency expired he received public addresses from all the State Legislatures which were convened within that period, and also from many other public bodies, expressing a cordial approbation of his conduct during the eight years that he had filled the office of Chief Magistrate, and deep regret that the nation was to be deprived of his services.

WEDNESDAY, DECEMBER 28.

At Philadelphia: "*December* 29.—Yesterday at 12 o'clock, a deputation from the Grand Lodge of the Ancient and Honorable Fraternity of Free and Accepted Masons in Pennsylvania waited on the President of the United States with an address delivered to him by the Grand Master [William Moore Smith]."—*Gazette of the United States.*

22

1797.

TUESDAY, JANUARY 3.

At Philadelphia : Visits the Globe Mills, situate at what is now the intersection of Germantown Avenue and Girard Avenue.*

"1797.—One of the earliest manufactories in the United States, of any extent, for spinning and weaving flax, hemp, and tow, by water power, was that of James Davenport, put in operation with patent machinery within the last twelve months, at the Globe Mills, at the north end of Second Street, Philadelphia. It was visited at the beginning of the year by Washington and several members of Congress, who were highly pleased with the ingenuity and novelty of the machinery. The President in particular expressed a high opinion of the merits of the patentee, Mr. Davenport;† and an earnest wish that a work so honorable to the infant manufactories of the Union might be extended to different parts of the country. The labor was chiefly performed by boys."—*Bishop's History of American Manufactures from 1608 to 1860*, vol. i. p. 71.

SUNDAY, JANUARY 8.

At Philadelphia : " The first thing I shall do, after I am settled at Mount Vernon, will be to adjust all my accounts of a private nature ; the doing of which, as they ought, has been prevented by public avocations."— *Washington to David Stuart.*

THURSDAY, JANUARY 12.

At Philadelphia : " *January* 13.—Yesterday the Senate of this Commonwealth waited on the President of the

---

* An interesting paper by Samuel H. Needles, entitled " The Governor's Mill and the Globe Mills, Philadelphia," will be found in vol. viii. pp. 279-377 of the *Pennsylvania Magazine.*

† James Davenport received (February 14, 1794) the first patent for any kind of textile machine issued in the United States.

338

United States and presented him with an Address."—*Claypoole's American Daily Advertiser.*

THURSDAY, FEBRUARY 9.

At Philadelphia: " *February* 9.—I saw the President and Mrs. Washington on Tuesday [February 7], and am to dine there to-day. They are both extremely well."—*James Iredell to Mrs. Iredell.*

" In private, as well as in public, his [Washington's] punctuality was observable. He had a well regulated clock in his entry, by which the movements of his whole family, as well as his own were regulated. At his dinner parties he allowed five minutes for the variation of time pieces, and after they were expired he would wait for no one. Some lagging members of Congress came in when not only dinner was begun, but, considerably advanced. His only apology was, ' Sir or Gentlemen, we are too punctual for you;' or in pleasantry, ' Gentlemen, I have a cook, who never asks whether the company has come, but whether the hour has come.' Washington sat as a guest at his dinner table, about half way from its head to its foot. The place of the chaplain was directly opposite to the President. The company stood while the blessing was asked, and on a certain occasion, the President's mind was probably occupied with some interesting concern, and on going to the table he began to ask a blessing himself. He uttered but a word or two, when bowing to me, he requested me to proceed, which I accordingly did. I mention this because it shows that President Washington always asked a blessing himself, when a chaplain was not present."—*Reminiscences of Ashbel Green.*

FRIDAY, FEBRUARY 17.

At Philadelphia: " *February* 20.—On Friday last [February 17] the House of Representatives of this Commonwealth waited on the President of the United States with an Address."—*Claypoole's American Daily Advertiser.*

SATURDAY, FEBRUARY 18.

At Philadelphia: " *February* 18.—At four o'clock I went with the following members of the [Pennsylvania] House [of Representatives] and dined with that great and good man, George Washington, President of the United States, who will retire from office on March 4th next, at which time John Adams, the present Vice-President, will take his place: Speaker [George] Latimer, [Joseph] Ball, [Francis] Gurney, [Robert] Waln, and [Lawrence] Seckel, of Philadelphia; [Richard] Keys, [Thomas] Boude, [Abraham] Carpenter, and [Jeremiah] Brown, of Lancaster; [John] Hulme, [Theophilus] Foulke, [Ralph] Stover, and [Isaac] Van Horn, of Bucks; [Robert] Frazer, [Thomas] Bull, and [James] Hannum, of Chester; [William] McPherson, [Alexander] Turner, [William] Miller, and [John] Stewart, of York; and [Samuel] Marshall, of Huntingdon. Our Speaker sat between the President and his lady, and I on the left of the President."—*Diary of Jacob Hiltzheimer.*

WEDNESDAY, FEBRUARY 22.*

At Philadelphia: "*February* 23.—Yesterday being the anniversary of the birthday of the President of the United States, in which he entered the 65th [66th] year of his age, it was observed here as a day of Festival and Rejoicing. It was ushered in by ringing of bells and firing of cannon. Most of the members of Congress and the Governor and the Legislature of this State in a body congratulated him on the occasion. The Officers of the Militia met at Eleven o'clock at the State-House, and marched from thence to the house of the President to whom they presented an address, and received his answer thereto. They then returned to the State-House, and accompanied the Society of the Cincinnati in their visit to the President, who also presented to him an address and received his answer. At twelve o'clock a federal salute was fired. The procession was attended by the uniform military corps, who performed a variety of evolutions on the occasion.

"This day has always been observed in this city by

---

* "*February* 24.—On Wednesday evening [February 22] arrived in town, on a visit to the President of the United States the famous Mohawk Chief Colonel JOSEPH BRANT, and the Seneka Chief Cornplanter."—*Claypoole's American Daily Advertiser.*

marks of joy and festivity; but this being the last birth
day which will return to GEORGE WASHINGTON, as Chief
Magistrate of the Union, it was not only honoured by out-
ward marks of joy, but by sensations of a peculiar kind,
which are better felt than expressed—they were those of
Gratitude and Esteem for Eminent Services.

"In the Evening there was a Ball on the occasion at
Rickett's Amphitheatre, which for Splendor, Taste and
Elegance, was, perhaps, never excelled by any similar En-
tertainment in the United States."—*Claypoole's American
Daily Advertiser.*

"*February* 24.—The President's birthday (the 22d) was celebrated here
with every possible mark of attachment, affection and respect, rendered
affecting beyond all expression, by its being in some degree a parting scene.
Mrs. Washington was moved even to tears, with the mingled emotions of
gratitude for such strong proofs of public regard, and the new prospect of
the uninterrupted enjoyment of domestic life : she expressed herself something to this effect. I never saw the President look better, or in finer
spirits, but his emotions were too powerful to be concealed. He could sometimes scarcely speak. Three rooms of his house were almost entirely full
from 12 to 3, and such a crowd at the door it was difficult to get in. At the
Amphitheatre at night it is supposed there was at least 1200 persons. The
show was a very brilliant one, but such scrambling to go to supper that
there was some danger of being squeezed to death. The Vice President
handed in Mrs. Washington, and the President immediately followed. The
applause with which they were received is indescribable. The same was
shown on their return from supper. The music added greatly to the interest
of the scene. The President staid till between 12 and 1."—*James Iredell to
Mrs. Iredell.*

"It was the usage, while Washington was President of the United States,
for the clergy of the city to go in a body to congratulate him on his birth-
day ; and on these occasions he always appeared unusually cheerful. The
last time we made such a call, which was about ten days before his retirement from office, he said with singular vivacity, 'Gentlemen I feel the
weight of years; I take a pair of sixes on my shoulders this day.' This
great man was not in his proper element when he attempted a pleasant con-
ceit. I never witnessed his making the attempt but on this occasion ; and
if his allusion, as I suppose must have been the case, was to the fifty-sixes
used in weighing heavy articles, it was surely far-fetched and not very obvious. He entered his sixty-sixth year at this time."—*Reminiscences of Ashbel
Green.*

FRIDAY, FEBRUARY 24.

At Philadelphia: " *March* 1.—An Address of the Legislature of the State of Massachusetts, was on Friday last [February 24] presented to the President of the United States by the Senators representing that State in Congress, accompanied by most of the Members of the House of Representatives, from that State."—*Claypoole's American Daily Advertiser.*

MONDAY, FEBRUARY 27.

At Philadelphia: " *February* 28.—Yesterday at twelve o'clock the Common Council of this city waited on the President of the United States with an address. And at half past twelve the Select Council waited on the President, and presented their address."—*Claypoole's American Daily Advertiser.*

" *February* 27.—We are informed that the President of the United States will be at the representation of the new comedy, *The Way to get Married,* this evening, at the New Theatre." *—Idem.*

TUESDAY, FEBRUARY 28.

At Philadelphia: " *February* 28.—The President and his family honor the Ladies Concert with their presence this evening."—*Claypoole's American Daily Advertiser.*

THURSDAY, MARCH 2.

At Philadelphia: " *March* 3.—Yesterday the Rector, Church Wardens and Vestrymen of the United Episcopal Churches of Christ Church and St. Peter's waited on the President of the United States with an Address."—*Claypoole's American Daily Advertiser.*

On the following day, March 3, a number of the clergy of the city and vicinity of Philadelphia also presented the President with an address. The

* " NEW THEATRE. THIS EVENING, February 27. By particular desire, will be presented, the last new Comedy. *The way to get Married ;* after the comedy the comic ballet *Dermot & Kathleen,* or *Animal Magnetism."* *Claypoole's American Daily Advertiser.*

Reverend Ashbel Green, referring to this in his *Reminiscences*, says, "On the 4th [?] of March, when he carried into effect his purpose of retirement, which he had previously announced, the city clergy waited on him with an address; which, with his answer, was published in the newspapers of the day. Mr. Jefferson in a letter published after his death, speaks of the design of this address, and of the character of its answer, as indicating that Washington was suspected of infidelity, and broadly intimates that such a suspicion was just. As to the design of the address, I may be allowed to say, that Mr. Jefferson's remarks are incorrect, since by the appointment of my clerical brethren, it was penned by myself, and I have not a doubt that the whole imputation was groundless."

FRIDAY, MARCH 3.*

At Philadelphia: "*March* 2.—To-morrow at dinner I shall, as a servant of the public, take my leave of the President elect, of the foreign characters, the heads of departments, &c., and the day following, with pleasure, I shall witness the inauguration of my successor to the chair of government."— *Washington to General Knox.*

Of this dinner, Bishop White, one of the guests, writes, "On the day before his leaving the Presidential chair a large company dined with him. Among them were the foreign ministers and their ladies, Mr. and Mrs. Adams,† Mr. Jefferson, with other conspicuous persons of both sexes. During the dinner much hilarity prevailed; but on the removal of the cloth it was put an end to by the President, certainly without design. Having filled his glass, he addressed the company, with a smile on his countenance, as nearly as can be recollected in the following terms: ' Ladies and gentlemen, this is the last time I shall drink your health as a public man. I do it with sincerity, and wishing you all possible happiness!' There was an end of all pleasantry. He who gives this relation accidentally directed his eye to the lady of the British minister (Mrs. Liston) and tears were running down her cheeks."‡

---

* " *March* 3.—This evening is Mrs. Washington's last drawing-room, and a very crowded one it will be, though extremely exciting to a person of any sensibility."—*James Iredell to Mrs. Iredell.*

† This is incorrect. Mrs. Adams at this time was at home at Quincy, Massachusetts.

‡ " Memoir of the Life of Bishop White," by Bird Wilson, D.D.   Philadelphia, 1839, p. 191.

SATURDAY, MARCH 4.

At Philadelphia : " *March* 6.—On Saturday [March 4], at
twelve o'clock, agreeably to the notification which he gave
to both Houses of Congress soon after his election, JOHN
ADAMS, as President of the United States, attended in the
Chamber of the House of Representatives, to take his Oath
of Office, according to the directions of the Constitution.
On his entrance, as well as on the entrance of the late President, and of Thomas Jefferson, the Vice President, loud
and reiterated applause involuntarily burst from the audience.   The President having taken his seat on the elevated
Chair of the Speaker of the House of Representatives,* the
Vice President, the late President, and the Secretary of
the Senate † on his right. the Speaker and Clerk ‡ of the
House of Representatives on his left, and the Chief Justice
of the United States § and the Associate Judges || at a table
in the centre, all the foreign Ministers and Ambassadors,
the Heads of Departments, General [James] Wilkinson, the
Commander-in-Chief, and a very crowded auditory of the
principal inhabitants of this city being present, the President proceeded to deliver his Speech. . . .

" After concluding his speech, the President descended
from his seat to receive his oath of office from the Chief
Justice, who pronounced the following constitutional oath
with great solemnity, which was repeated by the President
in an equally audible and solemn manner. 'I do solemnly
swear, that I will faithfully execute the office of President
of the United States, and will, to the best of my ability,
preserve, protect and defend the constitution of the United
States.'

---

* Jonathan Dayton, of New Jersey.

† Samuel Allyne Otis, of Massachusetts.

‡ John Beckley, of Virginia.

§ Oliver Ellsworth, of Connecticut.

|| William Cushing, of Massachusetts; James Wilson, of Pennsylvania;
and James Iredell, of North Carolina. The Judges not present were William Paterson, of New Jersey, and Samuel Chase, of Maryland.

"Having taken his oath, the President again resumed his seat, and, after sitting a moment, rose, bowed to the audience, and retired. After him, followed the Vice President (though not without a contest betwixt the late President and him with respect to Precedence, the former insisting upon the Vice President taking it, and he with great reluctance receiving it). Afterwards followed the members of the Senate, Foreign Ministers, Heads of Departments, Representatives, &c." *—Claypoole's American Daily Advertiser.*

"On Saturday [March 4] the Merchants of Philadelphia gave a Public Dinner, at Rickett's Circus,† to GEORGE WASHINGTON, in testimony of their approbation of his conduct as President of the United States.—The Company, among whom were all the Foreign Ministers, many of the Members of both houses of Congress, the Governor of the state, and all the principal merchants of the city, met at Oeller's hotel,‡ and marched in procession from thence to the place of entertainment. On their entering the Circus, *Washington's march* resounded through the place, and a curtain drew up which presented to view a transparent full length painting of the late President, whom Fame is crowning with a Wreath of Laurel, taking leave after delivering to her his valedictory address, of the Genius of America, who is represented by a Female Figure holding the Cap of Liberty in her

---

* "*March* 5.—Your dearest friend never had a more trying day than yesterday. A solemn scene it was indeed, and it was made affecting to me by the presence of the General, whose countenance was as serene and unclouded as the day. He seemed to me to enjoy a triumph over me. Methought I heard him say, 'Ay! I am fairly out and you fairly in! See which of us will be happiest!' When the ceremony was over, he came and made me a visit, and cordially congratulated me, and wished my administration might be happy, successful, and honourable. . . . In the chamber of the House of Representatives was a multitude as great as the space could contain, and I believe scarcely a dry eye but Washington's."—*John Adams to Mrs. Adams.*

† Rickett's Circus was first opened (April 12, 1793) at the southwest corner of Twelfth and Market Streets. In the fall of 1795 it was removed to a large circular building erected for the purpose at the southwest corner of Sixth and Chestnut Streets. This was known as Rickett's Amphitheatre.

‡ South side of Chestnut, west of Sixth Street, adjoining Rickett's Amphitheatre.

hand, with an Altar before her, inscribed PUBLIC GRATITUDE. In the painting are introduced several emblematic devices of the honours he had acquired by his public services, and a distant view of Mount Vernon, the seat of retirement.* Not less than two hundred and forty persons were present, and a most sumptuous entertainment was provided by Mr. Richardet,† which consisted of four hundred dishes of the most choice viands which money could purchase or art prepare, dressed and served up in a manner which did him the highest credit. Mr. Willing and Mr. Fitzimmons presided, and the whole was conducted with the greatest order."—
Claypoole's American Daily Advertiser.

THURSDAY, MARCH 9.

Leaves Philadelphia : " *March* 10.—Yesterday morning at 7 o'clock General Washington and family left this City for Mount Vernon."—*Claypoole's American Daily Advertiser.*

" *March* 9.—The President and Mrs. Washington go off this morning for Mount Vernon. Yesterday afternoon he came to make me his farewell visit, and requested me, in his own name and Mrs. Wᵃ, to present 'their respects' to Mrs. Adams."—*John Adams to Mrs. Adams.*

SUNDAY, MARCH 12.

At Baltimore : " *March* 13.—Last evening arrived in this city, on his way to Mount Vernon, the illustrious object of veneration and gratitude, GEORGE WASHINGTON. His Excellency was accompanied by his lady and Miss Custis, and by the son of the Unfortunate Lafayette and his preceptor. At a distance from the city, he was met by a crowd of citizens, on horse and foot, who thronged the road to greet him, and by a detachment from Captain Hollingsworth's troop, who escorted him in through as great a concourse of people as Baltimore ever witnessed. On alighting at the Fountain Inn, the General was saluted with reiterated and thundering huzzas from the spectators. His Excellency,

---

* This painting was the work of Charles Willson Peale. An engraving of it, executed by Alexander Lawson, was published in the *Philadelphia Monthly Magazine* for January, 1799.

† Samuel Richardet, "master of the City Tavern and Merchant's Coffee House, 86 south second st."—*Philadelphia Directory*, 1797.

with the companions of his journey, leaves town we understand this morning."—*Baltimore paper.*

WEDNESDAY, MARCH 15.

At Mount Vernon: " *March* 19.—We arrived here on Wednesday [March 15], without any accident, after a tedious and fatiguing journey of seven days. . . . Grandpapa is very well & much pleased with being once more *Farmer Washington.*"—*Nelly Custis to Mrs. Wolcott.*

SATURDAY, APRIL 1.

At Alexandria : Dines by invitation (at Abert's Tavern) with the Ancient York Masons of Alexandria Lodge, No. 22. Returns to Mount Vernon under an escort of mounted troops of the town.

MONDAY, APRIL 3.

At Mount Vernon: "I find myself in the situation nearly of a new beginner; for, although I have not houses to build (except one, which I must erect for the accommodation and security of my military, civil, and private papers, which are voluminous and may be interesting), yet I have scarcely any thing else about me, that does not require considerable repairs. In a word, I am already surrounded by joiners, masons, and painters; and such is my anxiety to get out of their hands, that I have scarcely a room to put a friend into, or to sit in myself, without the music of hammers, or the odoriferous scent of paint."—*Washington to James McHenry.*

MONDAY, MAY 15.

At Mount Vernon: " To make and sell a little flour annually, to repair houses (going fast to ruin), to build one for the security of my papers of a public nature, and to amuse myself in agricultural and rural pursuits, will constitute employment for the few years I have to remain on this terrestrial globe. If, also, I could now and then meet the friends I esteem, it would fill the measure and add zest to my enjoyments; but, if ever this happens, it must be under my own vine and fig-tree, as I do not think it probable that I shall go beyond twenty miles from them."— *Washington to Oliver Wolcott.*

MONDAY, MAY 29.

At Mount Vernon : " I begin my diurnal course with the sun; if my hirelings are not in their places at that time I send them messages of sorrow for their indisposition; having put these wheels in motion, I examine the state of things further; the more they are probed, the deeper I find the wounds, which my buildings have sustained by an absence and neglect of eight years; by the time I have accomplished these matters, breakfast (a little after seven o'clock) is ready; this being over, I mount my horse and ride round my farms, which employs me until it is time to dress for dinner, at which I rarely miss seeing strange faces, come as they say out of respect for me. Pray, would not the word curiosity answer as well? And how different this from having a few social friends at a cheerful board! The usual time of sitting at table, a walk, and tea, bring me within the dawn of candlelight; previous to which, if not prevented by company, I resolve, that, as soon as the glimmering taper supplies the place of the great luminary, I will retire to my writing-table and acknowledge the letters I have received; but when the lights are brought, I feel tired and disinclined to engage in this work conceiving that the next night will do as well. The next night comes, and with it the same causes for postponement, and so on. . . . Having given you the history of a day, it will serve for a year."— *Washington to James McHenry.*

SATURDAY, JUNE 24.

At Mount Vernon : " I am very glad to hear, that my old friend and acquaintance General Rochambeau is alive, and in the enjoyment of tolerably good health. It is some years since I had the honor to receive a letter from him; but, if it should fall in your way at any time to recall me to his remembrance by the presentation of my best regards to him, which I pray you to accept also yourself, it would oblige me."— *Washington to General Mathieu Dumas.*

THURSDAY, JULY 6.

At Mount Vernon : " On the 6th of July I set off, having a letter to the president from his nephew, my particular friend, Bushrod Washington, Esquire. Having alighted at Mount Vernon, I sent in my letter of introduction, and walked into the portico, west of the river. In about ten minutes the president came to me. He wore a plain blue coat; his hair dressed and powdered. There was a reserve, but no hauteur in his manner. He shook me by the hand, said he was glad to see a friend of his nephew's, drew a chair, and desired me to sit down."—BENJAMIN H. LATROBE (*Dunlap's Arts of Design*, vol. ii. p. 475).

" After conversing with me for more than two hours, he got up and said that, ' we should meet again at dinner.' I then strolled about the lawn, and took a few sketches of the house, &c. Upon my return I found Mrs. Washington and her grand-daughter, Miss Custis, in the hall. I introduced myself to Mrs. Washington, as the friend of her nephew, and she immediately entered into conversation upon the prospect from the lawn, and presently gave me an account of her family, in a good-humoured free manner, that was extremely pleasing and flattering. She retains strong remains of considerable beauty, and seems to enjoy good health and as good humour. She has no affectation of superiority, but acts completely in the character of the mistress of the house of a respectable and opulent country gentleman. His grand-daughter, Miss Eleanor Custis, has more perfection of form, of expression, of colour, of softness, and of firmness of mind, than I have ever seen before. Young La Fayette, with his tutor, came down some time before dinner. He is a young man of seventeen years of age, of a mild, pleasant countenance, making a favourable impression at first sight. Dinner was served up about half-past three. . . .

" Washington has something uncommonly majestic and commanding in his walk, his address, his figure, and his countenance. His face is however characterized more by intense and powerful thought, than by quick and powerful conception. There is a mildness about its expression, and an air of reserve in his manner which lowers its tone still more. He is sixty-four, but appears some years younger, and has sufficient vigour to last many years yet. He was frequently entirely silent for many minutes, during which time an awkward silence seemed to prevail in the circle. His answers were often short, and sometimes approaching to moroseness. He did not at any time speak with remarkable fluency; perhaps the extreme correctness of his language, which almost seemed studied, prevented that effect. He appeared to enjoy a humorous observation, and made several himself. He laughed heartily several times, and in a very good humoured manner."— BENJAMIN H. LATROBE.

FRIDAY, JULY 7.

At Mount Vernon: "Your 'View of the Causes and Consequences of the present War with France,' which you were pleased to send to me through the medium of Mr. Bond of Philadelphia,* has been duly received, and I pray you to accept my best acknowledgments for this mark of your polite attention, particularly for the exalted compliment which accompanied it."— *Washington to Thomas Erskine.*

The *exalted compliment* referred to by Washington consisted of the following sentiment written by Mr. Erskine, afterward the celebrated Lord Erskine, on a blank page of his pamphlet: "I have taken the liberty to introduce your august and immortal name in a short sentence which is to be found in the book I send to you. I have a large acquaintance among the most valuable and exalted classes of men; but you are the only human being for whom I ever felt an awful reverence. I sincerely pray God to grant a long and serene evening to a life so gloriously devoted to the universal happiness of the world."

SATURDAY, JULY 15.

At Mount Vernon: "Our crop of Wheat this year, from the best information I have been able to obtain, will be found very short, owing to three causes; an uncommon drought last autumn, a severe winter with but little snow to protect it, and which is still more to be regretted, to

---

* Phineas Bond, Consul-General from Great Britain for the Middle and Southern States.

what with us is denominated the Hessian fly, which has spread devastation, more or less, in all quarters; nor has the later wheat escaped the rust."— *Washington to Sir John Sinclair.*

SUNDAY, JULY 23.

At Mount Vernon : " Your mamma went from here (with your sister Nelly) to Hope Park, on Wednesday, and is as well as usual. Your sister Law and child, were well on that day; and Mr., Mrs., and Eleanor Peter are all well at this place now, and many others in the house, among whom are Mr. Volney and Mr. William Morris."— *Washington to George Washington Parke Custis.*

" General Washington, who hated free-thinkers, was of course not very disposed to caress Volney, and indeed, as President, had declined to notice the French emigrants. Volney, however, paid him a visit at Mount Vernon, where he was received *bon gré, mal gré,* and entertained with the usual kindness shown to strangers. When about to depart he asked the general for a circular letter that might procure him aid and attention on the long tour he was about commencing. Washington wrote a few lines, which Volney considered, it was said, either equivocal praise or much too feeble for his exalted merit, hence the degrading manner in which he speaks of that superlatively great man. As well as I remember, the note was in substance thus : ' Monsieur Volney, who has become so celebrated by his works, need only be named in order to be known in whatever part of the United States he may travel.' " *—Recollections of Samuel Breck* (1771-1862). Philadelphia, 1877.

TUESDAY, AUGUST 29.

At Mount Vernon : " Your grandmamma (who is prevented writing to you by General Spotswood and family's being here) has been a good deal indisposed by swelling on one side of her face, but it is now much better. The rest of the family within doors are all well."— *Washington to George Washington Parke Custis.*

---

* " C. Volney needs no recommendation from Geo. Washington" were the words used.

SUNDAY, OCTOBER 8.

At Mount Vernon: "*October* 8.—Gave G. W. La Fayette a check on the Bank of Alexandria for the purpose of defraying his expenses to France, $300." *—*Washington's Cash-Book.*

"*October* 8.—This letter I hope and expect will be presented to you by your son, who is highly deserving of such parents as you and your amiable lady. . . . His conduct, since he first set his feet on American ground, has been exemplary in every point of view, such as has gained him the esteem, affection, and confidence of all who have had the pleasure of his acquaintance. His filial affection and duty, and his ardent desire to embrace his parents and sisters in the first moments of their release, would not allow him to wait the authentic account of this much desired event; but, at the same time that I suggested the propriety of this, I could not withhold my assent to the gratification of his wishes to fly to the arms of those whom he holds most dear, persuaded as he is from the information he has received, that he shall find you all in Paris.

"M. Frestel has been a true Mentor to George. No parent could have been more attentive to a favorite son; and he richly merits all that can be said of his virtues, of his good sense, and of his prudence. Both your son and he carry with them the vows and regrets of this family, and all who know them. And you may be assured, that yourself never stood higher in the affections of the people of this country, than at the present moment."— *Washington to the Marquis de Lafayette.*

FRIDAY, OCTOBER 13.

At Mount Vernon: "I suffered every attack, that was made upon my executive conduct, to pass unnoticed while I remained in public office, well knowing, that, if the general tenor of it would not stand the test of investigation, a newspaper vindication would be of little avail; but, as immense pains have been taken to disseminate these counterfeit letters, I conceived it a justice due to my own character and to posterity to disavow them in explicit terms; and this I did in a letter directed to the Secretary of State, to be filed in his office, the day on which I closed my administration. This letter has since been published in the

---

* George Washington Lafayette and his tutor M. Frestel sailed from New York for France on the 26th of October.

gazettes by the head of that department."— *Washington to William Gordon.*

In allusion to the republication in 1796 of a series of letters originally published at London in June, 1777, under the title of " Letters from General Washington to several of his Friends in the year 1776, in which are set forth a fairer and fuller view of American Politics, than ever yet transpired or the Public could be made acquainted with through any other channel," none of which, however, were written by Washington.

These *spurious letters,* purporting to have been written in the months of June and July, 1776, were seven in number, five addressed to Lund Washington, manager of the Mount Vernon estate, one to Mrs. Washington, and one to John Parke Custis, her son ; "the first draughts, or foul copies," of which were said to have been found in a small portmanteau taken from a servant of the general, at Fort Lee, in November, 1776.

These letters were reprinted at New York in 1778, at Philadelphia in 1795, and at London and New York, with other letters, in 1796, with the title: " Epistles, domestic, confidential, and official from General Washington, etc." The appearance of the latter publication called out a letter from Washington (March 3, 1797) to Timothy Pickering, Secretary of State, in which he declared them to be base forgeries, and that he had never seen or heard of them until they appeared in print.

MONDAY, NOVEMBER 6.

At Mount Vernon : " An eight years absence from home (except occasional short visits to it), has thrown my building, and other matters of private concern, into so much disorder, that at no period of my life have I ever been more engaged, than in the last six or eight months, to repair & bring them into tune again."— *Washington to Sir John Sinclair.*

MONDAY, NOVEMBER 18.

At Mount Vernon : " The running off of my cook has been a most inconvenient thing to this family, and what rendered it more disagreeable, is that I had resolved never to become the Master of another slave by purchase, but this resolution I fear I must break. I have endeavored to hire, black or white, but am not yet supplied."— *Washington to George Lewis.*

23

SATURDAY, DECEMBER 2.

At Mount Vernon : "To have steered my bark amid the intricacies of variegated public employment to a haven of rest with an approving conscience, and, while receiving the approbation of my own country for the part I have acted, to meet similar proofs of it from many of the moderate and virtuous of other countries, consummates my greatest wish and all my ambition, and in my eye is more precious than any thing that power or riches could have bestowed."— *Washington to John Luzac*, Professor in the University at Leyden.

From the beginning of the American Revolution, Professor Luzac had acted a zealous part in favor of the friends of liberty ; and, as editor of the *Leyden Gazette* for many years, had ably promulgated the principles of freedom, and defended the cause and conduct of those who were struggling to establish them. To no pen in Europe were the United States so much indebted for a just representation of their affairs and defence of their rights as to that of Professor Luzac.

MONDAY, DECEMBER 4.

At Mount Vernon : "A very severe winter has commenced, since the first of November we have hardly experienced a moderate day ; heavy rains following severe frosts have done more damage to the winter grain now growing than I recollect ever to have seen—at this moment and for several days past all the Creeks and small Waters are hard bound with ice—and if the navigation of the River is not entirely stoped is yet very much impeded by it."— *Washington to John Marshall*, at Paris.

1798.

WEDNESDAY, JANUARY 3.

At Alexandria: " *January* 3.—M^n Washington, myself &c^a went to Alexandria & dined with Mr Fitzhugh."— *Washington's Diary.*

MONDAY, JANUARY 8.

At Mount Vernon : " *January* 8.—A Mr Marshall Music Master came here—Tuned Nelly Custis's Harpsicord & returned after dinner."— *Washington's Diary.*

" Nelly Custis's Harpsicord," which was presented to her by Washington, is now at Mount Vernon. Lossing, in his *Mount Vernon and its Associations*, says, " The best teachers were employed to instruct Nelly in the use of the harpsichord, and her grandmother made her practise upon it four or five hours every day. 'The poor girl,' says her brother, the late Mr. Custis, ' would play and cry, and cry and play, for long hours, under the immediate eye of her grandmother, a rigid disciplinarian in all things.' "

MONDAY, JANUARY 15.

At Alexandria: " *January* 15.—I went to Alexandria to a meeting of the Stockholders of that Bank to an Election of Directors."— *Washington's Diary.*

WEDNESDAY, FEBRUARY 7.

At George Town: " *February* 7.—Went to a meet^s of the Potomak C^o in George Town—Dined at Col^o Fitzgeralds & lodged at Mr T. Peters. *February* 8.—Visited the Public build^gs in the Morn^g met the Comp^y at the Union Tavern & dined there—lodged as before Weather very cold. *Februa-ry* 9.—Returned home to Dinner."— *Washington's Diary.*

MONDAY, FEBRUARY 12.

At Alexandria : " *February* 12.—Went with the family to a Ball in Alex* given by the Citizens of it & its vicinity in commemoration of the anniversary of my birth day."— *Washington's Diary.*

The Gregorian, or " New Style" of computing the length of the year, although promulgated in 1582, was not adopted by Great Britain until 1751, nineteen years after the birth of Washington. It was then enacted that eleven nominal days should be omitted ; Wednesday the *second* of September, 1752, being made the last day of " Old Style," and the next day (Thursday) counted the fourteenth instead of the third. After that date Washington's birthday would be February twenty-second instead of February eleventh. In some localities the " Old Style" remained in use for a long time, especially in the case of birthdays. The anniversary ball at Alexandria, it will be noticed, was held on the twelfth, in consequence of the eleventh of February, 1798, falling on Sunday.

WEDNESDAY, FEBRUARY 14.

At Mount Vernon : " *February* 14.—M* Alex* Spotswood & Wife & M* Field* Lewis * & M* Lear came to dinner the latter returned afterwards. *February* 15.—M* Field* Lewis went away after dinner. *February* 16.—M* & M* Spotswood left us after breakfast."— *Washington's Diary.*

SUNDAY, MARCH 4.

At Mount Vernon : " *March* 4.—Doct* Stuart came to dinner. *March* 5.—Doct* Stuart left this, to accompany Washington Custis to S* Johns College at Annapolis."— *Washington's Diary.*

SUNDAY, MARCH 18.

At Mount Vernon : " *March* 18.—M* Steer Sen* & Jun* Miss Steer & M* Vanhaven dined here & returned to Alex*

---

* Washington's sister Betty, who married in 1760 Colonel Fielding Lewis, of Fredericksburg, Virginia, had six children : Fielding (above mentioned), Betty, who married Charles Carter, George Fielding, Robert, Howell, and Lawrence. There were other children, who died young. Colonel Lewis died December, 1781, and Betty Washington, who was his second wife, died March 31, 1797.

afterwards. . . . *March* 19.—Dined with Mrs Washington &c^a at Mr Thomson Mason's."— *Washington's Diary.*

TUESDAY, MARCH 20.

At Mount Vernon: "*March* 20.—Mr Law^e Washington of Chotanck & Mr Law^e Washington of Belmont came to Dinner—Albin Rawlins came to live with me as Clerk."— *Washington's Diary.*

Lawrence Washington, of Chotank, was a descendant of Lawrence the Immigrant, the brother of John Washington, the great-grandfather of General Washington. In his will the General bequeathed him a gold-headed cane and also a spy-glass carried in the Revolution, designating him as the acquaintance and friend of his juvenile years. Lawrence Washington, of Belmont, Fairfax County, was probably another descendant of Lawrence the Immigrant.

TUESDAY, MARCH 27.

At Mount Vernon: "*March* 27.—Mr Charles Carroll Jun [son of Charles Carroll of Carrollton] & Mr Willm Lee came to dinner. *March* 28.—Mr Carroll & Mr Lee went away after breakfast & the family here went to dine with Mr Nichols."— *Washington's Diary.*

The visit of young Mr. Carroll having given rise at Annapolis to a rumor that it was made with the intention of paying his addresses to Nelly Custis, her brother wrote to the General in allusion to it, saying, " I think it a most desirable match, and wish that it may take place with all my heart." In reply, under date of April 15, Washington wrote, " Young Mr Carroll came here about a fortnight ago to dinner, and left us next morning after breakfast. If his object was such as you say has been reported, it was not declared here ; and therefore, the less is said upon the subject, particularly by your sister's friends, the more prudent it will be until the subject developes itself more."

But youthful alliances are not always made at the nod of Dame Rumor, nor are they always controlled by the wishes of relatives. Nelly Custis married, February 22, 1799, at Mount Vernon, Lawrence Lewis, a nephew of Washington; and Charles Carroll, Junior, found, in the following year, a bride at Philadelphia in Harriet, a daughter of Benjamin Chew.

SATURDAY, MARCH 31.

At Mount Vernon : " *March* 31.—A M' Tevot a French Gentleman recom⁴ by Count de Rochambeau dined here— & a M' [Jonathan] Freeman Member in Congress from N : Hamp. came in the afternoon & returned."— *Washington's Diary.*

FRIDAY, APRIL 13.

At Mount Vernon : "*April* 13.—Gen' Lee came to dinner & Col° Heath & son in the after". *April* 14.—Gen' Lee & Col° Heath went away after breakfast."— *Washington's Diary.*

MONDAY, APRIL 16.

At Alexandria : "*April* 16.—I went to Alex' to an Election of Delegates for the C'' of Fairfax—voted for Mess'' West & Jn° Herbert—returned to Dinner. *May* 9.—I went to the Proclam" sermon in Alexandria."— *Washington's Diary.*

WEDNESDAY, MAY 16.

At Mount Vernon : " A century hence, if this country keeps united (and it is surely its policy and interest to do it), will produce a city, though not as large as London, yet of a magnitude inferior to few others in Europe, on the banks of the Potomac, where one is now establishing for the permanent seat of the government of the United States, between Alexandria and Georgetown, on the Maryland side of the river; a situation not excelled, for commanding prospect, good water, salubrious air, and safe harbour, by any in the world; and where elegant buildings are erecting and in forwardness for the reception of Congress in the year 1800."— *Washington to Mrs. S. Fairfax.**

---

* Mrs. Fairfax (Sally Cary) was the widow of George William Fairfax, of " Belvoir," the neighbor and early friend of Washington. The Fairfaxes left Virginia in 1773, and settled at Bath, England, where Mr. Fairfax died,

SATURDAY, MAY 19.

At Hope Park : * " *May* 19.—About 8 Oclock in the forenoon Mrs Washington & myself sat out on a visit to Hope Park & the Federal City.—Got to the former to Dinner and remained there until Morning when we proceeded to the City."— *Washington's Diary.*

SUNDAY, MAY 20.

At Washington City: " *May* 20.—Dined at Mr Thos Peter's & remained there until Wednesday, and then went to Mr Law's & remained there until friday [May 25] when we sat out on our return home & called at Mount Eagle to take our leave of the Revd Mr Fairfax who was on the point of Embarking for England."— *Washington's Diary.*

SUNDAY, MAY 27.

At Mount Vernon : " An absence for more than eight days from home, on a visit to our friends in the Federal City, is offered as an apology for my not giving your polite and obliging favor of the 9th instant an earlier acknowledgment. I pray you now, my good Sir, to accept my best thanks for the pamphlet, and the song which accompanied it."— *Washington to Joseph Hopkinson.*

The song referred to in the above-quoted letter was the national air, " Hail Columbia," the words of which were written by Joseph Hopkinson, and adapted to the music of the " President's March," composed in 1789 by a German named Feyles, who at the time was the leader of the orchestra at the John Street Theatre in New York.   " Hail Columbia" was first sung at the Chestnut Street Theatre, Philadelphia, by Gilbert Fox on the evening of Wednesday, the 25th of April, 1798.† Judge Hopkinson, alluding to the

---

April 3, 1787. Mrs. Fairfax, for whom Washington in his early days had a sincere admiration, died at Bath in 1811.

* Five miles northwest of Fairfax Court-House.   Hope Park was the residence of Dr. David Stuart, who married the widow of John Parke Custis.   For some time after their marriage (1783) the Stuarts lived at Abingdon, near Alexandria.

† " New Theatre. MR. FOX'S NIGHT. This Evening, April 25, BY DESIRE. THE ITALIAN MONK. . . . End of the Play, ' More Sack.'

song in his letter to Washington of May 9, said, "As to the song it was a
hasty composition, and can pretend to very little extrinsic merit—yet I
believe its public reception has at least equalled anything of the kind. The
Theatres here and at New York have resounded with it night after night,
and men and boys in the streets sing it as they go."

TUESDAY, MAY 29.

At Alexandria : " *May 29.*—Went up to Alex* on business & returned home to dinner."— *Washington's Diary.*

THURSDAY, MAY 31.

At Mount Vernon : " *May 31.*—M' Delivs of Bremen &
a M' Pekmoller of Hamburgh dined here & returned afterwards."— *Washington's Diary.*

A letter from one of these gentlemen, written in 1858, at the age of eighty-
four, is quoted on page 460 of Custis's *Recollections of Washington,* in which,
after referring to some pictures of the Washington family which hung in
his hall, he says, "They vividly call to my mind the day—the proudest of
my life—that I passed upon the beautiful banks of the Potomac, in the
family of the best and greatest personage that the world has ever produced.
It was in May, 1798, now nearly sixty-one years ago. I was seated at his
right hand at dinner, and I recollect as distinctly his majestic bearing as if
it were yesterday. Though of mortality, his overpowering presence inspired an impression that he belonged to immortality. His stateliness, his
serene face, the perfect simplicity of his manners, his modest demeanor, and
the words of wisdom which he uttered, led me irresistibly to the belief that
he was an emanation from the Omnipotent, for the marvellous work that he
had just then consummated. It was my good fortune to contemplate him
in his retirement—after he had left nothing undone that he could perform
for the republic of his creation, and after he had quitted office for ever!
What a privilege I enjoyed in being his welcome guest! Of the 240,000.000
of people in Europe, I imagine I am the only person, since the death of Lafayette, who was so favored as to break bread and take wine with Washington at his own table."

_____

'An Epilogue, in the character of Sir John Falstaff, to be spoken by Mr.
Warren. After which, an intire new song, (written by a Citizen of Philadelphia) to the tune of the ' President's March,' will be sung by Mr. Fox ;
accompanied by the full band, and a grand chorus."—*Claypoole's American
Daily Advertiser,* Wednesday, April 25, 1798.

SATURDAY, JUNE 2.

At Mount Vernon : "*June* 2.—M* Law & a Polish Gentleman [Mr. Niemcewitz] the Companion of General Kosciaski came here to dinner, as did Miss Lee of Green Spring * with Nelly Custis who returnd to day [from Hope Park]."— *Washington's Diary.*

WEDNESDAY, JULY 4.

At Alexandria : "*July* 4.—Went up to the Celebration of the Anniversary of Independance and dined in the Spring Gardens near Alex* with a large Comp* of the Civil & Military of Fairfax County."— *Washington's Diary.*

" *Alexandria,* July 7.—The 23d Anniversary of American Independence was celebrated by the inhabitants of this town, on Wednesday last, with the greatest harmony and conviviality.—Every thing conspired to render the business of the day a varied scene of patriotism and social joy ; and the dignified presence of the beloved WASHINGTON, our illustrious neighbor, gave such a high colouring to the tout ensemble, that nothing was wanting to complete the picture. The auspicious morning was ushered in by a discharge of sixteen guns. At 10 o'clock the uniform companies paraded ; and, it must be acknowledged, their appearance was such as entitles them to the greatest credit, while it reflects honor on their officers and the town—it was perfectly military : . . . The different corps were reviewed in King street by General Washington, and Col. Little, who expressed the highest satisfaction at their appearance and manœuvring ; after which they proceeded to the Episcopal Church, where a suitable discourse was delivered by the Rev. Dr. Davis. Of this discourse I may say, with the expressive Collins, it was

" ' *Warm, energetic, chaste, sublime.*'

" A dinner was prepared at Spring Gardens by Mr. John Stavely ; which, considering the number of citizens and military that partook of it (between 4 and 500) was conducted with the greatest propriety and decorum.—Ludwell Lee, esq. presided at the head of the table—the foot was honored by Col. Charles Little. . . . GEN. WASHINGTON was escorted into town by a detachment from the troop of Dragoons. He was dressed in full uniform, and appeared in good health and spirits. The troops went through a number of military evolutions during the day, with all of which the General

---

* Cornelia Lee, daughter of William Lee, a brother of Richard Henry Lee.

was particularly pleased, and bestowed many encomiums on their martial appearance."—*Claypoole's American Daily Advertiser*, July 19.

THURSDAY, JULY 5.

At Mount Vernon: "The President's letter to me [of June 22], though not so expressed in terms, is nevertheless strongly indicative of a wish, that I should take charge of the military force of this country; and, if I take his meaning right, to aid also in the selection of the general officers. The appointment of these is important, but of those of the general staff all-important; insomuch that, if I am looked to as the commander-in-chief, I must be allowed to choose such as will be agreeable to me. To say more at present would be unnecessary; first, because an army may not be wanted; and, secondly, because I might not be indulged in this choice if it was."— *Washington to James McHenry.*

On the 28th of May a law was passed by Congress, authorizing the President, "in the event of a declaration of war against the United States, or of actual invasion of their territory by a foreign power, or of imminent danger of such invasion discovered in his opinion to exist, before the next session of Congress, to cause to be enlisted, and to call into actual service, a number of troops not exceeding ten thousand non-commissioned officers, musicians, and privates, to be enlisted for a term not exceeding three years." Authority was also given to the President to organize the army, with a suitable number of major-generals and other officers, into corps of artillery, cavalry, and infantry; and, in short, to make every arrangement for preparing the forces for actual service. This was called a *Provisional Army.* The measure was adopted in consequence of the threatening aspect of affairs between France and the United States. The causes and particulars are briefly stated in Marshall's *Life of Washington*, vol. v. pp. 735–746.

FRIDAY, JULY 6.

At Mount Vernon : "*July 6.*—Doctors Thornton * & Dalson—Mr Ludwell Lee, Lady & Miss Armistead, & Mr David

---

* Dr. William Thornton, a West Indian by birth. He was educated as a physician and lived for many years in Philadelphia. Dr. Thornton, who was a skilled architect, drew the plans and superintended the erection, in its early stages, of the first Capitol building at Washington City. He was the first head of the Patent Office.

Randolph & a Son of Col° R. Kidder Mead * came here to Dinner, the two last proceeded to Alex* afterwards. *July* 7.—M* R. Bland Lee & M* Hodgden came here to dinner & M* Ludwell Lee & Lady went away after Din."— *Washington's Diary.*

THURSDAY, JULY 12.

At Mount Vernon: " *July* 12.—The following Comp* dined here Col** Fitzgerald & Simms M* Herbert & Son— Doct* Craik & Son—M* L: Lee Col Ramsay—Cap Young & L* Jones M* Potts W* Wilson, M* Porter Doct* Cook M* Riddle M* Lear M* Tracy—& six Ladies & 4 Gent* from M* Rogers."— *Washington's Diary.*

FRIDAY, JULY 13.

At Mount Vernon : " I had the honor, on the evening of the 11*th* instant, to receive from the hands of the Secretary of War † your favor of the 7th. announcing that you had, with the advice and consent of the Senate, appointed me lieutenant-general and commander-in-chief of all the armies raised or to be raised for the service of the United States.‡

" I cannot express how greatly affected I am at this new proof of public confidence, and the highly flattering manner in which you have been pleased to make the communication ; at the same time I must not conceal from you my earnest wish, that the choice had fallen on a man less declined in years, and better qualified to encounter the usual vicissitudes of war."— *Washington to John Adams,* President of the United States.

---

* Richard Kidder Meade, an aide to General Washington in the Revolution, and the father of William Meade, Protestant Episcopal Bishop of Virginia, 1841–62.

† " *July* 11.—M* M°Henry—Sec* of War came in the evening. *July* 14.— The Sec* of War left this after dinner."— *Washington's Diary.*

‡ On the 2d of July the President nominated to the Senate " George Washington, of Mount Vernon, to be Lieutenant General and Commander in Chief of all the armies raised or to be raised, in the United States."   The nomination was unanimously confirmed by the Senate the next day.

In continuing this letter, Washington said, "It was not possible for me to remain ignorant of, or indifferent to recent transactions. The conduct of the Directory of France towards our country, their insidious hostilities to its government, their various practices to withdraw the affections of the people from it, the evident tendency of their arts and those of their agents to countenance and invigorate opposition, their disregard of solemn treaties and the laws of nations, their war upon our defenceless commerce, their treatment of our minister of peace, and their demands amounting to tribute, could not fail to excite in me corresponding sentiments with those which my countrymen have so generally expressed in their affectionate addresses to you. Believe me, Sir, no one can more cordially approve of the wise and prudent measures of your administration. They ought to inspire universal confidence, and will no doubt, combined with the state of things, call from Congress such laws and means, as will enable you to meet the full force and extent of the crisis.

"Satisfied, therefore, that you have sincerely wished and endeavoured to avert war, and exhausted to the last drop the cup of reconciliation, we can with pure hearts appeal to Heaven for the justice of our cause, and may confidently trust the final result to that kind Providence, which has heretofore and so often signally favored the people of these United States.

"Thinking in this manner and feeling how incumbent it is upon every person of every description to contribute at all times to his country's welfare, and especially in a moment like the present, when every thing we hold dear is so seriously threatened, I have finally determined to accept the commission of commander-in-chief of the armies of the United States; * with the

---

* "John Adams President of the United States of America To all who shall see these Presents Greetings : Know Ye, That reposing special Trust and Confidence in the Patriotism, Valour, Fidelity and Abilities of George Washington I have nominated and by and with the Advice and Consent of the Senate, do appoint him Lieutenant General and Commander in Chief of all the Armies raised or to be raised for the Service of the United States : He is therefore carefully and diligently to discharge the Duty of Lieutenant General & Commander in Chief by doing and performing all Manner of Things thereunto belonging : And I do Strictly charge and require all Officers and Soldiers under his Command, to be obedient to his orders as Lieutenant General & Commander in Chief: And he is to observe and Follow such Orders and Directions from time to time, as he shall receive from me, or the Future President of the United States of America, This Commission to continue in Force during the Pleasure of the President of the United States for the Time being. Given under my Hand, at Philadelphia this Fourth day of July in the Year of our Lord One thousand seven Hundred and ninety eight and in the twenty third Year of the Independence of the United States.

"JOHN ADAMS.

"JAMES McHENRY, Secry. of War."

reserve only, that I shall not be called into the field until the army is in a situation to require my presence, or it becomes indispensable by the urgency of circumstances."

FRIDAY, JULY 20.

At Alexandria: "*July* 20.—Went up to Alex^a with Mrs W. & Miss Cus[tis], dined at Doct^r Craiks ret^d in ye aft^n."— *Washington's Diary.*

WEDNESDAY, JULY 25.

At Mount Vernon: "I little imagined, when I took my last leave of the walks of public life, that any event could bring me again on a public theatre. But the unjust conduct of France towards these United States has been and continues to be such, that it must be opposed by a firm and manly resistance, or we shall not only hazard the subjugation of our government, but the independence of our nation also; both being evidently struck at by a lawless, domineering power, which respects no rights, and is restrained by no treaties, when it is found inconvenient to observe them."— *Washington to Dr. James Anderson.*

FRIDAY, JULY 27.

At Mount Vernon : "The *Greyheads* of Alexandria, pretty numerous it seems, and composed of all the respectable old People of the place; having formed themselves into a company for the defence of the Town & its Vicinity, are in want of Colors; and it being intimated that the Presentation of them by Mrs. Washington would be flattering to them; I take the liberty of requesting the favor of you to have made and sent to me as soon as it is convenient, such as will be appropriate to the occasion. Handsome, but not more expensive than becomes Republicans (not Bachite Republicans) is req^d. If you think a Motto would be proper, the choice of one ' chaste & unassuming' —is left to your own judgment."— *Washington to James McHenry.*

"ALEXANDRIA, November 1.—Tuesday last [October 30], being the anniversary of the birth day of our beloved and patriotic President John Adams, was observed in this town with military honours. The uniform companies of militia, and the company of Silver Grays, went through a variety of manœuvres and evolutions, under the command of Captain George Deneale. After firing several rounds in evidence of their attachment to this good man, as well as to shew that they approbated his conduct towards the insidious French Directory, they retired in the evening with the utmost decorum and harmony.

" A stand of colours, presented by the respected consort of our venerable Cincinnatus to the company of Silver Grays, was displayed for the first time on that day ; and, though a variety of incidents prevented their being entirely completed, they had a very elegant appearance. The colours are composed of white silk ; the device is, however, on an azure blue ground. The Golden Eagle of America has a portrait of General Washington * suspended from its beak, in one talon a bunch of arrows, in the other a branch of olive, and is surmounted by sixteen Stars, indicative of the number of States! The motto—'FIRM IN DEFENCE OF OUR COUNTRY !' "—*Claypoole's American Daily Advertiser*, November 6.

MONDAY, AUGUST 6.

At Alexandria : "*August 6.*—Went to Alex* to a meeting of the Pot° C°—M* Bur : Bassett came home with me."— *Washington's Diary.*

FRIDAY, AUGUST 10.

At Mount Vernon : "Little did I think when my Valadictory address was presented to the people of the United States that any event would occur in my day that could draw me from the peaceful walks and tranquil shades of Mount Vernon : where I had fondly hoped to spend the remnant of a life, worn down with public cares, in ruminating upon the variegated scenes through which I have passed and in the contemplation of others which are yet in embrio. I will hope however that when the Despots of

---

* " In the account of the presentment of a flag by Mrs. Washington, to the Silver Grays, published a few days since under the Alexandria head, in our paper, there was an error. Among other emblems, the flag contained a strong likeness of President Adams, and not of General Washington, as there stated. "—*Claypoole's American Daily Advertiser*, November 14.

France find how much they have mistaken the American character, and how much they have been deceived by their partizans *among us*, that their senses will return to them and an appeal to arms for the purpose of repeling an Invasion at least will be rendered unnecessary."— *Washington to William Vans Murray.*

MONDAY, AUGUST 20.

At Mount Vernon: "*August* 20.—No acc^t kept of the weather &c^a from hence to the end of the Month—on acc^t of my Sickness which commenced with a fever on the 19th & lasted until the 24th which left me debilitated."— *Washington's Diary.*

"*September* 3.—My last to you was dated the 20th of August; two days previous to which I had been seized with a fever, which I endeavoured to shake off by pursuing my usual rides and occupations; but it continued to increase upon me; when on the 21st at night Dr. Craik was called in, who it seems chose to have assistance, and on the 24th procured such a remission as to admit bark. Since which I have been in a convalescent state, but too much debilitated to be permitted to attend much to business."— *Washington to James McHenry.*

MONDAY, SEPTEMBER 3.

At Mount Vernon: "*September* 3.—In the Morning to breakfast came Genl [John] Marshall & Mr Bushrod Washington—and to dinner the At^y Genl Chas Lee Mr Herbert Mr Keith & Doc Craik."— *Washington's Diary.*

WEDNESDAY, SEPTEMBER 5.

At Mount Vernon: "*September* 5.—Genl Marshall & Mr B. Washington went to a dinner in Alex^a given to the former by the Citizens there & returned. *September* 6.— Mr Marshall & Mr B. Washington went away before breakfast."— *Washington's Diary.*

John Marshall (Chief-Justice of the United States, 1801-35) was appointed in June, 1797, an envoy to France, in conjunction with Charles Cotesworth

Pinckney and Elbridge Gerry. The envoys arrived at Paris in October, and were shortly approached by secret agents (X. Y. Z.) of Talleyrand with a demand for money,—fifty thousand pounds sterling for private account and a loan to the government. These suggestions were repelled with indignation, and a paper prepared by Mr. Marshall was sent to the minister, which set forth with great precision and force of argument the views and requirements of the United States and their earnest desire for maintaining friendly relations with France. But it availed nothing, and Pinckney and Marshall, who were Federalists, were ordered to leave the territory of France, while Gerry, as a Republican, was allowed to remain. The news of these events was received in this country with the deepest indignation, and when Mr. Marshall returned in June, 1798, he was everywhere received with marks of the highest respect and approval for the course he had pursued. The public dinner given to him at Alexandria, noted in the Diary, was one of other demonstrations of a like character, that given at Philadelphia on June 23 being noteworthy in consequence of the introduction of Mr. Pinckney's celebrated sentiment, "Millions for defence, but not a cent for tribute," as one of the toasts.

THURSDAY, SEPTEMBER 20.

At Washington City: "*September* 20.—Went up to the Federal City—Dined & lodged at Mr Thos Peters. *September* 21.—Examined in company with the Com^rs some of the Lots in the Vicinity of the Capital & fixed upon N° 16 in 634 to build on. Dined & lodged at Mr Laws. *September* 22.—Came home with Mr T. Peter wife & 2 children to Dinner."— *Washington's Diary.*

SUNDAY, SEPTEMBER 30.

At Alexandria: "*September* 30.—Went to Church in Alex^a."— *Washington's Diary.*

FRIDAY, OCTOBER 5.

At Mount Vernon: " *October* 5.—Doct^r Thornton—Mr Law and a Mr Baldo a Spanish Gentleman from the Havanna came to Dinner. *October* 6.—Mr Bushrod Washington & Captn Blackburn came to dinner & Mr Thos Peter returned in the afternoon from New Kent. *October* 7.— Mr B. Washington & Captn Blackburn went away after Breakf^t."— *Washington's Diary.*

TUESDAY, OCTOBER 9.

At Washington City: "*October* 9ᵗʰ 10 and eleventh absent
—in the Federal City."— *Washington's Diary.*

SATURDAY, OCTOBER 13.

At Mount Vernon: "*October* 13.—Genˡ Lee, Captⁿ Pres-
ley Thornton & Mʳ T. Peters came to dinner. *October* 14.—
Genˡ Lee & Captⁿ Thornton went away after breakfast &
Mʳ Booker came at Night."— *Washington's Diary.*

TUESDAY, OCTOBER 16.

At Mount Vernon: " *October* 16.—The Attorney Genˡ of
the United States Lee and Lady & Mʳ Wᵐ Craik dined
here & retᵈ."— *Washington's Diary.*

THURSDAY, OCTOBER 18.

At Mount Vernon: " My opinion always has been (however necessary to be in a state of preparation) that no
formidable invasion is to be apprehended from France,
while Great Britain and that country are at War; not from
any favorable disposition the latter has towards us, but
from actual inability to transport Troops and the Munitions
of War, while their ports are blockaded. That they would
willingly, and perhaps necessarily, employ their forces in
such an enterprise in case of Peace I have little doubt, unless adverse fortune in their foreign relations—a Revolution at home—or a wonderful change of sentiment in the
governing powers of their country, should take place."—
Washington to Timothy Pickering.

SUNDAY, OCTOBER 28.

At Mount Vernon: " *October* 28.—The Attʸ Genˡ U. S.
Mʳ Jnᵒ Hopkin & Mʳ Chˢ T. Mercer dined here & returned."
— *Washington's Diary.*

MONDAY, NOVEMBER 5.

Leaves Mount Vernon: " *November* 5.—I set out on a
journey to Philᵃ about 9 oclock with Mʳ Lear my Sec-

24

retary—was met at the Turnpike by a party of horse &
escorted to the Ferry at George Town where I was rec⁴
with Military honors lodged at M⁺ T. Peters."— *Washington's Diary.*

" *Alexandria*, November 6.—Yesterday about 11 o'clock, arrived in town,
on his way to the seat of the Federal Government—his excellency Lieutenant-General GEORGE WASHINGTON, accompanied by his Secretary
Colonel Lear. He was met at West End and escorted into town by Colonel
Fitzgerald's and Captain Young's troops of cavalry, and the company of
Alexandria blues, under the command of Captain Piercey. When he
alighted at Gadsby's tavern, the blues fired a continental salute of 16 rounds.
The troops of horse escorted the General to the ferry at George Town where
the George Town troop were in waiting to pay him the same token of respect."—*Claypoole's American Daily Advertiser*, November 10.

" *George Town*, November 6.—Lieutenant General WASHINGTON arrived on the Virginia shore of the Potomak, yesterday, about 1 o'clock; to
which place he was escorted by a party of horse from Alexandria. Five
gentlemen of George Town, in uniform, received him into a yawl and passed
the river while the infantry and artillery on the Maryland side by several
discharges, honoured their illustrious chief. The George Town troop of
horse and the other military companies then escorted him into the city of
Washington, and after firing a number of rounds, they and the whole assemblage of spectators retired. This morning early he who 'amidst all
plaudits takes command' resumed his journey, attended by the horse.

" The warriors of Homer were aided by the Gods—oratory and poetry
awoke the spirits of ' departed heroes ;' and perhaps nothing on earth more
nearly resembles obtaining the aid of the immortal heroes of Elysium, than
when a WASHINGTON, venerable from age, from experience and from
former services—surrounded by virtues and glory, leaves ' his choice retreat' and ' blest abode,' for the cares of mortals and military scenes."—
Idem.

TUESDAY, NOVEMBER 6.

At Spurrier's Tavern : " *November* 6.—Breakfasted at
Bladensburgh—dined & lodged at Spurriers Escorted by
horse."— *Washington's Diary.*

WEDNESDAY, NOVEMBER 7.

At Baltimore : " *November* 7.—Breakfasted at Baltimore
—dined at Websters, & lodged at Hartford—Met at Spurriers by the Baltimore horse & escorted in and out by the

same—Viewed a Brigade of Militia at Balt*."—*Washington's Diary.*

"*Baltimore,* November 7.—This morning arrived in town, the Chief who unites all hearts. He left Spurriers pretty early, and lighted at Bryden's about 8 o'clock, escorted in by Captains Hollingsworth's and Bentalon's troops, who went out last evening for that purpose. About 10, the 5th and 27th regiments (as many as from the shortness of the notice could get ready) had the gratification of being reviewed by him in Market street, much to the satisfaction of a large concourse of spectators who thronged around him, again to behold at once the venerable Cincinnatus and commander in chief of America. The City Company, capt. Harris, waited on the general at his quarters, personally to congratulate him on once more seeing him among them in health, and made open ranks for him to pass through as he came out to review the troops. He was accompanied, as he marched in front of the line, by generals Smith and Swan; his secretary, Mr. Lear; judge Chase, and several other gentlemen. About 11 he proceeded on his way to Trenton, escorted out by the Fell's Point troop.

"The object of the commander in chief in going to Trenton, is, we understand, to attend a grand council of the executive and general military officers of the union. The president, and the three late unsuccessful ambassadors to France, we also learn, are to be present.*

"Americans! what measure of gratitude is not due to a man, loaded with years and glory, who so ardently wished to terminate his days in the peaceful shades of Mount Vernon, again coming forth, to sustain the thought of council and the fatigue of war, to perpetuate that liberty which he so gloriously achieved for his country."—*Claypoole's American Daily Advertiser,* November 10.

THURSDAY, NOVEMBER 8.

At Elkton, Maryland: "*November* 8.—Breakfasted at Susquehanna escorted by the Hartford horse—dined at

---

* Shortly after the adjournment of Congress, on the 16th of July, the public offices were removed to Trenton, New Jersey, in consequence of the prevalence of yellow fever in Philadelphia. The President also went to Quincy, Massachusetts, and did not return to the city until November 23, having been detained by the illness of Mrs. Adams. All danger from the fever was, however, over by the end of October, and a proclamation to that effect was issued by the city authorities on the first day of November. Washington, therefore, met the Secretary of War and Major-Generals Hamilton and Pinckney at Philadelphia to make the necessary arrangements for the provisional army.

Elkton and lodged at Christiana brdge."—*Washington's Diary.*

" *November* 9.—Breakfasted in Wilmington & dined & lodged at Chester —waited at the latter the Return of an Exp⁸, at this place was met by sev¹ Troops of Phil⁴ horse."—*Washington's Diary.*

SATURDAY, NOVEMBER 10.

At Philadelphia : " *November* 10.—With this Escort I arrived in the City about 9 oclock & was rec⁴ by Gen¹ M°Phersons Blues & was escorted to my lodgings in 8ᵗʰ Street (Mʳˢ White's *) by them & the Horse."—*Washington's Diary.*

" *November* 12.—Lieutenant General WASHINGTON Commander in Chief of the Armies of the United States, arrived here on Saturday morning last [November 10], escorted by the different troops of horse—and, notwithstanding the short notice which had been given the [Macpherson] Blues, almost the whole of that corps, with an alacrity which does them honor, were drawn up on the commons,† to receive their beloved General.

" On his arrival, the cavalry and infantry were drawn up, and the General, having passed in review down their front, is said to have expressed the highest satisfaction at their soldierly and elegant appearance. The procession then moved from the commons, the General accompanied by his secretary Mr. Lear, in the centre of the cavalry. On his arrival at his lodgings in Eighth-street, he was saluted by the acclamations of the citizens who had collected once more to behold their Chief. The General was dressed in his uniform, and is apparently in good health and spirits."—*Claypoole's American Daily Advertiser.*

SUNDAY, NOVEMBER 11.

At Philadelphia : " *November* 11, 12, & 13.—Dined at my Lodgings receiving many Visits."—*Washington's Diary.*

" *November* 14.‡—Dined at Maj^r [William] Jackson's [187 South Third Street]. *November* 15.—Dined at Mr Tench Francis's [Market between

---

* " Rosannah White, widow, boarding house, 9 north eighth street "— *Philadelphia Directory*, 1798.

† The vacant ground west of the built-up portion of the city was known as the commons.

‡ " *November* 14.—We are informed, that the governor as commander in chief of the state militia, attended by the officers of the city and county brigades, will pay their respects to the Commander in chief of the armies of

Eleventh and Twelfth Streets]. *November* 16.—Dined at the Secret⁷ of the Treas⁷ [Oliver Wolcott, Junior, 91 Spruce Street]. *November* 17.—Dined at Mʳ [Thomas] Willings [100 South Third Street]. *November* 18.—Dined at my lodgings. *November* 19.—Dined at Doctʳ Whites—Bishop [of the Protestant Episcopal Church of Pennsylvania, 89 Walnut Street]. *November* 20.—Dined at the Secretary of Wars [James McHenry, 113 South Third Street]. *November* 21.—Dined at Majʳ Reeds—Senator's [Jacob Read, of South Carolina, corner of Eleventh and Chestnut Streets]. *November* 22. —Dined at Mʳ [William] Binghams [South Third, near Spruce Street]. *November* 23.—Dined at Mʳ Samˡ Merediths Treasurer [of the United States, 171 Chestnut Street]. *November* 24.—Dined at the Secretary of States [Timothy Pickering, corner of Sixth and Arch Streets]. *November* 25.—Dined at my Lodgings. *November* 26.—Dined at the Presidents of the U : States [190 High Street].* *November* 27.—Dined in a family with Mʳ [Robert] Morris.† *November* 28.—Dined with Judge [Richard] Peters [85 Walnut Street]. *November* 29.—Dined with the British Minister [Robert Liston, 217 Arch Street]. *November* 30.—Dined with the Govʳ of the State Govʳ Mifflin [250 High Street]. *December* 1.—Dined with Mʳ [William] Rawle [260 High Street]. *December* 2.—Dined with Bingham. From hence until my leaving the City on the 13 I dined at my lodgings."—*Washington's Diary.*

TUESDAY, DECEMBER 4.

At Philadelphia: "*December* 6.—Last Tuesday [December 4] the Potawatamy, Chippawa, and Ottawa Chiefs paid their respects to the President of the United States, and to Lieutenant General Washington."—*Claypoole's American Daily Advertiser.*

SATURDAY, DECEMBER 8.

At Philadelphia: Present at the delivery of the President's address to both Houses, Third Session, Fifth Congress.

----

the United States at 10 o'clock this forenoon."—*Claypoole's American Daily Advertiser.*

* No. 190 High or Market Street was the house occupied by Washington when residing in Philadelphia.

† Robert Morris was imprisoned for debt February 16, 1798, and was not released until August 26, 1801. This family dinner must therefore have taken place in the debtors' apartment of the Old Walnut Street Prison at Sixth and Walnut Streets. The debtors' apartment was situated on the north side of Prune, now Locust Street, east of Sixth Street. The buildings were taken down in 1836.

" At twelve o'clock, Lieutenant General Washington, with his Secretary, Colonel LEAR, Major Generals [Charles Cotesworth] PINCKNEY and [Alexander] HAMILTON, entered the Hall [of the House of Representatives], and took their places on the right of the SPEAKER's Chair. The British and Portuguese Ministers, and the British and Danish Consuls, with the Secretaries, had their places assigned them on the left of the Chair.

" A few minutes after twelve, the PRESIDENT OF THE UNITED STATES, accompanied by his Secretary, and the Heads of the several Departments of the Government, appeared. The PRESIDENT having taken his seat, and the officers of Government theirs, near the general officers, he rose and addressed the two Houses.' —*Journal of Congress.*

FRIDAY, DECEMBER 14.

Leaves Philadelphia : " *December* 14.—After dinner set out on my journey home—Reached Chester."— *Washington's Diary.*

" *December* 15.—Yesterday morning Lieut. Gen. WASHINGTON left this city, on his journey to Mount Vernon, Virginia. The General was accompanied by his Secretary, Col. Lear."—*Claypoole's American Daily Advertiser.*

SATURDAY, DECEMBER 15.

At Elkton : "*December* 15.—Breakfasted at Wilmington bated at Christiana—and dined and lodged at Elkton."— *Washington's Diary.*

" *December* 16.—Set out after a very early breakfast;—and was detained at Susquehanna from 10 Oclock until the next morning—partly by Ice and Winds—but principally by the Lowness of the tides occasioned by the N⁰ Westerly Winds. *December* 17.—Breakfasted at Barney's—bated at Hartford—Dined at Webster's and Lodged at Baltimore."—*Washington's Diary.*

TUESDAY, DECEMBER 18.

At Washington City : " *December* 18.—Breakfasted at Spurriers—dined at Rhodes's—and lodged at M⁺ Laws in the Federal City."— *Washington's Diary.*

" We had an invitation to dine with Doctor Thornton [at Washington City]: and the Doctor having a public dinner on that day, I got introduced to many respectable characters; and among the rest to Mr. Law, a gentleman married to the granddaughter of Mrs. Washington. Mr. Law is an Englishman, and brother to Lord Ellenborough. He gave Colonel Lyles and myself an invitation to go to sleep at his house; but we were prevented by General Washington coming to sleep there that night, and Colonel Lear, his Secretary. I had, however, the gratification to be introduced to the General; and Colonel Lyles being a neighbour and a particular acquaintance of his, a most pleasing evening I spent. The General was quite sociable, and received me very kindly. After supper, at nine o'clock the General went to bed, as that was his hour; for the supper in most houses being tea, and some broiled fish, sausages, steaks, &c., it is generally introduced between six and seven o'clock, which was done that evening. Doctor Thornton, Colonel Lyles, Mr. Law, and myself, sat some hours after; and the Colonel and I went to sleep at a tavern in the city, which was kept by an Englishman named Tunnercliffe. We were asked the next morning to breakfast at Mr. Law's, with the General; which we did: and the General gave me a most kind invitation to go to see him in a few days.* After breakfast, he set off in his carriage for Mount Vernon."—RICHARD PARKINSON, *Tour in America in 1798*, etc. London : 1805. Vol. i. p. 59.

WEDNESDAY, DECEMBER 19.

At Mount Vernon : "*December* 19.—Stopped at Doct' Thornton's and M' Peter's & dined at home."—*Washington's Diary.*

MONDAY, DECEMBER 24.

At Mount Vernon : "*December* 24.—Doct' Craik came to D[inner] & Judge Cushing & lady in the Afternoon—as did a M' Dinsmoor Agent in the Cherokee Country on his way to Philadelphia."—*Washington's Diary.*

"We reached Mount Vernon," wrote the wife of Judge Cushing, in February, 1799, "the evening before Christmas, and if any thing could have added to our enjoyment, it was the arrival of General and Mrs. Pinckney the next day, while we were dining.† You may be sure it was a joyful

---

* Mr. Parkinson, referring to the visit to Mount Vernon made in consequence of this invitation from Washington, says, "I dined with him ; and he showed me several presents that had been sent him, viz. swords, china, and among the rest the key of the Bastille. I spent a very pleasant day in the house, as the weather was so severe that there were no farming objects to see, the ground being covered with snow. The General wished me to stay all night ; but having some other engagements, I declined his kind offer."

† "*December* 25.—Gen¹ Pinckney Lady & daughter came to dinner."—*Washington's Diary.*

meeting, and at the very place my wishes had pointed out. To be in the company of so many esteemed friends, to hear our good General Washington converse upon political subjects without reserve, and to hear General and Mrs. Pinckney relate what they saw and heard in France, was truly a feast to me. Thus the moments glided away for two days, when our reason pointed out the propriety of our departing and improving the good roads, as the snow and frost had made them better than they are in summer."— *Lossing's Mount Vernon*, p. 309.

WEDNESDAY, DECEMBER 26.

At Mount Vernon: "I returned a few days ago from Philadelphia, whither I had been for the purpose of making military arrangements with the Secretary of War, respecting the force which is about to be raised."— *Washington to William Vans Murray.*

THURSDAY, DECEMBER 27.

At Mount Vernon: "*December* 27.—The following Gentlemen dined here the 27th viz—Mess" Wᵐ Fitzhugh—Wᵐ Herbert Potts—Wilson—Doctʳ Craik & Son Geo: Washington Craik, Heath & Doctʳ Greenhow of Richmond."— *Washington's Diary.*

1799.

WEDNESDAY, JANUARY 16.

At Mount Eagle: "*January* 20.—On Wednesday last [January 16] M⁰ Washington & myself took a family dinner at Mount Eagle *—and left all the family in good health & Spirits in the afternoon—Miss Custis was, at that time, with her mother [Mrs. Stuart], at Hope Park, or she would have accompanied us on that visit."— *Washington to Bryan Fairfax.*

WEDNESDAY, JANUARY 23.

At Mount Vernon : "Your letter of the 10ᵗʰ instant I received in Alexandria, on Monday, whither I went to become the guardian of Nelly, thereby to authorize a license for your nuptials on the 22ᵈ of next month."— *Washington to Lawrence Lewis.*

SUNDAY, FEBRUARY 10.

At Mount Vernon : " *February* 10.—Wind shifted in the Night to N. W. blew fresh & turned cold—Mer at 30 in the morning & 34 at Night—clear all day."— *Washington's Diary.*

Washington's custom of recording the state of the weather will be noticed in nearly all of his diaries. Indeed, one kept at Philadelphia in 1796, with the exception of two entries, one referring to receiving the national colors of France from M. Adet on January 1, and the other to George Washington Craik having joined him as private secretary on April 12, is entirely devoted

---

* Mount Eagle, on the old road from Alexandria to Mount Vernon, was the home of Bryan Fairfax, rector of Christ Church, Alexandria, 1790–1792, and afterward Lord Fairfax. The house is still standing. At the date of the above-quoted letter Mr. Fairfax was in England on a visit.

to that subject. This diary, the handwriting of which is peculiarly neat and
distinct, is in the possession of the Historical Society of Pennsylvania. It
runs from January 1 to June 21.

MONDAY, FEBRUARY 11.

At Alexandria: " *February* 11.—Went up to Alexandria
to the celebration of my birth day—Many Manœuvres were
performed by the Uniform Corps—and an elegant Ball &
supper at Night. *February* 12.—Return'd home."—*Washington's Diary.*

SATURDAY, FEBRUARY 16.

At Mount Vernon: "*February* 16.—M^r and M^m Peters
came to dinner. *February* 18.—M^m Stuart and her 3 daughters came here in the afternoon."—*Washington's Diary.*

TUESDAY, FEBRUARY 19.

At Mount Vernon: " You will please to grant a license
for the marriage of Eleanor Parke Custis with Lawrence
Lewis, and this shall be your authority for so doing."—
Washington to Captain George Deneale, Clerk of Fairfax
County Court.

THURSDAY, FEBRUARY 21.

At Mount Vernon: " *February* 21.—Mr Ch^s Carter wife
& daughter came to dinner—& Mr Robt Lewis in the Afternoon."—*Washington's Diary.*

FRIDAY, FEBRUARY 22.

At Mount Vernon: " *February* 22.—The Revd Mr Davis
& Mr Geo: Calvert came to dinner & Miss Custis was mar-
ried ab^t Candle light to Mr Law^e Lewis."—*Washington's
Diary.*

" An event occurred on the twenty-second of February, 1799, that, while
it created an unusual bustle in the ancient halls, shed a bright gleam of
sunshine on the last days at Mount Vernon. It was the marriage of Major
Lewis, a favorite nephew, with the adopted daughter of the chief. It was
the wish of the young bride that the general of the armies of the United

States should appear in the splendidly embroidered uniform (the costume assigned him by the board of general officers) in honor of the bridal; but alas, even the idea of wearing a costume bedizened with gold embroidery, had never entered the mind of the chief, he being content with the old Continental blue and buff, while the magnificent white plumes presented to him by Major-General Pinckney he gave to the bride, preferring the old Continental cocked hat, with the plain black-ribbon cockade, a type of the brave old days of '76."—GEORGE WASHINGTON PARKE CUSTIS, *Recollections of Washington.*

MONDAY, FEBRUARY 25.

At Mount Vernon: "*February* 25.—River nearly closed with Ice.—M^r L: Lee Mrs Lee & Miss French—Mr Herbert, M^r Jn° Herbert & Miss Herbert.—Doct^r Craik & Mr G. W. Craik—Miss Fitzhugh Miss Moly Fitzhugh & Miss Chew— & Col° Fitzgerald dined here & returned."—*Washington's Diary.*

"*February* 26.—Mrs Potts—Mrs Fendall—Mr And^w Ramsay & Wife— Mr Wm Ramsay—Mr Edm^d Lee & Sister Lucy—and Mr Hodgden dined here & returned—and Mr Bushrod Washington came in the afternoon. *February* 27.—Mr Thomson Mason & Wife and Mr Nicholls & Wife dined here & returned."—*Washington's Diary.*

SUNDAY, MARCH 3.

At Mount Vernon: "*March* 3.—Mrs Stuart & her 3 daughters (Stuarts) * and M^r & Mrs Peters went away after breakfast. *March* 4.—M^r & Mrs Carter went away after Breakfast. *March* 6.—M^r & Mrs Law went away to day."— *Washington's Diary.*

SUNDAY, MARCH 31.

At Mount Vernon: "Mr Lewis & Nelly Custis fulfilled their matrimonial engagement on the 22^d of February. In consequence the former, havg. relinquished the lapp of Mars for the Sports of Venus, has declined a Military appointment."— *Washington to Charles Cotesworth Pinckney.*

---

* By her second marriage Mrs. Stuart had seven children,—five daughters and two sons.

WEDNESDAY, APRIL 3.

At Four Mile Run: * "*April* 3.—Went up to four mile Run to Run round my land there—Got on the gr^d about 10 Oclock and in Company with Captn Sterret and Mr Luke commenced the Survey on 4 mile run & ran agreeably to the Notes taken—In the evening went to Alex^a & lodged my self at Mr Fitzhugh's."— *Washington's Diary.*

> "*April* 4.—Recommenced the Survey at the upper end where we left off in company with Col^o [Charles] Little—Capt^a Sterret and Mr Willm Adams —& cont^d it agreeably to the Notes until we came to 4 Mile run again which employed us until dark—Returned to Alex^a and again lodged at Mr Fitzhughs. *April* 5.—Returned home to Breakfast."— *Washington's Diary.*

FRIDAY, APRIL 12.

At Mount Vernon: "*April* 12.—Spread Plaster of Paris this Morning on the circle & sides before the door—& on the Lawn to the Cross Path betw^n the Garden gates—& on the Clover by the Stable."— *Washington's Diary.*

WEDNESDAY, APRIL 24.

At Alexandria: "*April* 24.—Went up to Alex^a to an Election of a Representative from the District to Congress & from the County to the State Legisla^a."— *Washington's Diary.*

MONDAY, APRIL 29.

At Four Mile Run: "*April* 29.—Went up to run round my land on 4 Mile run. Lodged at Col^o Littles [at Alexandria]. *April* 30.—Engaged on the same business as yesterday & returned home in the afternoon."— *Washington's Diary.*

TUESDAY, MAY 14.

At Mount Vernon: "*May* 14.—Maj^r Wm Harrison came here to dinner. *May* 15.—Mr Thomson Mason came here

---

* Four Mile Run empties into the Potomac about three miles above Alexandria. See note to May 4, 1786.

to breakfast and attended Majʳ Harrison & me on the
Survey of the latters land & both dined here, as did a Mʳ
Season."— *Washington's Diary.*

John Searson, whose visit to Mount Vernon is noted in the Diary under
the name of Season, was the author of a disjointed composition (the result
of this visit) entitled "MOUNT VERNON, A POEM: Being the seat
of his excellency George Washington, in the STATE OF VIRGINIA;
Lieutenant-general and commander in chief of the land forces of the United
States of America. This rural, romantic and descriptive Poem of the seat
of so great a character, it is hoped may please, with a copper-plate likeness
of the General. It was taken from an actual view on the spot by the
author, 15th May, 1799. BY JOHN SEARSON, formerly of Philadelphia, merchant." This *remarkable* attempt at verse was published at Philadelphia in September of the same year.

THURSDAY, MAY 16.

At Alexandria: "*May* 16.—Went up to Alexandria to
the Purse Race, & returned in the Evening Mʳ Law &
Doctʳ Thornton here."— *Washington's Diary.*

THURSDAY, MAY 23.

At Mount Vernon: "*May* 23.—Mʳ Thoˢ Adams third
son to the President & Mʳ Joshua Johnson, Lady & son
came to dinʳ."— *Washington's Diary.*

FRIDAY, MAY 31.

At Washington City: "*May* 31.—Went up to the Fed¹
City—dined & lodged with Mʳ Peter. *June* 1.—Dined &
lodged at Mʳ Laws. *June* 2.—Returned home to dinner—
takˢ Church at Alexˢ in my way."— *Washington's Diary.*

Edward C. McGuire, on page 154 of his work entitled "The Religious
Opinions and Character of Washington,"* quotes the following narrative
"from a valued female friend, now numbered with the dead," which evidently refers to Washington's attendance at Christ Church, Alexandria, on
Sunday, June 2, recorded in the Diary. "In the summer of 1799," said Mrs.
M., "I was in Alexandria, on a visit to the family of Mr. H., with whom I was
connected by the ties of relationship. Whilst there, I expressed a wish to

* Published at New York in 1836.

see General Washington, as I had never enjoyed that pleasure. My friend
Mrs. H observed, ' You will certainly see him on Sunday, as he is never
absent from church when he can get there ; and as he often dines with us,
we will ask him on that day, when you will have a better opportunity of
seeing him.' Accordingly, we all repaired to church on Sunday, and seated
in Mr. H's large double pew, I kept my eyes upon the door, looking for the
venerable form of him I had so long desired to see. Many persons entered
the doors, but none came up to my impressions of General Washington's
appearance. At length, a person of noble and majestic figure entered, and
the conviction was instantaneous that I beheld the Father of his Country.
It was so!—my friend at that moment intimated the fact to me. He walked
to his pew, at the upper part of the church, and demeaned himself throughout the services of the day with that gravity and propriety becoming the
place and his own high character. After the services were concluded we
waited for him at the door, for his pew being near the pulpit he was among
the last that came out—when Mrs. H. invited him to dine with us. He
declined, however, the invitation, observing, as he looked at the sky, that he
thought there were appearances of a thunder-storm in the afternoon, and he
believed he would return home to dinner."

THURSDAY, JUNE 20.

At Mount Vernon : " *June* 20.—The following company
dined here—Chief-Justice of the U. S. Ellsworth, M^r & M^rs
Steer Senr—M^r & Mrs Steer Junr Mr Van Havre—M^r & M^rs
Ludwell Lee—Mrs Corbin Washington M^r & Mrs Hodgson
& Miss Cor Lee M^r & Mrs Geo. Calvert and a Captn Ham-
ilton & Lady from the Bahama Islands."—*Washington's
Diary.*

TUESDAY, JUNE 25.

At Mount Vernon : " Your favor of the 18th of September last, with the small box containing four pairs of prints,
came safe to hand, but long after the date of the letter."—
Washington to John Trumbull.

In April, 1790, Washington subscribed to four sets of engravings after
Trumbull's pictures, " The Battle of Bunker Hill" and " The Death of
General Montgomery." They were published in London, the former exe-
cuted by J. G. Müller, of Stutgard, Germany, and the latter by J. F.
Clemens, of Copenhagen, Denmark. These are the *four pairs of prints*
referred to in the above letter.

THURSDAY, JULY 4.

At Alexandria: "*July* 4.—Went up to Alex² and dined with a number of the Citizens there, in celebration of the anniversary of the declaration of american Independᵉ at Kemps Tavern."— *Washington's Diary.*

"*Alexandria*, July 6.—The 23d anniversary of the American Independence was celebrated in this town with the greatest harmony and decorum. The military commands agreeably to orders previously given, mustered in the court house square, and the line was formed in Fairfax street. After going through the manual, which was performed with the strictest exactitude, Col. John Fitzgerald, accompanied by John Potts, Esq., passed the line in review, and expressed his satisfaction at their military and elegant appearance. The battalion then marched, by sections, up King street, and formed the line there to receive their beloved Chief General GEORGE WASHINGTON. On his passing the line the usual military honors were paid; and it is with pleasure I remark, that the Cincinnatus of America appeared in excellent health and good spirits.

"Lieutenant General Washington dined at Col. Kemp's tavern, with a select party of friends."—*Claypoole's American Daily Advertiser*, July 11.

TUESDAY, JULY 9.

At Mount Vernon: On this day Washington executed his Last Will and Testament, consisting of twenty-nine pages of manuscript, written entirely by himself; and at the bottom of each, with the exception of page twenty-three, he affixed his signature. To this he added a schedule with descriptive notes of the property included in the will, which was directed to be sold, making thirteen additional pages.

WEDNESDAY, JULY 17.

At Mount Vernon: "*July* 17.—Colonels Powell & Simms and Mʳ Herbert—and Judge Washington * Captⁿ Blackburn & Mʳ H. Turner dined here—the three first went away in the afternoon. *July* 18.—Slow rain with the wind at Sᵒ Eᵗ & contᵈ until I went to bed a 9 oclock. . . . Captⁿ

* Bushrod Washington was commissioned an Associate Justice of the Supreme Court of the United States, December 20, 1798.

Blackburn went away after breakfast. *July* 19.—Judge Washington & Mr H. Turner left this after dinner."— *Washington's Diary.*

MONDAY, AUGUST 5.

At George Town: "*August* 5.—Went up to George Town, to a general meeting of the Potomac Company—dined at the Union Tavern & lodged at Mr. Laws. *August* 6.—Returned home to dinner—found Genl Wm Washington* of S^o Carolina and Son here."— *Washington's Diary.*

WEDNESDAY, AUGUST 7.

At Mount Vernon: "*August* 7.—The following Gentlemen dined here—viz. Col^o Fitzgerald—Doct^r Craik & son —Mr Wm Craik—Mr Herbert & Son J^{no} C. Herbert—Col^o Ramsay—Mr Potts—Mr Edm^d Lee—Mr Keith—Lieut Kean of the Marines—and Mr Ch^s Fenton Mercer. *August* 8.— Gener^l Washington & son went away after breakfast."— *Washington's Diary.*

SATURDAY, AUGUST 24.

At Mount Vernon: "*August* 24.—Mr White came to dinner—as did 4 Gentlemen from Phil^a viz—Young Mr Meredith (son of the Treasurer) Mr Clifton, a Mr Walter & —— the 4 last returned after dinner."— *Washington's Diary.*

SUNDAY, SEPTEMBER 1.

At Mount Vernon: "*September* 1.—Doct^r Craik dined here—sent for to Mrs Washington who was sick. *September* 6.—Doct^r Craik who was sent for in the night to M^{rs}

---

* Colonel William Washington, a distinguished cavalry officer in the Revolution, was appointed a brigadier-general July 19, 1798. He was born in Stafford County, Virginia, February 28, 1752, and was a descendant of Lawrence Washington the Immigrant. General William Washington died at Charleston, South Carolina, March 6, 1810.

Washington came early this morning."— *Washington's Diary.*

SATURDAY, SEPTEMBER 7.

At Mount Vernon : "*September* 7.—M^r & Mrs Peter and Genl Washington came in the afternoon. *September* 8.— Genl Washington went away after breakfast—& M^r & Mrs Law came to dinner."— *Washington's Diary.*

THURSDAY, SEPTEMBER 12.

At Mount Vernon : "*September* 12.—Cap : Truxton [Thomas Truxtun] came to dinner."— *Washington's Diary.*

SUNDAY, SEPTEMBER 22.

At Mount Vernon : "The death of near relations always produces awful and affecting emotions, under whatsoever circumstances it may happen. That of my brother [Charles] has been so long expected, and his latter days so uncomfortable to himself, must have prepared all around him for the stroke, though painful in the effect.

"I was the first, and am, now, the last of my father's children by the second marriage, who remain. When I shall be *called upon to follow them* is known only to the Giver of Life. When the summons comes I shall endeavor to obey it with a good grace."— *Washington to Colonel Burgess Ball.*

FRIDAY, SEPTEMBER 27.

At Mount Vernon : "*September* 27.—Governor Davie on his way to the Northward to Embark as Envoy to France called, dined & proceeded on."— *Washington's Diary.*

William Richardson Davie, Governor of North Carolina in 1798, was appointed, in conjunction with Oliver Ellsworth and William Vans Murray, Envoy Extraordinary and Minister Plenipotentiary to France. The envoys reaching Paris in March, 1800, found Napoleon Bonaparte at the head of the new republic, and soon concluded a satisfactory adjustment of all disputes ; the result of which was the convention signed September 30, 1800, which included a recognition from France of the rights of neutral vessels, and an indemnity for depredations on American commerce.

TUESDAY, OCTOBER 1.

At Mount Vernon : " *October* 1.—M*rs* Fairfax sister and daughter—and M*rs* Herbert & M*rs* Nelson—M*r* Jn° Herbert & two of M*rs* [Warner] Washington of Fairfields Sons dined here."— *Washington's Diary.*

TUESDAY, OCTOBER 22.

At Mount Vernon: " *October* 22.—M*r* Liston (British Minister) & lady came to dinner. *October* 25. M*r* and M*rs* Liston left this after breakfast."— *Washington's Diary.*

MONDAY, OCTOBER 28.

At Mount Vernon : "*October* 28.—M*r* Ridout an English Gentleman and his Lady dined here as did M*r* G. W. Craik —M*r* Lear set out for Harper's Ferry to make some arrangement with Col° Parker respecting Cantoning the Troops."— *Washington's Diary.*

TUESDAY, NOVEMBER 5.

At Difficult Run, Virginia: " *November* 5.—Set out on a trip to Difficult Run to view some Land I had there & some belonging to M*r* Jn° Gill who had offered it to me in discharge of Rent which he was owing me—Dined at M*r* Nicholas Fitzhughs and lodged at M*r* Corbin Washingtons. *November* 6.—Set out from thence after 8 Oc*lk* being detained by sprinkling Rain, & much appearance of it until that hour—reached Wiley's Tavern near Difficult Bridge to Breakfast and then proceeded to Survey my own Land." — *Washington's Diary.*

In the notes to the schedule of property directed to be sold by his executors, the land on Difficult Run, Loudoun County (three hundred acres), is described as follows : " It *lyes* on the great Road from the City of Washington, Alexandria and George Town to *Leesburgh* & Winchester, at Difficult bridge—nineteen miles from Alexandria—less from the City & George Town, and not more than three from Matildaville at the Great Falls of Potomac."

THURSDAY, NOVEMBER 7.

At Difficult Run: "*November* 7.—Finished Surveying my own Tract & the Land belonging to Gill—returning, as the Night before to Wiley's Tavern. *November* 8.—Morning very heavy and about 9 oclock it commenced Raining which it continued to do steadily through the day—notwithstanding which I proceeded to ascertain by actual measurement the qualities [? quantities]—this being finished betw^n 12 & 1 oclock I returned to Wiley's Tavern & stayed there the remainder of the day."—*Washington's Diary.*

SATURDAY, NOVEMBER 9.

At Washington City: "*November* 9.—Morning & whole day clear warm & pleasant set out a little after 8 oclock—viewed my building in the Fed^l City—Dined at Mr Laws—& lodged at Mr Thos Peter's. *November* 10.—Returned home about noon."—*Washington's Diary.*

TUESDAY, NOVEMBER 12.

At Mount Vernon: "M^m Washington and myself have been honoured by your polite invitation to the Assemblies at Alexandria this winter, and thank you for this mark of attention. But, alas! our dancing days are no more. We wish, however, all those who have relish for so agreeable and innocent an amusement all the pleasures the season will afford."—*Washington to the Gentlemen of the Alexandria Assemblies.*

FRIDAY, NOVEMBER 15.

At Mount Eagle: "*November* 15.—Rode to visit M^r now Lord Fairfax who was just got home from a Trip to England—ret^d to dinner."—*Washington's Diary.*

SUNDAY, NOVEMBER 17.

At Alexandria : " *November* 17.—Went to Church in Alexandria & dined with Mr Fitzhugh."— *Washington's Diary.*

FRIDAY, NOVEMBER 22.

At Mount Vernon : " *November* 22.—Col° Carrington * & Lady came in the aftern°.—*November* 23.—Col° Carrington & Lady went away after Breakfast."— *Washington's Diary.*

" *Mount Vernon,* November 22.—We arrived at this venerable mansion in perfect safety, where we are experiencing every mark of hospitality and kindness that the good old General's continued friendship to Colonel Carrington could lead us to expect. His reception of my husband was that of a brother. He took us each by the hand, and, with a warmth of expression not to be described, pressed mine, and told me that I had conferred a favor never to be forgotten in bringing his old friend to see him ; then, bidding a servant to call the ladies, entertained us most facetiously till they appeared."—*Mrs. Edward Carrington to Mrs. George Fisher.*†

WEDNESDAY, NOVEMBER 27.

At Mount Vernon : " *November* 27.—Doct^r Craik who was sent for to Mrs Lewis (& who was delivered of a daughter ab^t — oclock in the forenoon) came to Breakfast & stayed dinner."— *Washington's Diary.*

THURSDAY, NOVEMBER 28.

At Mount Vernon : " *November* 28.—Col° & Mrs Carrington came to Dinner. *November* 30.—Col° & Mrs Carrington went away after B^t."— *Washington's Diary.*

" *Mount Vernon.*—After visiting my numerous friends, we returned to this revered mansion. . . . Everything within doors is neat and elegant, but nothing remarkable, except the paintings of different artists which have been sent as specimens of their talents. I think there are five portraits of

---

* Colonel Edward Carrington, a Virginian by birth (February 11, 1749), was Quartermaster-General under General Greene in the Revolution. He commanded the artillery and did good service at the battle of Hobkirk's Hill, April 24, 1781, and also at Yorktown. He was a member of Congress 1785–86, and was foreman of the jury in Burr's trial for treason in 1807. Colonel Carrington died at Richmond, Virginia, October 28, 1810.

† Anne Ambler, a sister of Mrs. Carrington.

the General, some done in Europe and some done in America, that do honor to the painters. There are other specimens of the fine arts from various parts of the world, that are admirably executed and furnish pleasant conversation. Besides these, there is a complete greenhouse, which at this season is a vast, a great source of pleasure. Plants from every part of the world seem to flourish in this neatly finished apartment, and from the arrangement of the whole I conclude that it is managed by a skillful hand, but whose I cannot tell: neither the General nor Mrs. Washington seem more interested in it than their visitors. We have met with no company here, but am told that scarcely a week passes without some, and often more than is agreeable or convenient. Transient persons, who call from curiosity, are treated with civility, but never interfere with the order of the house, or with the General's disposition of time, which is as regular as when at the head of the army or in the President's chair. Even friends who make a point of visiting him are left much to themselves; indeed, scarcely see him from breakfast to dinner, unless he engages them in a ride, which is very agreeable to him. But from dinner to tea our time is most charmingly spent; indeed, one evening the General was so fascinating, and drew my husband out into so many old stories relating to several campaigns where they had been much together, and had so many inquiries to make respecting their mutual friends, particularly Kosciusko and Pulaski, who have always corresponded with Colonel Carrington, whose characters afford great interest, that it was long past twelve when we separated. At breakfast I feel quite at home, everything is so plain."—*Mrs. Carrington to Mrs. Fisher.*

SUNDAY, DECEMBER 1.

At Mount Vernon : " *December* 1.—Morning clear & but little W^d—that Southerly—Mer 26—Lowering towards evening—Mer 36.—Mr Foot dined here."—*Washington's Diary.*

MONDAY, DECEMBER 2.

At Mount Vernon : " *December* 2.—Rained in the Night— Morning heavy—Wind Southerly—and Mer at 36.—afternoon calm & less clouded—Mer 38—Lord Fairfax, Lady, Daughter & Miss Dennison dined here."—*Washington's Diary.*

TUESDAY, DECEMBER 3.

At Mount Vernon : " *December* 3.—Morning extremely foggy—Mer at 38 and wind what there was of it Southerly

—Ab' 2 oclock the fog dispelled and it became extremely pleasant—Mrs Stuart & daughters went away after breakfast." *— *Washington's Diary.*

WEDNESDAY, DECEMBER 4.

At Mount Vernon : " *December* 4.—Morning clear—Wind at N° W' and Mer at 36—From 10 oclock until 2 very like for Snow—it then cleared & became mild & pleasant Mer 38 at N :"— *Washington's Diary.*

THURSDAY, DECEMBER 5.

At Mount Vernon : " *December* 5.—Morning raining, and it continued to do so moderately through the day with the Wind at S° E'—Mer 38 in the Morning & 36 at Night."— *Washington's Diary.*

FRIDAY, DECEMBER 6.

At Mount Vernon : " *December* 6.—Morning heavy, with appearances of clearing now & then, but about 2 o'clock it set in to raining—Mer 34 in the Morning & 37 at Night." — *Washington's Diary.*

SATURDAY, DECEMBER 7.

At Mount Eagle : " *December* 7.—Rainy Morning, with the wind at N° E' & Mer at 37—afternoon clear & pleasant wind westerly—Mer 41 at Night— dined at Lord Fairfax's." — *Washington's Diary.*

SUNDAY, DECEMBER 8.

At Mount Vernon : " *December* 8.—Morning perfectly clear, calm and pleasant ; but about 9 o'clock the wind came from the N° W' and blew fresh. Mer 38 in the Morning—and 40 at Night."— *Washington's Diary.*

---

* " *November* 21.—Mrs Stuart and the two eldest Miss Stuarts came here to dinner."— *Washington's Diary.*

MONDAY, DECEMBER 9.

At Mount Vernon : "*December* 9.—Morning clear & pleasant, with a light wind from N° W' Mer at 33—pleasant all day—afternoon Calm Mer 39 at Night—M' Howell Lewis & wife set off on their return home after breakfast— and M' Law° Lewis and Washington Custis on a journ' to N : Kent."— *Washington's Diary.*

James K. Paulding, in his " Life of Washington" * (vol. ii. p. 195), gives a statement made to him personally by one of the favorite nephews of Washington, describing his last parting with the General. This nephew was doubtless Howell Lewis, who, by the above-quoted entry in the Diary, left Mount Vernon on December 9, after a ten days' visit. The statement is as follows :

" During this, my last visit to the general, we walked together about the grounds, and talked of various improvements he had in contemplation. The lawn was to be extended down to the river in the direction of the old vault, which was to be removed on account of the inroads made by the roots of the trees, with which it is crowned, which caused it to leak. ' I intend to place it there,' said he, pointing to the spot where the new vault stands. ' First of all, I shall make this change; for after all, I may require it before the rest.'

" When I parted from him, he stood on the steps of the front door, where he took leave of myself and another, and wished us a pleasant journey, as I was going to Westmoreland on business. It was a bright frosty morning, he had taken his usual ride, and the clear healthy flush on his cheek, and his sprightly manner, brought the remark from both of us that we had never seen the general look so well. I have sometimes thought him decidedly the handsomest man I ever saw; and when in lively mood, so full of pleasantry, so agreeable to all with whom he associated, that I could hardly realize that he was the same Washington whose dignity awed all who approached him.

" A few days afterwards, being on my way home in company with others, while we were conversing about Washington, I saw a servant rapidly riding towards us. On his near approach, I recognised him as belonging to Mount Vernon. He rode up—his countenance told the story—he handed me a letter. Washington was dead !"

TUESDAY, DECEMBER 10.

At Mount Vernon : "*December* 10.—Morning clear & calm—Mer at 31 afternoon lowering—Mer at 42 and wind

---

* Published at New York in 1835.

brisk from the Southward—A very large hoar frost this Morn^e."— *Washington's Diary.*

On this day (December 10) Washington completed a plan or system, which had been under consideration for some time, for the management and cultivation of the Mount Vernon farms for several successive years. In this paper, which occupies thirty closely written folio pages, the most minute and detailed instructions are given as to the cultivation of the land, with tables designating the rotations of the crops. This was accompanied by a letter of the same date to James Anderson, his manager, with a request that the instructions be "most *strictly* and *pointedly* attended to and executed, as far as the measures required will admit."

As an example of his remarkable powers of application and life-long attention to detail, and also as showing the soundness and vigor of his intellect at this period of his life, the document possesses considerable interest.

WEDNESDAY, DECEMBER 11.

At Mount Vernon: "*December* 11.—But little wind and Raining—Mer 44 in the Morning and 38 at Night.—About 9 oclock the Wind shifted to N° W^t & it ceased raining but cont^d Cloudy.—Lord Fairfax, his Son Tho' and daughter— Mrs Warner Washington & son Whiting—and M^r Jn° Herbert dined here & returned after dinner."— *Washington's Diary.*

THURSDAY, DECEMBER 12.

At Mount Vernon: "*December* 12.—Morning Cloudy— Wind at N° E^t & Mer 33—a large circle round the Moon last Night.—about 1 o'clock it began to snow—soon after to Hail and then turned to a settled cold Rain—Mer 28 at Night."— *Washington's Diary.*

"On Thursday, December 12, the General rode out to his farms about ten o'clock, and did not return home till past three. Soon after he went out, the weather became very bad, rain, hail, snow falling alternately, with a cold wind. When he came in, I carried some letters to him to frank, intending to send them to the post-office in the evening. He franked the letters, but said the weather was too bad to send a servant to the office that evening. I observed to him, that I was afraid he had got wet. He said, No, his great-coat had kept him dry. But his neck appeared to be wet, and the snow was hanging upon his hair. He came to dinner (which had been waiting for him) without changing his dress. In the evening he appeared as well as usual."—TOBIAS LEAR. (Sparks, vol i. p. 555.)

FRIDAY, DECEMBER 13.

At Mount Vernon : " *December* 13.—Morning Snowing & ab^t 3 Inches deep *—Wind at N° E^t & Mer at 30—cont^s Snowing till 1 oclock—and ab^t 4 it became perfectly clear— wind in the same place but not hard—Mer 28 at Night."— *Washington's Diary.*

This, the final entry of the Diary of 1799, was the last piece of writing executed by Washington. On the following morning, Saturday, December 14, between two and three o'clock, he was taken seriously ill from a cold incurred on the morning of the 12th, while taking his usual ride, and died that night of quinsy, between ten and eleven o'clock.

At three o'clock in the afternoon of Wednesday, December 18, 1799, all that was mortal of George Washington, soldier, statesman, and patriot, the foremost man in American history, was deposited with Masonic ceremonies in the family vault at Mount Vernon. He had passed from the sight of man; but his fame, so long as virtue, truth, and sincerity shall be guiding principles, will increase with the gathering years!

---

* " A heavy fall of snow took place on Friday, which prevented the General from riding out as usual. He had taken cold, undoubtedly from being so much exposed the day before, and complained of a sore throat. He, however, went out in the afternoon into the ground between the house and the river to mark some trees, which were to be cut down in the improvement of that spot."—TOBIAS LEAR.

INDEX.

395

THE END.

www.ingramcontent.com/pod-product-compliance
Lightning Source LLC
Chambersburg PA
CBHW030812110726

47900CB00006B/1596